HIS LONGING HEART

BOOKS BY JAN THOMPSON

CITY/COASTAL/BEACH ROMANCE

Seaside Chapel (7 Books)

JanThompson.com/seaside

Savannah Sweethearts (12 Books)

JanThompson.com/savannah

Vacation Sweethearts (8 Books)

JanThompson.com/vacation

ROMANTIC SUSPENSE/THRILLERS

Protector Sweethearts (6 Books)

JanThompson.com/protector

Defender Sweethearts (6 Books)

JanThompson.com/defender

Binary Hackers (4 Books)

JanThompson.com/binary

JanThompson.com/books

HIS LONGING HEART

SEASIDE CHAPEL
BOOK ONE

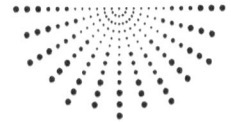

JAN THOMPSON

GEORGIA
PRESS

To my Lord and Savior, Jesus Christ, who died on the cross to save me from my sins and rose again from the grave to give me eternal life in heaven.

For God so loved the world that He gave His only begotten Son, that whoever believes in Him should not perish but have everlasting life.
—John 3:16

READ A FREE EBOOK IN THE
SAME STORY WORLD

Set in Georgia, South Carolina, and Tennessee, this clean and wholesome Christian romance tells the story of art gallery archivist Sheryl Breckenridge and world-famous sculptor Winton Pace. Read this ebook for free!

Time for Me (A Vacation Sweethearts Prequel)
JanThompson.com/time-free

ABOUT THE SEASIDE CHAPEL SERIES

Welcome to *USA Today* bestselling author Jan Thompson's **Seaside Chapel** Christian beach romance series. These novels are set on real-life St. Simon's Island, Georgia—a beach town where history is all around and the future is a moment away—and the neighboring fictitious Seaside Island, where the rich and famous in Jan's story world live.

Savor the small-town atmosphere and the warm southern beaches of St. Simon's Island and the idyllic Golden Isles along the Atlantic Ocean. Enjoy the music of the orchestra and hymns of the church, and hang out with our Christian friends who attend Seaside Chapel, a little church by the sea known for its beach weddings and fair share of love and life.

As these Christians grow in their knowledge and understanding of God, they are tested in their spiritual maturity, their love lives, and their relationships with others. Share their heartaches and healing, and cheer them on as they celebrate faith, family, and friends.

JanThompson.com/seaside

- Book 1: His Longing Heart
- Book 2: His Wake-Up Call
- Book 3: His Morning Kiss
- Book 4: His Quiet Serenade
- Book 5: His Waiting Love
- Book 6: His Beach Retreat

While Seaside Chapel novels can be read as standalone stories, you can see a bigger picture of the Seaside Chapel community and get a glimpse of the futures of previous characters if you read Books 1-6 in order.

A FREE EBOOK FOR YOU!

A Christian beach romance novel, *Ask You Later* is the story of artist Leon Watts, who returns to Tybee Island and Savannah to jump-start his fledgling career. This novel is a part of the Savannah Sweethearts collection, and happens one year before the Seaside Chapel series begins.

Download this FREE novel now:
JanThompson.com/ask-seaside

YOU ARE READING HIS LONGING HEART

SEASIDE CHAPEL BOOK 1

He is a struggling violinist living in poverty. She is a billionairess violin collector with a trust fund. Living in two different worlds, will their unexpected romance last?

THE MUSICIAN...

Six years ago, Ivan McMillan was a budding cross-over violinist on a world tour with his pianist sister. His career was cut short when Grandpa Otto died suddenly, leaving Grandma Yun saddled with enormous medical bills that ate up all their savings. In the midst of Ivan's struggle to provide for his elderly grandmother and to save their family home from foreclosure, he finds himself falling in love with his billionairess friend, whose lifestyle he cannot afford.

THE MUSE...

After Brinley Brooks's ex-boyfriend abandons her due to her vow of purity, the twenty-something heiress goes home to St. Simon's Island to spend time with her family and to accept her life as a single woman. At her sister's birthday party, Brinley is mesmerized by a violinist friend, Ivan, when he plays one of Bach's orchestral suites. Music therapy or not, her heart starts to seek its own second movement in her love life. Or is she just lonely? One thing leads to another, and Brinley enters Ivan's world of material poverty and spiritual wealth.

THE MINUET OF THEIR LIVES...

When one of Ivan's worst fears comes to pass, he feels obligated to show Brinley what it means to be a Christian living through adversity. However, trusting God is the last thing on his mind as the crisis affects his career, his life, his family, and his relationship with Brinley. Ivan cannot let her see how far he has sunk. What is a Christian man to do?

His Longing Heart is the first novel in *USA Today* bestselling author Jan Thompson's Seaside Chapel Christian small-town beach romance series. This book is the updated second edition of the previously published *Share with Me*.

His Longing Heart (Seaside Chapel Book 1)
JanThompson.com/longing

Seaside Chapel
JanThompson.com/seaside

Sign up for Jan Thompson's mailing list:
JanThompson.com/newsletter

HIS LONGING HEART

CHAPTER ONE

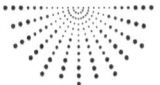

"*B*rin! There you are. I thought you weren't going to make it to my birthday party."

Brinley Brooks watched her sister strut toward her in a shimmering purple-and-black Valentino topped off with a choker of diamonds around her neck. Zoe looked rested and perky and full of life.

As for Brinley—

Never mind.

She shut the French door to the loggia behind her, closing out the sounds of the Atlantic Ocean that she had enjoyed in the few minutes it'd taken her to walk from their parents' seaside cottage to this guesthouse. She had arrived on Seaside Island no more than half an hour before, jumped into her evening gown, and headed here.

Alone.

The ballroom that had turned into a dining room tonight was loud and permeated with laughter that Brinley was too jet-lagged to share. In the backdrop was what sounded like the last measures of Felix Mendelssohn's orchestral "Octet in E flat major." Live orchestral suites were some of her favorite music.

Brinley stepped toward her sister and hugged her tightly.

"I can't believe you made it." Zoe sniffed. "Dad said you had unfinished business in Zurich."

"All done." Brinley had pulled an all-nighter, but the merger was complete, and Brooks Investments, Inc., had added another subsidiary in Ireland. Zoe didn't need to know the details. She also didn't need to know that it was the last business deal Brinley would do for Dad's company.

And the last time she'd live in Zurich.

Too close to the mess, the hurt, the pain. Well, the pain was easing off; it had been three months and a few days since her break-up with her ex-fiancé.

"It's good to be home," Brinley declared.

"I'm happy for you. You've always been a home-body. In fact, I was surprised when you agreed to head up sales for Dad in Zurich."

It wasn't for Dad.

Brinley drew in a deep breath. "It was only for a year."

"It feels like forever not having you around." Zoe lifted her skirt to expose a pair of glittery five-inch

Jimmy Choo platform sandals. She shook a foot so the diamonds on the straps could sparkle under the chandeliers twenty feet above them. "Thank you for my birthday gift, Brin."

To Brinley, it looked like the same pair Zoe had bought last year. And the year before. Only this time it was in another shade of purple.

"Love it, Zoe," she said, anyway. It made her sister happy.

"I do have great taste, don't I?" Zoe pirouetted around Brinley. "And you? What's this?"

Brinley felt self-conscious as Zoe tugged at her midnight blue silk patchwork gown. She hoped none of its many seams ripped.

"Azaria? Marc Jacobs? Dolce? Vera Wang?"

"Peterson."

"Peter who?" Zoe tsk-tsked the same way Mom did when she didn't approve. Zoe had taken after Mom in every way from her lithe beauty to her ability to spend out of a bottomless purse. Must be nice to live rent-free in their parents' guesthouse and eat out of the Brooks family kitchen without touching a dime of her trust fund.

"He's a new designer out of London." Brinley knew she didn't have to explain.

"Never heard of him."

"I told him I'd wear it. It's quite comfortable."

"Quite? *Quite* doesn't cut it. He's still a nameless nobody." Zoe smiled as if with pity. "It's so you, Brin. Always saving homeless cats."

Brinley bristled. "He's up-and-coming. He just needs a chance."

"Sure. But I still like my Valentino over a no-namer." Zoe swished her evening gown.

That was when Brinley saw that her slim sister was filling out. *Is that a tummy or...?*

"Come. I want you to meet Quincy." Zoe locked arms with Brinley, ushering her along through the tables swarming with servers in white gloves.

"Quincy? What happened to Oleg?"

"Oleg? I've been going out with Quincy since October. Didn't I tell you?"

"I don't remember."

"I'm sure I did." Zoe laughed. "You know what they say. Stress can make you forgetful. You work too hard, Brin."

"Work is good for you."

"I'm working too. Practicing for SISO takes a lot of time."

"I'm sure."

"What's that supposed to mean, Brin?"

"Take it literally."

"Oh? I thought you might have some hidden meaning."

"I meant what I said. I agreed with you that SISO takes a lot of time. Petrocelli emails me every now and then. A lot goes on."

"Conductor Petrocelli? Why does he communicate with you?"

Brinley shrugged. "Something to do with Grandpa."

4

"Ah. Did Petrocelli ask you to help underwrite SISO? You know funding is down across the board? They had to let a few percussionists go."

Brinley wasn't sure how much to say. Grandpa Brooks and his friends had started the Sea Islands Symphony Orchestra some twenty years before, but he'd died halfway through that period. Mom and Dad had continued to underwrite the small regional orchestra only to give Zoe something to do as she figured out the rest of her life. There must be more to it than sitting pretty at fashion shows in Paris and Milan. SISO would put her years of contrabass clarinet lessons to good use.

"I'm taking a break, though," Zoe said. "Can't be in Paris and in SISO at the same time."

"Well, you paid for them to be here tonight. That's helping them tremendously." Brinley glanced in the direction of the live orchestra on a platform beyond the sea of round tables as the fourth and last "Presto" movement began.

"Quincy's brother is the concertmaster." Zoe pointed with her purple fingernails.

"Ivan McMillan?"

"You know him?"

"We've met."

"Really?" Zoe's eyebrows rose.

"Can't remember when we first met, though. I've met everybody in SISO at one point or another." Brinley followed her sister as they zigzagged around full tables.

"Ivan is how Quincy and I became an item." Zoe

tipped her head back. "Where's Phinn this Christmas?"

"Probably in Courchevel, but do I care?" Every few months her ex-fiancé had thrown bashes on the French Alps. While they had been together, he had insisted that Brinley accompany him to party with people she didn't know, didn't care for, and hoped never to see again. All to show off the pink diamond ring he'd bought for her at Sotheby's.

It seemed silly that it had taken Brinley more than a year to see through it all. She and Phinn had such contrasting tastes and opinions that she wondered how they'd lasted two years.

"I know he's your ex, but you guys have broken up so many times it's hard to tell if it's on or off. Tell me he won't be back."

"I'm not letting him back, Zoe." There was no way Brinley could have gone on with Phinn. They had parted ways numerous times in their rocky relationship, each time reconciling after he'd crawled back with an offering she couldn't refuse. Things like he'd stop his hard partying after they married, they didn't have to live in Zurich if she didn't want to, or they could move to Seaside Island to raise their future kids.

Each time she had bought the sales pitch, there remained a warning light as bright as the one that said *Exit* in his Boeing Business Jet. She knew that Phinneas Farragut IV had not been groomed for a laid-back lifestyle.

"You sure, Brin?"

"Oh yes. It's unsustainable."

"Unsustainable? Listen to you, Brin. Love is not a business transaction." Zoe tsk-tsked again. "Someday you'll meet the love of your life, and you'll know what I mean. Maybe you'll have something special like Quincy and I do."

"Maybe. Maybe not. Perhaps I'm meant to be single the rest of my life."

"I'm sure you're independent enough for that. But I know you, dear Brin. You're meant to love and be loved. Wait and see."

Brinley didn't say anything. Up ahead the "Brandenberg" concerto started. The program was beginning to sound like something Zoe usually arranged. A mish-mash of random classical pieces. Much like the way her sister had practiced her clarinet back in the days when Brinley accompanied her on the piano.

Someday Brinley hoped to play more piano, but for now it was all work and no play.

"So. What was the final straw?" Zoe asked.

"Inquisitive, aren't we?" Brinley thought about whether it was too personal to share. She kept her voice down. "If you must know—don't tell Mom and Dad—Phinn wanted us to have an open relationship."

"An open marriage too?"

Brinley nodded.

Zoe laughed so loudly several dinner guests turned their heads in her direction. "That fool. You kept the ring, of course."

"Why should I? If I did, he'd think we're still

engaged." Besides, its history was morbid. An ancient Indian maharaja had killed countless tribal leaders to get the pink diamond for his bride, who then promptly died at childbirth.

"Twenty-five million dollars say you shouldn't have. Tell me you didn't throw it across the room at him."

"Nope. FedEx goes to France."

"I'm glad it's over, Brin, for your sake. I don't know what you saw in him in the first place." Zoe leaned her pretty copper curls against Brinley's straight brown hair. "You deserve better than him."

"And you know what's best for me?"

"Maybe not what's *best*, but I do know what's *bad*."

"You're right. You know how to spot a loser."

"Thank you. Let's not think about exes anymore."

The orchestra stopped playing. All Brinley heard now were the clinks of glasses amidst a sea of voices. The plush carpet beneath her was comfortable to her tired feet. She tried not to trip on her long gown.

Zoe chattered on, something about her beau. Brinley refocused.

"I want you to meet Quincy's entire family. Grandma Yun is such a dear. She likes old things too. You'll get along with her. And she makes the best gingerbread cookies—oh, look, Brin. There's Ivan." Zoe pointed.

Brinley stopped walking the moment she heard the familiar first four bass clef staccato notes on the piano. She had played that many times on the piano herself. She turned toward the orchestral platform up ahead—

And saw him.

He was all she saw.

Ivan McMillan.

He looks different from last summer.

Perhaps it was the way his left hand brushed against the neck and fingerboard of the violin. Or the way his right hand moved the bow over the strings. Perhaps it was that fresh haircut, perfectly trimmed sideburns, clean-shaven face, Mona Lisa smile. Or the way he stared right at her as Johann Sebastian Bach's "Air on the G String" rose from his violin and filled the entire ballroom.

Brinley had heard him play the violin before.

Why does he look different tonight?

The rest of the Sea Islands Symphony Orchestra faded away into the *trompe l'oeil* wall behind the platform and the antique copper ceiling above them as the clarity of that violin reached Brinley's ears. She couldn't help it if her heart wafted toward the threaded consonance of violin and piano, two of her favorite instruments. She'd been to many orchestral performances elsewhere. Yet something about this *espressivo* delivery tugged at her.

"Air" had come alive and swirled around her.

An anodyne for her painful weeks, months, years...

She closed her eyes to savor the notes from the second movement of "Suite No. 3 in D major." For a moment, Brinley felt that the evening was meant for her.

How would "Air" sound if it were played on one of her Stradivarius violins that Grandpa Brooks had given to her from his personal collection?

Perhaps it was time to take those old Strads out of the vault and let them make music again. They had been hidden away too long. But she hadn't done anything with them because they were common Stradivarius specimens. The pièce de résistance was the stolen 1698 Damaris Brooks Stradivarius that still hadn't been recovered after seventy years.

I'd like to hear him play "Air" on that.

When she opened her eyes, Ivan was gazing at her, a glint of surprise in his own eyes. Something passed between them, something she could not explain. They'd known each other for a year or there-abouts. Always in passing. And often through oblique references in those emails that Conductor Petrocelli had sent her in Zurich to keep her updated about life in SISO, emails the conductor had sent to Grandpa Brooks when he had been alive.

But she knew one thing. This *Air* had become their song.

Our song.

How could this be? There had been nothing going on between her and Ivan.

Why does he look different tonight?

Before Brinley could dissect the vagaries of that moment in time, Bach wrapped up. Brinley didn't want it to end, but end it did.

Was it the violinist or was it the violin?

Brinley's eyes were still on the platform as stirrings roiled in her heart. She watched Ivan bow and return to the first violin section. He sat down in the concertmaster's chair and nodded to her.

That was all it took.

Her breath caught.

CHAPTER TWO

*B*efore Brinley and her sister could reach
the family table, a tall, lanky man with his
hair tied up in a ponytail jumped in front of them, his
arms immediately going to Zoe's waist and his lips on
hers in ways that were so intimate Brinley had to
avert her eyes. She'd seen a lot of things, but not this
slobbery-smooching-whatever that the lovebirds were
trying to claim in public. Brinley backed away, trying
to give her sister some privacy.

Right. In front of hundreds of dinner guests.

When they separated, they left a smacking sound
in their wake, the same kind of sound one heard
when a suction cup came off a piece of glass. Zoe's
eyes, all occluded, were on Brinley, who was still
stepping back.

"Brin, meet Quincy McMillan."

One arm on Zoe, Quincy reached toward Brinley
with his long, spindly fingers that were surprisingly

well-manicured. Brinley guessed that he must be at least six-five, a whole foot and a half taller than petite Zoe in her Jimmy Choo heels. As for Brinley, the top of her head came up to his neck.

"I know who you are. Brinley Brin, your dad calls you."

Brinley chuckled. "Nice to meet you, Quincy."

"Did you see Ivan, my brother? He plays a smashing violin, doesn't he?"

"Yes, he does," Brinley replied.

"You'd never know he was once a crossover violinist."

"Really."

Quincy seemed to study Brinley. "That haircut frames your face well. Who is your stylist?"

"Whoever is available." Brinley had never been particular about grooming.

"Lovely. Brown hair looks good on you." Quincy waved his free hand at Brinley's head. "Hope there isn't too much chemical in that dye."

Brinley glanced at Zoe. *Where did you dig up this guy?*

Zoe waved her off. "Quincy is a hairstylist. Can you tell?"

"This is my original hair color," Brinley explained. Yep. Straight brown hair. Dull, plain, not glamorous enough to keep Phinn happy.

"Au naturel. I like that." Quincy leaned toward Zoe. "Since you're half as lovely as your sister here, I'm confident we're going to have some pretty kids. Isn't that right, sweetie pie?"

Half as lovely?

Brinley's eyes darted toward her sister. *Seriously?*

Zoe couldn't stop laughing. "Isn't he funny?"

Sure. Funny.

"You know what Quincy bought me for my birthday?" Zoe asked Brinley. "A Maserati Quattroporte GTS."

On his hairstylist's salary?

"She picked the color and chose the model all on her own." Quincy grinned. "While she was at it, she paid for it on my behalf. She sent me a thank-you card. Isn't that sweet?"

Sweet? Brinley didn't know how to respond.

Zoe patted Quincy's chest. "Let's get to dinner before you put the other foot in your mouth."

"Ladies first." Quincy stepped back but still held Zoe's hand.

It was endearing. Brinley couldn't remember the last time Phinn held her hand. Every time they'd been together they'd done nothing but argue and bicker about one thing or another. That went on for two whole years.

"I'd like to do your hair," Quincy suddenly said to Brinley. "I think I can get some curls in there."

"I like it straight. Thank you, though."

At the table near the orchestra platform, Brinley spotted her parents conversing with a couple of people who'd stopped by the table. Brinley waited until Dad saw her.

"Brinley Brin!" Dad leapt out of his chair.

Brinley was glad to see that Dad continued to

recover well from his stroke. His speech had improved in the last few months, and now he was looking more like himself. She wondered whether this was a good time to talk to Dad about the changes in her life, her desire to take a break from Brooks Investments, a sabbatical to find herself.

Brinley hugged both of them. It had been six months since she last saw Mom and four months since she last saw Dad. Funny how it went. In high school and college, she couldn't wait to get out of her parents' hair. Now that she was out in the corporate world and traveling eighty percent of her time, she missed home. Missed eating dinners with her parents. Missed chatting with Dad. And sometimes she even missed going shopping with Mom.

"Where's Phinn, dear?" Mom dabbed her lips gently with a gold-threaded napkin.

"We broke up in the summer, remember?"

"I thought he'd be back by now."

"It's really over, Mom." *Finally.*

Mom knitted her eyebrows. "I can't believe you let him go. He's quite a catch."

Dad cleared his throat. "Guess what, Brinley Brin?"

"What, Dad?" It was a game they had played since she was four years old. *Guess what, Brinley Brin? What, Dad?*

"Aunt Ella is here."

"Is she?" How did Aunt Ella get here from West Palm Beach? She hated long road trips, but she hated flying even more. It would take her at least nine or ten hours with frequent stops on the way to get from West Palm to Seaside Island. "Did someone drive her up?"

"Her caregiver. Apparently she has friends on Hilton Head. After Christmas she'll come back here and pick up Ella and they'll go home."

"Here she comes now." Mom pointed with her chin.

Brinley turned. There she was. Aunt Ella, coming across the plush carpet with a piece of toilet paper trailing behind the sole of her Mary Jane shoes.

Someone ought to tell her.

Sure enough, a server did. He squatted down to remove the stuck paper, and was rewarded with a *whack-whack-whack* on his shoulders.

Aunt Ella retracted her massive purse. Brinley figured that her hard-of-hearing Aunt Ella must not have heard him tell her that he was trying to help.

Dad moaned. "Great. Another lawsuit coming up."

Brinley rushed to Aunt Ella's side. The octogenarian paused for a split second. Then she lurched forward with her arms open wide and hugged Brinley before she could say anything.

Eccentric she might be, Aunt Ella was still Grandpa Brooks's younger sister. Yes, she was technically Great-Aunt Ella. And her name wasn't really Ella either. It was Ursula. Grandpa Brooks had liked to tell that she became Ella when none of her siblings —all gone now—could pronounce Ursula when they were kids.

Any interaction with Aunt Ella only reminded Brinley of lost memories and happy days with Grandpa Brooks back when he was still alive and well and eager to show her his private collection of musical instruments. Yes, he'd bequeathed the collection all to Brinley. At a very high price and at a cost to her relationship with Phinn and all the other boyfriends before him.

"Do you still drive?" Aunt Ella asked.

"Pardon me?" Brinley was taken aback by the question.

"Can you handle a vehicle?" Aunt Ella emphasized each syllable slowly.

"Yes, ma'am. Why?"

"I need a ride to a Christmas luncheon. Will you take me?"

Saying "I don't feel like it" to Aunt Ella was like saying no to Grandpa Brooks. "If I'm around, of course. When is it?"

"Saturday."

"This Saturday?"

Aunt Ella nodded.

"I guess I'll be here."

"Thank you, Brin. You know this could be the last time I see you."

"You said that last year, Aunt Ella." And every year before that since Grandpa Brooks had passed away.

A flurry of server activities around them caught Brinley's attention. "Let's get to our seats, Aunt Ella."

"Time to eat!" Aunt Ella's eyes positively sparkled. She shuffled forward more quickly.

"Yes, ma'am." Brinley matched her pace.

Dear Aunt Ella. No husband. No children. No grandchildren. She lived in a big old house that Grandpa Brooks had bought for her. It came with a housekeeper, a cook, a round-the-clock caregiver, and all the money in the world she could spend.

Alone.

All alone.

Brinley wondered if she might end up like that. She held her great-aunt's wobbly, fragile elbow. "Where are you sitting, Aunt Ella?"

Aunt Ella pointed to the empty seat two place settings away from a diminutive silver-haired lady smiling at something Quincy said to her. She was wearing a dress that Brinley thought she'd seen in World War II museums. It looked like cotton. Maybe it was from the era. A history buff, she had to know. Dad had often teased her about the misappropriation of her MBA because she was more at home as a historian and preservationist than as the top sales executive at Brooks Investments.

"I'll sit next to you," Brinley offered.

"Where's Phinn going to sit?"

Phinn?

"Phinn and I are not together anymore, Aunt Ella."

"Good for you. Everybody, but you, knew he's a loser."

CHAPTER THREE

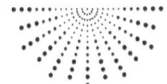

*I*van McMillan wasn't entirely certain what had transpired. He hadn't intended to play "Air" for Brinley Brooks. He and Petrocelli had planned the three-and-a-half-minute movement as an interstice to give the rest of the orchestra a break.

But she had walked into his line of sight at that moment.

Our moment.

Was it possible for something like this to happen? If so, why now? He had met Brinley the year before. Between then and now, nothing had happened. No connection, no circumstances, no calling to bring them together. Obviously, they had lived in different worlds.

They still lived in different worlds.

Ivan reached for his beard but it wasn't there.

Oh yeah. I shaved it off this morning.

His eyes found Brinley again. She was sitting next to Grandma Yun at the Brooks family table. She had a somewhat understated beauty about her and a face so pleasant to look at that all Ivan could think about were breezy summer days—

Tap! Tap!

Ivan heard a throat clearing and more taps.

What?

Ivan looked up. Conductor Petrocelli inhaled noisily and his eyes shot him darts of "I will fire you" as his right hand tapped his baton so hard on the music stand that Ivan thought the man's favorite control stick was going to break in two.

Ivan snapped to attention. Any misstep and Petrocelli would yank that concertmaster chair out from under him. He needed this job. Between his SISO first violin and concertmaster salaries and his music studio income, he was barely able to support himself and Grandma and pay off all those debts, let alone find a girlfriend to—

Girlfriend?

Nah.

He couldn't help looking at her, though. Brinley was talking to Grandma Yun, who looked a bit tired. It had been a mistake to drag the nonagenarian to this dinner party. He had thought Grandma might enjoy some free food, spend some time with her two grandsons, and listen to him play in SISO.

Grandma hardly ever got out of the house these

days except to go to church and the doctor's. Doing things cost money that they didn't have, and Grandma would rather they put every penny toward paying off the three mortgages that Grandpa Otto had left them and those remaining medical bills from her hip replacement.

Yet, looking at Grandma in that straight-back chair put a strain on Ivan's shoulders in that tight thrift shop tuxedo jacket he was wearing, as if he should take Grandma home right away so she could be more comfortable in her rocker. Unfortunately, he knew he couldn't leave. The dinner party for Quincy's girlfriend wouldn't end for a couple more hours though Quincy had promised to take Grandma home at nine o'clock before the after-party began.

Ivan prayed to God that Grandma would last another two hours. She'd been there with him since six o'clock when SISO gathered for a preconcert warmup. Grandma had graciously sat through the rehearsal, a smile on her face the entire time.

She still wore that sweet smile as she chatted with Brinley.

Brinley, who had stood there rooted to the carpet when he played "Air on the G String."

He could play it again and again for her the rest of his—

What am I thinking?

It can never be.

Two different worlds, remember? Even here, the situation was clear. Across from Grandma at the table, the parents of the birthday girl held court, a steady stream of people stopping by to hug them or shake their hands. All of coastal Georgia probably knew them for their generosity to the communities but also for their historical preservation efforts, not to mention their underwriting SISO. It was all chump change to them, probably, as was this guest cottage.

Only a guest cottage. Imagine that.

These people have money coming out of their ears.

He wondered what could happen to the Brooks family now that his brother, Quincy, was dating one of their daughters. Quincy wasn't exactly the epitome of steady income-producing men. He'd gone from job to job, from being a roofer to a student and now a hairstylist.

It was Ivan's fault, really, that Zoe somehow ended up with his brother. Some months before, Zoe had fired her hairstylist. Ivan happened to mention that his older brother was a hairstylist. Next thing he knew, Quincy was jet-setting around the world with Zoe, her money tap flowing non-stop.

As for Ivan, he couldn't imagine not being self-made. All his life he had worked hard. It had paid off with a full scholarship to Juilliard. For a season he was here in a small coastal orchestra instead of being in the Atlanta Symphony or Boston or Vienna, but only for a season. Ivan was proud that he'd worked hard and made a living and was taking care of his grandma. Grandpa Otto, now walking the streets of gold in heaven, would be happy to know he was keeping his promise.

Still, Ivan hoped it hadn't been a mistake to introduce a fellow orchestra member to his brother who had dropped out of cosmetology school at least twice. Maybe it worked out after all in Ivan's favor. It was Zoe's twenty-fifth birthday today. And she had paid SISO generously to add this event to their December calendar. Conductor Hank Petrocelli hadn't minced a word when he said they'd be able to keep renting their rehearsal studio for months to come. That much, huh?

Well, as long as the Brooks family paid SISO for this gig, that was all that mattered to Ivan's financial well-being. Five concerts and soirées done since the Thanksgiving weekend, they had about seven more to go with the last SISO performance on New Year's Eve at the City Hall in downtown Brunswick. After that he had five days off before the winter season began. A small town orchestra, SISO only paid its musicians for rehearsals and performances, so the more events they had, the more Ivan got paid.

Thank God for my music studio or we'd be out in the streets.

Still, his exposure as a member of SISO would go some ways to get him back on the world stage. For that, he had Petrocelli to thank. The conductor had put a lot of faith in him to promote him to concertmaster.

"Vivaldi," Petrocelli spat out at Ivan.

Nervously, Ivan lifted his borrowed 1850 Vuillaume to his left shoulder and placed his bow on the strings. The music sheets were in front of him on the music stand but all he saw was the face of a certain lady superimposed on Vivaldi's *Winter*.

He blinked but her face was still there.

Focus, Ivan. Focus.

CHAPTER FOUR

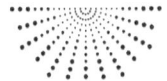

Kobe steak flown in fresh from Hyogo Prefecture, Japan, notwithstanding, Brinley couldn't eat a bite of it. She nibbled on a piece of roasted asparagus. Drank water with lime from a cobalt blue goblet. Stared into space, oblivious to the chatter around her. Her eyes were on Zoe and Quincy on the other side of the table, loving and cozy and rubbing foreheads together.

Was that what being in love looked like?

Brinley had nothing of that sort with Phinn. Or any of the guys before him.

This is all my fault.

When Brinley had been a teenager, she was fascinated by Grandpa Brooks's vast collection of fifteenth- through nineteenth-century musical instruments. On her sixteenth birthday, Grandpa had made her an offer she almost refused. He would bequeath to her his entire music collection valued at millions of dollars at auction, including all the Stradi-varius violins he had already owned and had continued to buy, if his favorite granddaughter would do one thing: take a vow of purity until her wedding night.

With an eye on the private collection and what a teenager could do with all that money, she'd said yes. And then spent the next ten years regretting it. Grandpa Brooks had suffered a brain aneurism and died suddenly. In memory of him, she couldn't possibly break her vow. After all, she bought his reli-giosity—sort of.

And Brinley always kept the promises she made.

Because of that vow, she'd lost Phinn, Crispin, Xander, and that cute cross-country skier from college who'd all wanted more than what she could give them.

Didn't they all understand that she was saving herself for her future husband? But Grandpa Brooks wasn't here to give her support on her cause. What had she done, really, but only exchanged herself for a collection of violins and pianos and things?

Then again, Grandpa Brooks had said that personal purity and good works earned points with God. Even after he'd been gone a decade, Brinley still wanted him to be proud of her, to call her worthy of her special inheritance. Good works, she could do all day long. But what about personal purity? It had begun with that vow, didn't it? It went from there to all the things that Grandpa Brooks had said would get her God's approval for her life. Then she'd be fulfilled and would have peace in her heart. No one else had told her otherwise, so what Grandpa had said must be true.

For now, she knew she had done the right thing to let Phinn go. *Finally*.

"—the rest of that?"

Brinley turned toward Aunt Ella's voice. She was spooning mashed potatoes from her dinner plate into a ziplock bag that she then carefully arranged into her oversized purse.

"What are you doing, Aunt Ella?" Sotto voce. And where did she get the ziplock bag?

Aunt Ella pointed to Brinley's plate. "I like asparagus."

Seriously? "They'll bring you seconds if you like."

"Hate to let *that* go to waste." Aunt Ella's knobby fingers were on the edge of Brinley's dinner plate. All Brinley could think of were her fingerprints everywhere.

"Willard always said to eat up," Aunt Ella said.

Willard. Grandpa Brooks.

Brinley remembered those holidays with Grandpa, how he had grilled the snapper and bass he had caught at sea. How he had always told his grandkids to "eat up" and "don't let it go to waste."

Across the table Quincy remarked to Mom something about Kobe. Next to him, Zoe's seat was empty. Brinley didn't wonder where Zoe had disappeared to because she could never sit still. Always up and about, doing something. As for Brinley, she could sit in the same spot for hours reading a book.

"Well, it would've cost us more if we'd flown *everyone* to Paris and put up *everyone* at the castle." Mom's voice carried across the table. She patted Dad's arm. "This dinner party is cheaper than our new Bugatti Veyron."

"Frugal is good." Dad gave Mom a peck on her cheek.

Her parents sure had a different definition of frugal, Brinley thought. She had spent her twenty-sixth birthday at work in Zurich this summer. Dad knew she had been homesick. He had Chef Pierre bake a homemade apple pie which he personally flew to Zurich. It was the most expensive pie Brinley had ever eaten. But it was her comfort food, and Dad knew it.

Now that Brinley was home, she wasn't getting any apple pie this time. Mom had let Chef Pierre take the rest of the year off so he could go home to Toronto to be with his family and relatives for Christmas and New Year's Day.

Brinley nudged her plate away from Aunt Ella's prying fingers. She picked up her fork and knife, and dug into the steak. The steak was delicious. Lukewarm now, but still, the flavor was there. Whoever the caterers were, they did a great job.

Truly, she had always had good food here in coastal Georgia. She loved going out to eat by the ocean, walking about the shops, reading a book on the beach. She made a mental note to call up her sister-in-law for lunch before she had to go back to Atlanta again the first week in January.

Riley had turned into a hermit since her husband, Brinley's oldest brother, Parker, had passed away suddenly some five years before. Brinley had made it a point to have lunch with Riley at least once whenever she was in town. Not that Riley had always shown up, but Brinley tried.

Oh, Brinley wished she didn't have to go back to a big city with its traffic and smog. If she could have her way, she'd move to Seaside Island or St. Simon's Island and never leave.

With her own trust fund available to her since she had turned twenty-six, Brinley didn't have to earn a salary a single day the rest of her life. She could do pet projects, like those historical preservation projects Dad had been neglecting since his stroke. She'd been helping him out in Brooks Renovations on and off the last several years. Maybe she could do more.

She wondered how she could broach that subject with Dad, how he was going to take it, and what it would do to her brother, Diehl. Would it add more work to his already stressful load as CEO of Brooks Investments if she bailed out and worked for Brooks Renovations instead?

Would it have been easier had Parker been alive? Her two brothers had been very close and had managed the family businesses together. Now Diehl was alone, and as his sister, she must put in her fair share of work since they didn't expect Zoe to have a mind for business though she'd often surprised them with her acuity.

Aunt Ella was now taking her own pulse and feeling her own forehead. On the other side of Aunt Ella, the other elderly lady looked concerned.

"Are you all right, Ella?" Her voice was soft-spoken.

They'd been briefly introduced. Yun McMillan had lived all her life on St. Simon's Island, yet Brinley had never seen her in town. She thought it was nice of Zoe to invite Quincy's family to her birthday party.

"Looks like I'm fine," Aunt Ella declared.

"Glad to hear that," Yun said. "Don't want you to be sick and miss the Christmas luncheon on Saturday."

"My grand-niece here is taking me to it."

"Is she?" Yun dug into her vintage purse with intricate beadwork on it, fished out some sort of post-card, and passed it on to Brinley with a freckled hand protruding out of a frayed sleeve.

Couldn't she have found a newer dress?

"It's at Seaside Chapel." Yun retracted her hand.

Brinley looked at the postcard. The date and time were printed on it together with a Bible verse. *Does Aunt Ella know what she's getting into?*

"Do you know where the church is?" Yun asked. "By Massengale Park near East Beach."

"Yes, I know. I've attended beach weddings there a couple of times."

"Our church is known for that."

How many of those marriages lasted? "In fact, my

brother Parker married his wife there. And his funeral was also at Seaside."

"I'm sorry to hear that." Yun's voice sounded genuine.

"Life and death." Brinley sat back. "Part of what we have to deal with, right?"

CHAPTER FIVE

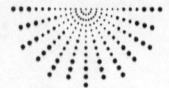

"*D*id you enjoy the orchestra, Grandma?" Ivan asked, hands on Grandma Yun's shoulders.

"Yes, dear." She reached back to tap one of his hands. "You always do such a marvelous job, Ivan. I enjoyed it tremendously and I'm sure Brinley here did too."

Brinley.

Ivan was acutely aware that Brinley, sitting next to Grandma Yun, was not paying any attention to him as her fingers pecked away at her iPhone.

She gasped.

"Are you okay?" Ivan asked.

"I will be. Soon." Brinley looked across the table. "Mom. Dad. Guess what?"

Ned and Rose Brooks stopped talking.

"Helen says an art thief told Interpol that he saw

what looked like the Damaris in a private collection in Vienna."

"Vienna. Of all places." Ned shook his head. "How many times have we been there?"

"Interesting, isn't it?" Brinley's eyes brightened. Under the chandeliers, Ivan thought there were specks of gold in them. He was too close for comfort, but she was smiling and beautiful and—

"Have you ever played a Strad?" Brinley asked him.

"No. I've heard of your Damaris."

"Then you know that one of my paternal ancestors, Jeremiah Brooks, bought that straight from Stradivari's shop in Italy."

Ivan nodded. "A wedding gift for Damaris Brooks in 1698. Wasn't there another?"

"She reciprocated twenty years later with a Strad for him, a 1714 model. The two violins were passed on as a pair down the generations until 1893 when there was a bitter fallout among the brothers. The 1698 Strad was taken by one of the brothers and sold to an anonymous buyer. It was never seen again until now. See here."

Brinley handed her iPhone to Ivan. He caught a breeze of light perfume, so light he wouldn't have noticed had her wrist not been this close to him.

He stared at the Strad. Wow. It had some sort of intricate carvings on the side. And the initials DLSB.

"LS?" Ivan asked.

"La Salle. Damaris La Salle Brooks." Brinley seemed excited. "The La Salles were indigo planters living next door to the Brooks, who planted rice. The two plantations merged after the marriage, but just so you know, they did marry for love."

"That's always good," Yun said.

"So where's the other Strad?" Ivan was interested now. All he had was someone else's Vuillaume.

"It's safe." Brinley said no more and Ivan decided not to pry though he wanted to know where it was kept.

"And is it called the Jeremiah Brooks Strad?"

"No, actually it's the Lord Sterling Strad because Damaris bought it from a Lord Sylvester Sterling. She was too frail to travel to Italy at that time."

Ivan handed Brinley's iPhone back to her. Their fingers touched. It was accidental. He tried not to read too much into it. "You know a lot about your family history."

"She's our family historian," Ned said from across the table. "I often wondered why she's in marketing instead."

Brinley frowned. "Oh, am I sitting in your chair?"

"No, Miss Brooks. I'm not at this table." He pointed to a table farther away marked SISO.

"Call me Brinley. Your brother is dating my sister. Let's not use titles."

"Okay. Brinley." For a year they had not been on a first name basis. Did he have Quincy to thank for this?

"Your brother is tall," Brinley said.

"Yeah. Well, he lords over all of us." Ivan laughed.

"You're pretty tall, so don't sell yourself short."

"Haha."

"Thank you for "Air." It was beautiful." Brinley's eyes were faraway all of a sudden. "I wonder how it'd sound on the—never mind."

"Get it back and I'll play it for you." Ivan had no idea how those words formed themselves and tumbled out of his mouth.

"You will?"

"It'll be our song—oops! I don't mean—uh—"

"Our song," Brinley said. That faraway look again. "Grandpa Brooks spent a lifetime looking for it. Now it shows up. A blip."

"A blip of hope."

"And you will play our song."

Our song.

Ivan caught a movement at the corner of his eye. Conductor Petrocelli was waving to him. "Back to work. Good to talk with you."

Ivan's patent black leather shoes developed a bit of a bounce on his way back to the platform. Not sure what that meant. Must be the thick padding on the carpet.

Brinley was easy on his eyes, but they were in two different worlds with little in common between them. He'd always be the hired court musician, nothing more, and she, the noble lady, nothing less.

Sure, he'd just promised to play "Air" on the grand old Strad for her. If she ever recovered it. Some stolen Stradivarius violins were never found. He prayed she didn't get her hopes up too high.

Still...

Our song.

It had a nice ring to it.

How sweet it was that the pair of violins had belonged to a married couple. He hoped they did get the Damaris Strad back. Ivan wondered how much the violins were worth. He had heard about the search but hadn't bothered to dig up more information. Tonight he was more curious than ever, perhaps because Brinley was interested in it.

He made a mental note to google later. *Well, here.* His iPad was on the music stand in front of him. Every SISO member had an iPad so that they could play impromptu requests. He sat down and logged into his iPad. He googled both violins. There were people out there who had no life outside cataloging Strads.

His eyes widened when he saw that the stolen 1698 Damaris Brooks was listed at twenty-two million dollars.

Are they kidding? That had to be the priciest violin in the world, more expensive than the 1721 Lady Blunt auctioned off at sixteen big ones several years before. He wondered what the 1714 Lord Sterling would fetch.

A whopping seven point nine million dollars.

Didn't Brinley say she had it still? Why wasn't it played? Maybe it was on loan to a music museum? How sad. Violins were meant to be played, not kept somewhere "safe." What was the point of a musical instrument if it were never heard?

Is that what rich people do? Buy things that never get much use?

Ivan's eyes scanned the room. Such opulence. From the chandelier to the plush carpet, from the painted walls to the big French doors. All felt foreign to him though he'd played in many concert halls and private parties before. Back in his Juilliard days, he had dreamed of touring the world as a concert violinist and playing in rich settings the rest of his life.

Unfortunately, after two years of trying, everything had ended abruptly. So much for earning enough income to own his own Strad. Maybe not the Damaris Brooks or the Lord Sterling, but something he could pay cash for.

Not gonna happen.

Nope. Not since Grandpa Otto had that massive heart attack when he was out shopping.

Grandpa Otto had been quite a historian himself, and Ivan imagined he would get along with Brinley as they talked history—

Brinley? How did she pop into my head?

His eyes came upon hers, twenty feet of space between them. She quickly looked away. How long had she been looking this way? What for?

Ivan felt self-conscious. But there was no time to ponder why she had been staring as Conductor Petrocelli tapped his baton. Ivan led the tuning but his mind was on a certain seat. She made him unable to focus. He struggled through the simple process.

The Sea Islands Symphony Orchestra rivaled

that of other small orchestras. Maybe some day SISO might play with the Atlanta Symphony Orchestra. Ivan had thought of auditioning for a position in the ASO, even if it was only second violin. Then again, he'd have to move Grandma Yun all the way to Atlanta and settle her into a new town, a new place, a new hassle. In the end he had given up on that, and simply stayed on St. Simon's Island.

Thank God he had not moved because Grandma Yun preferred to recover from her hip surgery in a small town rather than in a big city. Her rehabilitation had taken a lot of time. After that, Ivan continued as Grandma Yun's primary caregiver, and took over the management of the family finances. And debts.

Six years.

Six long years.

Gustav Holst's "Jupiter" theme soon filled the entire ballroom. When SISO was done, Ivan watched as his brother Quincy walked up onto the platform, hand in hand with Zoe. The other hand held a microphone.

"That was my brother, Ivan, and SISO giving Holst a run for his notes, y'all," Quincy said. "Was that amazing or what?"

Ivan cringed as Quincy yelled into the microphone, his voice echoing off the plaster walls. Everyone clapped and cheered.

Ivan spotted his friend from the Seaside Chapel men's Bible study group, Chef Sebastian Langston, restaurateur and caterer, roll a giant purple-and-black cake toward the platform. Ivan wondered if the cake was even edible. He thought that the small little cake he'd bought for Grandma Yun from Publix looked more delectable than that ghastly creation. Sebastian lit the candles, all twenty-five of them.

Quincy beamed. "We're going to sing happy birthday to my sweetie pie, Zoe!"

The orchestra began to play a boisterous jazz accompaniment to the singing of a wild and off-key "Happy Birthday" to Zoe who was beaming with delight.

After the crowd calmed down, Zoe took the microphone, Quincy's gangly arms hanging over her petite shoulders.

"Before we have our cake and eat it too, I want you to be the first to know..."

Uh-oh. Ivan braced himself.

"Mom, Dad, everyone." Zoe drew a deep breath. "Quincy and I are married, we're having a baby, and we're moving to Paris!"

A hush swept through the ballroom.

Ivan's eyes immediately shot to where Grandma Yun was sitting. She had spilled her water on the table. Around the table, Aunt Ella, Ned, and Rose looked stunned.

And Brinley. She was reaching toward the floor to pick up her iPhone. Then she stared at her sister and her now husband.

As for Ivan, he didn't know what to think.

Moments later, the entire room erupted in a cacophony of confused applause.

CHAPTER SIX

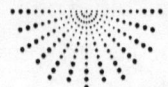

$\mathcal{T}$he birthday cake was more fluorescent purple than black, and Brinley would have none of it. She watched Yun McMillan inch toward it with a tremulous fork gripped in her right hand. The fork never made it to the rectangular piece of cake on the gold-trimmed dessert plate. It clattered to the table. She pushed away what turned out to be cheesecake.

Behind Yun, SISO continued playing an eclectic mix of selections that Brinley was sure wasn't her sister Zoe's doing. Might be Quincy's musical taste.

"I wonder which came first." Yun shook her head.

"Excuse me?" Brinley sat back a little as a server came by to fill her water goblet. When she left, Brinley had a clear view of Yun, who seemed to have aged in minutes.

Yun pointed to Quincy and Zoe making the

rounds through other tables, where they were continuously congratulated.

For the first time in her life, Brinley realized she didn't know her sister all that well. Whatever happened to childhood innocence and carefree days on the sand and surf? All that insulation was gone. Here was the harshness of time.

"I was hoping for a church wedding." Yun dabbed her eyes. "I can't keep up with him."

"Quincy is not a little boy anymore. He and Zoe are consenting adults."

"I guess I just have to trust God for my grandchildren."

Trust God.

Yun placed a hand on Brinley's wrist. Her fingers were cold. Very cold. "What time is it, please?"

"Eight-thirty."

"Only eight-thirty?" Her shoulders sagged. "It's nearly my bedtime."

"Who did you come here with?"

"Ivan. Quincy was supposed to take me home."

Well, Ivan was busy with SISO and Modest Petrovich Mussorgsky's *Pictures at an Exhibition.* Brinley noticed that his demeanor had remarkably changed. The glint in his eyes was gone. He looked spent sitting there at the edge of the orchestra.

Brinley heard crackles of laughter and followed the sound to Zoe sprouting from Quincy's lap at another table, a sloshing Bordeaux glass in her hand as she drank from his. It was the wrong time for Brinley to talk to Zoe about fetal alcohol syndrome.

And the wrong time to give either of them the car keys.

Back at their table, Aunt Ella was missing. Brinley didn't remember seeing her leave the table. The rest of the table was empty. Mom and Dad had left minutes after Zoe had dropped the baby bomb on them.

"What time did Ivan say SISO would be done tonight?" Brinley asked.

"Not sure exactly. When the party's over, I guess." Yun had weary eyes. Red eyes. Sad eyes. "Zoe, or maybe Quincy, is taking me home."

No way was Brinley going to let either one of them drive. And she couldn't sit there looking at the little lady like that either. "You know what? I'll take you home."

"Oh no, please don't bother. I can wait."

"It's no trouble at all. Where do you live?" Brinley dug into her purse for the spare key to Dad's Bugatti Veyron. Every time she was in town, Dad let her drive his Bugatti. Diehl didn't get the same privilege because he'd wrecked his Ferrari two years before and Dad was leery of his touching his BV.

"Off Old Demere and the marshes."

"We've worked on some houses on Old Demere. We'll plug your address into the GPS and get you home." Whenever Brinley was in town, she'd follow Dad around on his pet project renovating old houses and buildings to keep the history of coastal Georgia alive from Savannah to Cumberland Island and beyond.

In fact, that was one of the things she had wanted to talk with Dad about during this vacation.

Yun told her the street address. Brinley knew exactly where that was. Her house was one street over from the block that Dad had been bidding for. He had been trying to prevent overzealous developers from turning the entire oceanfront north of the lighthouse into a series of pastel clustered villas devoid of native trees. Two blocks from the beach, Yun's neighborhood was next in the developers' teardown list. Dad and Brinley were determined to preserve old houses and the green spaces around them the way they'd been the past century.

"Fifteen minutes tops." She pushed back her chair.

"Are you sure?"

"Yes, Yun. I'm sure. I need some fresh air myself."

"We have to tell Ivan."

"Text him."

Yun dug around her old beaded purse. "Oh, I left my cell phone at home. Could you?"

"Sure. What's the number?" Brinley tapped it in and sent Ivan a text message. "This is Brinley. Your grandma is tired. I'm driving her home."

Brinley was on her feet, ready to get out of there. "Yun, I'm going to get our coats and the car. I'll drive it out to the front door over there, and then come back in here to get you. Okay?"

"Yes." Yun seemed to like knowing what was happening.

There was an elevator to the basement near the

butler's pantry. The coatroom was nearby. Brinley was putting on her fur coat when a server passed by. It was the same server whom Aunt Ella had bashed. He was walking with one shoulder up and the other down.

Brinley felt sorry for him. She pressed a twenty into his palm. He was very surprised. Brinley didn't explain.

She entered the elevator as SISO began a Schumann sonata. She looked that way but only saw Ivan's side as the elevator door closed.

In the basement, Brinley found Dad's Bugatti in the private garage not open to guests. Since Dad hadn't driven it in a year since his stroke, the mechanic had taken it for a few spins to keep the engine going.

She drove it up the ramp, went around the building, and parked it at the porte cochère where the valet eyed the car, all two-point-something million of it.

This Bugatti was one of the main reasons Dad had agreed with Mom to purchase this guest cottage a few years ago to complement the Brooks's winter home next door, another original Addison Mizner design from the twenties. Word was Mizner himself had seen the finished cottages before he passed away. Brinley wondered if he ever thought of the misnomer.

While the main house had eleven thousand square feet, this guest cottage only had nine. It boasted an imposing twenty-car underground garage that sold the house, setting Brinley's parents back thirty-two million dollars.

Dad only laughed, saying that Mom's true economic purpose in life was to leave nothing for posterity, though no matter how many houses she bought here and abroad, no matter how much she spent, Dad's accountants almost always managed to level off the Brooks family fortune at twenty-seven billion dollars, give or take a few billion dollars due to stock market fluctuations, the income stream coming from the international Brooks Investments as well as the smaller, more regional Brooks Renovations.

When Brinley got out of the car, she could see Yun through the glass doors, walking toward her, holding on to Ivan's arm. SISO must be taking a short break.

The valet opened the door for Brinley. Brinley entered the foyer and walked toward Yun. Between her and Ivan they managed to get Yun's old coat on her. Then they continued the walk of ages toward the great cold outdoors. Brinley wondered if Yun had a walker she wasn't using.

"I'm ninety-seven," Yun declared. "I can take my sweet old time."

"Yes," Brinley said. "You've earned it."

Ivan smiled an affable smile. "Thanks for taking Grandma home."

"No problem at all. After that announcement I needed to get out of here myself."

Silence. Then: "My brother is full of surprises."

"My sister too."

Ivan seemed to cheer up that it wasn't all his family's fault. "Are you coming back? SISO will be done shortly, and then Quincy's jazz band is playing."

"You're in it?"

"Just for tonight. Subbing for their pianist sick with stomach flu."

"Looks like they're working you hard." Brinley laughed.

"Getting paid helps."

"That does, doesn't it?" "Air" was on Brinley's mind. That alone was worth the price of admission.

The front door opened into the cold night.

"Wow. What car is this?" Ivan asked.

"Dad's car." Brinley realized something bad. The Bugatti only had two doors. Oops. The passenger side was on the other side, so they had to go around the bumpers. It took a while but Yun was determined to make it on her own two feet.

With Yun safely seated and belted, Brinley found herself escorted by Ivan to the driver's side.

"Please drive slowly," Ivan whispered into her ear. "Grandma doesn't need more excitement tonight."

Brinley nodded.

He opened the car door for her. "Will you come back to the after-party?"

"That's the second time you asked the question."

"And the second time you didn't answer."

"I'm not all that into parties, Ivan." Ivan. She liked saying his name.

"Neither am I."

"But you have to be here. I don't." Brinley got into the car.

"Ah, I'm sorry I asked."

"Don't be. We're family now, aren't we?"

"Scary thought, isn't it?" Ivan chuckled. "So will you come back?"

"Okay." But she wasn't sure why she wanted to.

CHAPTER SEVEN

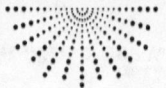

*B*rinley drove Dad's Bugatti onto Tenth Street and made the turns she knew well in the area. It was dark and there were no streetlights. She didn't like that but here they were now. She wondered whether she could reach into her purse fast enough for her pepper spray.

Then again, there was nothing to worry about. St. Simon's Island had always been laid-back and safe. Hardly any crimes ever happened around here. But with the mass presence of the newly rich buying up cottages on Seaside Island and spending their time on St. Simon's and Jekyll, crime was bound to rise. Dad had told them that the islands wanted to raise property taxes so they could expand the police force and fire department. Nothing new, really. They had expanded once in 2004 when the thirtieth G8 Summit was held on Seaside Island with fortress-like security.

Brinley hit the gas pedal.

"Oooh, please slow down." Yun's hand was on her forehead.

The speedometer said Brinley was going thirty-five miles per hour, well within the speed limit of forty this side of town. She wondered how she could petition for streetlights to be built in the area.

As she was thinking, the GPS said, "Your destination is on the right."

Yun McMillan lived one block from the beach and three doors down from the house that Dad and Brinley had salvaged from foreclosure two years before. They'd renovated it and rented it out. It was a lovely cottage from the thirties, but they'd opened up the inside space and added a spectacular deck to bring in the outdoors. Dad was into outdoor fireplaces and kitchens. Each house that he and Brinley had bought and redone under Brooks Renovations had reflected Dad's mood at that point in life.

With his stroke, Dad would be hard-pressed to continue the pet project. Brinley's remaining brother, Diehl, ran the worldwide headquarters of Brooks Investments, and truly, he didn't need Brinley anymore to bring in sales or to run the marketing department. Diehl could handle it, even without Dad. So maybe Brinley could take over this renovation business after all.

"Here we are." Yun McMillan's voice was fatigued.

Brinley coasted on the driveway and cut off the engine in front of the porch. When she turned off the headlights, they were sitting in darkness. She flicked on the headlights again.

"That's kind of you, Brinley. Our porch lights are broken." Yun struggled to get out of the car.

"Hold on." Brinley went to her, helped her out of the car and up the rickety steps onto the porch. The floorboards rattled and creaked, and Brinley thought she was going to fall through.

How could anyone live here?

Yun's keys jingled from her hand. Brinley glanced all around for shadows as Yun patiently reached for the keyhole. The headlights were bright, but when Yun stood in front of the door, she blocked most of it from the keyhole. Brinley turned on the flashlight app on her iPhone to help Yun see enough to get the key into the front door.

Yun flicked on the living room lights.

Brinley surveyed the room. It was all fifties furniture. Maybe even forties. Sparse, dusty, vintage. Old things were everywhere. Brinley spotted an old upright piano. Her eyes lit up. The wood was dark honey. She was sure it was Brazilian rosewood with its rich burls and rings. The piano legs were ornately carved. There was a pair of fretwork on the top above the keyboard.

The fallboard was down, covering what should be keys underneath, but if this piano was what Brinley suspected, there should be a decal on the fallboard.

"Go on." Yun seemed to know what Brinley wanted to do.

Brinley lifted the fallboard. There they were. Old words she was pleased to see.

Steinway & Sons.

Brinley knelt down on the old oak floor and peered under the keyboard to confirm. Sure enough. Inscribed on the fretwork above the pedals were the initials "S&S."

"I haven't seen a prettier Victorian upright," she said.

"Why, yes." Yun took off her coat and hung it on the coat rack in the coat closet. Then she reached for her walker. "I like old things."

"I do too." Brinley was all over the piano. "What year was this made?"

"Take a guess."

"Late 1800s?"

"Very good. You do know your pianos. It was built in 1877."

Brinley sat down on the piano stool. It felt original. "Fully restored?"

"Yes. That's what the second mortgage—oh dear. I wasn't supposed to tell anyone. My Otto said not to."

"I won't say anything. May I?" She reached for the keys.

"Of course. It would be nice for someone else other than Ivan and me to play it sometime."

And inevitably, Brinley played a minuet until she stopped abruptly. "I can't remember the rest of the notes."

Yun clapped when Brinley was done. "You're pretty good."

"All the piano lessons paid off." Brinley laughed. "Well, I must go."

"You're welcome to come here anytime to play my Steinway." Yun handed Brinley a business card. "Ivan had these made for me."

Brinley read the card. "Tea for Two at Two."

"Every weekday afternoon at two, I will be available for tea here. Would you come this week?"

At first Brinley wanted to say no. But then she thought of the piano. "I'm not sure how often I could come. I'm going back to Atlanta the first week of January."

"We don't have much time then. How about tomorrow at two, if you like."

"Tomorrow?" Without further thought, Brinley checked her iPhone. Lunch with her sister-in-law was at noon, but they would be done before two o'clock because Riley had to go pick up her son from school. And she didn't have other plans. "What can I bring?"

"Yourself. And whatever you want to play on the piano."

Brinley had plenty of music sheets on her iPad currently in her suitcase at the big house. "Well, I guess I'll see you at two tomorrow."

"Sounds good. I'll have tea ready. Do you like chai?"

"Love chai tea."

"Organic."

"Even better." Brinley walked toward the front door. "Now be sure to lock up when I leave."

"I will."

"Don't forget to text your grandson to tell him you're home safely. He was a bit concerned with the car."

Yun laughed. "He worries about me all the time."

They passed the coat closet again. Brinley remembered Yun's coat. She wanted to take her synthetic fur coat off and give it to Yun, but the lady probably wouldn't take it, and it would look like charity. Besides, the coat would be too long for Yun. Perhaps Brinley could give her a brand new coat for Christmas instead of the coat off her own back. Christmas was in fifteen days. Plenty of time for her to find a nice coat.

Ah, better yet, she'd take her shopping. She couldn't be presumptuous about what Yun wanted.

Brinley waved to Yun, reminded her again to lock the doors, and nearly sprained her ankle on a shifting floorboard on her way across the porch. Good thing her dress shoes had a chunky heel instead of the usual stilettos she wore to dinners.

She backed out of the driveway. She felt sleepy. She'd been flying all day across time zones. Right now it would be way past her bedtime in Zurich. However, she'd given Ivan her word that she'd return to the party.

So return she must.

When she gave her word, she kept it.

CHAPTER EIGHT

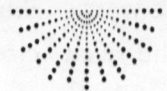

*T*he music of Wynton Marsalis was the king of the after-party, bursts of brass and percussion and New Orleans, with Zoe's new husband off to one side, standing tall with the bass he seemed to be enjoying thwacking and thumping.

Jazz might've been Quincy's thing, Brinley thought. Zoe was more into Béla Bartók and Antonín Dvořák. Not jazz.

On the platform were a couple of trumpet players, a man and a woman. Brinley didn't recognize the man, but she'd seen the woman in the brass section of SISO this evening. Her eyes on the jazz band, Brinley strolled nonchalantly toward the front to get a closer look at the pianist in the fedora with his tuxedo jacket off and white oxford shadowing toned arms. His straight back, shoulder width, and that slight leaning forward told her that it was unmistakably Ivan McMillan.

Unmistakably?

Brinley caught herself. She'd only known Ivan for what? A year? And not even on familiar terms. How could she have spotted him in a crowd?

An empty table opened up in front of her, beckoning her to sit and stare. She shed her coat and piled it onto a seat. And sat down. And stared. Unabashedly. Ivan's back was turned toward her, anyway, and he wouldn't have known she was enjoying more than just the music. Besides, he seemed to be single, and so was she now.

Then again, so what? They were strangers.

Brinley's iPhone pinged at the same time the jazz band finished the number. She checked her email. Helen Hu said the Stradivarius trail had gone cold. Brinley emailed back asking her to keep at it.

A wail and a shriek startled Brinley. Her head snapped up and she stared incredulously as Quincy McMillan began to sing something that sounded like a cross between a wolf howling and a rooster crowing. The piano bench was empty. Staggering up to the platform, Zoe nearly tripped on the steps.

Brinley watched Zoe and Quincy give karaoke a really bad name, slurring lyrics to indiscernible songs, transposing the tunes into what sounded like a five-car pileup on Interstate 285 back in Atlanta. And the baby—

"Are you thinking what I'm thinking?"

Ivan.

His voice caused Brinley's heart to flutter a bit or she thought it did.

"You mean fetal alcohol syndrome?" Brinley offered.

"I'm thinking my brother is making a fool of himself."

"So is my sister."

"But we can't babysit them."

"They're above the age of consent."

"I concur." He sat down on the chair and threw his tuxedo jacket over the back of another chair. "Glad you came back."

"I don't know why I did."

"Hope you didn't feel pressured."

"I can still hear Bach in my head. You really made that violin come alive."

"I credit God for that."

Brinley hesitated with what she was about to ask. She went back and forth in her mind and then she decided there was no harm asking. "You and Yun talk about God all the time."

"God is very important to us."

"I can see that."

"If you love someone you keep talking about that person. Grandma and I love God, so we talk about Him all the time. What do you talk about all the time?"

"Work. Food. Work. Food."

Ivan looked at her like he couldn't believe how shallow she was.

"I suppose those are essentials," Ivan said. "What about the intangibles?"

"We all have our own beliefs."

"Exactly." Ivan paused long enough for Brinley to wonder what he was going to say next. "As for me and my house, we will serve the Lord."

"You're religious, like your grandmother."

"I'm not into religion."

"No? God. Lord. Aren't those religious words?"

"I'm just a Christian who loves God."

Brinley leaned toward him. "As opposed to a Christian who doesn't love God?"

"I don't want to get into a debate."

"I didn't mean to start one."

"Are we fighting?"

"How can we? We barely know each other."

Ivan leaned back in the chair and folded his arms. "Have you ever tried to wind down and were unable to?"

"With that cacophony?" Brinley pointed her chin at Zoe and Quincy. Suddenly she realized that was what Mom did a lot. She pointed with her chin.

Fortunately the song was short. Amidst claps and catcalls, another dinner guest went up to sing her favorite number, something mellower. *Thank God.*

"SISO did a great job tonight, I must say. You're good with the violin. Way better than karaoke."

Ivan smiled. Something about that smile tugged at Brinley's heart. It was both glad and sad.

"How long have you been playing the violin?"

"Since I was four. Grandma Yun was my violin teacher. She retired some years ago." A glint in his eye hinted at memories that Brinley wasn't privy to.

He quickly changed the subject. "Anymore news about the Strad?"

"We don't have it yet."

"What are you going to do if the collector won't give it back?"

"There's always compensation." Brinley would pay anything to get the 1698 Damaris Brooks Strad.

Ivan chuckled. "Who has that kind of money? It's only a violin."

"It's history, Ivan. Keeping memories alive, you know."

"Memories are intangibles."

There it was again. Fleeting sorrow in his eyes.

"Some old things are reminders of moments lost and time gone." Brinley had many old things from old books to old Stradivarius violins and old Steinways to old whatnots handed down to her from Grandpa Brooks who seemed to be a hoarder of all things historical about the Brooks family. That was why she had to get the Strad back. Even if Grandpa was gone, this was his legacy of handing down history to the next generation. Besides, that one empty case in the art and music vault must be filled.

"Are you all right?" Ivan's voice was soft, uplifting almost, like a strand of sea oat grass floating on the sea breeze. A kite in the air. Then coming down, he lowered his voice even more. "Don't worry. We'll pray that you'll get the Strad back."

Pray.

"Do you think prayer works?" Brinley asked.

"If I pray to the wind, what good is it?" Ivan

replied. "If I pray to my God, it means something because my God, to whom I pray, is the One who works. Speaking for myself, of course."

"Grandpa Brooks used to take us to church."

"Grandpa Otto used to take us to church."

Brinley understood. "We all have losses."

"Some more than others."

Brinley rubbed her forehead. "Sorry. I'm just tired."

"Me too." Ivan waved down a server. "Want coffee or hot cocoa?"

Brinley shook her head. "No, thanks. Don't want to be up all night."

"I'm driving home. I need caffeine."

"For a ten-minute drive?" Brinley laughed.

"See. Made you laugh." When the server came by, Ivan asked for two cups, one for here and one to go. "But truth be told, anyone can fall asleep behind the wheel."

"It's a ten-minute drive, Ivan."

"That's what happened to a friend of mine. Heart attack at the wheel."

"Oh, I'm sorry."

"It does happen." Ivan left it at that.

As he sipped coffee, Brinley swiped her iPhone and texted Malik Medcalf, Director of Security for all of Brooks properties worldwide. He texted back that the security personnel assigned to Zoe was in the ballroom. She turned around to find him. The crowd had dwindled to Zoe's friends. There at the back of the ballroom, the security personnel looked up from his iPhone and waved to her. Funny how he was as far away as possible from the couple. Brinley felt sorry for his having to put up with Zoe.

"Well, I'd better be going." Brinley started to rise.

Ivan helped Brinley with her chair. "Grandma texted me. She said you were kind to her."

"It was nothing."

"I—we—appreciate it."

"No problem at all." Brinley thought it was nice of Ivan to help her with her coat even though she didn't need any help at all.

"May I walk you to your car?" Ivan asked.

"I'm just going back to the cottage next door."

"That's nice. When I visit my sister in Atlanta, she makes me stay in a hotel most of the time. That way she doesn't have to clean up after me."

"Well, it's nice to have some space sometimes."

"I'll walk with you." He put on his tuxedo jacket, slung his backpack violin case over his shoulders, and grabbed the hot paper cup.

Brinley hesitated. "It's just a short sprint."

"I'll sprint with you, then. Is that okay with you?"

Oh, more than okay.

~

*B*rinley led Ivan through the French doors and loggia and across the grass now a strange green under the floodlights. The stone path was lit with solar-powered luminaries curving parallel to the ocean beyond the sea oats. They walked quietly together, savoring the night.

The ocean with its waves of the night sloshing and swishing on the Atlantic sands evoked memories in Brinley's mind of Grandpa Brooks's animated voice regaling tales of worldly nonsense. She could hear her brothers, Parker and Diehl, and her baby sister, Zoe, laughing at Grandpa's jokes as they picked up seashells on the beach. Brinley was the quiet child who'd soaked up everything he'd said with intrigue, meticulously arranging his words in a mental treasure chest as though they were rare jewels.

All forgotten now.

Sometimes in desperate nights, her regret of not having written down Grandpa Brooks's wisdom gnawed at her, little painful nibbles here and there, plaguing her. Those walks on the beach could never be rewound and replayed, and eventually they ebbed away, as with all things, returning to the nebu-lousness.

If only a great palm could scoop up what she had lost and bring them back to her.

"Cold night." Brinley tugged her coat around her.

"Forties, I think." Ivan sipped more coffee. "Want some?"

"I don't share cups, not knowingly."

"Generally, I don't either. But you're freezing to death."

"I'm not." Brinley unlatched the painted gate.

There it was. Grandpa's pool, an eyesore to some but a gem to others.

"What in the world is that?" Ivan spread his arms and headed for the edge of the lighted pool.

Brinley watched him walk around the violin-shaped pool. He seemed fascinated by the black tiles at the bottom of the pool that stretched like strings from the tailpiece on one end of the pool to the other end where the scroll was. On both sides of the pool were the violin F-holes, also carved with tiles. Tiles from Italy, of course, where the luthier Antonio Stradivari lived until the eighteenth century, making his namesake violins.

"The springboard is in the chin rest. This is crazy!"

Brinley felt his amusement. "Grandpa Brooks was a bit eccentric. He was obsessed with Strads."

"Only violins?"

"Well, he collected pianos and other musical instruments too."

"Where did he keep all those things?"

"In a safe place."

"So you've said." Ivan was still walking around the pool. "You know, musical instruments are meant to be seen and played, not locked in vaults."

Ivan squatted down and touched the water. "It's warm."

"They filled it up because they thought my brother, Diehl, was coming today. He didn't make it."

"Why didn't they make this an indoor pool? You could use it all year round."

"Grandpa could see it better from his chopper if it were outdoors."

Ivan stood up, straightening his tuxedo. "This must've cost a fortune."

"Not as much as the money he spent hunting down the lost Strad."

"I bet."

"No need to bet." Brinley started to shiver. "I told you."

Ivan frowned at her. "Let's get you inside. You're shivering."

"Don't mind me. I'm always cold." Brinley could have gone up the stairs by the pool to the balcony that was a shortcut to her room, but she decided that it would be too close for comfort. She went around the stairs to the terrace instead.

The door was unlocked. Brinley opened it to chimes. That was good that the chimes worked, but it was bad that the door was unlocked. She'd have to speak to Dad about it. He'd probably say she had lived in Atlanta way too long, where she locked everything, and that Seaside Island, as she should have remembered, wasn't infested with crime.

"Good night," Brinley said, warming up as the indoor heat permeated her coat through the open door.

"You have a good night too."

"I will."

"See you around?" There was hesitation in Ivan's voice.

"I'm sure we will. We're family now with our siblings married to each other."

Ivan shook his head. "I still can't believe they eloped."

"At least the baby will be born to married parents. That's not always the case these days."

"Somehow I don't think Quincy had social causes in mind when they ran off."

"And who knows what Zoe had in mind." Brinley extended her hand. "Do you want me to take that?"

Instead of handing her the empty paper cup, Ivan stepped toward Brinley. In the dim light of the terrace and the moon, Ivan reached for her chin. The pads of his fingers felt rough and calloused against her face, probably from his years of contact with violin strings.

He lowered his lips.

She didn't protest.

Before he reached her, he hesitated. Stepped back. Drew a deep breath. "I don't know what overcame me."

"'Air.'"

"What? Yeah. The air is cold."

"No. Bach's 'Air.' That overcame you."

Ivan didn't say anything to that. Brinley wasn't sure why. Did he think she was accusing him of being emotional? Well, he could be. What about that split second of something or other between them back at the dinner party?

"I'd better go. It's late. Good night, Brinley Brooks. Have a nice life."

Have a nice life?

Brinley wasn't sure what to make of that. Ivan wasn't making any sense. Did he talk gibberish when he was nervous? He didn't look nervous. Just a bit confused about his feelings.

So was she.

She felt a twinge of loss as she watched Ivan walk away into the December night.

He didn't look back.

CHAPTER NINE

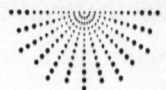

*B*rinley nearly collided with Mom in the hallway connecting the sunroom to the living room. It looked like Mom had come out of the living room in a desperate attempt to get away from Dad. Her voice was harsh.

"There's nothing wrong with having a baby, Ned."

"It's her portfolio I'm worried about." Dad went after her, but Mom walked faster than his walking stick could catch up.

"They're in love, Ned."

"Without a prenup, it's just lust."

"You're impossible!" Mom disappeared into the elevator in the kitchen they'd added to the house after Dad's stroke.

Brinley didn't go after her. Mom could take care of herself. Dad was the stability of the Brooks family. Mom was the sinew of persistence in the family. It was Dad whom Brinley was worried about. He'd shown himself strong through the stroke recovery, but he tired more easily these days, couldn't remember things sometimes, and preferred an uncomplicated life.

Those years of his being on the go and multi-tasking in several companies were gone. Dr. Endecott had insisted the family kept Dad's life simple so he could heal. His speech and physical therapy were coming along very nicely, but there were still other internal recoveries and discoveries to come.

Dad made a U-turn in the hallway, heading for the family room. "See what I had to put up with the last forty years?"

Brinley followed. Fake skinny Christmas trees were here and there, framing large windows that opened to the dark outdoors. In the daytime there was a bougainvillea garden outside those windows.

Dad took up his usual seat on his old leather smoke chair circa 1880. It'd been reupholstered. If Mom had her way, it would've been gone, replaced by some European finds. Mom was allergic to smoke, and the whole idea of where the chair had been in the past somehow made her quite pixilated. Dad just laughed it all off. He hadn't smoked in years and had no intention of going back to that old habit.

Brinley sat across from Dad on a more modern sofa. Still antique but more Edwardian. From where she was sitting, she spotted the Napoleon chess set to Dad's right. It had been Grandpa Brooks's, the same one he'd taught Dad and then Brinley to strategize life on. Dad and Brinley used to play chess a lot. And then she went to college. Now it was Dad's travel chess set. He never went on vacation without it.

To Dad's left there used to be a tray of imported spirits, but it was gone, replaced now by a couple of books and Dad's iPad where he checked stocks and kept tabs on his international corporations.

"What do you think?" Dad asked.

"About Mom?" Brinley kicked off her shoes.

"About Zoe."

Oh. The elopement. Dad wanted her to take sides. "Well, it's Zoe's way of doing things. Spontaneous, vagarious, skittish."

"You agree with her."

"No, Dad. I don't. I only respect her freedom to choose."

"Freedom to choose poorly." Dad was beside himself. "With my money."

"You gave her a trust fund."

Dad winced at Brinley. She saw it then, his continued efforts to keep the family stable in spite of his own medical conditions. The stability had rested on his shoulders, like it or not, but tonight it had begun to fray. Not enough to disintegrate the family, but Dad had always wanted to keep the Brooks ship sailing on an even keel, and to have everyone in their proper little rowing spot, working in unison to move forward.

Zoe had upset that equilibrium.

"Why can't she be like you, Brin? You're easy to live with, demanding little. I don't worry about you."

He paused. "Except for that violinist. What's his name?"

"Ivan."

"Yes, Quincy's brother. What was he doing on our terrace?"

"You don't miss a thing, do you, Dad? Ivan walked me home. That's all."

"That'd better be all. Those McMillans are dirt poor. Who knows what they want."

Brinley gathered her thoughts. Both Yun and Ivan McMillan didn't seem like gold diggers. Quincy might be an oddball, but he seemed harmless. What was Dad worried about?

Before she could retort, Dad continued. "I'm calling June."

Ah, bring in the family attorney.

"She should be able to help us figure this out."

"I'm not involved, Dad. Please."

"You're in it, whether you like it or not. If she loses her trust fund, you and Diehl are going to have to support her when your mom and I are gone."

"Dad."

"It's hard to talk about, but we'll all die one day, Brin."

Brin blinked.

"And Zoe is going to be the death of me."

"No, Dad. Please don't talk like that."

"It's the truth."

Then Brinley realized Dad wasn't really talking about his children. It was his fortune he was referring to. Somehow he must not have approved of Quincy, and perhaps his entire family. Dad must not have met Yun or Ivan.

Or Dad had already called Helen Hu, the private investigator who was ensconced in Vienna tracking down her violin, to look into the McMillans' background. He had done that when Brinley was dating her ex-boyfriends, and most recently, Phinn.

"What's the matter with her?" Dad droned on.

"Mom?" Brinley asked.

"Your sister. She can't keep a relationship. Why is *whatshisname* any different? Why did they have to get married?"

"For love?"

"Love?" Dad burst out laughing. "You're not that naive, Brinley."

"My generation is returning to that which used to work, Dad. Like Grandpa's generation. Love, marriage, children."

"Seriously?"

Brinley wasn't a hundred percent sure she was right, but she wished it. Believed it. "A fifth grandchild, Dad. Won't you be happy?"

"I will be as soon as I see a prenup." Dad's shoulders slumped.

"Kind of late for that, don't you think?"

"We can work it in."

"The prenup?" After the fact? "If Quincy will sign it."

"Is that his name?" Dad rubbed the back of his neck. "I've worked hard to maintain the family fortune. I don't want to see it disappear into a black hole because I haven't been paying attention to what my youngest daughter is doing."

"She's twenty-five as of this morning, Dad."

"Acting like fifteen."

Brinley didn't want to go there. She walked around the ottoman and rubbed Dad's shoulders.

"You've always been good to me, Brin." Dad reached for her hand. His was warm and big and getting stronger every day.

"I love you, Dad."

"I know."

"We all love you, even Zoe."

"Sure. For portfolios, we can all love."

"It's not like that at all, and you know it, Dad. Family is family. That's what Grandpa Brooks had taught us. Even if we were poor, I'd still love you, Dad."

"And you'd be the only one." Dad chuckled. "Mark my word, Brin. You'd be the only one."

Brinley didn't believe him. She released Dad's shoulders. As she was walking back to the sofa, she passed by the side table with the two books on top that had replaced Dad's liquor. Right on top was an old Bible that looked awfully familiar. Brinley opened it. Sure enough, it was Grandpa Brooks's Bible that his great-grandmother had given him in 1930. The Bible had been printed in 1823.

It should be in a museum.

"Are you reading this Bible?" Brinley asked Dad.

"Every day."

"When did you start reading the Bible?"

"Since Argo Perry invited me to his church."

"He always invites people to his church. What changed?"

"I changed, Brin. I met Jesus."

Brinley was stunned. "When did this happen?"

"Maybe five or six weeks ago."

"What church are you attending? Better be sure it's not a cult, Dad."

"Seaside Chapel is not a cult."

"Is it the same church the McMillans attend?"

Dad paused for the longest time. "I see your point, Brinley Brin."

"You needn't worry about any ulterior motives on their part, right?" Brinley plopped back onto the sofa.

"You'd be surprised at what people who call themselves Christians do." Dad raised a hand. "I'm not saying the McMillans can't be trusted but it's human nature we're dealing with."

"Yeah. That ubiquitous problem. Just don't get conned or scammed."

"I won't. Don't worry."

"Don't you think it's odd that Argo and the McMillans go to the same church?" Brinley asked.

"What do you mean?"

"You trust Argo Perry, but you don't trust the McMillans."

"I've known Argo for some thirty-odd years. I didn't know the McMillans until Zoe came home one day with this green-haired fellow."

"Quincy had green hair?"

"He cleaned up." Dad sighed. "What are you doing in the morning?"

"Sleeping in."

"Could you do me a favor?"

Uh-oh.

"I need you to check on the reno on Second Street. If you get there at six, you can see if they put down the bathroom tiles properly."

"Did you say six?" Brinley glanced at her watch. "Don't you have Toby to do that sort of checking for you?"

"I want you there before Toby gets there."

"You don't trust him anymore?"

"I do, with my life even. In fact, he was the one who saw that I was having a stroke. He called 911. He saved my life."

"But you want me to micromanage your GC." Brinley knew her dad too well. She'd been tagging along his pet projects since she was a teenager and Dad was trying to build up Brooks Renovations, Inc. Basically he flipped old houses, renovating them in period style in the process. Since his stroke, he had to hire a general contractor, Toby being his third and, hopefully, the one to keep.

"Well... He wouldn't mind you on the job site." Dad pressed his temple again. "Bring a box of Dunkin' Donuts and all will be well."

"I think he's a Krispy Kreme sort of guy."

"And how would you know that?"

"He told me."

"When?"

"I can't remember. Why?"

"Just wondering."

"Dad, I've known Toby since we were in high school."

"He has a girlfriend."

Brinley rolled her eyes. "We're talking doughnuts here. Nothing personal."

"Let's keep it that way. I don't want anyone breaking your heart again."

"I'm a happy single at the moment." Brinley retrieved her iPhone from her purse. "Oh, lookee there. Nothing scheduled at the crack of dawn except life-saving sleep."

"You can take a nap later. Will you do this for me?"

Brinley considered it. "You know I love this stuff."

In a corner of her luggage she'd brought with her for the holidays was her tool belt. She brought it every time she came to Seaside Island. *In case Dad lets me go to the job sites.*

Dad flinched.

"What's wrong, Dad?"

"This headache. Comes and goes."

Brinley glanced at her watch. "What were we thinking, Dad? It's almost midnight. Let's get you to bed."

"I guess I could go to the job site to see how Toby is doing." Dad struggled to get out of that big old chair.

"Don't worry about it. I'll go."

"You sure?"

"Positive." Brinley tried to help Dad to his cane. At first he didn't want Brinley's help. Maybe he thought that since his stroke had been somewhat mild that he'd bounce back. The recovery had taken a bit longer and Dad's patience was running out. He wasn't a hundred percent and everyone knew it.

Brinley waited until Dad didn't resist her holding his arm. His other hand was on the cane. They'd barely reached the hallway when the doorbell rang.

Brinley glanced at her watch. Midnight. Who could it be?

"Will you get that?" Dad asked.

"Me? Shouldn't we call security?"

"It's probably them." Dad inched his way toward the elevator. "Take care of it, Brinley Brin."

CHAPTER TEN

*I*n the foyer, Brinley's head spun. There were Christmas trees everywhere, tall and fake, and twinkling pine trees rising some five, ten, twenty feet into the air, and backing up against the walls, million-dollar paintings, and the grand staircase. It looked like a forest in there. And smelled like it too, as much pine scent as Brinley's nose could bear.

Brinley hadn't seen it earlier this evening when she had arrived from the airport because the chauffeur had dropped her off in the basement garage and she'd taken the elevator directly to her room on the second floor of the family cottage. Then it was a quick jaunt from the upstairs balcony, around the pool, through the gate and backyard to the guest cottage.

Between two Christmas trees in giant urns trimmed with birds, nests, and Swarovski eggs, the front door with its Italian stained glass looked strangely nondescript even though the custom-made glass had cost her parents a pretty penny.

It was signature Rose Brooks. In previous years, it wasn't uncommon for Mom to drop fifty thousand or more in decorations, mostly going to high-priced interior decorators for their gaudy labor. A small price to pay for the praise of Mom's guests.

If it were up to Brinley, she'd give that money to the local homeless shelter or some poor senior citizen living in a dilapidated old home with rotting porch floorboards.

But that wasn't Mom.

Brinley tapped a few times on the security panel near the front door. It came to life, but she didn't like what she saw on screen. The front door camera framed an officer and one of the security staff members. Sure, police always made her feel safe, but at this time of night, it could only mean trouble.

She pressed a button.

"What's up, Chaz?" Brinley braced for the worst.

"I'm here with some officers from the GCPD and Aunt Ella."

What does the Glynn County Police Department—

"Did you say Aunt Ella?"

Brinley couldn't unlock the front door fast enough, but it was bolted down five ways to Fort Knox and then some. It seemed silly since the back terrace door had been unlocked. The reason for the heavy security was Grandpa Brooks's art and music collection in the basement. The vault, as they called it.

When she finally yanked open the front door, Brinley gasped. Standing behind two stout officers and wrapped in a blanket was someone she had never expected to see in that condition. Her hair was matted, her mascara smudged on her cheekbones, lipstick on her chin. She was wearing only one slipper.

"Aunt Ella! What happened to you?"

Aunt Ella pushed past Brinley. That was when Brinley saw a sprig of something sticking out of Aunt Ella's disheveled hair. She quickly removed it. Aunt Ella didn't seem to notice.

"Would you like to come in, Chaz, officers? It's chilly out." Brinley stepped aside.

"Thank you, ma'am." They entered the foyer into Mom's winter wonderland.

Brinley thought they were trying not to laugh out loud, but it might just be her imagination.

"They found Aunt Ella loitering on Seaside Island Drive." Everybody called her Aunt Ella, even Brooks employees.

"Loitering?" Brinley's knees went weak. "As in wandering around?"

"Yes, ma'am. Someone called in. Said she was trying to use their yard as her bathroom."

Brinley's cheeks flushed. Her head snapped toward Aunt Ella quailing by the Christmas trees, hanging on to flimsy ornaments. Those were probably made of real gold filigrees.

She rushed to her. "What were you doing out there, Aunt Ella?"

Sheepishly she began to speak. "I was looking for my old bed."

"Your old bed?"

"I don't want to sleep in the guest cottage. Willard gave me a bedroom to put my old bed. Where is the big house and where is my old bed?"

What?

"This is the big house," Brinley reminded her.

"But my old bed is gone."

"What are you talking about, Aunt Ella?"

"Go upstairs and see."

Brinley held Aunt Ella's arm. "We'll find your bedroom, okay? I'm glad you're safe."

She turned to the officers. "Thank you."

"The neighbors are mad their flower beds have been trampled on and, uh, you know."

Brinley wanted to run and hide her head in those big urns. She was speechless.

"They're pansies," Aunt Ella whimpered.

"The flowers or the neighbors?" Brinley asked. "Never mind."

One of the officers spoke. "Trespassing is trespassing, ma'am. So is vandalism."

"I'll call her doctor in the morning to see what's going on."

"Malik has already texted her doctor, Miss Brinley," Chaz said.

"Thank you."

Brinley offered all three men coffee, but they

declined. After the men left, Brinley went around the house, locking the doors and windows. When she returned to the foyer to set the house alarm, Aunt Ella was still standing in the same spot.

"I want to sleep in my old bed." Spindly fingers pointed upward. Upstairs.

Brinley hadn't paid any attention in years past because it hadn't been a problem. The renovation that her parents had done to the house this year had apparently not considered Aunt Ella's needs. Frankly, Brinley hadn't opened any other door upstairs besides her own bedroom door since she arrived. She wondered what happened to Aunt Ella's bedroom.

Aunt Ella mentioned earlier that she had come from the guest cottage. This must be the first year they'd moved her there. Aunt Ella didn't like changes.

Well, neither did Brinley.

"Let's go find your bedroom, Aunt Ella."

They took the grand staircase with Aunt Ella clutching her one slipper. The rest of her was cocooned in the blanket.

"Whose blanket is that?"

No answer.

Brinley noticed that Aunt Ella's heels and soles were filthy. All that tracked on the marble stair treads.

They reached the top floor, but they couldn't find Aunt Ella's room. Brinley hadn't been up here in ages as her bedroom was on the second floor overlooking the violin pool. Walking down the hallway, Brinley realized that in her parents' renovation euphoria, they had knocked down walls, merged bedrooms, and transformed the entire third floor. What used to be Grandpa Brooks's bedroom—where he'd passed away —now looked like a library with comfortable reading chairs.

Aunt Ella became frantic. She ran up and down the hallway, opening and closing doors. No one was in any of those rooms. "Where's my bed? Where's my bed?"

Brinley hushed her and locked her arms into hers. "Why don't you sleep in my bedroom, Aunt Ella? We'll sort it out in the morning."

Aunt Ella seemed to think about that proposal. Slowly, she yawned and nodded.

Brinley took her to the elevator, where they went down one floor. She opened her bedroom door. She heard the ocean waves again, and now Aunt Ella also did, apparently, because she walked across the plush carpet floor to stand at the tall windows next to a pair of locked doors.

Outside, the sky was clear and the moon was out. The sound of the ocean grew stronger even through the closed doors and windows.

Brinley picked up her blouse and jeans from the bed, and rolled her suitcase out the door. She came back to get Aunt Ella settled.

Aunt Ella looked sickly. "Where's my old bed?"

"You can have my bed. It's the same one Grandpa Brooks bought for me."

"Willard bought this for you?" Aunty Ella shed the blanket and sat down on the comforter.

Brinley realized then that Aunt Ella had been wearing nothing more than a flannel nightgown on her tear through the neighborhood. She felt sorry. She hoped the doctor had something to say about the poor woman's condition.

If Brinley knew how to pray to God—if she remembered how Grandpa Brooks had said they ought to pray—then she would ask God to make Aunt Ella well.

Perhaps tomorrow—today!—afternoon she'd ask Yun McMillan about it. Better yet, she'd bring Aunt Ella to tea with Yun, and Yun could pray to her God for Aunt Ella.

Aunt Ella now looked around, confused. "This will have to do."

"Just for tonight."

"Yes. Just for tonight." Aunt Ella pulled back the comforter.

Brinley helped her get into bed, grime and all.

"Good night, Aunt Ella." Brinley closed the door gently. It clicked. She rolled her suitcase to Diehl's bedroom, but it was locked. She rolled it the other way and heard Dad snore. She rolled her suitcase back to the elevator and went upstairs. In the library, she shed her evening gown, changed into her flannel pajamas, and discovered that the library had no bathrooms or half bath or anything. She had to go down three floors to brush her teeth in the half bath near the family room, wash off her makeup, and get ready for bed.

Bed? What bed?

Back in the library, Brinley sat down on what seemed to be an antique—Mom detested reproductions—Grecian couch. If Brinley were to hasten a guess, she'd say it was pre-Civil War. Reupholstered, the couch was quite comfortable, and Brinley fell asleep wondering whether she was ever going to get up in four or five hours to beat Toby to the renovation site.

CHAPTER ELEVEN

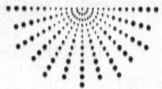

$\mathcal{N}$othing matched on the long twin bed, not the pillowcase or bed sheets or the old thrift-shop blanket that Ivan had used since he was in high school. It kept him warm through cold winter nights when they turned down the heat to save money. With a roof over his head—not leaking now that it hadn't rained in the last few weeks—there was no reason for Ivan to complain.

He sat down on the edge of his bed and swiped his iPad to get to his Bible app. At six o'clock the next morning, it would be his turn to teach in the Seaside Chapel men's Bible study group. He should have swapped teaching time with someone else, but it was too late by the time he realized it was the morning after the Thursday night SISO gig. He should learn to be more organized with his schedule.

Still, he was working off some talking points he'd discussed with Grandma Yun, so it wasn't like he had to come up with a completely new exposition of the two verses in Proverbs. Besides, Pastor Gonzalez at church had preached on that verse when he challenged everyone to memorize it for the entire year.

This is a recap. Piece of cake.

He found the highlighted Proverbs 3:5-6 passage in the bookmarked page in his Bible ebook. There it was.

> *Trust in the Lord with all your heart,*
> *And lean not on your own understanding;*
> *In all your ways acknowledge Him,*
> *And He shall direct your paths.*

Ivan wondered if he had trusted God lately. Didn't trusting God bring peace? Then why had he been feeling a lot of stress lately, especially in his financial shambles?

Everything he had done these years was to pay off the family debt and provide a decent life for Grandma Yun. He wondered if that singular focus—his own understanding of what he needed to do—was in line with God's will for his life.

If it were, then why did he feel as if the bottom of this box he was trying to hold together would disintegrate and everything fall out? Any day now they could miss a payment and Grandma's house would go into foreclosure. He'd have to sell Grandpa's 1945 Chevrolet truck. His part-time SISO job only paid him whenever he attended rehearsal or a performance, nothing more. No healthcare. No 401(k). No retirement.

How was he qualified to teach other men about trusting God when his own life was falling apart?

As Ivan stretched his arm to put the iPad back on the side table, he heard a ripping sound. The underarm seam on his undershirt came apart. Well, considering there were other holes and rips in this old shirt, the new tear didn't make any difference. In a few months the shirt would be a rag, anyway.

He shut off the light. He lay down on his bed and stared up at the ceiling. Through the rectangular windows, the grayish moon spilled some light into the room, creating geometric shadows in the room that still looked the same since his senior year in high school some twelve years ago now.

It had been an amazing ride, but it probably would never happen again. That four-year scholarship to Juilliard School had been a godsend. He'd made the best of it, even performing at Lincoln Center for Itzhak Perlman. That single encounter, a divine intervention, no less, had opened doors he hadn't seen before.

After graduating from Juilliard, he had started Jade Strings with his pianist sister, Willow. Their crossover ensemble with orchestral accompaniment had toured the world for two years. Three CDs later, he had realized that he hadn't taken full advantage of his classical training during the time Jade Strings had been on the road touting its showmanship to standing-room only audiences.

Then Grandpa Otto had passed away, leaving him and Quincy to care for Grandma Yun.

Ivan had scrambled home only to fall out with the other Jade Strings members, particularly his sister, Willow, who still hated him to this day for disbanding the group. Ironically, the timing of Grandpa Otto's death had coincided with Ivan's feelings of being worn out after two years of non-stop traveling across twenty-four time zones. He had welcomed the time off to help Grandma Yun through her grief.

Well, then she had gone and broken a hip getting down the front porch steps.

Six years later, Ivan was still here on St. Simon's Island.

Stuck.

Life had changed. Someday he'd go back to being a concert violinist. For now, being the concertmaster in SISO and teaching violin seemed to be where God wanted him to be. It was certainly not his first career choice, but Grandma's well-being was paramount. Taking care of Grandma was what Grandpa Otto would have expected him to do.

In a way, it seemed like Ivan had never left town, and that his world tour had been nothing but a dream.

Above his bed, the dark painted beams across the ceiling made the attic room look taller and more imposing. He remembered helping Grandpa paint this room.

He and Quincy were horrible painters but they

had been good company for Grandpa, the consummate do-it-yourself type. The entire house had been in perpetual renovation year after year as Grandpa had always found something to fix or update with money he didn't have, bankrolled on jobs he couldn't keep.

If Grandma Yun's music studio hadn't been as successful as it was, they would never have been able to afford to keep this house.

All in all, it had been twelve years since high school and he was still nowhere near his dream job. Pushing thirty, he felt like he had never really left home.

So much for wanting to be a concert violinist.

With Quincy uninterested in keeping the McMillan Music Studio going, it was up to Ivan to take over the violin and piano lessons six days a week and juggle his hourly position as first violin in the Sea Islands Symphony Orchestra. He'd fought for that position and was good enough to get it, but his longevity there was tenuous and depended on his ability to play the violin well.

One full-time job and one part-time, and yet he still couldn't pay off the mortgages that Grandpa Otto had taken out to fund various harebrained "investment" projects, that was, after he'd raided their retirement funds. Grandpa had been a wonderful man but he had no head for finances.

Not that I'm doing any better.

Nevertheless, Grandpa had left him that old 1945 Chevy truck.

Ivan wondered how much it would fetch at auction if he were to sell it. It had the original frame with a rebuilt engine. Never mind. He would never find out. Grandpa wouldn't have wanted him to sell the truck as much as Grandma wouldn't want to part with her old Victorian piano.

"Lord..." Ivan began to pray, but no further words came out of his mouth. No words.

He closed his eyes.

Can't sleep.

Maybe it was too much coffee from the after-party. Maybe it was adrenaline. It had been quite a night.

He opened his eyes.

Moving clouds outside obscured the moonlight. The darkening night didn't help him feel sleepy. At all. Maybe if he thought of some pleasant memories, prayers would come and sleep would follow.

Pleasant memories?

Of what? Of debt and drudgery? Of pain and pressure? Of life and labor?

And love.

Ivan thought of Brinley Brooks and their near-kiss.

She had seemed receptive to his desire, but he hadn't gone through with it because it had dawned on him, standing there alone with her on the terrace, that he didn't know Brinley Brooks at all, and it wasn't in his nature to kiss strangers.

She might not be a Christian. Ivan didn't know where she was coming from or where she was going.

It was as if they had just run into each other at the bus stop waiting for buses going on different routes.

And he didn't want to jeopardize his hard-earned new job as concertmaster at SISO.

Nope. Can't pursue anybody now. Look what happened with Emmeline.

Well, dating that harpist had been a mistake, however brief it had been. Ivan vowed never to date a fellow orchestra member again.

He tried to sleep.

He still couldn't.

All he saw when he closed his eyes was Brinley's face.

Was it possible for a pretty lady like Brinley to go out with a man in such a sorry state as he? Maybe just for lunch? Or coffee since he might not be able to afford the lunch she was accustomed to.

Just once? It would make his day.

They had something in common, though.

Our song.

Ivan wondered if there was something more between them than Bach. What was the probability of—

Ivan cringed and covered his face with both palms. "I can't believe I tried to kiss her."

I have to apologize to Brinley Brooks.

"Lord, please forgive me for my indiscretion." Once Ivan began praying, the rest of his prayers tumbled out, prayers for Grandma and prayers for Brinley, and he fell asleep with songs of praise to God on his lips.

CHAPTER TWELVE

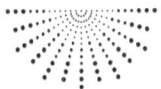

*T*he air was nippy as Ivan McMillan pedaled his bike to the Seaside Chapel men's Bible study group at Argo Perry's independent bookstore by the pier surrounded by numerous cafés. He had sometimes taken his dates to those cafés. The cafés were still there, but Ivan's relationships had been short-lived.

He couldn't date anyone long-term at this time. He had Grandma Yun's mortgages to pay off, an old house to save from foreclosure, massive medical bills to settle, and a music studio to maintain. Earning money was all he could think of right now.

It had been a mistake to go out with Emmeline the summer before. The harpist had just arrived on St. Simon's Island and had no friends. Ivan decided not to repeat the same mistake again with newcomers.

Brinley Brooks is not a newcomer to the islands.

Brinley? How did she enter his mind?

Ivan hit the brakes. He chained his old bicycle outside the bookstore. The word *Scrolls* was etched on the old door under the *Closed* sign. During warmer months, the men's Bible study group often met at the Seaside Chapel beach pavilion every Friday morning at six o'clock if no wedding was being conducted in the vicinity that day. In the winter, they met in any available heated room that generous church members could offer them to use for free.

When Argo Perry, one of the deacons at Seaside Chapel, had found out about the need, he said they could meet at the café nook inside his bookstore from six to seven every Friday morning.

Once inside the bookstore, Ivan made a beeline for the coffeemaker. Sitting at the counter and chatting with Argo Perry's daughter, Talia, was his friend Sebastian Langston, restaurateur and caterer. Sebastian always made it a point to show up at the Bible study, especially now that it was held in his future father-in-law's bookstore.

Sebastian and Talia had been dating on and off, and had been engaged on and off. Ivan wasn't sure if it was Talia's indecisiveness or Sebastian's assertiveness that had caused the two of them to go nowhere. Perhaps it was God's intervention to prevent a disastrous relationship.

"Coffee!" Ivan embraced the cup as the door chimes went off a couple of times. Matt Garnett, whose antique store was a few blocks away, filed in, followed by a couple of other guys who weren't regulars, Gunther and another guy whose name escaped Ivan. He was glad to see them attend more frequently now.

"Several guys are out of town so attendance is going to be a bit thin this morning," he said.

The door chimed again. A couple more guys trudged in.

"Coffee, bagels, whatnots are on the counter here," Sebastian said from his perch. "If you need anything else, speak up now before Talia leaves."

No one needed anything else.

Ivan watched Talia give Sebastian a peck on the cheek. Sebastian grabbed her and kissed her soundly before letting her go.

"Let's not forget we're in a Bible study here." And Ivan wasn't joking.

"Shut up, Ivan," Sebastian said. "You don't know what it means to be in love."

The hoots and howls were too much to bear. Ivan tried to take the high road and not respond, but Sebastian's words grated him. He counted to ten and then some and then prayed for the right response. He loved his brothers in Christ.

"I'm glad you brought that up, Seb. It's exactly what we're talking about this morning." Ivan swiped his iPad. "Turn with me to Proverbs 3:5-6 as we focus on how to trust God no matter what people say or do to you and no matter how difficult life is day by day."

There was near silence in the café save for the flipping of pages in Bibles or stray notification sounds from iPads and Galaxy tablets.

"Let's open with prayer before we check out these verses." Ivan looked at each face. "Matt, would you pray for us?"

Matt Garnett. Such a good friend to him when Ivan had struggled both emotionally and spiritually. He was getting out of the funk now and things were looking up. Although not the life he had planned for himself, he felt that what he was doing, where he was on St. Simon's Island, was where God had wanted him to be at this time of his life.

For such a time as this, God had chosen to deny his request to tour the world as a concert violinist.

And yet...

Taking care of Grandma Yun after Grandpa Otto died should be more fulfilling for Ivan though he didn't feel it. Not yet. Some days he felt that he was just going through the motions of family obligations. And there was no one to talk to about it except his best friend from high school, Matt. He couldn't broach the subject with Grandma Yun because it was about her.

"Let's pray." Matt closed his eyes and everyone else followed. "Father God, thank You for another day. Help us to listen to Your Word and learn from You. In Jesus' name I pray. Amen."

Matt had come a long way, Ivan thought. Back in high school, Matt hadn't been saved, but he didn't shun Christians either. Later on, after his divorce, Matt drew closer to God. Several men witnessed to him, and Sebastian led him to Christ. Matt got saved, grew spiritually very quickly, and now he was a Bible study leader at Seaside Chapel.

Ivan straightened up as he read Proverbs 3:5-6. "'Trust in the Lord with all thine heart; and lean not unto thine own understanding. In all thy ways acknowledge him, and he shall direct thy paths.'"

Ivan checked off his outline. "Thing is, I'm still learning about this. You know my grandma reads the Bible all the time and this is her favorite verse. I wrote down what she highlighted in a devotional book she was reading about this verse." He lifted up the book so that everyone could see the title, *Writing Days*.

"Let me read it to you. 'Unless I trust God with all my heart, I would fall back to trusting my own finite vision. If I fall back on human understanding, I would be too proud to acknowledge the Hand of God and His Lordship over my life. As a result, I wouldn't have God's perfect navigational skills applied to my life's paths.' Does anyone have examples you'd like to share?"

"I'm trusting God for Talia," Sebastian Langston said. "Pray for me that she'll come around and marry me. This on-again, off-again thing is wearing me down. I want a long honeymoon and at least six or seven kids."

Ivan gagged, and started to cough and choke as the coffee went down the wrong way. Sebastian scooted over and slapped him hard on his back. Ivan elbowed him away.

"Do you see the progression?" Ivan asked after he cleared his throat.

No one said anything.

"There are four steps to Proverbs 3:5-6. Let me paraphrase the verse." Ivan scrolled down the screen on his iPad and read aloud. "Firstly, I trust in God with all my heart. Secondly, I don't depend on my own understanding. Thirdly, I acknowledge God at all times. Fourthly, He will direct my steps."

"So it begins with trusting God and ends with His direction for our lives," Matt said.

"Exactly. It's not the other way around. We aren't going to get directions from God if we don't trust Him. We trust Him first and then He'll show us what His perfect will is, and we'll know where to go and what to do."

"What if we already know what to do?" Sebastian asked.

"I would want to be sure that what I want to do lines up with God's best for my life." Ivan paused at his own words. *Wow. I need to hear that myself.* "Okay, guys. Excellent discussion. Any praises and prayer requests?"

"I have another one." Sebastian raised his hand. "Most of you know that my sister, Skye, is a personal chef. One of her clients moved away, so she needs a new client."

"Pray for Skye." Ivan tapped his iPad.

"Business is going well at my antique store," Matt said. "Things could be better at my thrift shop next door. Not sure if it's too late to pray that I had made the right move buying the thrift shop. If not, I need to get this straightened out so I can have God's will for my life."

Everyone made notes.

Ivan had a prayer request too, but he wasn't sure how to say it.

I'm interested in a nonbeliever, so help me, God?

"My grandma is witnessing to my brother's sister-in-law," he said instead. "Please pray for her to be saved. Her name is Brinley Brooks."

"Oh, super rich heiress," Gunther said. "Twenty-six years old. Trust fund material. Very eligible."

Ivan ignored him. "And I need more students for my music studio and more gigs for SISO. No work, no pay."

"I know what you mean," Sebastian said. "Same here with Saffron on Jekyll and Sage Café down at the Village. I need more customers. No cooking, no pay."

Ivan's iPad said that it was already 6:40 a.m. "Let's be thinking about Proverbs 3:5-6 and ask God to show us points of application this week. You know what's going to happen if we do that?"

"We're gonna be tested," one of the other men replied.

"We have less than twenty minutes to pray and then we're out of here," Ivan said. "Who wants to start?"

CHAPTER THIRTEEN

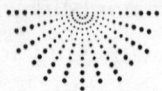

*A*s far as Brinley could tell, the bathroom floor in the house looked fine. She had inspected it, poked at it, taken photographs on her iPhone, spoken to the installers, and eaten enough doughnuts to warrant multiple laps around St. Simon's Island.

She knew that "everything is fine" wasn't what Dad wanted to hear. He wanted to hear that somehow the tiles were uneven, the installers had messed up, and general contractor Tobias Vega had failed to deliver. In other words, Dad wanted affirmation that he was needed at Brooks Renovations and that the company couldn't continue without his imposing, in-your-face presence.

Tobias, all six feet and two inches of him, was leaning against the marble vanity, amused. "Papa sent his princess to check up on the minions."

"So make this easy for me, Toby." Brinley placed her hands on her hip. The low-rise jeans now had dust marks on them. She was glad she'd worn boots because she could've stubbed her toes in the gutted house had she been in sandals. She knew better than to wear open-toe shoes at renovation sites.

"Tell me something that I can take to Dad." It'd better be something good. Brinley had overslept and arrived forty-five minutes late. For some reason Tobias had arrived early by fifteen minutes. They had pulled in at the same time, both surprised to see each other at 6:45 a.m.

"I saved him seven or eight thousand dollars on the kitchen cabinets by refinishing the surface, but I bet he doesn't care about that." Tobias's hair was still wet from his shower. And it was forty-eight degrees outside.

"You know Dad is a hands-on guy, Toby."

Tobias nodded. "Do me a favor, Brinley. Please don't call me Toby anymore. It's Tobias from here on out."

"Why?"

"Toby was me when we were little kids."

"But you've been Toby to me since the day you built me a chicken coop." Brinley laughed. "Diehl would never let you forget it."

"Considering you had no chickens. How's Diehl, by the way?"

"Workaholic." Brinley reached for another Krispy Kreme. "Same old, same old."

"You might want to cut back on that or I'll have to give you some work to do here to work off that sugar from your system."

"What? Are you my big brother now?" Brinley almost had the box when Tobias yanked it away. He handed it to his workers. "Get it out of here before she puts on more weight."

More weight? "I'm going to let that roll off my shoulder."

Tobias adjusted his tool belt. "When we were kids we could eat anything we wanted. Not anymore."

"So you're my nutritionist now? My adopted brother and my nutritionist?"

"Don't you see? Lots of people care about you."

Too much sometimes.

"Now, about this floor. Tell your dad it's perfect. Tell him not to worry. He needs to get better, and then he can come here and run the show. Meanwhile, he paid me to do this and I'll try to do my best."

"So I came here for nothing?" Brinley sighed.

"You want a tip for delivering the doughnuts, is that it?" Tobias's cell rang and he took the call.

Brinley wandered off to the other parts of the house. Upstairs, the view was gorgeous. The panoramic window frames were in, but the glass hadn't been installed. If it had been up to her, she'd want the wall replaced with French doors to make the entire floor an indoor-outdoor room. She wondered how many bedrooms this house had. If this were her house, she'd be happy with three bedrooms.

She walked out onto the balcony. Beyond the construction equipment and workers coming and going below was a stretch of the usual sea oats, protected dunes that laced the coastline. A small boardwalk—it needed to be restrained—led over the dunes to the fine sand. The tide had receded. Sandpipers were running back and forth on the sand at the ocean's edge.

Above them an occasional brown pelican or two glided in the wind. Brinley remembered her childhood days when flocks of pelicans flew by her window. Endangered, the brown pelicans had to make a comeback soon or they'd be extinct.

It was a little past 7:20 a.m. when the sun rose over the Atlantic. With picture-perfect puffy clouds in the morning sky, the sun was in brilliant hues of orange and yellow and blue and white. Brinley took photos of the sunrise on her iPhone and sent them to Diehl and copies to Mom and Dad.

"Look what you're missing, bro. When are you coming home for Christmas?"

She stood there for the longest time. She didn't hear Tobias come up to her until he spoke. "The view will sell the house."

"Any idea what the listing price will be?"

"At least a million. It has an acre lot." He put both hands on the balustrades. "A few blocks away a three-story with a crow's nest went for three million earlier this year. And no yard space. Bidding war and all that."

Really.

"Will you show me the rest of the house?" Brinley asked.

"Sure. Maybe you'll find more good things to report to your dad. Anything to appease the boss."

That isn't why I want to see what else is in this house.

There were two other large bedrooms on the second floor, each with their own baths. The colors were all off-white or cream, island style. If she were to take over the project, she'd want more blues.

When they went back downstairs, Brinley saw the kitchen again. It looked bigger a second time. Spacious. A chef's kitchen. The open floor plan was exactly what she liked. The breakfast nook was another indoor-outdoor room leading to a porch where the boardwalk began.

Brinley thought she could cycle from the bicycle shed across the boardwalk and down to the beach. The packed sand of St. Simon's Island, especially this side of the northern beach, was perfect for cycling.

Just then a cat crossed the backyard and jumped on the railings of the boardwalk where it was highest over the dunes.

I could get a cat and—

Tobias stepped into her view. "No."

"What?"

"No, Brinley. You're not taking over this project. If you do, I'll quit."

"I didn't say a word."

"Exactly. I can see that look on your face. The last time you took over from your dad it was a nightmare to make all the changes you wanted. You and I don't work well together. We bite each other's heads off. We're night and day. Good and evil—"

"Don't overreact, Toby." Brinley gently punched his arm.

"Tobias."

"Last time I was in Europe. I'm here now. I can see this through in person."

"And you're here for how long?"

"A few more weeks."

"Not enough time. I'm taking Christmas week off." Tobias paused. "I don't know which is worse, working with your dad or with you. I think with you because you'll bring that interior designer from h—"

"I was just asking questions."

"That's how nightmares begin. Questions. Now go home. Tell your dad I'll call him tomorrow." Tobias turned and walked away.

"I'll check in tomorrow," Brinley said.

"No need. We're fine." He didn't even look back. He lifted his arm above his head and waved her off.

CHAPTER FOURTEEN

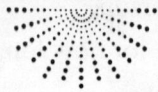

*B*rinley's plan to go back to bed was dashed when she arrived home to a dissonance of voices coming from the sunroom. Mom and Dad were at it again over Zoe's elopement and pregnancy.

Brinley had parked the Bugatti in the three-car garage of the main house, where she always parked when she was in town. But now she wondered if the garage door opening and closing had alerted her parents to her being home.

She closed the door to the garage quietly, took off her Keen boots, and tiptoed down the hallway to staccato pitches and fits and repeated emphases of the words "your daughter" and "reckless."

Somehow the daughter committing the crime was always the other's offspring and the daughter getting the accolades was one's own.

"Brin, get in here!"

Mom.

Brinley hadn't even reached the double doors to the sunroom that she must pass to get to the stairs up to the library, where she had hoped to catch a few more hours of sleep. She counted to eleven, maybe twelve, and braced herself. Really, she didn't want to be dragged into Zoe's affairs and her parents knew it. Ironically, her neutrality had caused her to be summoned many times to arbitrate disputes in the family.

Slowly, she dragged herself to the sunroom. Her parents were sitting adjacent to each other in a couple of armchairs facing her. Behind them a row of windows separated them from the brown bushes in the yard lining up like tumbleweeds. They had been cut down some time in the fall, but left to sit through the winter. Somewhere out there the distant surf peppered the quiet morning under the sun, now midway up the sky.

"If it's about Zoe, keep me out of it." Standing under the tall doorframe, she looked helpless with nowhere to hide.

"It's not about Zoe," Dad said. "We're turning all this over to the lawyers. What did Toby say?"

"I was going to tell you later after you two finished fighting." Brinley stifled a laugh. "He's fine. The floors are fine. The entire house is gorgeous. If I were living here, that's the kind of house I would live in."

"Seriously?" Dad asked.

"I mean, what's not to like? The second floor master has a balcony that overlooks the ocean, the living room opens up to a covered porch that connects to a boardwalk taking you to the beach. It's a nice retreat."

"Make me an offer, Brinley Brin."

"What?"

"Make me an offer before I list it. I don't want a bidding war."

Brinley put down her boots next to the armchair closest to her, poured herself some Kona coffee from the carafe on the antique butler tray table, and sat down thinking about that house.

"Let me call my agent," Brinley said. "Do some comps."

"Good answer."

"Well, I don't want to pay you more than the house is worth." Brinley sipped more coffee.

"That's my girl."

Brinley watched Dad and Mom look at each other and then back at her.

"You tell her," Dad said to Mom.

"Tell me what, Mom?" Brinley asked. "You're pregnant too?"

Dad spewed coffee out his mouth.

"Ned! Don't be melodramatic." Mom nudged him. "Well, we're going to Paris for a week and then we'll be back Christmas Eve."

"Didn't you just go to Paris last month?"

"Yes, but we're going to help Zoe settle into her new house and shop for the baby."

"The baby? Zoe's baby? Don't they have stores in the United States?"

Mom waved her off as if Brinley was being silly. "This is our first grandchild."

"When do you leave?" Brinley asked.

"Tonight as soon as Gene fuels up."

Tonight.

"There's more," Dad said.

"Okay. What?"

"Cara's out of town next week to visit her family in Arkansas."

"And?"

"So you'll have to keep an eye on Aunt Ella."

"No way, Dad. Call her caregiver. Have her come down here." *Why me? Haven't I done enough?*

"She gets the holidays off. It's in the contract."

"I've got things to do."

Mom smiled. "Take Aunt Ella with you. She'll enjoy it."

What about me?

"One more thing." Dad shifted in his seat.

Brinley groaned.

"I have a fundraising event next week I need you to attend in my place."

"I can't take Aunt Ella with me."

"You'll figure out something, Brinley Brin."

Take care of it, Brinley Brin.

"Monday night at The Priory," Dad continued. "You could even walk there."

"You know I'll drive."

"It's the annual Oglethorpe Charity Dinner."

"I remember that one."

"You'll like this. Two violins are going to be auctioned off. One Guarneri and the other... Guess."

"A Strad."

"Got your attention." Dad nodded. "The proceeds will benefit the Sea Islands Preservation Society. Do you still have your colonial garb?"

"Sure do, but the question is whether I can still fit into it." The silk dress was patterned after something that her colonial ancestor, Rosemary Larkin Brooks, would've worn to her wedding in 1734.

Could have. Nobody knew what she had worn, really.

Brinley had it made the year before when she began attending the Oglethorpe Charity Dinner. Dad would've gone as General Oglethorpe, but that was already reserved for a paid interpreter. Instead, Dad went as Jeremiah Brooks, that rice planter who'd gone to Savannah to help Oglethorpe cultivate the land and who'd fallen in love with the indentured servant his cousin had died freeing.

It was a long story and someday Brinley would write a book about everything that happened and how Jeremiah Brooks had married Damaris Larkin, and how their 1698 Stradivarius had come to be handed down from generation to generation until Grandpa Brooks's generation.

And now, they were closer than ever to getting it back. Brinley had been waiting patiently as Helen Hu remained in Vienna to coordinate with Interpol and the FBI interrogating the art thief. Brinley had instructed Helen to do whatever she could to get the

Strad back. If she had to sell some of her other violins, she would.

And if she had that Strad back, she would soon find out how "Air" sounded on it in Ivan McMillan's hands.

Why am I thinking of him?

"Cara and her daughter can work with you on your costume if you need the hem taken out." Mom finished her coffee. "By the way, who put your suitcase and clothes in my new library?"

"Aunt Ella has my room, so I slept in the library last night. I'll go to the guest cottage tonight."

"We can move Ella there anytime," Mom said.

"Or maybe I can have Diehl's room."

"Good idea, Brin. Cara has the key."

"Good to know." Brinley looked around. "Speaking of whom, where's Aunt Ella?"

"Cara's taken her to see Dr. Endecott. Maybe he'll find out what's going on with her. Wandering around like that, scaring the neighbors." Mom poured more cream into her coffee cup. Then two cubes of sugar. "Good thing whatever it was happened last night and that Dr. Endecott has a cancellation today. He's leaving tomorrow for Vail, as you know he does every December. He'll be gone until after Christmas."

Brinley slid her feet into her Keen boots. "Thank you for the coffee. I'm going to pack up my things and vacate your library, Mom."

"Don't forget to call Pace if you want the house before we list it."

"Right. What's his number?" Brinley jotted it down on her iPad and made a note to herself to call her real estate agent before the end of the day. "When does it go on the market?"

"First week of January, I hope."

"Dad."

"What?"

"You can't make Toby work through Christmas and the New Year."

"Have a soft spot for him, don't you?"

"Only as a brother. He's got his family. And it's Christmas."

"Tell you what, Brinley Brin. Make me an offer I can't refuse. Then you can finish the house whenever you want."

CHAPTER FIFTEEN

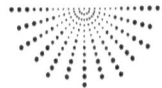

*B*rinley was picking up her evening gown and packing up her suitcase in Mom's library when her widowed sister-in-law messaged her an apology. She couldn't make lunch. Again. This was the umpteenth time Riley Brooks had canceled.

Every time Brinley was in town she tried to get together with Riley because she and her two kids were the closest connection she had left with her older brother, Parker, who had died in a drowning accident about five years before.

Brinley messaged back a quick "No problem!" but she didn't like it. Riley had been cooped up in her sprawling estate on Seaside Island for a long time now. She and Parker had used to go to church but she didn't anymore. The last Brinley had heard, the kids still went but only if someone else gave them a ride back and forth. Brinley didn't know how to help

Riley get out of her unhealthy and protracted grieving period.

Perhaps she could ask Yun McMillan this afternoon when she had tea at her house. Perhaps she had some sort of sagacious wisdom for her about matters of life and death. She'd find out.

Brinley rolled the suitcase toward the door and turned off the light on her way out. The hallway was quiet. Twenty years ago it wasn't. As a precocious six-year-old child she had tried to keep up with her older brothers Diehl and Parker as they played cowboys up and down this very hallway back in the days when the floor was then new parquet and running on it made a lot of noise. Considering that Brinley was cattle while her older brothers were cowboys, she did a lot of running if she didn't want to be lassoed.

Today, the floor was a darker tone of hickory wood. So many layers of history there.

She left her suitcase and the pile of evening gown outside Diehl's door and then headed for the elevator rather than the stairs because the former went downstairs to the hallway outside the gourmet chef's kitchen.

She headed for the refrigerator. Chef Pierre had surely stocked it before he left town. Yes, there was food on every shelf.

Brinley was foraging for said food in the double-wide Sub-Zero when she heard the sound of clogs getting louder in the French country kitchen.

She spun around. She was right. It was Cara. She

was wearing what looked like Mom's old pink lamb-swool sweater. Mom usually cleared her wardrobe once a year, and Cara and her teenage daughters got first dibs.

"My sweet Brinley!" Cara opened up her arms and waited for Brinley to hug her. "I didn't see you last night after the party since I had to leave early."

Brinley smiled. *Early* to Cara meant she left the house before midnight.

"My husband is still sick with the cold and he's very needy when he's sick."

"I hope he feels better, Cara."

"He will be. I made him chicken soup last night. Then he slept like a baby."

"There you go," Brinley said. "What did Dr. Endecott say about Aunt Ella?"

"She's disoriented and confused, probably because she's not taking her medicine properly. Might also be an early onset of dementia."

"Oh, I'm sorry to hear that."

"We just need to keep an eye on her until her caregiver comes back to get her. Then she can go home to her regular physician and they'll take care of it." Cara walked past Brinley. "What are you looking for? Lunch?"

"Yes."

"What did you have for breakfast?"

"Coffee and doughnuts."

"Doughnuts!" Cara made a *tsk-tsk* sound. "How about chicken curry with saffron rice for lunch? Salad on the side. Homemade dressing. And your favorite apple pie, baked from scratch just the way you like it. All organic."

Cara had prepared for Brinley's arrival. "I feel loved."

Cara seemed pleased to hear that. "They just opened a new organic grocery store on Demere. It's a hit."

"You bought and cooked my favorite food. Why are you always so good to me?"

"Don't tell the chef." Cara hadn't changed. She had always been like that. She would feed the Brooks kids around the clock, even if the chef said it was his job to cook for the family.

If not for the high Brooks metabolism, Brinley and her siblings would not have been able to work off the high carbohydrates and sugar. Overall, Cara had cared for the four of them better than Brinley's parents could ever do with their jet-setting lifestyle. When not running global companies or campaigning for their favorite political candidates, they'd be on vacation.

Parker, Diehl, Brinley, and Zoe, in that order, grew up with Cara. She had bathed them, driven them to school, helped them with homework, taken them to soccer and swimming and field trips. She had been their surrogate mother.

When Parker died, Cara was so distraught that she passed out at his funeral.

To be fair, Brinley's parents had done the best they could. They loved the kids in their own special way. What they couldn't provide, Grandpa Brooks had made up for the lack. What Grandpa couldn't be there for—which was most of the time with his own busy schedule—they had Cara to fall back on. The erstwhile nanny and current housekeeper had always been there for the kids.

Quietly, Cara took out containers of food. When she turned around, Brinley thought she saw tears in Cara's eyes.

It made no sense. Brinley hadn't been away that long. This year had been the longest but she called home to the cottage every month, and usually ended up talking with Cara since nobody else was around most of the time. Brinley's parents had often spoken of making the Seaside Island home their main residence, but inevitably they'd end up in Europe somewhere.

"Is everything okay?" Brinley asked.

Cara looked at Brinley with sorrowful eyes. "Every time I see you, little one, I see Grandpa Brooks. You have his eyes. His chin."

Brinley choked up.

"Someday we'll see him again." Cara came over to hug Brinley again.

"How can we be sure? Did he earn enough good points to get to heaven?"

Cara went around the island to make a plate of food for Brinley. "Well, your grandpa was a very good man. He did so much philanthropy in the communities up and down coastal Georgia. Restored historic buildings, preserved history, protected the environment, promoted the arts. Future generations will thank him for all those wonderful things he did in his lifetime."

"But the one thing he couldn't do was find the Damaris Brooks Stradivarius."

"As expensive as that is, as old as that is, it's only a thing, you know." Cara stuck the plate into the microwave. "As we always say, people are more important than things."

Brinley sat at the island and ate the reheated food silently.

"Your grandpa's death was a loss to all of us, not just to you. But we have to carry on. Like your sister-in-law, Riley, has to carry on after her husband died."

And just as Yun McMillan had to carry on alone for many years. She still talked about Otto.

I guess the memories don't fade as quickly as some say.

"If you ever need to talk, little one, come to me, okay? You can tell me anything."

Brinley nodded.

"We all go in different ways," Cara continued.

"Do we all end up in the same place, though?" Brinley asked between bites.

"What do you mean?"

"After death?"

Cara looked at Brinley. "I don't know, to be honest. I don't think that far ahead, Brin. I've been busy living in the here and now."

"Me too. But if you ever have to think about it—"

"I don't." Cara snapped the lids on the containers

and put them back neatly into the refrigerator. "Why worry about it? There's no certainty, anyway."

"That's the point, Cara. Don't you want to be certain where you're going?"

"This is getting into religion, and you know me. I don't talk about religion. I tell my entire family to keep it practical."

"It's life and death. I'm just looking for answers."

"I don't even know what your question is." Cara slid a plate of apple pie in front of Brinley. "Here. Have some pie."

CHAPTER SIXTEEN

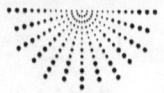

*B*rinley walked around the McMillan family room past the old Steinway upright piano as Yun boiled water in the kitchen nearby. Peeling paint on the wall was somewhat masked by rows and rows of photographs from years gone by. Some were black and white and some were in faded sepia colors.

Brinley moved from photo to photo, studying old childhood pictures of Ivan and Quincy and of a girl whom Yun had identified as Ivan's sister, Willow, who now lived in Atlanta and owned a piano studio. The two boys looked like two happy twins until Quincy outgrew the other.

Yun had briefly mentioned that her husband, Otto, had been a photographer of some repute. Apparently he couldn't keep down a job for long, and the entire family—two adults and three grandchildren—had depended primarily on Yun's music studio to make ends meet.

Yet while Otto still had his photography equipment he had taken most of these pictures. There were photos of the Frederica Middle School, which Brinley had also attended. She had no recollection of the McMillan brothers. At the bottom of the photograph, Brinley could see Ivan's name scrawled there —maybe by himself—and the year in faded ink.

1996.

Ivan was in middle school then. That would make him about thirty years old now. Four years older than Brinley was.

She heard the tea kettle whistle, followed by the clicking sounds of cups. Coming out of the kitchen and toward her, Yun was rolling an old cart with a tray on it. The tray had a teapot covered by a frayed quilted cozy, two cups on their saucers, and a small platter of macadamia cookies.

"Please let me get that." Brinley took over the cart. She rolled it to where Yun told her, right next to her rocker.

"I'm sorry your aunt can't make it today," Yun said.

"She's drowsy from her medication, but there's always next time." Brinley took her seat in an old armchair that had seen better days. It was more comfortable than it looked. It faced windows with faded drapes overlooking a patch of grass and the marshes.

The afternoon sun illuminated everything in the

room, defining the age of the house and the nostalgia on those walls.

"Nice photos of your family," Brinley said.

"The grandkids are my pride and joy." Yun beamed. "I'm looking forward to meeting my first great-grandchild. I never expected to be a great-grandma, and here I am."

Brinley was surprised Yun had brought it up. Not twenty-four hours before, Yun had been visibly shaken by the announcement that one of her grandsons had not only eloped but was going to be a dad. Perhaps she had gotten over the initial shock of it.

"If only Ivan had children too, but he's not eager to marry."

Does he have a girlfriend?

Brinley decided not to ask. Instead she watched Yun pour tea. Brinley reached for her own cup so that Yun didn't have to get out of her rocker.

"He's too busy trying to make ends meet," Yun continued. "Did you know he was a concert violinist for two years after Juilliard?"

"Juilliard. He must be very good." Brinley smelled the fragrance of chai with its spices. *Delish.*

"Full scholarship."

"Why didn't he continue being a concert violinist?"

"My Otto died. Seventy years. I married him when I was only twenty. He had just come home from the war. I was a music teacher in Boston, and I sang in the choir. His first Sunday back at church, he saw me. That was all it took."

"I thought love at first sight is a myth."

"We didn't fall in love right away. We went out to the movies and spent time with each other's families. Our love grew as we got to know each other."

"Over time."

"Right. Over time. How's your tea?"

"Very good. Love loose-leaf tea."

"No bags for me either."

"Seventy years of marital bliss." Brinley pondered that over her steamy tea, but she didn't even know where to begin to think of such a possibility. Could the love between a husband and wife last that long? "Is it possible for that to happen anymore?"

"Yes, Brinley. It's possible. It takes a lot of effort, but you have to be determined to make it work."

"Did you and Otto ever fight?"

Yun laughed, stray silver curls on her head bobbing slightly. "Yes, we did. Believe me. We had to learn the hard way to differentiate behavior from personhood."

"I'll try to remember that."

"Sadly, Otto passed away six years ago. We were shopping and he had a heart attack right there in the book aisle. We had so many dreams unfulfilled."

"I'm sorry."

"Nothing to be sorry about, Brinley. My Otto is in heaven now, and someday I'll join him there."

Brinley couldn't finish her tea fast enough. "How do you know Otto is in heaven? How do you know he earned enough points to make it in?"

"Eternal life in heaven is a free gift that God

gives to us through Jesus Christ. My Otto couldn't earn a single brownie point even if he lived ten thousand years. You should see the mess he made which Ivan and I are still cleaning up. None of us is perfect. That means all of us have sinned." Yun placed both hands together on her lap. "By believing that Jesus died on the cross to pay the penalty for his sins, and rose again three days later to give him eternal life, Otto was saved. It wasn't his works that saved him but Jesus Christ. He's the only ticket to heaven."

"So all he did was believe in Jesus?"

"For the forgiveness of sins, yes. You see, the whole world has sinned and fallen short of the glory of God. But God loves us so much that He sent His only begotten Son, Jesus Christ, so that anyone who believes in Him will not perish but have eternal life. That's essentially what John 3:16 says."

Yun dug around the side pockets hanging over her rocker arm, pulled out a small business card and handed it to Brinley.

Brinley read the verse quietly.

For God so loved the world that He gave His only begotten Son, that whoever believes in Him should not perish but have everlasting life.

"Thank you. I'll keep this in mind."

"No need to collect points, Brinley. Simply believe in Jesus, and you will go to heaven."

"Then where is Grandpa Brooks now?" Brinley stared at her empty teacup.

"If he had believed in Jesus Christ as his Lord and Savior, he is in heaven today."

"I hope so."

"Only God knows our hearts, whether we are saved or not."

"Saved from what?"

"Saved from sins, of course. You see, God is holy and cannot fellowship with sinful man. But when Jesus came, he washed all our sins away, and now we can have a relationship with God through Jesus."

"Grandpa Brooks used to take us to church." Brinley poured herself and Yun their second cups. "I was sixteen when he died suddenly. Aneurism."

"That can take you quickly. At least, he didn't suffer."

"The doctors didn't think he even knew it. One moment he was here, the next he was gone."

Brinley thought Yun had compassion on her face. "Suffering is part of life. We grieve. And we grieve."

Brinley couldn't hold it in. She reached for the box of tissues on the scratched side table between her armchair and Yun's rocker.

"When Quincy was eight, Ivan was six, and Willow was five, their mother showed up one rainy day and dropped them off on the front porch. She didn't come into the house. We never saw her again."

"Their father?"

"The kids—don't tell Ivan I told you this—had different fathers. Ivan and his sister, Willow, had the same father, some live-in boyfriend who dumped her. Quincy's dad died in a car wreck some twenty years ago. As for Ivan's dad, we heard from him once when Ivan graduated from high school. A small card to congratulate him. Nothing since then."

"That's a lot of pain for you to bear," Brinley said.

"Well, my daughter is—assuming she's still alive —an adult. She has to make her own decisions. I can't make any decision for her. God sees our hearts. We choose a path and we live with the consequences of our choices."

"You seem to know a lot about God, Yun."

"Everything I need to know about God is in here." Yun patted the worn-out leather-bound Bible on the side table next to her rocker. "God is patient, Brinley. God will wait patiently until my Jade comes home."

"Jade. That's an interesting name."

"You know what's even more interesting? Do you know the name of Ivan's tour group of concert musicians?"

"The one after Juilliard?"

Yun nodded. "The one that lasted only two years."

"Let me guess. Jade something."

"Jade Strings. Willow came up with the name. She was the piano accompanist in the group. She suggested the name so that maybe someday Jade would see them in the news and contact them."

"She never did."

"You guessed it, Brinley."

"So we don't know if she's dead or alive?"

"No."

"And she goes by Jade McMillan?"

"Yes. Jade Ji-Yun McMillan."

Brinley made a mental note to call Helen Hu, the private investigator who could find anything and anyone. She might have to talk with Yun to get more information so she could find the missing mother. It would take time, but it could bring closure for Yun. She wasn't getting any younger. She was older than Grandpa Brooks. Any day now, Yun could die. It would be a tragedy for her to die without knowing where her daughter was.

The same way it had been a tragedy for Grandpa Brooks to die without ever seeing his quest fulfilled.

"More tea?" Yun asked.

"No, thanks. But I'll have a shortbread."

"Oh yes, we forgot about that." Yun smiled. "Better eat up. That's Ivan's favorite and it'll be gone before you come back next."

"I've enjoyed tea with you, Yun. It's nice and quiet out here."

"Only now because Ivan's music studio is on break for two weeks. When it starts back up again, it's violin and piano music all day long."

"Let's have tea again before I go back to work." Brinley bit into her shortbread.

"When is that?"

"First week of January."

"That soon."

Too soon indeed.

CHAPTER SEVENTEEN

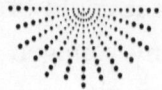

"*Y*ou can't use that one. It's broken."

Upon hearing the embarrassed voice, Brinley stepped back from the powder room door. "When's the plumber coming?"

"Ivan's going to take care of it."

"He's going to fix it himself?"

"I'm assuming that's what he meant. Just use mine." Yun tipped her chin toward a long hallway. There was a bedroom at the end of it.

All that chai tea she drank made Brinley rush toward where Yun had directed her.

The entire hallway was covered with more photographs of Yun and her deceased husband when he had been young and in the service, when they married and fed each other wedding cake, and when they held their children in their arms. The gallery was an extension of what was in the family room though going back further in time.

Yun's bedroom was another snapshot of the past. Faded curtains, worn bedspread neatly made and tucked into an iron bed frame, a frayed house robe hanging off an antique coat tree. The afternoon sunshine came into the room obliquely today, but Brinley could imagine how bright it must be in the summer time.

She found the bathroom. A small little one off to one side. She wondered how Yun and Otto had made do with this tiny space where a cast-iron tub took up half the floor. A small pedestal sink, chipped and stained, squeezed in between the tub and a small toilet.

Brinley flushed it to see if it worked and immediately regretted it as she had to wait a long time for the water to fill up again. A short while later, she turned off all the lights, went down the hallway and found Yun back in her rocker.

"Yun, I would like to get someone to fix your toilet." There, she said it.

"Oh, we should let Ivan handle it."

"How long has the commode been broken?"

"Well, it hasn't worked right since the last time Ivan tried to fix it."

Ha. Ivan the violinist and plumber. "And when was that?"

"About a couple of months ago, maybe."

"Sixty days."

"Oh, at least, but really, it just broke again two weeks ago. Not long." Yun shrugged. "I go to my bedroom, and Ivan goes to his in his bedroom upstairs. Don't worry."

Ivan lives here? In this dump?

"It's a long walk for you down the hallway." Somehow Brinley felt that she had to make it all better for Yun. The poor elderly lady didn't have to live in a ramshackle house.

Brinley could fix it. She could fix that porch, repaint this whole room, give Yun a new bedroom, renovate the dumpy kitchen, give them a new roof, a new house, and make it all better.

"How about this? I came to your house. I didn't bring a hostess gift. Let me do this for you."

"Well..." Yun looked concerned. "Let's think about this. The toilet's been having problems on and off for two months and completely broke two weeks ago. Ivan doesn't have time to fix it, with all his rehearsals. Besides, how expensive could it possibly be?"

"There you go. So let's get it taken care of, and Ivan needn't worry."

"If you give us the bill."

Without committing to being reimbursed, Brinley was on her iPhone right away, calling the plumber who worked with Brooks Renovations. After getting to the owner, who happened to be Tobias's younger brother, she was given the runaround.

"What do you mean you can't send someone right now? Get someone from the job site. Toby's there. Ask him. He'd understand—what? No one's available? Seriously, Felipe?"

Brinley raised an index finger to signal to Yun that she needed a minute, then went outside to the front porch.

"Tell you what. I'm going to tell your *older* brother everything you told me. And I'll call Always Flush and tell them you're short of plumbers. I'm sure Adam over there would be glad to send me someone right away. Yes, now."

She paced up and down the creaky porch, walking past two dirty white plastic chairs and a side table up against a window. Between the plastic chairs was a low plastic side table. On top of it someone had placed a small flower pot of what looked like silk flowers.

"What about you? Send yourself. I'm sure you still remember how to fix—What? You need to answer the phone? Am I hearing this right?"

Brinley stopped at the edge of the stairs. The floorboards needed new nails. "This is too funny, Felipe. I'm sure Dad would get a kick out of—oh, you can send someone? When? Twenty minutes? Very good. No, I don't care what your super emergency rate is."

Brinley's iPhone told her it was three o'clock. It wasn't like she had all afternoon to spare, but it was best if she were here when the plumber showed up, considering that Ivan wasn't home. She'd rather not leave Yun alone with a stranger. Felipe was Brinley's business associate, not Yun's.

She went inside and sat with Yun in the family room.

Rocking in her chair, Yun seemed to have second thoughts. "Maybe it's not a good idea. Ivan would be mad."

"We're helping him. Why would he be mad?"

"He doesn't like handouts."

"If he wants to pay me back, that's fine, but the bottom line is that your commode will be fixed today."

~

*B*rinley heard the crunch of gravel. Like the sound of a heavy truck rolling on it.

"Must be them now," Yun declared.

"I'll get the door." Brinley opened it only to find it wasn't Felipe but an older version of him. "I don't believe this. Felipe's grandfather to the rescue."

"Alonzo Vega at your service, Miss Brooks."

Brinley laughed. "So Felipe is sitting in the office answering the phone and he sends his grandpa?"

"Don't forget. I'm still a master plumber. I taught him everything he knows."

"I know." Brinley held the door. "Come on in."

Alonzo stepped in and stopped right there with his heels on the rotting threshold.

Oh no. His knees have gone arthritic.

Then Brinley heard Yun's voice in the background.

"Thank you for coming." It was in a sweet, low voice.

Alonzo began to stutter something unintelligible.

"Alonzo, this is Yun McMillan," Brinley said as stoically as she could. "She owns this house. I'm helping her fix the toilet her grandson doesn't have time to work on. Yun, this is Alonzo Vega, master plumber at Plumb Good."

"That should be Plumb Well, don't you think?" Too sweet.

"Grammar's not my forte, ma'am."

Brinley's eyes darted between the two of them. *Something's going on, but I know not what.*

Alonzo's knees unlocked themselves and he propelled forward, except in the wrong direction.

"The powder room's over there." Brinley pointed.

Alonzo must not have heard her. He went straight into the family room. "A pleasure to meet you, Mrs. McMillan."

"Yun."

"Yun. Pretty."

They stood there smiling at each other.

Brinley cleared her throat.

Alonzo snapped to attention. "If you'd just show me the offending commode, I will resolve the issue for you."

Offending commode? Brinley's eyes widened. *Resolve the issue?*

"Come with me, then, Alonzo."

Come with me?

Alonzo?

And off the two of them went down the hallway. Brinley thought Yun stood a little taller, walked a little more purposefully. And hey, she wasn't using her walker.

"Uh, don't mind me." Brinley plopped down on the flat couch in the family room. She could feel the hard springs underneath the cushion. "I'll just chaperone from over here."

CHAPTER EIGHTEEN

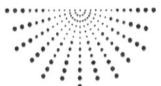

$\mathscr{T}$he rain came down in sheets of ice-cold water that Ivan's cheap plastic poncho could barely hold off as he hunkered down over the handlebars, pedaling as fast as he could toward the house. What had been no more than a mile and a half of cycling now turned into a dangerous low-visibility ordeal as vehicle headlights and swerving bad drivers filled both sides of Old Demere Drive at rush hour.

What did he expect? It was five o'clock on a Friday. He could have left earlier, but the opportunity to play again and again on the violins for auction at the SISO fundraising dinner Monday night was too good to pass up.

Two violins, can you believe it?

He wasn't sure which he preferred. The 1721 Schoenberg Stradivarius had a bold voice that filled the practice room, but the 1736 Guarneri del Gesù wanted to sing. Conductor Petrocelli had left it to

Ivan to pick which one to play what. They'd agreed on two pieces, one slow and one fast, both of which Ivan could easily accomplish.

That was, if he didn't get into an accident on the way home.

At least his borrowed Vuillaume was safely tucked away in the hard-case backpack under the plastic poncho. He was sure it was all right. He wondered when he'd be able to afford his own Vuillaume. Or Guarneri. Or Tononi.

Or even a Stradivarius.

Nah.

Never gonna happen.

When Ivan cycled onto the gravel driveway of the McMillan family home, he expelled a heavy load of relief. "Thank you, Lord! I made it home safely."

He got off the old bike, whose wheels needed oiling, and wheeled it to the carport. He chained it, just in case, and shed his poncho. Shook it a bit and hung it over the rung of a ladder to dry.

The same porch floorboards creaked as usual when Ivan stepped on them with squishy tennis shoes soaked all the way through socks and soles. He could have taken them off but not on this porch with its splinters that he had known too well as a kid. Someday when he had more money he'd fix this entire porch. All those rotting floorboards would be gone, replaced by brand new treated pine boards that he'd stain the original color, some kind of brownish tone that Grandma Yun had picked out the last time they'd cleaned the porch.

He could see Grandpa Otto hammering down the new boards. Quincy and Ivan had helped some though most of the time they were playing and acting silly. Just keeping Grandpa company.

Ivan turned the key in the front door keyhole. He took off his wet shoes and socks before he stepped on to the linoleum foyer, chipped in places from years of heavy use. "Grandma, I'm home!"

Oh, there she is.

Coming out of the kitchen, Grandma came shuffling toward him on her walker, one cut tennis ball glide almost coming off a back wheel. He'd have to get more tennis balls for that two-wheeler.

As he watched her, Ivan realized that Grandma could barely press down on the front-wheel release button. He'd been noticing sapping strength by the week.

Lord, please sustain Grandma.

"You're all wet, dear," Grandma Yun remarked.

"I made it home."

"Thank God."

"How was tea with Brinley?"

"It went well."

"And?" Ivan wiped some rain off his face and neck. He felt a bit chilly, but he was more curious about Brinley being here in their home. He wondered what she had thought about the house and their living conditions. Some people didn't care, but Ivan was a bit sensitive about it since it showed his poverty more than Grandma's. Compared to Seaside Island opulence, the contrast was stark between the

Brooks family home and the McMillan hole-in-the-ground.

"She asked a lot of questions about heaven." Grandma looked like she was about to get into the details of her afternoon when she stopped abruptly. "You need to dry off, Ivan. Don't want you to catch a cold. I'll tell you more over dinner. Spaghetti okay with you?"

"Yum. My comfort food."

"Whoever marries you better know how to cook spaghetti."

"Haha, Grandma. I don't think you need to worry about that for a very long time. I'm not marrying anytime soon."

Ivan dropped off his violin in his basement studio before heading up two flights of stairs, two steps at a time, to his attic bedroom overlooking the live oak grove and the rest of the marshes. After a long hot shower, he donned an old sweatshirt and sweatpants, and padded downstairs.

He heard the toilet flush.

Oh no. Not again.

Grandma had been forgetful lately. Had she forgotten that the commode was broken? He stopped in the hallway, expecting toilet water to spill over the bowl, across the floor, and out to the hallway.

No such thing.

Grandma came out of the bathroom.

Is she humming?

"He fixed it all right, that whipper-snapper." Grandma made her way to the kitchen.

"Whipper-snapper?" Ivan followed her.

"Alonzo Vega. He's a master plumber, you know."

Ivan stopped at the door. "You called the plumber?"

"I didn't. Brinley did, but I agreed to it." Grandma pressed a palm to her chest and nodded once. "Do not make a fuss, dear."

A fuss? "How much did it cost?"

"I don't know. Brinley told me not to worry about it."

Ivan raised an eyebrow. "Brinley Brooks paid for it?"

"She said we're practically family since her sister is now my granddaughter-in-law." Grandma was still smiling. "Besides, there was nothing on the bill except Alonzo's phone number."

Alonzo? First-name basis now? "What about his phone number?"

"Don't worry, dear. I'm not going to call him. Say, did you know that Alonzo served in the US Army too? Just like my Otto, but on different continents and about ten years apart." Grandma's eyes were far away. "I enjoyed meeting Alonzo."

Ivan saw the sparkle in her eyes. A moment of happiness? He wished he were able to provide more for Grandma Yun. Fix the leaky roof, for example. Or those creaky floorboards on the porch. Or that back door that was always stuck.

But his paycheck from the Sea Islands Symphony Orchestra was only supplemental to his music studio income. He wished for more performances with more income. Then again, SISO was a small private orchestra, unlike big city ones such as the Atlanta Symphony Orchestra, where salaries were higher.

Yeah, he'd been thinking he needed more students. Or go work for a bigger music studio that could pay him a second salary.

Perhaps someday he could play in the ASO. But for now Ivan felt at peace staying on this small St. Simon's Island, taking care of Grandma Yun. God would provide for them as He had always provided. They hadn't had to go hungry yet, and that in itself was a lot to be thankful for.

"Grandma?" Ivan walked up to her. "What's Brinley's number? I'll call her and arrange a reimbursement."

"You have her number. I asked her to text you last night, remember?"

Oh yeah.

"Why don't we eat first while the spaghetti is hot and then you can call her?" Grandma stirred her meat sauce on the stove.

Ivan watched that spindly hand grasp the wooden ladle and wondered how long Grandma would keep her strength. The money he had been secretly squirreling away from extra SISO gigs to buy her an electric mobility scooter must now be portioned off to pay for the commode.

He had no idea how much the plumbing had cost. He hoped it wouldn't be more than a few more hundred dollars. He read the bill from Plumb Good company again, but couldn't guess the cost of any of the parts or labor. Give him a music manuscript in German and he could read it. But these plumbing jargons looked like Greek to him.

~

*D*inner filled Ivan after the third helping of pasta. He scraped the bottom of the pan to get all the sauce out onto his plate. After telling Grandma that he'd take care of the dishes as soon as he called Brinley, Ivan went to his music studio to find his cheap prepaid phone.

He tabbed through the text messages until the one from last night's party came into view.

This is Brinley. Your grandma is tired. I'm driving her home.

Mentally he rephrased it.

This is Brinley. Your grandma's commode is broken. I'm fixing it.

He got it that Brinley wanted to be helpful but—

"Hello?"

A pleasant voice.

Ivan felt so nervous he had to sit down. "Uh, er, uh, is this Brinley Brooks?"

"Yes. Who is this?"

"Ivan McMillan. Quincy's brother."

"Oh. I didn't recognize your voice. You sound like you're in a cave. How are you?"

Ivan gulped and felt like a giddy schoolboy. For a

moment there he couldn't remember why he had called or what question she had asked him.

"You didn't have to fix my commode," he finally said.

"Your commode? I thought that's Yun's commode. She agreed to have me call the plumber."

What a mess. "I would've fixed it two weeks ago, but I was busy rehearsing and teaching."

"Your studio closed for the holidays last week."

"But SISO gigs and string ensemble performances pick up every Christmas season, and we're busy through New Year's Day."

"And I want to know your schedule because...?"

"I'm saying that we can take care of our own problems. We're not charity cases."

"Did I say you were?" Brinley said. "You're making a big deal out of nothing. I was trying to use your bathroom and it was broken."

"So you have to do something about it."

"Wouldn't anyone?"

"I don't want us to take advantage of your kindness and generosity." Ivan tried to calm down.

"It was nothing. Really, Ivan. Don't worry about it."

"I can take care of it."

"Uh-huh."

"What's that supposed to mean?" Ivan had to know.

"You're both a violinist and a plumber. You can do it all."

"How hard can it be to fix the commode? Home Depot has kits."

"But when can you get to it?"

Ivan went silent. She was right. He had no time. And if he did, did he really know how to use those kits?

"You have to admit that your grandma was pretty happy it's all taken care of," Brinley said.

"It will be your fault if Grandma has a new boyfriend."

Over the phone, Brinley guffawed. "You think too much, Ivan."

"I do appreciate your help in getting a plumber, and thank you."

"Welcome."

"But I'll reimburse you."

"It's all taken care of."

"I insist."

"Stubborn, are we?"

"Like I said, we're not taking handouts." Ivan braced himself. "So if you can send me the bill, I won't hound you again."

"Well, if you must, you can buy me lunch and we'll call it even—oops—I didn't—what did I say?"

"You asked me to buy you lunch."

"I didn't mean—"

"You can't retract it now. When do you want to do lunch?"

"I don't know."

"All right. Do you like home-cooked meals?"

"I *love* home-cooked meals."

"Anything specific that you like?"

"I'm not allergic. Whatever you want is fine."

Easy to please. "Great. Grandma and I would love to have you over. Unfortunately, I'll be in Savannah most of next week. Can you do Monday lunch? I'm gone Tuesday onwards."

"Let me check my calendar." Brinley said nothing for a while.

"I will too." Ivan waited. Tensed. He walked toward the calendar he had nailed to the wall, and sat down at his computer desk next to his MIDI keyboard. He stared at his giant wall calendar. Yes, he had an iPad, but there was something about seeing the whole month on the wall. Something tangible and visual, not in pixels on a too-small screen. The calendar showed that all next week he either had rehearsals or performances. Working in a free day would be hard.

He wanted to get it over and done with before Brinley changed her mind or left town. If she had asked for a restaurant dinner, it could be more expensive than fixing the commode. He knew those people, those rich and famous patrons of SISO. Nothing was too expensive for them, it seemed.

Throw a soiree, invite SISO, splash down half a million dollars, and no one bats an eye.

All that money could pay off his family debts and send him back on tour.

Tour?

Ivan wondered why he had thought of that. As long as Grandma was still alive he could never leave town. And Grandma could live a long time. His great-grandma had passed away at a hundred and two years old. Longevity ran on the maternal side of the family.

"You there?" Brinley was back.

Ivan really loved to hear her voice. *Lord, is that good or bad?*

Ivan sighed. *Probably bad.*

"Monday sounds good."

"Glad that works out. Otherwise we'll have to wait until I get home from Savannah, and then the weeks are pretty much filled up." Whenever SISO wasn't playing as a full orchestra, either the SISO Strings or the SISO Brass were. They played in hotel lobbies and restaurant foyers throughout the Christmas and New Year for the tourists.

"I'll see you Monday, then," Brinley said.

Ivan hoped to see her sooner than that, and he didn't know why. Somewhere deep in his heart was a longing that he couldn't place. It couldn't possibly be for Brinley, could it? He stared at his phone. The call had ended.

He wanted to talk to her again.

It seemed silly at first, but he was sure he wanted to hear her voice again. It was pleasant.

Pleasant.

Pleasant like springtime and wide open meadows covered with blooms as far as the eyes could see.

Ivan could hear a new tune in his head. He had to write it down. He swiveled in his chair, faced his laptop, and booted it. The song just came to Ivan, flowing on the keyboard and then onto the music notation software on his laptop. He wrote about thirty measures before he printed out the music sheet, picked up his Vuillaume, and began to play.

He grabbed a pencil and jotted the title on the top of the page.

"Pleasant Days."

Then he added more notes to the printout.

Ivan played some more, bow and string from the violin that the luthier Jean Baptiste Vuillaume had constructed in 1850 bearing witness to his creativity. He closed his eyes to let the sound wash over him, a meadow breeze basking in sunshine.

Thank You, God, for strings.

CHAPTER NINETEEN

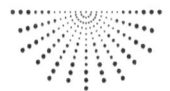

*C*hopin's "Fantaisie Impromptu in C Sharp Minor" was difficult to play, but Brinley was determined to finish. It was her parents' favorite opus. They were listening to her and drinking their usual Kona in the adjacent sunroom. Grandpa Brooks's Steinway grand, now Brinley's, helped her along, masking her rusty dynamics and her lack of musicality.

Brinley supposed she was more self-conscious than she ought to be. She hadn't been home in months, hadn't practiced the piano for as long, and her fingers were locking up, so to speak. They stretched not. They kept playing *andante* and *largo* when she had to go *allegro*.

With great effort, Brinley clawed and mangled her way to the last note.

She heard applause coming through the house-plants behind her. "Thanks, Dad!"

Dad had always been her unconditional encourager. She could play like a kindergartener, and he'd clap like she had just performed at Carnegie Hall. Brinley didn't hear Mom in the sunroom. She might have left.

She moved on to something simpler. *Thank you, Sergei Rachmaninoff.*

To her right, the grand stone staircase framed Aunt Ella waltzing down the stairs. She was wearing something in Christmas green, topping it off with bright pink lipstick. Outfit notwithstanding, Brinley thought that Aunt Ella must've been quite a beauty in her heyday. She had that Brooks elegance that Brinley had seen in paintings of Damaris Brooks when she was nineteen years old, the same year she was gifted the Stradivarius. As Brinley was thinking that, Aunt Ella continued to descend.

Brinley half-played "Piano Concerto No. 2" and half-watched Aunt Ella tiptoe toward the Christmas trees near her. Aunt Ella reached into the lower branches of a twelve-foot Colorado blue spruce and plucked off ornaments, stuffing them into a plastic bag in her hand.

Brinley hit a bad note.

She sprinted to Aunt Ella's side, thinking her great-aunt was having another episode. "What are you doing?"

"It's an ornament exchange party."

"A what?"

"Yun's Christmas luncheon today. We have to bring ornaments."

Brinley had forgotten about it. She glanced at her watch. The party started at 11:30 a.m. They had forty-five minutes to get there.

Aunt Ella was now holding a Swarovski crystal ball in her hand. *Mom's favorite.*

"Stop, please," Brinley said.

"You're driving me there, aren't you?" Aunt Ella kept bagging ornaments.

"Yes, as agreed." Brinley gently pried the bag away from Aunt Ella and rehung the ornaments. "How many ornaments do you need?"

"Just one, but I thought I would bring some spares."

"If you need ornaments, we can stop at the store."

"These are more expensive. More valuable."

"Precisely why we need to not steal them from the owner."

"Willard owns this house."

Owns? Uh-oh. "Grandpa Brooks gave this house to my parents, so everything in it belongs to my parents now."

"They're used ornaments." Aunt Ella scooted close to the Christmas tree. "They won't be missed. Your mom has plenty more in boxes in the basement."

"Aunt Ella, I don't think you should give people used ornaments."

"New ones cost money."

"Come on, Aunt Ella. I'll pay for them." Brinley knew Aunt Ella could afford the ornaments herself, but it didn't matter. These were just things.

147

Brinley was happy to know that Cara had been assigned to make sure Aunt Ella took her medications properly. Brinley wished that Aunt Ella's caregiver would show up, but she understood that she had her own family to return to at Christmas.

"That's nice of you." Aunt Ella backed away. "Will you wrap them up for me?"

"Of course. Or we could toss them into gift bags. Whichever one is fastest."

Aunt Ella seemed satisfied. "We should go to Walmart. There's always a sale there."

"Walmart it is, Aunt Ella. I'll get my purse and coat." And a book or ebooks to read in case she had to wait.

～

*I*van and Brinley arrived at the same time at the Seaside Chapel parking lot. Ivan watched Brinley help her great-aunt—Aunt Ella?— out of the Bugatti at the covered porch entrance to the Fellowship Hall. They looked lost, like they didn't know what to do or where to go.

Ivan pulled up behind the sleek Bugatti and stopped his clunky Chevy. He picked up the aluminum walker from the truck bed, opened it up on the sidewalk next to the truck, and helped Grandma Yun get out of the passenger side. Behind him a few more vehicles were coming up, waiting for them to drop off their passengers.

He waved to Brinley and pointed to a garden

bench next to the entranceway. "Why don't we let the ladies sit there and wait while we park our vehicles? Then we'll come back and help them get to the Fellowship Hall."

"Sounds like a plan." Brinley looked visibly relieved. "Nice truck."

"Nice car."

Smiles.

They found parking spaces not too far from each other. Ivan got out first and waited for Brinley to lock her car. Brinley's charcoal peacoat looked regal over matching indigo jeans. She looked like a million-dollar model while Ivan's old barn jacket and twice-patched jeans—*well, can't have holes in my pockets*—made him look like a poor man living under a bridge.

"Glad you came by when you did. I didn't want Aunt Ella to walk across the parking lot, and I didn't want to leave her there by herself." Brinley filled him in on what happened Thursday night.

"We'll be praying for her safety."

At first Brinley didn't seem to know what to do about that. Then: "Thanks."

When they reached the entrance, Grandma Yun and Aunt Ella were chatting away with newly arrived senior adults from Seaside Chapel. They were all decked out in Christmas colors. All were carrying little gift bags or boxes for the ornament exchange.

Ivan was glad that the Fellowship Hall door was inside a wide hallway. He found two wheelchairs in the coatroom, but both Grandma Yun and Aunt Ella refused them. They wanted to walk on their own volition. So they did, all the way to the Fellowship Hall, where Ivan could hear "O Come, All Ye Faithful" in the background.

When Ivan ushered Grandma Yun into the hall, he realized that the music hadn't come from a CD, but from Seaside Chapel's youth orchestra. He thought they'd taken a winter break. He hadn't kept up with them as much as he should.

"I see a couple of your students in the orchestra, Ivan." Grandma beamed.

"Yes. Glad to see they're keeping it up even when the studio is on break."

Ivan saw Brinley put a business card in Aunt Ella's pocket.

"Call me if you need anything," she was saying softly. "I'll be back in three hours to pick you up."

Grandma put her hand on Aunt Ella's sleeve. "Ella, I want you to meet some of my friends."

Ivan didn't leave because he was watching Brinley watch her great-aunt and Grandma mingle.

"We can go now, you know," he finally said.

"I hope she'll be okay. Nobody to watch her. Hope she doesn't wander off."

Ivan pointed to people at the doors. "See those volunteers? They're going to help the seniors get around, cut their food for them, or help them go to the bathroom. So don't worry. It's only for three hours."

"Your church does take care of its seniors."

"We do ministry at the nursing home near here

too. You could come along if you like. Some of my SISO friends and I are going to play some Christmas music on Christmas Day."

"Christmas Day? Sorry. It's the only day everyone in my family comes together."

"Good for you." Ivan was turning to leave when he decided to put the question out on a whim. "What are you doing the next three hours while they're partying here?"

"I don't know. Grab lunch, read a book."

"I know you're coming for lunch at our house on Monday, but how about let's do lunch now, too?"

Brinley seemed to study him.

"It's not a date. We don't even have to sit at the same table."

No response.

"Or in the same restaurant."

Brinley laughed.

"Made you laugh."

"I'm not even hungry," Brinley said. "I had a late breakfast."

"We'll have a late lunch."

"You're stubborn."

"Persistent."

"Well..." Brinley stretched the word. "I don't know if I should leave Aunt Ella. Uh-oh. Lookee there."

Ivan followed Brinley's line of vision. There was Aunt Ella sitting at a table glancing repeatedly in the direction of several smiling senior gentlemen. Ivan watched Brinley's eyes widen at the sight of a man in plaid tweed leaving his seat and heading for Aunt Ella, hat and walking stick and all. It took him a while to get from his table to Aunt Ella's table, but when he arrived he started chatting with Aunt Ella right away. She seemed completely enthralled as she patted the empty seat next to her. With difficulty and slowness of movement, the man sat down.

"Oh dear," Brinley said.

"It's all right." Ivan chuckled. "That's Hiram Jacobs. He's safe."

"Safe as in how?"

"Safe as in harmless. Hiram's the perfect gentleman. Lost his wife a few years ago to cancer. Sixty-plus years of marriage."

"Okay."

"He lives in the Brunswick Senior Living Community down the road here."

"Uh-huh."

"Our church is actively involved there. We bring meals, do activities, spend time with the seniors there. It's safe." Ivan touched her arm. "Let's go before you get too worried."

"I don't know..."

"All right." Ivan sighed. "You can drive my 1945 Chevy truck."

"You have a 1945 Chevy?"

"Yep."

"You should meet my dad—uh, what did I say?"

"You want me to meet your dad. I gather he's into antique cars?"

"Yes—I mean—never mind. So what did you say about your Chevy?"

"I'll let you drive it."

"To lunch and back?" Brinley's eyes widened.

Ivan dangled the truck key in front of her eyes.

"You're very persuasive, Ivan McMillan." She grabbed the key from him.

CHAPTER TWENTY

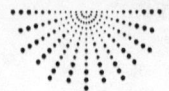

*I*n fits and starts, Brinley backed out Ivan's Chevy truck, cringing that she would probably lose control of it and hit those rows of cars behind them. The stick shift sort of stuck, the weird buttons and old speedometer looked like they shouldn't be working anymore, the thin steering wheel was a bear to grip and turn, and the bench was uncomfortable. The restored 1945 hunk drove like a tank.

They barely barreled out of the Seaside Chapel parking lot when Brinley slammed on the brakes.

"Okay. That was fun." Brinley was surprised she actually broke a sweat. The tension on her shoulders eased up. She opened the door with great difficulty.

"What? That's it?"

"That's it, dude. All yours. Thank you." She came around to the passenger side and climbed in as

Ivan, head still shaking, slid over the bench seat to the driver side and reached out to pull the door shut.

"Maybe I should've backed it out first and then let you drive," Ivan said.

"You mean let me drive forward only?" *Like that's going to help?*

Ivan shrugged. "I guess I didn't think it could be hard since I've been driving this truck since I was fourteen."

"Your grandpa let you drive it then? Underaged?"

"Up and down the driveway. I got my learner's at fifteen, so it all worked out." Ivan joined the traffic on Ocean Boulevard heading toward the pier. "Where would you like to go eat? I'm at your service, ma'am."

"Don't expect me to tip you."

"I'm partial to shortbreads."

"Ha. That's what your grandma told me. She saved some for you Friday."

"Y'all didn't have to."

"Your grandma is such a considerate person."

"That she is. So. What do you want to do? Go to the pier, park and walk around?"

"Sure. We have time. After that, we could grab a quick lunch—or not—and then go back to pick up the party girls."

Ivan chuckled. "You should've seen your own face when Hiram quickstepped toward Aunt Ella."

Brinley rolled her eyes.

She ran her fingers over the bench seat. It felt like leather.

"It's fake leather, if you must know." Ivan leaned back against the seat as he stopped at a red light.

Brinley glanced at his long legs and what looked like brawny thighs underneath the tight jeans. "Do you cycle a lot?"

"Yes. Why?"

"Just wondering." She looked out the clean windshield as Ivan turned onto Beachview. The busy Pier Village district came into view, and Ivan slowed down to let jaywalking tourists cross the street.

"There's my favorite restaurant." Brinley pointed at Barbara Jean's at the end of Beachview.

"Yours too? How interesting. We should grab lunch there." Ivan put on his left turn signal. "And over there is Scrolls."

"Yes. Argo Perry's bookstore. My dad plays chess with him."

"He has a chess club there. Every Friday morning before the bookstore opens, the Seaside Chapel men's Bible study group meets in the bookstore."

"So you study the Bible every Friday?" Brinley should've suspected that Ivan was as religious as his grandma.

"And at church and at home. I study the Bible every day." Ivan coasted down Mallery Street. "It's my compass. What's your compass, Brinley?"

"Myself, I guess." Brinley pointed to a car leaving a parking spot near the covered pier on top of which a single brown pelican perched. Decades before there would have been many of them. Now they were fewer in spite of their having been delisted as an endangered species.

After the car left, Ivan parked the truck. Brinley sprang out of the truck before he could offer to help her.

"Can you believe this weather? It's actually warming up." Brinley took off her peacoat, revealing a raspberry-colored fisherman sweater. She folded the peacoat and placed it neatly on the bench seat. The whole domestic activity didn't seem to be lost on Ivan. Brinley ignored his stares as she tried not to slam that old door. Any moment now, she expected the passenger door to come right off its hinges.

When Brinley turned around, she saw that they had parked across the street from her sister-in-law's gallery two doors down. "The Sandpiper Gallery is just over there."

"Something special about it?"

"Not really. My sister-in-law owns it, but you won't find her there. She rarely leaves her home since my brother died."

"I'm sorry to hear that. How long ago was this?"

"Five years."

"Long time to be grieving."

"They say if it's true love, you never really get over it."

"Is that right?" Ivan pocketed the truck keys into his jeans pocket. "What was your brother's name?"

"Parker. He drowned in the ocean trying to save his daughter when she fell overboard from their fishing boat. Sadly, they'd both perished." In fact, the junior high schooler had taken off her life jacket and jumped in, but that wasn't the cover story the Brooks family wanted disseminated among Mom's neighbors and friends. So Parker Brooks, thirty-six years old, became a hero and had been so for five years. His other daughter, a witness to the entire traumatic event, had been under psychiatric care ever since.

"Do you want to check out the gallery?" Ivan seemed relaxed, like they had all the time in the world.

Brinley hadn't noticed until now that Ivan was quite tall, at least six-one. She supposed that on Thursday night when they both helped his grandma out of the dinner party that they had to lean down as they walked and such. And when he had spoken to her briefly, she was in heels and taller than she really was. Today she was in her usual Keen boots, and her eyes came up to where his lips were—

Don't go there!

They crossed the road and walked down the sidewalk to Sandpiper Gallery. The only person working there was a college-aged girl with hot pink hair working on a laptop. Brinley had never seen her before. She looked up from her keys and greeted them.

"Welcome to Sandpiper Gallery. We have some new pottery pieces from local potters along that window, and also new art pieces by some area watercolorists. Feel free to browse around and let me know if you need anything."

"Sure. Thanks."

Brinley noticed that Ivan followed her around through the gallery, as if he didn't have his own plans. She went to the pottery pieces first, wondering if Riley Brooks had made those. There were wash-bowls, platters, and the usual coffee mugs. They were all in some swirly brown and burnt sienna patterns.

She picked up a mug and turned it over. It wasn't Riley's piece, but another local artist had signed and dated it this year. The coffee mugs were thirty dollars.

"That's almost the same color as your hair," Ivan said. "I like it."

"The mug or my hair?"

"Will you think poorly of me if I said both?"

"No. I don't care either way. I do like these mugs." Brinley picked up another one. It had a bit of a heft to it. The handles were made well, sturdy and wide enough for her to put four fingers through. The dab of clay on top of the handle was perfect for her thumb. She held it up. "Good balance."

Ivan picked up one. "Nice handle. Good hold."

They both looked at each other, mugs in their hands.

"We should each get one," Ivan said.

Brinley thought a moment. "Okay. Let's do it."

Hot Pink wrapped up the mugs in too much newsprint. Brinley and Ivan each had a paper bag to carry their coffee mugs home. They paid separately, Ivan using a debit card, and Brinley paying in cash.

"Too bad we won't be using these mugs together," Brinley said as they left the store.

"But I'll remember the color of your hair when I drink my coffee in the morning."

Brinley wondered whether that was good or bad.

The sun shone somewhere above their heads, not directly, but still warm enough to counter the soft breeze coming ashore from St. Simon's Sound. They dropped off their mugs in the truck, then decided to walk toward the pier and then to the lighthouse. Crossing Neptune Park afterward, they could make their way to Barbara Jean's, where their little walking tour would end.

End.

Such a definitive word.

Brinley didn't want her time with Ivan to end. She felt like she wanted to get to know Ivan more but was afraid of what she might find. Her tea time with Yun McMillan had revealed a deeply religious woman with a broken family that she and her husband had pieced together and weathered for years. In spite of living in a rundown house that ran the risk of collapsing—especially that front porch—Yun had been adamant that her God was still good and that He still dispensed blessings.

Brinley wondered what sort of blessings Yun meant when the McMillans' lives looked pretty rough.

Well, looks like Ivan turned out okay.

Maybe that's one blessing.

One.

∼

*I*van felt self-conscious next to Brinley as they walked through the covered portion of the St. Simon's Island Pier, as if this scene, this surreal time with a lovely lady, was too good to be true. Here was a pretty girl strolling with him like she belonged with him.

She seemed to be taking it all in despite the smell of squid, shrimp, and other fish bait around them. In front of and behind them, more island residents with fishing poles, folding chairs, and rolling coolers appeared, together with multilingual tourists in their sun hats, sunscreens, excited faces, and digital cameras, all heading in the same direction as Ivan and Brinley, toward the edge of the T-shaped pier.

They passed a police officer patrolling the pier, then by people who had already cast their lines over the side of the pier.

"We used to say it's shaped like a hammerhead shark," Ivan said.

"You and Quincy?"

"And Willow too. Did Grandma tell you about my sister, Willow?"

Brinley nodded. "She plays the piano."

"She's still somewhat mad at me because I disbanded Jade Strings when we were at the peak of our careers." *Now why would I tell Brinley that?*

"After how many years?" The wind blew Brinley's hair here and there, and she tried to pull it all back behind her ears.

"Six years."

"A grudge?"

"I'm sorry," Ivan added. "Too much information."

"Yun is fortunate to have you, Ivan. It's hard to be widowed, for sure. Grandpa Brooks was lonely for many years after Grandma passed away."

"He didn't remarry?"

"No. He was on a quest. You know, that one."

"Ah, the Strad."

"It was an endless pursuit."

Ivan didn't say anything. He didn't want to cast the first stone. He had enough things to worry about. Family debts to pay off, Grandma Yun to provide for, those performances coming up next week he had to rehearse for. He had been so busy he hadn't even thought much of his brother and his sudden marriage to Zoe. The thing was, the couple had all but moved to Paris. Out of sight and all that jazz. He wished his brother well.

Ivan and Brinley stopped at the wood railings at the edge of the pier. Ivan looked down at the water splashing about the pillars in greenish and brownish hues. He couldn't see any fish or barracudas.

"Jekyll over there looks peaceful." Brinley put on her sunglasses.

Facing the wind, it swept her hair back. Ivan saw little baby hair at the edge of her forehead. And a tiny little brown spot—a mole or a birthmark—on her right earlobe. She had no earring holes in her ears. In fact, she wasn't wearing any necklaces that he could see.

All she had on was a watch and a small cross-body purse.

"SISO will be playing there New Year's Eve. I hear most of the board members will be there together with some guests from ASO."

"ASO?" Brinley raised an eyebrow. "Scouting for talented musicians?"

"One never knows." Ivan glanced at his old watch, its surface scratched and the leather straps falling apart. Matt's thrift shop probably had some straps he could swap these out with. It was almost one o'clock.

There was commotion all around them. Words in Korean filled the air. He knew it was Korean, but he couldn't understand it in spite of it being Grandma Yun's mother tongue. He looked to see if he could tell what was going on. Tourists and locals were pointing toward the Sound and cameras were clicking.

"Look, Brin!"

They both looked in the same direction as everyone else on the pier. There between Jekyll and the pier, a pod of whales breached the surface tension of the water. They screeched and dropped back into the water on their swim south.

"Oh, wow. All the way from Greenland." Brinley dug for her iPhone and tried to snap a picture as another North Atlantic right whale breached the waterway.

"And Canada." Ivan was so excited he didn't realize his left arm had gone over Brinley's shoulders and was sitting there around her neck.

Apparently, Brinley didn't either as she kept taking photos.

Then she snapped a close-up photograph of Ivan's face.

He hadn't expected that. "What was that for?"

"A moment with the whales."

"And with you," Ivan whispered.

Brinley didn't reply. She snapped one more time. "I'll email these photos to Zoe, and your brother can look at it."

The whales moved on, but the moment remained.

Ivan wanted to retract his arm, but it wasn't cooperating. Brinley didn't seem to mind or notice. Either that or she had quickly become so comfortable with him that she had expected it.

Expectations?

This can't happen.

They were of different faiths. Ivan was a Christian and Brinley wasn't, as far as he knew.

Grandma Yun had mentioned briefly that Brinley had been asking about heaven.

Good.

That meant she didn't know much about it.

Not so good.

This trajectory he was on could only end badly because he couldn't give her what a non-Christian might expect out of a relationship.

Relationship? What relationship?

We're just keeping each other company.

Sure. And they had bought twin coffee mugs. His and hers.

But we're accidental chaperones and chauffeurs for our elderly relatives.

Sure. And they had planned on eating lunch. Together.

But it's lunchtime. Everyone has to eat.

Ivan kept telling himself it wasn't a date. Not. A. Date. Still...

What's happening, Lord?

Ivan prayed quickly for relief.

The fisherman sweater felt soft in his hands as he rounded his arms around Brinley's waist and gathered her toward him. He didn't hesitate this time, and Brinley closed her eyes when their lips touched, gently and tentatively at first, then deepening and yet with guarded ardor.

What am I doing?

Ivan's eyelids blinked when those same tourists who went crazy over the whales now snapped their cameras incessantly at them, all the while chattering in rapid Korean.

"Kiss, kiss," one of them said in English. "Again."

Brinley buried her face into Ivan's barn jacket. "Help."

She felt nice and warm against his chest. But...

What in the world overcame me?

"Guess we'd better get out of here," Ivan said, pushing through the crowd toward shore. In minutes they were off the pier and walking along the shoreline past the public library and Neptune Park and its live oak trees.

"At least you finished what you started."

Brinley's voice was quiet, but Ivan heard her as they passed by children playing among the oaks. In his heart, he didn't agree with her.

Some things should never be started at all.

He felt like Tevye in *Fiddler on the Roof*, sitting on his milk cart and having a conference with God.

Lord, was that a mistake?

What am I going to do now?

CHAPTER TWENTY-ONE

"*W*hat? Twelve dollars per person?" Ivan shoved his hands into his barn jacket pocket. "I can't believe it."

They were standing outside what used to be the lighthouse keeper's dwelling built in 1872, now a museum. Brinley wasn't sure if Ivan was only joking about the cost of admission. She pointed to the next line in the brochure in her hand. "Free for kids six and under."

"It'll be a long time before we—" Ivan clamped up abruptly.

We?

Brinley dared not look at him so he didn't feel anymore embarrassed than he probably already was. They had only started spending more time with each other for three days. Maybe less than three full days. Then again, they had known each other casually for a year.

And he's talking we?

Maybe it was a universal *we*, as in "we people at our age." *That must be it.*

After all, a kiss does not children make.

"For free, we could walk around the gazebo and along the shoreline. Save us a hundred and twenty-nine steps." Ivan turned to leave.

"Twelve dollars will get you the lighthouse, the museum, and the Coastguard Station." Brinley reached for his arm. "Come on, Ivan. Let's do it. Just this once."

Forty-some steps up the steep spiral lighthouse stairs later, Brinley wondered why she had even insisted. She was a student of Georgian history, yes, but only when it didn't hurt her calves and thighs this much. Her knees seemed to be holding up, but that was no consolation.

"They did this all the time back in the days." Ivan reached for her hand. "Imagine the hard life."

"Hard life? Not *harder* life? How ironic."

Brinley thought Ivan's life was hard enough. The day before, Yun let it slip that they had multiple mortgages on that dumpy old house of theirs. If Ivan had more income, wouldn't he have fixed up that house? Replaced the floorboards on the porch, and repainted the interior of the house, at least? Brinley remembered pulling out of that driveway on Friday afternoon, wondering whether their roof also leaked. It had looked old and run-down with a few pieces of shingles missing.

Brinley let Ivan help her up the next steps. She

looked down. It looked like a nautilus spiral all the way down to the bottom of the lighthouse. "Did you realize once we reach the top, we have to come back down?"

"We can't go down now," Ivan said. "We have six more dollars to go."

"Are you blaming me?" Brinley stopped at a window to catch her breath. They were about halfway up. That window faced the pools, the park, and the pier where they had kissed for the first time.

Brinley still felt the tingle on her lips from his soft kiss.

It was just a kiss.

And they were both single, unattached, free to date.

Nothing to it.

Right. Keep telling myself that.

Brinley sat down on a cool stone step. There wasn't anyone else around. "I used to be able to climb these steps. I guess I'd better hit the gym more often."

"Do you work a lot?" Ivan asked, sitting down next to her.

They were shoulder to shoulder. Brinley welcomed his nearness. He felt comfortable to her.

"I'm in sales," she said.

"You must work like a dog."

"And then some."

"You don't sound enthused."

"Dad said work is good for the soul." It wasn't much of a defense, but it was all Brinley had. She had wanted out of Brooks Investments for a long time.

She had taken Parker's place after he passed away suddenly. She should have said no. But her MBA had said yes. Dad knew sales wasn't her forte nor point of interest.

Truth be told, she'd rather be a historian. That didn't bring in any income, did it? But who cared, really? Her inheritance would be enough for her to live at least five lifetimes over. She could buy up the entire St. Simon's Island if she wanted to.

"But you don't enjoy it," Ivan said.

"It has ups and downs."

Ivan seemed to be waiting for more.

Brinley didn't give it to him. "You're a curious guy, aren't you?"

"I'm curious about you."

"Well, I don't particularly love being in sales, not the least bit all the traveling I have to do to get new clients for Dad's company, but I enjoy the independence and I'm sort of good at it."

"You can be good at things you like to do too, you know. Why choose something you don't like?"

"I'm doing this for my brother, Diehl, so the burden wouldn't be entirely on his shoulders after we lost Parker."

"And it makes you happy to help others."

Brinley shrugged. "Let's get to the top."

"So we can get back down again."

"Haha."

The door opened to a blustery December. The sun was up in the sky, but the winds were swirling all around them. Above them was a smaller balcony encircling the giant Fresnel lens, out of use since ages past.

"I'm glad they rebuilt this lighthouse," Brinley said.

"They did?"

"There're probably some old photographs downstairs. I don't recall much since it's been a while since I visited the museum. All I remember is that the original lighthouse was built in 1810 and destroyed during the Civil War, you know."

"I didn't know that."

"And how long have you been living on St. Simon's?"

"I'm more into music history."

"Can't put on blinders. History is all around you."

"So if you could do anything, you wouldn't be in sales. You'd be doing something related to history." Ivan stopped walking and reached for the iron railing.

"Not just any history but the history of coastal Georgia." Brinley stood next to him.

"That specific. So why not do the career you like?"

Brinley wondered how much to tell him. She decided not to say anything. Didn't want to get his hopes up about her leaving Dad's company and moving to St. Simon's permanently. They just started to know each other.

Still, they had kissed, if it meant something.

"Obligations," Brinley said.

"Obligations? I know how that is."

Brinley couldn't read his face. "Love this place. I can't imagine living anywhere else. Don't get me wrong. I love Atlanta and all, but if I had to choose between the two, I'd leave the big city for this seaside town any day."

"I'm the opposite. Once my obligations are done, I'm gone. Out of here."

"You mean leaving St. Simon's for good?"

Ivan nodded. "My sister and I were on tour for two years in our crossover orchestra."

"Yun had mentioned it, though not in details."

"Much about me you don't know."

"Likewise."

Ivan reached for her hand. "I'd like to know you more."

"If our paths cross again." Brinley started to feel something akin to a loss, but she wasn't sure. She tried to make light of it. "Maybe I'll see you perform at Carnegie Hall?"

"I'll make sure you have front-row seats."

"Promise?"

"Promise. If I make it." Ivan held her hand. "God has changed my plans at least once before. He might change them again."

"God doesn't let you get what you want?"

"I didn't say that. If it's bad for me or for my family, I don't want it." Ivan pointed toward the village. "See over there, behind that row of shops where your sister-in-law's gallery is?"

"One street over?"

"Yes. Past those trees? See that three-story building?"

"Brick? Old warehouse?" Brinley asked.

"Yep! It has been on the market since June." Ivan shook his head. "If I were to stay put here and not go back on tour with my sister, maybe someday I could rent space in that building for a music studio."

"Have you been inside?"

"No. Can't afford it." Ivan looked resigned.

"But aren't you a bit curious about how it looks inside?"

"What do you mean?"

"If the building is on the market, my agent can get us in." Brinley reached for her iPhone. "When do you want to see it?"

"Uh, well... I don't know. SISO is busy through New Year's Day."

"Okay." Brinley pocketed her iPhone. "Let me know and we'll go see your future music studio."

Ivan laughed. "It's just a dream, Brinley. It's never going to happen. Plan A for me is to get back on the road."

All Brinley thought was she wanted to give Ivan the world if she could. She wasn't sure if it was because he looked like he was needy, or that she felt something for him she had not felt for anyone else.

"Regardless of my own plans, I want God's best for my family, most of all."

"Grandpa Brooks often said that God knows best." Only Brinley wondered now whether it had always been Grandpa Brooks rather than God who had called the shots in the Brooks family.

Ivan was still holding her hand. "You seem to know more about God than you let on."

"Only what Grandpa Brooks told me. Then, of course, I found out from Yun yesterday that some of what Grandpa said to me didn't match up with her Bible."

"That's Grandma for you. You should see what she tells Pastor Gonzalez from time to time. *It doesn't match up!*"

"Pastor Gonzalez? Seaside Chapel?"

Ivan nodded.

Brinley thought it was interesting that he didn't invite her to his church.

"Speaking of which, what time is it?" Ivan asked.

She checked her watch. "Only two thirty."

"Only? You don't enjoy being with me?" Ivan released her hand and folded his arms across his chest.

"I'm saying we'll have enough time to get lunch—if Barbara Jean's is not too crowded—and then get back to church."

"It could take us fifteen or twenty minutes to get down, unless we tumble down, in which case we could be dead."

Brinley punched his arm playfully. "This high elevation doing a number on your head?"

"The proximity with a beautiful lady is."

"I'm not—"

"Yes, you are." He lifted her chin. "Don't short-change yourself. God made you beautiful and that's the way it is."

"He made me plain."

"You're not plain. The word that has been in my mind is *pleasant*. You're pleasantly beautiful."

Brinley looked up into his eyes in interesting colors of light brown and dark green hues with specks of gold. Hazel eyes. She could easily stare at them for hours, but he didn't let her as he closed his eyes and stopped her further thoughts with a lingering kiss so sweet and light and full of promises of more to come.

She thought about all that on the way down the steps, noisy now with thumping sounds and chattering voices coming up toward them. They passed the same tourists they had met at the pier earlier. When they reached the ground floor, they decided to skip the museum and go eat.

Pleasantly beautiful.

And lovingly kissed.

Twice.

What did it mean? Ivan had called her beautiful. Everyone knew she was plain Jane with the straight brown hair. If not for her bank account, she'd be a spinster like Aunt Ella.

But Ivan?

He was poor. Had to be.

He probably didn't know, but coming down the stairs, she had spotted the loose threads at the seams on the back of his barn jacket that looked old, like maybe he got it from his grandfather. He should patch that rip up, but if it were up to her, she'd chuck it and buy a new one.

Maybe I could get him a new—

No.

She had revealed too much of herself to Ivan as it was. Getting someone to show up in twenty minutes to fix his family home commode had cost more than the usual call to a plumber. Driving Dad's million-dollar Bugatti Veyron about town like it were some putt-putt car made the Brooks family look like they threw money around.

Surely his brother, Quincy, by way of her sister, Zoe, had told Ivan a lot more than he needed to know about the Brooks family, their holdings, estates, global empire—whatnots, really, compared to the meaning of life, whatever that was.

Ivan McMillan could be like Phinn, Crispin, or Xander. Or worse.

At least her ex-boyfriends had their own fortunes and inheritance. Ivan had nothing.

If you were dirt poor, wouldn't you want money?

It was time for Brinley to run back into the castle where no one could touch her. It was safe inside the fortress. Out here in the wild, among the peasants, she could get robbed blind.

But the kisses...

His kisses.

They were real.

CHAPTER TWENTY-TWO

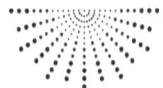

On Sunday morning, it wasn't lost on Brinley that Seaside Chapel was constructed to look like a little country church by the sea, complete with a cross on top of the steeple and a garden out in the back, a photographer's paradise with a meandering boardwalk leading to a pavilion and the beach where Seaside Chapel had conducted many weddings in the years the church had been in existence.

For some reason Aunt Ella wanted to get to the church service early. Reluctantly, Brinley pulled into the parking lot, thinking the entire time that she had had too much church this weekend. Yet she was happy that Aunt Ella was pleased she had obliged her. The church website didn't say how long the service would last, only that it began at eleven o'clock.

The front entrance of the church was easy to find, unlike the Fellowship Hall tucked away in a separate building adjacent to the church. God must be smiling down on them because when Brinley coasted to the front entrance, greeters pointed her toward an empty parking spot marked *Visitor* right around the fountain, close enough for Aunt Ella to walk in. *Score!*

The oblique morning sun came into the sanctuary through the open French doors. The sunlight rested where the ushers seated them in the last row. They would have sat closer to the front if not for Aunt Ella's complaining about the long walk down the aisle. When Aunt Ella spent a considerable time looking around, Brinley realized that the reason her great-aunt had wanted to sit in the back was to spot a certain someone inside the church.

Might it be a certain elderly gentleman with the dashing walking stick?

The pipe organ began to play a medley of Christmas carols as the congregation filled up the pews flanked by stained-glass windows that looked older than the church, and painted French doors here and there. Between doors and windows were fresh wreaths with simple red ribbons reminding everyone that Christmas was still around the corner.

Next to her, Aunt Ella's face brightened considerably.

"Saw him?" Brinley asked.

"He's over there." Badly applied pinkish nail polish was splattered on Aunt Ella's nails as she pointed with tremulous fingers.

Ha! What did I say?

Brinley couldn't see anyone she recognized, but she peered anyway.

That pleased Aunt Ella to no end. "I hope he says *hello* to me after the service."

"If not, we'll go find him." Brinley hid her grin in the bulletin.

The program listed all the hymns they were going to sing this morning, plus special music by ensembles and trios and the choir and such. She recognized many Christmas hymns she had sung since childhood and around the fireplace at Christmas time with Grandpa Brooks. Too bad she never knew Grandma Brooks. She had passed away when Dad was young.

The welcome message and announcements dispensed with, the platform cleared for an ensemble.

A string quintet!

Brinley's heart skipped a beat when she saw Ivan McMillan among the violinists and viola players. A cellist and harpist were in chairs and Brinley could only see the tops of their heads from where she was sitting. The church floor sloped to the front, so even the back pews could see the people on the platform, but not by much. With Ivan being tall, he was hard to miss.

"O Holy Night" resonated throughout the entire sanctuary.

Pretty good acoustics in this little place.

Aunt Ella was singing along with the instru-mental arrangement of the Christmas carol. Pretty soon, Brinley was joining in, humming the nine-teenth-century hymn.

His law is love and His gospel is peace...

The tune was still ringing in Brinley's ears later on in the service when Pastor Tom Gonzalez stepped up to the podium to deliver his sermon. First thing he did was to ask everyone to turn to John 3:17. Brinley found it on her iPhone. It was the verse after John 3:16, which Yun had shared with her on Friday.

She followed the words as Pastor Gonzalez read John 3:17 with his expected pastoral gravity.

"Let's read. 'For God did not send His Son into the world to condemn the world, but that the world through Him might be saved.' If you miss anything else I say this morning, don't miss what God says."

When the sermon finished and everyone stood up to sing another Christmas carol, Brinley was still thinking of one phrase that Pastor Gonzalez had repeated in his sermon.

Not condemnation, but salvation.

She recalled what Yun had said about Grandpa Brooks.

If he had believed in Jesus Christ as his Lord and Savior, he is in heaven today.

So simple.

Well, many things in life were simple. Grandpa Brooks said that humankind had an innate ability to overcomplicate life.

Still, Brinley felt she had much to think about. Much to mull over. She had more questions she'd have to ask Yun on Wednesday.

~

"*I* can't believe she's here at church," Ivan said to Matt Garnett after they exited the side door of the sanctuary. When he was standing up there playing in the string quintet, he'd looked all the way across the sanctuary and saw her sitting in the last pew with Aunt Ella.

"You said that many times," Matt said. "What was Pastor Gonzalez's key verse?"

"John 3:17. Why?"

"Just checking if you were paying attention. Look, I have to run. A few things to do before the evening service. Why don't you go talk to her?"

"Now?"

"Now, Ivan. Don't be shy."

Shy? If he were shy he wouldn't have kissed Brinley. Twice. "All right. Talk with you later."

Ivan looked for Grandma Yun in her usual seat with the senior adults—she liked to chat with her buddies—but she wasn't there. He found her talking with Aunt Ella and Brinley instead. In fact, the entire senior adult section—including Hiram Jacobs—was gabbing with Aunt Ella. Something about the Christmas luncheon the day before. They'd probably be talking about that for weeks and possibly months to come.

Ivan sneaked in behind Brinley and whispered in her ear, "I'm glad you're here."

She smiled.

They both stepped back to give Aunt Ella's fan club more room.

"Aunt Ella insisted on coming," Brinley said. "She's made some new friends, as you can see."

"I see that. And I see you. I like your outfit." Red turtleneck and black pants. "Go Dawgs."

"Your quintet did a great job."

"Thank you."

"How did you find time to practice? You must have performances almost every day this holiday season."

"We start right after Thanksgiving and don't let up until the first of the year. I rehearse all the time."

Brinley looked thoughtful. "Yesterday. You lost three hours of rehearsal."

She was right, but Ivan wasn't going to admit it. "I gained time with you. Not enough, but I'd rather be with you."

"Than play violin?"

"I can always practice later." Ivan had more to say but here came Grandma and Aunt Ella.

"Would you two like to come over to our house for lunch?" Yun asked. "I think we have enough food for everyone."

"I'm sure we do, Grandma." He tried not to frown when thinking of the ramifications of Brinley coming over to lunch at their home. He wished they had a proper dining table but the kitchen table was all they had. If he put Brinley in the seat facing the wall, then she wouldn't be spending the entire time looking in the direction of their old stove and sink.

That's it.

"Today instead of tomorrow?" Brinley asked.

"We can do both days if you like." Ivan touched her elbow.

"What are we having for lunch?" Aunt Ella asked before Brinley said anything.

"Spaghetti," Yun said.

"I love spaghetti." Aunt Ella turned to Brinley. "Let's."

"Well..."

Ivan wondered what she was going to say.

"I hate to impose." Brinley looked at him.

"You won't be, Brin. It'll be our pleasure." Ivan realized he had called her Brin.

"I'll be over for lunch again on Monday."

"Oh, we might have spaghetti again Monday." Ivan grimaced.

"How about if I come over today and cancel tomorrow's lunch?" Brinley turned to Yun. "We can still have tea at two, if you like."

"I'd like that very much, Brinley." Grandma Yun was all smiles.

Ivan tried to hide his disappointment. "We can do that."

"Okay. Since we're the only ones in town and we have to reheat whatever Cara cooked last week, I guess spaghetti sounds good."

Aunt Ella clapped her hands.

Ivan was relieved. He reached for Brinley's hand. "Where are you parked?"

"Out front. Almost curbside by the fountain."

"We're in the back lot," Ivan said, letting go of Brinley's hand. "We'll see you at our house, then."

"Should we pick up something on the way? Desserts?"

"Don't worry about it," Grandma said. "I made a new batch of cookies. Gingerbread, this time."

Yep. Cookies that I like. Maybe Brin could learn how to make—

What am I thinking!

Ivan realized he didn't know much about Brinley. Did she cook? What did she cook? What were her interests besides history and old things? What about hobbies? How well did she play the piano? Did she play any other musical instruments? What were her pet peeves? Things she absolutely loved? Hated? Everything in between?

I know so little about her.

And yet I have kissed her twice.

CHAPTER TWENTY-THREE

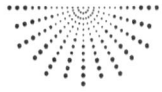

$\mathcal{B}$rinley wasn't sure what had gotten into Ivan. He had seemed antsy the entire time they ate lunch. Sure, the McMillan kitchen was small. It wasn't like she hadn't been in a small kitchen before. Her apartment when she was at UGA wasn't any bigger.

Still, his behavior was suspicious. He had made her sit facing the wall and away from the rest of the galley kitchen and refused to let her get up to do anything. She had wanted to help and he had made it look like she was useless. Couldn't get the silverware or plates. Couldn't fill glasses with water. Couldn't dish out the spaghetti. Couldn't do a thing.

In the end, Brinley waited until Ivan had sat down to eat his lunch before she made her move. He wasn't going to get away with making her look like she was too fragile for kitchen duties. She wanted to show him that she could help in the kitchen, load the dishwasher, wipe down the counters, domestic stuff that she had seen Cara do. How hard could it be?

She finished her small portion of spaghetti before everyone else and was the first one on her feet as soon as Yun finished her plate.

"Seconds, Yun?" Brinley asked as calmly as she could.

"Yes, please."

Ivan was on her case again. "I'll do it. Please sit down, Brin."

What has gotten into him?

"Ivan, dear." Yun's voice was quiet but firm.

"Yes, Grandma?"

"Let Brinley help."

When Ivan didn't respond, Brinley did. "Thank you, Yun."

Brinley carefully carried Yun's plate to the stove. *Don't drop the plate! Have to show Ivan—*

She was blanking out as she tried to remember the order of things. Put the spaghetti on the plate first. Then the meat sauce. Then cheese on top.

Seriously, Brin!

She almost laughed at herself, but the plate rocked in her hand and she nearly freaked out. *Boy, these stoneware plates are heavy.*

"How much do you want, Yun?" Brinley showed Yun her plate. "This enough?"

"More than enough."

Brinley didn't dare look at Ivan as she sprinkled parmesan cheese on top. Back at home, they'd be shredding imported Parmigiano-Reggiano, not this whatever-it-was. Then it was back to the table.

Whatever you do, don't drop the plate.

Aunt Ella also wanted seconds. And thirds. By the time lunch was over, there was nothing left to eat on the stove.

"We still have cookies," Yun said.

Everyone groaned.

"Maybe in a little bit." Ivan started clearing the table.

Brinley wasn't going to let him get away with it anymore. It felt like a domestic squabble and she had to win this. Without asking Ivan, Brinley helped to clear the table. Ivan said nothing to her as they piled up dirty plates on the Formica counter next to the two sinks. In the sinks were colanders, ladles, pot covers. Brinley wondered how he was going to rinse out the plates before putting them into the dishwasher if he couldn't turn on the single faucet.

He seemed to hesitate. Then he cleared the sinks. That was when Brinley saw that the porcelain sinks were old and stained. In a reno house, that would be the first thing she'd throw out into the dumpster.

In fact, she'd rip up this entire kitchen and throw everything out. Those four-ton dumpsters could take quite a load.

But they live here.

People actually live here.

Brinley remembered the corner stain on the popcorn kitchen ceiling when they had arrived from church for lunch. Probably a leaky roof up there. And before that, Aunt Ella had almost tripped on those unnerving loose pine boards on the porch. If Brinley had her way, she'd call Tobias Vega right away—

This is not my house.

Why did she feel strongly, then? In her heart, she knew she couldn't help it. She wanted to make life easier for him, for his grandma. Yet what Dad had told her when they went around St. Simon's and Brunswick and Jekyll buying up foreclosed properties came to mind.

Sometimes the best way to help people is to let them go through the difficulties. Bailing them out would short-circuit their life lessons.

"I'm sorry, Ivan."

"What for?" Ivan was running water over a large pot.

"I'm only trying to help."

"I know."

Brinley watched Ivan squirt dish liquid into the large pot. He swirled the soapy water with his hand.

"Let me help load the dishwasher." Brinley reached for the door.

"The dishwasher is broken." Ivan dropped forks and knives into the large pot that he had turned into a washbasin.

"Oh."

"It has been broken for years."

Years? "Why is it still here?"

"There'd be a hole there if we take it out." He paused. "And I don't know how to remove it."

"That's easy. I'll call Toby—"

"No. Don't call anyone."

Brinley remembered overstepping with the plumber. "I'm sorry."

Ivan stopped what he was doing and wiped his hands on the dishcloth hanging off the door pull below the sink.

"I'm the one who should be sorry. Ever wonder why I didn't date for six years? I can't afford it, Brin. I can't bring a girl to this dump. I can't let her see where I live. And here you are."

And here I am.

Brinley tried to choose her words carefully. It seemed to be a touchy issue. What could she say to ameliorate his angst? Maybe something Yun would say? Well, Yun would refer back to God.

"What do you think your Bible would say about it?" Brinley caught herself by surprise at what came out of her mouth, but it seemed to surprise Ivan more.

"My Bible?"

As if he was asking, "What do you know about my Bible?"

"I was thinking that when I had tea with your grandma on Friday, she talked about the Bible a lot. Seems to me it would have the answer to your po— uh, problem."

Whew. Good thing she didn't say poverty.

"The Bible says I should trust God." Ivan started washing the silverware. "I've been trusting God for years and still things have been bad for us."

"Let me try to understand this," Brinley said.

"Trusting someone implies trusting his take on things, right?"

"Pretty much."

"Therefore, trusting God means trusting His take on things."

"You said that."

"Maybe you need to wait it out."

"Meaning what?"

Brinley stepped closer to Ivan. Rubbed his flannel sleeve. His arm was rigid underneath. She kept stroking his arm until he eased up.

"You know Dad and I do a lot of renos—renovations—up and down the coast," she said.

"I have no idea what you do, Brinley, other than sales. What do you do exactly?"

"Well, I work for my father in the family business. Brooks Investments has several subsidiaries. Some are in Atlanta and some on St. Simon's. I'm quitting my job in the marketing department in Atlanta. Don't tell Dad yet. When he comes home from Paris next week, I'll talk to him about it." Brinley sighed. "When I'm in town here, I love doing stuff with Dad in one of our smaller entities, Brooks Renovations. Have you heard of it?"

"No."

"Doesn't matter. Dad flips houses as a hobby, you know."

"Flips? Like buying and selling?"

"Yes. We go to these houses. Maybe they have good bones, but the houses could be wrecks otherwise."

"Like this one."

"Worse."

"Is that possible?"

"Better believe it. Sometimes we have to gut the whole structure and rebuild from the foundation up. All that takes time. Sometimes I disagree with Dad about how we should fix the house. But in the end, I trust his judgment. I trust his take on things. So I wait and see what he does. And usually he's right. It almost always turns out better than I thought."

"Your point is?"

"Don't you get it? My dad is not perfect and I trust him and he comes through. Imagine if you trust your perfect God and He comes through. If He's God, He's perfect, and He's always right. Imagine the results."

"Yes."

"So trust your God. Wait it out. It will turn out better than you thought."

Silence.

"Say something, Ivan."

"I'm speechless."

"Why? Did I say something wrong about your God?"

"No."

"Then what? Don't look at me like that."

"You said that if God is God, then He is perfect and He is always right." Ivan was inches away from Brinley's face. "If He is perfect and right, I can trust Him for the situations in my life."

"Makes sense to me."

"If He's perfect and right, why are you not trusting Him for the salvation of your soul?"

Now it was Brinley's turn to be silent.

"Is that not logical?" Ivan pressed.

Slowly, Brinley nodded. "I guess it is. In my mind, I see what you mean. In my heart, I don't feel it."

"Brin, salvation is not by *feel*. It's by *faith* in God."

"I'll think about it."

"And I'll think about what you said too." Ivan let her go. "Now how about I wash these silverware and you dry them?"

"Sounds good. Where's a clean dish towel?"

"In that drawer over there."

Brinley opened the drawer at the island. The dish towels were clean but frayed at the edges. When she tried to close the drawer, it caught. It looked like the drawer slides were grimy and some parts had worn out. She couldn't get the drawer back in place.

"Let me get that." Ivan stepped in and jiggled the drawer. He slammed it shut. "Nothing sheer force can't fix."

"Uh-huh. Maybe I'll get you a can of WD-40 for Christmas."

"That would be a nice domestic gift." Ivan laughed.

Brinley blinked. *Domestic?*

CHAPTER TWENTY-FOUR

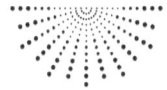

*T*he percussion of pattering shoes opened Ivan's eyes. Coming down the stairs into his basement studio, his domain, his man cave, Brinley stepped onto the worn carpet. She didn't seem to notice big old ugly stains beneath her dress shoes.

"That was beautiful." Brinley walked toward him. "What is it?"

"Something I'm composing."

"For?"

You. "Just a tune."

He had sneaked out of the after-lunch conversation to get some breathing space. His basement was where he could unwind from a long day, his favorite place to cool off. He had been up since five o'clock studying his Bible to get direction from God for his life. He had written some more of his song for Brinley. He and Grandma Yun had arrived at Seaside

Chapel at nine o'clock because he had an early rehearsal with the string ensemble for the offertory. Sunday school and service and then the whole tension of having Brinley in their house for lunch had all worn him out.

He could use a nap. But couldn't until Brinley and Aunt Ella had left.

"They're done gabbing up there?" Ivan asked.

"I told Aunt Ella we're leaving in fifteen minutes. She's eating her last cookies. Speaking of which, Yun said gingerbread is your favorite."

Only Grandma's gingerbread.

"She said she'll give me the recipe someday."

"Someday?" Ivan laughed. "Yeah. Wait for it."

"I wish I could cook. I'm reheating frozen food all week."

"Oh, you poor thing." Ivan almost reached for her, but he decided not to because they were alone in the basement and he didn't want to get into trouble with impropriety. Better let her stand there. "You can always learn, Brin."

Brinley shrugged. She opened up the paper napkin in her hand to reveal two nesting cookies. "Want some?"

"Can't. My hands are clean." Ivan picked up the violin again. "Can't get grease on this. It's not mine."

"Not yours?"

"Nope. This belongs to Conductor Petrocelli. Jean Baptiste Vuillaume made it in 1850."

"What did you play previously?"

"An assortment of violins." He didn't want to say more.

He felt that Brinley didn't need to know he had to sell his Gagliano to pay off part of the three mortgages on Grandma's house. The second mortgage was Grandpa Otto's fault, but the third was his to deal with Grandma's broken hip and the subsequent hospital bills and physical therapy not covered by his music studio insurance.

If he had the SISO job then, they would've been better off. But it was two years too late when SISO finally hired him as one of the first violinists. When the concertmaster left for greater venues, he had to compete for her position. Thank God he got it now and their income situation had improved.

Ivan was relieved when Brinley said nothing. He watched her break off a third of Grandma's homemade cookie and lift it toward his mouth.

"Open up," she said.

Are you kidding me?

But he did what she told him to do, and she stuffed the piece of cookie into his mouth. She didn't touch his lips or chin or cheek at all. Her movement was graceful, like she had done this before. He felt a bit jealous.

Of what? Of whom?

But why would he be jealous? Unwarranted, he chided himself.

Nothing could ever happen between him and her. Different worlds. Different circles. Different beliefs. Grandpa Otto used to stress how important it was for the husband and wife to be on the same spiritual page—

What did I say? Husband and what?

He stood there, violin in hand, speechless at what had crossed his own mind, all the while chewing on a piece of cookie that a woman he had only gotten close to for fewer than three days had hand-fed him. Granted, they'd known each other in passing for about a year. But they hadn't been on first name basis until the week before.

It felt so wrong.

"Want more?" She broke off another piece.

"No. Thank you. I'd better not." He swallowed the last bit of crumbs. "Want to hear my composition?"

"Absolutely."

Ivan put his chin on the violin chin rest. He began to play "Pleasant Days" as Brinley ate the rest of the cookies. He improvised a bit but she didn't seem to notice.

In the middle of it, he lost track of what he was doing. The rest of the tune in his head was ebbing into forgetfulness. After the thirty-fifth, measure the music manuscript blurred and all he could see was Brinley standing right in front of him, holding the rest of the cookie in her hand.

He stopped playing.

"I'm still working on the rest of it." It was somewhat true.

"I like what you have so far. Sounds like a quiet

walk on the beach in the morning with a cup of coffee."

"Seriously?"

Brinley nodded. "What is it called?"

"I titled it 'Pleasant Days.'"

"There you go." Brinley bunched up the paper napkin. "Are you going to write the accompaniment?"

"Yeah. Or maybe turn this into a sonata for two violins."

"You play it well."

"Thank you."

"I wonder how that would sound on a Strad."

Ivan shook his head. "Petrocelli is only letting me play one composition on the Strad for tomorrow night's auction."

"Oh, the fundraiser is tomorrow. I forgot. Just as well that we canceled lunch tomorrow. Busy day for you."

"Yeah. And I'd better rehearse that piece too."

"So we'd better leave."

"No. No. That's not what I mean." Ivan placed the Vuillaume into its case. "I practice every day. Maintenance, you know. So it's not a big deal if I don't rehearse this afternoon."

"You make the violin look easy to play." Brinley smiled.

Ivan shrugged.

"You said you might go back on tour, but is that around the world or just regionally?"

Ivan hesitated. *That's a loaded question.*

"Once upon a time I thought I would. Reality is, I can't go back. In any case, I can't think that far now. I need to focus on SISO and my music studio." And taking care of Grandma, the whole reason he was stuck on this island.

"I guess you're not sure, after all."

"I guess not." Ivan recalled what he had said to Brinley in passing. Yet they were only possibilities. There was no way he could leave Grandma Yun alone on the island. Anything he wanted to do would have to be after she passed away. However, he could not imagine life without her.

Brinley looked around. "Is this your music studio?"

"I know it's small, but it's thriving." Ivan snapped shut the violin case. He pointed to a wall of glass doors behind which were music stands and an upright piano. "This used to be one giant room, but I walled it off over there. That's sort of semi-soundproof."

"That's where you teach violin."

Ivan nodded. "All day long, year-round, except Thanksgiving and Christmas. Our Christmas break is longer because I can't juggle all these SISO performances and rehearsals and teach violin at the same time."

"SISO keeps you busy this time of year."

"Through New Year's Eve." Ivan plucked a flyer off a cork-board on the wall. "Here are all our performances if you want to come and listen. Some are open to the public. Some are private soirees."

Brinley took the paper from him, read it, then folded and pocketed it. "Do you have many students?"

"Enough to keep me busy, though some of them are not coming back after the Christmas break. I'll have to try to get new students in the spring or for next year."

"Not coming back?"

"Violin isn't the easiest instrument to learn. They hear me and they want to play like that. It takes years to get there. Sometimes people, especially kids, lose their patience."

"I used to hear Grandpa Brooks on his Strad."

"The Lord Sterling Strad? The one that's now in a safe place where nobody can play it?"

"I know what you said. Musical instruments are not meant to be locked in vaults."

She was listening!

Brinley nodded. "I think when the SISO Museum of Musical Instruments is done, I'll loan some of them to it. What do you think?"

"Some? How many Strads do you have?"

Brinley didn't say. "Grandpa would have traded them all—except the Lord Sterling—for the Damaris Brooks."

Wow. She is so outside my league.

CHAPTER TWENTY-FIVE

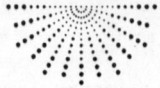

*B*rinley woke up with the sun when the beams beat down on her covers. From her brother Diehl's bed, she watched two—no, three, but no more—brown pelicans fly by. Over many summers in her childhood, she used to see flocks of them flying up and down the Atlantic coastline. These days if Brinley saw a few flying together, it was yet another sign of progress in recovering the species.

She plopped her feet on the heated hardwood floor in the bedroom, smaller than hers next door now occupied by Aunt Ella. Brinley had locked all the doors and windows and had warned her to stay put. The nurse would be coming in at ten to administer Aunt Ella's medications. Then it was up to Brinley to take care of her until Aunt Ella's caregiver returned from her own Christmas break.

Brinley brushed her teeth and showered quickly. She threw on a sweatshirt and a pair of sweatpants.

She peeked into her old bedroom to find Aunt Ella still asleep. Good. She was concerned she had run away again.

She padded downstairs to forage for breakfast. Before she could even reach the kitchen, she smelled the fragrant aroma of pancakes. She quickened her steps.

"Cara! What are you doing here?" Brinley gave the housekeeper a quick hug at Mom's La Grand Palais 180 range. Mom wanted the best range and hood though she never cooked in her life. In the end, it was for Cara's use and Brinley and her siblings' benefit.

"I can't let you eat last week's frozen food. I brought you some food for the next several days. I'll bring you some more at the end of the week."

"Cara, you don't have to." Brinley wasn't sure how to tell her. Didn't want to hurt her feelings. "I should've called you yesterday."

"About what?" Cara flipped the pancakes.

"I want you to have Christmas and New Year's off, Cara. Spend time with your husband and kids and your new grandbaby. Even Chef Pierre has three weeks off. So I'm having a personal chef come in twice a week until you come back."

"A personal chef?" There was some sort of edge to Cara's voice that Brinley couldn't make out.

"Skye Langston. You remember her? She fills in for Chef Pierre from time to time."

"Ah." Cara looked relieved.

"She's not taking your place, Cara. You're still in

charge of our menu. Skye is just going to make sure Aunt Ella and I have food for some of the days we don't eat out. Then you'll be back, and so will Chef Pierre."

"Promise?"

"Promise. And you know I always keep my promise."

"I know, but it's no trouble at all for me to drop off a few dishes."

"Who cooks those dishes?" Brinley opened a cabinet door to retrieve a dinner plate. She placed it on the granite counter next to the stove.

"Well, I do."

"Exactly. So you're at home cooking for me when you're supposed to be relaxing."

"I don't mind."

"I mind." Brinley watched Cara place several pancakes on her plate. Her mouth started to water when she smelled the buttermilk.

Yet she wished Cara had not come. "Like right now. Shouldn't you be having breakfast with your husband?"

"I've been here at six o'clock every morning since you were a little kid."

"Except at Thanksgiving and Christmas. Go home, Cara."

"Not until I make you pancakes for tomorrow morning." Cara poured more batter in the pan.

"I hope that God blesses you for your caring spirit, Cara."

Cara stopped what she was doing. "God? You believe in God now?"

"I don't have a problem with God. It's Jesus I can't get past." Brinley found organic maple syrup in the refrigerator.

"Do you want that heated up?" Cara asked.

"No time. I'm famished. Do you have coffee?" Brinley sat down on a barstool at the island, poured cold syrup on her hot pancakes, and dug in.

She remembered how Ivan had thanked God for the food, but she wasn't sure if God would hear her prayers if she did the same. Maybe it had more effect if Ivan or Yun said it instead of her. She'd ask Yun about it this afternoon when they met for tea.

"Where's Aunt Ella?" Cara asked as she poured Brinley black coffee.

"Still sleeping upstairs."

"Your parents left you to babysit her?"

"I don't mind." Brinley breathed in the aroma of coffee before she poured enough cream into it. "It's only for a week. Mom and Dad will be home next Tuesday, in time for our annual Christmas Eve dinner."

Sometimes Brinley wished they would eat at home like they used to do when Grandpa Brooks had been alive, but since he passed away, the Brooks family Christmas Eve dinner had been at The Priory. Only minutes from here and everything ready to go by the time they got there. It was easier on Cara, for one thing, because she didn't have to stay up all night cleaning up the kitchen and then rush home for her own family Christmas.

"And besides, the security people will be here in case we need to round up Aunt Ella."

"You're always helping others, Brin," Cara said. "What are you doing for yourself?"

I'm enjoying Ivan's company. "Taking it easy this Christmas."

"My daughter is so disappointed she doesn't get to work on your costume for the dinner tonight." Cara started cleaning up the pancake pan and ladles in the sink.

"Well, that's because she's such a good seamstress. I'm glad that she made the gown loose enough for me to fit in even a year later. The stretchable stomacher was a brilliant idea."

"I'll tell her." Cara loaded the dishwasher.

Brinley remembered Ivan in Yun's kitchen doing dishes by hand.

"Are you going alone tonight?"

"Well, Aunt Ella is going to spend the evening at my friend's house, so we're going to go from there."

"We?"

"Ivan and I."

"Ivan? I've never heard of him before."

"Ivan is Zoe's brother-in-law." Brinley was surprised Cara didn't know.

"Oh. He's special?"

Yes. Very special. "We started—I don't know what we started, Cara. We went out to eat, we spent time together. Not sure where it's going."

"But you like him."

Maybe more than like. "I'm going back to Atlanta in three weeks. It's not going to last."

Cara wiped the stove with a damp cloth. "But you like him."

"Yes. Like I said, it might not last." Like all the other boyfriends. They came and went like clockwork.

"Maybe this time it will." Cara picked up Brinley's empty plate. "For your sake, I hope so. That good-for-nothing Phinn! I hope he never comes back. You find yourself a nice man who can love you and take good care of you."

Take care of me? Ivan could barely take care of Yun and himself.

"I hope you find a good man, dear Brinley."

"I hope so too, Cara." Brinley wanted to say more, but her iPhone rang. She retrieved it from her sweatpants pocket. "It's Dad. I have to take this."

on't worry about me, Dad. I'm going to be fine."

No, I'm not.

Brinley couldn't believe what she had heard, but there was nothing she could do about it. Mom and Dad had made up their minds, and that was the way it went. They had kept busy and that prevented Mom from meddling in her life. Yet the irony was that they were too busy now to get the family together for Christmas.

This would be the first Christmas in Brinley's entire life where everyone was everywhere else but Seaside Island.

Even in years past when her brother, Diehl, had worked up to Christmas Eve, he'd flown in the next morning to have Christmas brunch with the family and to open presents. Though he'd fly back to Atlanta that very evening, at least he had not missed out. They were together. They laughed and had their photos taken. Brinley had kept photo albums of every Christmas since she was a little girl.

Now Dad was telling her something else.

"Are you sure, Brinley Brin?" Dad's voice had always been calm.

She could hear voices in the background on Dad's end of the phone. Some sort of announcements in French over the public address system. A Christmas carol in French began playing. They were probably out shopping somewhere, but Dad didn't say and Brinley didn't ask.

Seriously, she didn't care anymore. What happened to the idea of family and holidays and Christmas meals together?

She wanted to weep but it would be juvenile.

Those family Christmases. They are gone.

Gone!

"How about this, Brin? I'll send the BBJ to pick you and Aunt Ella up, and you can join us here for Christmas?"

"That sounds like an option, Dad. But you know how Aunt Ella feels about flying. She's going to freak out for eight or nine hours."

"We'll have her sedated."

"You mean like a pet?"

"Well, it's only for eight hours."

"Or nine." Brinley paced the sunroom. Outside, the sky was still clear, but in the distance she could see some dark clouds. "Let me ask Aunt Ella what she wants to do. It's not a problem for me to fly out to Paris for Christmas Day, but I'm not sure if Aunt Ella is up to it. We can't leave her behind. She has no one, Dad."

Oh. This is all so last minute.

"So when are you planning on coming home?" Brinley asked.

"After New Year's Day."

"Two and a half weeks from now?"

"You'll have the whole house to yourself, Brin."

"An empty house, Dad."

"Nice and quiet, then. You can read, nap, take it easy. Just don't throw any parties in the big house."

"You know how I feel about parties, Dad."

"I know. I'm sorry about the change of plans. I feel that your mom and I need to spend more time together."

"I totally understand, Dad." In her heart, Brinley wished that Mom would give too. She had always been a taker. *Do it her way or not at all.*

Brinley resolved that if and when she married that she and her husband would be more balanced in their approach to their lives together. Not one of those "give and take" maxims but more like each would give all to the other and be generous and flexible and—

A tear fell.

"Dad, go enjoy your time with Mom. Life is short, you know."

Sniff. Boy, this sunroom is dusty!

"Yeah, since my stroke, I've been thinking of that."

"Tell you what, Dad. Aunt Ella's going home the day after Christmas. How about I catch a flight out to see you and Mom for New Year's?"

"I'd like that, Brin."

"So meanwhile, it'll be only Diehl, Aunt Ella, and me for Christmas here."

"I'm glad you're not alone. And I love you, Brin."

"Love you too, Dad." Brinley heard women's voices and they sounded like Mom and Zoe talking at the same time.

"Your mom's done shopping, so we're going to go back to the chateau now," Dad said. "Mom said she bought you something. I'll tell her to wrap it up and she can give it to you when you get here."

"Sounds good, Dad. I'll ask Diehl if he wants to fly out with me to Paris."

"He might not. Tell him I'm upset he's working too hard."

Brinley found that ironic. Dad was the one who had decided to leave the entire company in Diehl's hands.

Brinley was only working in the sales department. Sadly, the more sales she brought in for Brooks Investments, the harder Diehl had to work. She wondered now whether she should even broach the subject of her departure from the company. How was that going to affect Diehl?

She decided to talk to him when he came for Christmas.

I hope he doesn't cancel it too.

Brinley and Dad said their goodbyes and the usual "I love you" and then she swiped her iPhone to look at her calendar.

Eleven days more with Aunt Ella.

It wasn't that she minded being with Aunt Ella, but Brinley wasn't cut out to be a full-time caregiver. The nurse who came to administer the daily meds only came for half an hour a day. It was ridiculous how expensive she was.

So this was how it could be if Brinley ever ended up alone in her life. She wondered how Aunt Ella felt being elderly and dependent on other people's mercy and time and, possibly, decisions that affected her well-being and care.

She heard the pattering of heavy clogs on the slate floor. The clop-clops sounded louder.

"I'm not going home after Christmas."

Aunt Ella.

Brinley tried to remain calm. "Have you been listening the entire time?"

Aunt Ella shuffled forward. "Most of it."

"Where were you? Outside the door?"

"Behind the wall. It's sturdy so I could lean on it."

"Okay. But you heard my voice, and not Dad's. So you didn't hear the entire conversation, not truly." Brinley pocketed her iPhone. "Didn't Grandpa Brooks say it's not good to eavesdrop?"

"Willard is dead and he doesn't care," Aunt Ella said.

Brinley laughed.

"Bottom line. I'm not going home to West Palm."

"I heard you."

"I want you to take me to see the director of Brunswick Senior Living Community."

"Isn't that where Hiram lives?"

Aunt Ella's face changed. "He's the one who told me about it. They have assisted-living facilities. I want to move there."

"What about your house in Florida?"

"All my friends in West Palm are either dead or dying. I'm alone there."

Oh.

"Would you take me? Hiram says they have fully furnished apartments. Three meals a day, snacks, and games all day long. Friends everywhere."

Aunt Ella might have had some memory lapses the week before, but she seemed fine now once her medications were regulated. As far as Brinley knew, Aunt Ella was fit enough to make her own decisions.

If she didn't want to go home to West Palm, then who was Brinley to stop her? After all, Brinley herself wanted to stay on St. Simon's Island. Something about the place. Something about the people.

Something about someone.

"Hiram said the director is in all week. Would you call them and make me an appointment for today?"

"Today? We're kind of busy today, remember?"

"Busy? I like busy. What are we doing again?" Aunt Ella perked up and moved her elbows in a back and forth motion. "I'm ready to go."

"Well, Yun invited us over to tea at two."

"Yes! I'm staying through dinner."

Brinley nodded. Yun had insisted that she and Aunt Ella could spend the evening together while Brinley went to the Oglethorpe Charity Dinner tonight.

An idea struck her. She would take the meals that Cara brought over this morning. Then Yun and Aunt Ella didn't have to worry about foraging for food.

She glanced at her watch. "Have you had breakfast, Aunt Ella?"

"Cara fed me."

"Pancakes?"

"And ice cream."

"She didn't feed you ice cream for breakfast."

"Well, I helped myself." Aunt Ella turned to leave. "I'm going to get ready now for tea."

"That's not until two, Aunt Ella. There's lunch before that."

"Are you taking me out to lunch?"

"Cara brought us some roast beef. I'll make you a sandwich."

"Thank you. You're so good to me, Brin. Willard would be so proud of how you turned out."

Brinley couldn't speak.

If only Grandpa Brooks were here.

All she had left now were memories of what once was.

The Brooks Christmas traditions were slowly falling apart. They might have already fallen apart with her parents in Paris and Diehl in Atlanta. Brinley felt alone, and yet, here with Aunt Ella, she felt obligated to keep up the holiday spirit and retain whatever remnants of Christmas they had. Even if it were just the two of them left in town, they were still Brooks. And they could have their Brooks family Christmas.

So there.

"Is Cara still here?" Brinley locked step with Aunt Ella.

"She left. I sent her away. I told her to go home to her family."

Family.

CHAPTER TWENTY-SIX

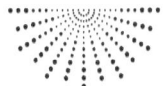

*D*ad called again right in the middle of tea time at Yun's house. Brinley threw on her jacket and went outside to the dilapidated porch to get some privacy. It was a bit chilly in mid-December. Must be the cooler Atlantic winds sweeping onshore and through those live oak trees.

Inside the house, Aunt Ella was getting louder by the minute. Brinley wondered if Aunt Ella's hearing was going but if she kept up the racket, her own hearing would go too. She closed the front door gently.

The once-white plastic chairs looked grimier than last week when she had first seen them. She didn't want to sit on either one. She went up to the edge of the porch where the steps faced the covered carport. She sat down on the pine boards, rotted in some places. She wondered if these had ever been pressure-treated.

"Dad, no need to apologize."

"We shouldn't have left you behind," Dad said. "Maybe you can go home to Atlanta."

"If I'm in Atlanta, I'm going to think about work. Here, I'm getting some peace and quiet."

"I feel bad."

"Don't. I've been working all year long. I need to stand still for a moment and not run around all the time. This is good for me."

"Don't get all philosophical on me, Brin."

"You're funny, Dad."

"We shouldn't have come to Paris. It was so spontaneous—"

"Dad, stop. I'm fine and you need to take my word for it. Where are you?"

"At the Palais Garnier."

"Only your favorite opera house in all the world." Brinley could hear faint applause on the phone. Those nearby doors leading to the theater must be opening and closing. She had been there before once. Opera wasn't Brinley's thing, but Mom and Dad had season tickets for operas up and down Europe, especially in Vienna. Tonight though, it was in Paris where they had spent their honeymoon some forty years ago.

"Dad, is the performance starting? I heard people clapping."

"Just about. I want to make sure you're all right."

"Don't worry about me, Dad."

"Are you sure?"

"A zillion times sure. Go enjoy the opera."

"In a minute."

"Go now, Dad. I'm sure the tickets are expensive."

"You know I don't care about that. But I can't get back the time we're losing with you."

He's right. But nothing can be done now.

"Right now, Aunt Ella and I are having tea with Yun McMillan," Brinley offered.

"Yun? Quincy's grandmother?"

"Yes. We're at her house. Yun brews some good tea."

That seemed to allay Dad's stress over the matter. She hadn't known Dad to be such a worrier, but he'd been more so after the stroke. And now, he'd called her from the opera house. He'd never done that before.

"I'll let you go before your tea gets cold. I'll call you tomorrow." Dad relented. "Don't forget to check your email. My agent sent you a counteroffer."

Ah, yes. The oceanfront house she wanted. "I know you're a fair businessman, Dad."

"I wish I could be a fair dad."

"Stop worrying. You're missing your opera."

"All right. I'll go now. I love you, Brinley Brin."

"Love you too, Dad."

Brinley hung up and stared at her iPhone.

Something caught her attention past her iPhone and lap and where her shoes rested on the steps. Rotting wood. She stepped off the porch and peered.

Are those...?

She found a twig nearby and started poking at the shredded wood. More wood crumbled off. As soon as the first layers fell away, thousands of bloated and blind little white-and-cream colored creatures greeted her with frenzied scurrying, possibly angry that she'd disturbed their winter hideout.

Termites!

Eating up Yun's house.

She pried and found that the porch was almost missing part of its foundation.

Jump on top of this corner and this end would cave in. Yikes.

She was shaking her head when she felt warm breath on her neck.

Uh-oh.

"What are you doing?"

His voice was soothing and calm and quiet, but Brinley was sure his face wouldn't register the same. Slowly, she turned around. Sure enough. Standing there on the cracked concrete driveway leaning over her, Ivan wasn't too happy to catch her digging into his collapsing porch.

"You have a termite infestation." Brinley tried to remain calm.

"And you have to do something about it?" Ivan's voice was curt.

"Someone has to."

"And it's your business?"

"No, it's not—"

"Exactly." Ivan extended his hand to help Brinley get to her feet.

"But—but this entire porch—"

"I'll get something from Home Depot and it'll take care of it."

"You have no idea—"

"And you do?"

"As a matter of fact, I do. My dad and I reno—"

"Not this house, you don't."

"What if Yun steps here and falls over?"

"She's not going to."

"How would you know that? Prevention is—"

"None of your business."

"Stop cutting me off!" *What in the world is wrong with you, Ivan?* "Trying to help, you know."

"Don't."

Brinley tried counting to ten but didn't get past two and a half. "You're going to lose your porch."

"So let me lose it."

"You're stubborn."

"So are you," Ivan snapped.

"Are we having a fight?"

"I don't know. You tell me."

"How can we have a fight? We hardly know each other."

"It feels like we've known each other a while." Ivan reached for her shoulder.

Brinley stepped back. "We're taking separate vehicles to the fundraiser tonight is all I can tell you right now, Mr. McArrogant."

She stalked back up the porch, careful to avoid

any soft and spongy boards. The boards were probably okay since they had been treated, but whoever had replaced those steps and their surrounding supporting beams had cut corners.

Ivan's long strides beat her to the front door. He blocked her from entering the house.

Brinley stared at her own shoes. They were new and clean against the weathered pine beneath.

"Brin." His voice was soft. "Look at me."

She couldn't.

"I'm sorry."

She should say something, but she decided that she had done enough.

"I'm sorry, Brin."

Well, at least he's trying.

"I really am." He reached for her again and wrapped her in his arms. "There's much I can't tell you. If you knew, perhaps you wouldn't think so unkindly of me."

"Unkindly? You're the one being unkind."

"Poor choice of words. I stand corrected."

They said nothing for a while.

"What's going on with you, Ivan?"

No answer.

"Why are you against everything I'm trying to do for you?" Brinley eased away.

"If you must know, Brin, I'll explain."

〜

*A*nd so Ivan explained on his 1850 Vuillaume with an improvisation that pushed and pulled at Brinley's heart, a mournful dirge entombed in his small basement studio, diminuendo measures fading into the old walls, then accelerating to a rabid presto that gnashed at her before it fell again into a sorrowful remorse.

Brinley listened, sniffled, and listened some more at Ivan's acute enumeration of things past, things lost, things gone, and things never to come. She hoped she wasn't somewhere in the recital, interlaced into his emotions of pain and fear and longing. The bow and string tore at her heart. Then finally it died away, repeats exhausted, the end of the pages in Ivan's mind accomplished.

He put down his violin. "That is my life on earth."

Brinley's impuissant arms, body, and mind all suspended in a vortex of opacity, imploding into a heavy chest constricted with agonies she had not known since the day they buried Grandpa Brooks. She understood now that Ivan had opened up a window into his personal space, letting her in to see the difficulties of his life that she had never ever known or hoped to ever experience.

Poverty.

Adversity.

Suffering.

Loss.

Yet somewhere in there were strands of hope,

measures in the key and time signature where bright silver linings had erupted, short-lived staccatos that fell back into the maddeningly funereal march toward death, that ending on earth that no human could avoid.

Ivan carefully placed the violin back into its case. "Don't get me wrong. There is a grand finale in heaven, a rapturous joy like we will never know on earth."

"But until then, this is how you view your life on earth?" Brinley asked.

"That was how my life *is* on earth."

"What about the crescendos of hopefulness in there?" Brinley stepped forward and snuggled into Ivan's flannel plaid shirt. And stayed there. She loved the warmth of his chest, the smell of fresh laundry and dryer sheets. She closed her eyes and tried to commit to memory this moment with him.

"Those are the times when I'm reminded that I have peace with God even if I don't always have peace on earth. Someday when I get to heaven, everything will be fine. No more troubles, no more losses."

"No more termites or broken toilets." Brinley's voice cracked.

The light in Ivan's eyes returned. "I have hope for the future. Do you, Brin?"

"Only for the here and now." She understood now where Ivan was coming from. All the inheritance in the world could not compare to the promise of heaven in his heart. That space was reserved for God alone.

"But you can have hope for the future too, Brin."
Ivan kissed her forehead, accepting, welcoming.

"Maybe we can help each other."

"We can?"

"Yes, Ivan. You tell me about the peace of God, and I help you with your peace on earth."

Ivan groaned. "You want to fix my porch."

CHAPTER TWENTY-SEVEN

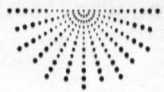

*W*hen the reproduction eighteenth-century boned stay dug into Brinley's ribs again, she knew that she wasn't going to be able to eat much tonight at the Oglethorpe Charity Dinner, colonial food notwithstanding. She placed a hand on her laced stomacher, its embroidery textured under her fingers. The salmon-colored *robe à l'anglaise* barely fit her, but if she survived the evening with the gown and petticoat intact, she'd be a happy camper.

She was glad she had snacked on Yun's gingerbread cookies before she came. Those cookies could hold her over for quite a while.

Hmm... Maybe those cookies are why my waist feels a bit tight right now.

She lifted the mineral water to her lips and looked around. She found Ivan chatting away with the harpist, who was in a pretty colonial costume herself. Ivan looked rather period-authentic and so did the entire SISO in their colonial garb.

Bravo, Conductor Petrocelli.

Someone waved to her.

Brinley waved back. Not the person she wanted to see tonight. But there he was in his three-piece hunter green silk damask colonial suit. "Jared."

"Brinley Brooks. I'm surprised to see you here." Jared Urquhart kissed her cheek lightly. "Is Phinn here with you?"

"No. We're no longer together."

Jared lifted her left hand. "I see you returned his ring. When did this happen?"

"Summer."

"He doesn't deserve you, you know."

"Some best friend you are, badmouthing him."

"We were best friends until... Water under the bridge." Jared's smooth, manicured fingers, went up her forearm. "You here alone?"

She pulled away. "I'm here with someone."

"Right. She's here with me."

Ivan.

He came up to Brinley in his dark blue waistcoat that brought out the color of his eyes. His coat was off, and Brinley could see the ruffles on his shirt under his cravat. His sleeves were crumpled, but Brinley didn't care. She felt his left arm going around her waist though the stiff stay prevented her from feeling his touch.

Ivan extended his other hand toward Jared as if he was parrying an opponent with his fencing sword. "Ivan McMillan. You are?"

"Jared Urquhart, an old friend of the Brooks family."

Brinley could feel the tension as the two men shook hands, eyeball to eyeball in their staring-down contest. Jared was a bit more willowy than Ivan, but they were both about as tall as each other in their colonial stacked heels. And both looked spiffy in their costumes, from their cravats down to their breeches, white stockings, and buckled black shoes.

She tried to muffle her chuckle.

"Are you okay, Brin?" Ivan turned to look at her.

You blinked.

Brinley could imagine Jared saying that.

Jared had always been competitive even when they were kids playing in Grandpa Brooks's backyard, though Brinley had never gone out with him. He seemed to find her refusal of him a missing notch in his totem pole and had made it a point to remind her. They would always be in the same circles, it seemed, with Jared's company hiring Brooks Investments for their many development projects all around the world. She wouldn't be surprised if he offered to buy Brooks Investments someday.

"I'm fine." Brinley stepped closer to Ivan.

Jared smiled. "I'm going to outbid you for the Strad, Brinley."

"Who says I'm going to bid for it?" Brinley had

put her West Paces Ferry house on the market so she could buy that oceanfront house that Tobias Vega was renovating for her on St. Simon's Island. There was no money leftover in that swap for her to do any frivolous spending. She was her father's daughter through and through, and he had taught her never to spend what she didn't have in cash. The lesson had been so ingrained in her such that even with liquid cash, Brinley was loathed to spend a dime. She'd rather keep the cash, thank you very much.

Except...

She would give Ivan anything.

Oddly enough, he hadn't asked for anything at all. She had given him whatever she thought he needed except for this afternoon when Ivan had personally called pest control. He had insisted at the compromise or else she would have sent Tobias Vega to fix his porch. They settled in the middle. Ivan would get the termites exterminated, and she would stop asking to fix his porch.

She wanted him to have a nice porch.

And a nice house.

A home?

"Sure, Brinley. Point is, you don't need another Strad."

"You're right, Jared," Brinley said. "I don't even play the violin. I'm only here at the ball representing Dad."

"Who is out of the country." Jared smiled. "Maybe I could come over, have lunch, and talk about Brooks Investments. Hate to see you all by yourself in that big old cottage."

Ivan cleared his throat. "She's not by herself."

"Oh, a live-in."

"That's not what I meant." Ivan's face turned red.

"Then what do you mean?"

"It means that we need to go." Brinley started walking, pulling Ivan along. "See you later, Jared."

Moments later, they were far enough away for Ivan to vent. "Who is that jerk?"

"He's not a jerk."

"Are you defending him?"

"No. I'm saying don't worry about him." Brinley placed a palm on his chest. She could feel his heartbeat underneath that white shirt.

"I saw him kiss your cheek and touch your arm." Ivan reached up and held Brinley's hand in place with his.

Now Brinley felt his heartbeat increase. "Are you jealous, Mr. McMillan?"

Before Ivan could answer, the harpist he had been talking to earlier appeared out of nowhere, holding his navy blue coat with gold buttons. Brinley watched her hand it to Ivan, telling him in a dulcet twang that Conductor Petrocelli had given them a two-minute warning.

"Thanks, Em." Ivan threw on the coat.

"Em?" Brinley asked. Their familiarity with each other bothered her a bit.

Only a bit.

Not!

"Are you jealous, Miss Brooks?" Ivan countered.

~

*I*van couldn't believe his ears when the professional benefit auctioneer rattled off increasingly bigger numbers for the 1736 Guarneri del Gesù violin after he had played the fastest "Flight of the Bumblebee" he'd ever played on any violin. The Guarneri held flawlessly against Nikolai Rimsky-Korsakov's original composition.

But that was over now. The Guarneri had been taken away from him forever, laid down to rest in that old case before the bids had begun.

He knew that Brinley's table was somewhere away from his line of sight in the large ballroom, but he was glad she wasn't at the same table as Jared Urquhart. Ivan watched Jared flick his bid paddle, smirking as he showed off how much money he could burn on that Guarneri. Ivan would like to take that paddle and swat that smirk off Jared's face.

Very unchristian-like.

Grandma would be disappointed.

When the frenzy died down, the hammer price was over three million dollars. The Guarneri was sold to someone from out of state. Ivan was happy—so happy—it wasn't that Jared fellow.

Three-point-two million dollars.

Ivan was stunned. He couldn't even count that high. To think he had played the Guarneri before it was auctioned off. What a privilege.

His eyes darted to the violin in his hand. This would be the last time he'd play this one too.

The lights dimmed in the ballroom as a video flashed across a big screen, a woman's voice adulating the 1721 Schoenberg Stradivarius violin about to be sold off to another highest bidder. The sound of that Strad was bold on the video, but Ivan didn't think it could compare to hearing it live.

After the video infomercial was over, Petrocelli nodded to Ivan.

He walked to the front of the podium like he had rehearsed countless hours before, the Schoenberg Strad in his hand. Somehow it felt different this time. He wasn't sure why. He breathed in and out slowly as there was silence in the entire ballroom.

Silence.

Somewhere in the ballroom, Brinley Brooks was listening to him play. He still couldn't see her for the bright lights on him. He could feel her presence in the room. The more he thought of it, the worse it got.

Lord, I shouldn't be this nervous.

All eyes were on him as if saying, "Any day now."

This is for Br— No.

Lord, this is for You. Thank You for the gift of music.

Nothing else mattered now as Ivan plunged wholeheartedly into executing Niccolò Paganini's "Caprice No. 24" on that old Stradivarius that he also would never see again after tonight. Better make it good. Make it memorable. He thought of nothing else but to get to the end of the piece without missing a note. All four years of Juilliard came to the fore, wrapped up in that almost three-hundred-year-old violin.

His left fingers danced nimbly on the strings, his right fingers sure and steady. He could see the music in his mind, the triplets, the slurs, pizzicatos, the rise and fall of sixteenth notes, and the sadness that filled his spirit when he reached the finale.

The ballroom shook with whistles and applause. Ivan's fingers trembled as he took his seat. A gloved assistant yanked—no, firmly took—the violin from him, bow and all.

Goodbye, Strad.

Ivan sat there, breathless.

He had never, ever been this nervous his entire life, and he knew it wasn't because of the violin. He felt that he had given the performance of a lifetime to show his worth as one of the best violinists in the region. Playing violin was all he ever knew and ever wanted to do. He wanted to make a living off playing the violin, support a family on it, and now he felt he had proven he could. The rest of his life hinged on this piquant fact. Without the violin—

Lord, don't let me be without a violin.

∽

"The bidding war did me in," Jared Urquhart told Brinley after the auction.

She was waiting at the ballroom entrance for Ivan to bring his pickup around. He had insisted they drive one vehicle. Then when they had arrived at The Priory, he didn't want to pay for valet parking. Now he had to walk across the parking lot to get the pickup in some forty-degree winds, leaving Brinley standing there by the door waiting and getting accosted.

"The Guarneri, we know who bought it." Jared didn't seem to be in a hurry to leave. "I guess the Nashville Symphony will put it to good use. But the Strad?"

"An anonymous telephone bidder. What do you care? Try again next time, Jared."

"For a long time in there, I thought it might be you."

"Don't you think five-point-four mil is overpriced for even a Strad?" Brinley asked. "It's not even the Lady Blunt." *Or the Damaris.*

"It's for charity. I suspect the buyer wanted to make sure nobody else had it."

Brinley nodded only slightly.

"But even if it weren't, I would pay that much myself." Jared stroked Brinley's hair before she could stop him.

"You would?" Brinley changed position on her heels to move her head away from Jared's roving fingers.

"For love, I'd pay any price."

Love?

At the corner of Brinley's eye, that old Chevy pickup came into view. "Oh, my ride is here. Bye, Jared."

"That old piece of junk?" Jared's jaw dropped. "You should let me take you home. I bought a new 458 Spider convertible."

"You can keep your new Ferrari." Brinley walked away, looked back and smiled. "As for me, I like old things."

CHAPTER TWENTY-EIGHT

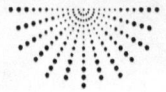

"*D*ude, that can only end badly." Matt emphasized *badly* as if it were the end of all things.

Ivan knew Matt was serious. But what did Matt really know about such things? He couldn't even keep his own marriage together.

"I'll take that under advisement." Ivan folded his arms across his chest and sat back.

The Scrolls bookstore was eerily silent this morning save for the occasional hum of the heating unit. They almost cancelled their Bible study this week because almost everyone was out of town save for Matt, Sebastian, and Ivan. But since they wouldn't meet until the first of the year, Matt decided they'd have one more this Tuesday morning before Ivan went to Savannah with SISO for the rest of the week.

Maybe Ivan shouldn't have come. He was

exhausted from last night's fundraising event. It had been a mixed bag of emotions for him. Exuberance at being able to hold the Stradivarius and Guarneri in his hands. Exasperation that it was over and he was back to borrowed violins. Cheaper violins.

Such is my life. Always stuck with cheap.

He chided himself. The Vuillaume wasn't cheap. He couldn't even afford it.

It wasn't the violin. He was cranky because he was exhausted. And the week wasn't even over. Waking up at four o'clock with Brinley on his mind and being unable to sleep was already a bad start to his long day. After this Bible study he had to go home, pack up his bags, and head for the SISO studio for a final rehearsal. Later this afternoon they had to catch the bus for their string of holiday concerts in Charleston and Savannah, wrapping up Saturday night.

Long week.

So. The last thing Ivan needed now was for his old buddies to excoriate him and intervene in his relationship with Brinley Brooks.

"Didn't you hear a thing Pastor Gonzalez said?" Matt asked.

"Yep. What he said." Sebastian didn't look up from his iPad.

"Better yet, what the Bible said." Matt threw his arms up.

"Yep. What the Bible said."

"Stop echoing Matt, Seb." Ivan hadn't been more

irritated with his friends than this morning. *Maybe I need more coffee.*

"Two words. Unequal yoke." Matt shook his head at Ivan. "You cannot fall in love with an unbeliever, Ivan. It will hurt both of you. Ask me how I know."

"I hear you, Matt—"

"I don't think you do, Ivan. When Giselle and I married, I was unsaved. We couldn't agree on anything. Whether we should go to church at all. How we were going to raise our future kids—which we ended up not having. See what I mean? If you can't agree on the basics, your marriage has no foundation. Don't make the same mistake I did."

"Marriage?" Ivan asked. "We're just going out. Nothing might come of it."

"So you're just friends?"

"Pretty much."

"Haven't held hands? Kissed?"

Ivan knew he couldn't tell Matt. It would only work against him. Matt was on a roll here.

"Dude, all I'm saying is that, inherently and innately, you two come from different perspectives. It's inevitable that you'll disagree on God, on Jesus, on church, on life, on everything."

"Not everything." They seemed to agree on their comfort level with each other though Ivan would have to admit that was basal and physical. Then again, the kisses meant something to him. "She came to our church Sunday. You saw her."

"Whether she went to church or not, her heart is not in it." Matt didn't let up.

"You don't know that, Matt."

"She is unsaved. Her heart does not belong to Jesus."

Well, okay. Matt has a point there.

"When did you meet this woman?"

"Brinley, Matt. Her name is Brinley."

"When did you meet this Brinley woman?"

"Last year, but we were dating other people. We saw each other again at my sister-in-law's birthday party last week. That's when things happened."

"Like what things?"

"Matt."

"Come on."

"Dude, your sister-in-law's party was Thursday." Matt ticked off his fingers. "Not even five days ago."

Only five days? "It felt longer than that."

"You're putting a new spin on whirlwind, dude."

Next to Matt, Sebastian slid his iPad across the table toward Ivan. "Check that out."

Ivan looked at the iPad screen as Sebastian kept talking. "She made the news. See the headline? *Buddy Billionaires.*"

Ivan frowned as he scrolled down the entertainment web page. The photograph of her dancing with Jared Urquhart six months before messed with Ivan's head. He didn't want to look at it, but Brinley was quite photogenic.

"Read it," Sebastian said.

"No." Ivan put the iPad down. He had to admit

he was curious, but he didn't know if he wanted to know whatever it was Sebastian was trying to tell him. Sebastian often agreed with Matt, and this time, Ivan knew they were right.

It's inevitable that you'll disagree on God, on Jesus, on church, on life, on everything.

Still...

"Says here that Jared Urquhart is the poorer one. He's got a billion dollars to his name."

"One billion dollars?" Ivan tried not to freak out.

"Got your attention, huh?" Sebastian went on. "Says here that Brinley Brooks stands to inherit nine billion dollars from the Brooks family fortune."

Nine billion dollars.

That was news to Ivan. "No way. She looks so..."

"Plain? Looks can be deceiving," Matt said. "Ask me how I know."

"I was going to say normal, man. Normal."

"What are you going to do?" Sebastian interjected. "Her family could say you're a gold digger. Sure, we know you don't care about money. That's how you ended up in that hole you're in, but they don't know you as well as we do."

"Is that supposed to be a compliment, Seb?" *Some friends I have.*

"You tell us," Matt said.

"Nothing is going on." *Uh, other than the two kisses.*

Ivan couldn't remember the last time he had tried to kiss a woman he had barely known, and then did it two days later, twice.

Only Brinley.

Something about Brinley had drawn him to her. He prayed to God it wasn't the attraction of wealth. She seemed unassuming, honest, brave enough to eat in his run-down kitchen. She even helped to dry the silverware and plates.

All in all, Brinley was very down-to-earth.

Strip away all that money, and she's just a commoner like the rest of us.

Only she wasn't common or ordinary.

Something about her tugged at Ivan's heart.

"Dude, I don't want you to get hurt, and I don't want you to hurt the girl," Matt finally said.

"Yep, don't get hurt."

Ivan glared at Sebastian. Mr. Echo was still glued to his iPad.

"Whoa," Sebastian said. "Look at all the men she has dated."

"I don't care." *Yes, I do.*

"She was engaged to one Phinneas Farragut IV, another bazillionaire. They broke off dramatically in the summer." Sebastian looked up. "Ivan, you sure she's not going out with you on the rebound?"

Rebound? "Can't be if it's been months."

"I don't know," Sebastian said. "Sometimes people never quite get over someone. Ask me how I know."

"We're not attached to other people."

"How do you know you're not a filler, Ivan? Maybe she's waiting for a better offer later and you're available now."

Available? I'm easy?

"I don't have to listen to you insult Brin." Ivan dropped his iPad into his shoulder bag.

"Brin? It's one syllable now?" Matt looked worried. He had never looked worried. "Sounds dangerous."

Ivan ignored him. He glanced at the clock. It was past seven. "You two are going to have to pray without me. I have to run. Have a bus to catch."

"You said that's not until after lunch."

Ivan could see that Matt was getting into his big-brother mode. He looked for a way out. "I have to pack and we have a rehearsal at ten. I'm telling the truth."

"With lots of hours to spare," Matt said. "I'm saying that you're not facing the problem."

"Brinley is not a problem." *Or is she?*

"Famous last words." Sebastian whistled.

"Some friends you are. Look in the mirror, you two." Ivan got up and walked off.

He could hear their voices behind him as he opened the glass door to the sidewalk. Something about "praying for him big time" and "thinking with his emotions."

He grunted.

What do they know?

CHAPTER TWENTY-NINE

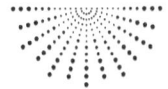

$\mathcal{M}$att's words ricocheted in Ivan's mind all the way to the SISO studio off Frederica Road. He chained his bicycle inside the building by the stairwell. What Matt had said still bothered him as he pounded the steel treads up the stairwell to the third floor, where the string section was rehearsing.

Dude, I don't want you to get hurt, and I don't want you to hurt the girl.

Ivan knew that Matt meant well. He always did. He had been a better older brother to him than Quincy could ever be.

Still...

Brinley isn't a Christian.

That was Matt's whole point.

Ivan flung open the door to the third floor. He panted and stopped to catch his breath, his violin case heavy on his back. As he dragged himself across the old harlequin floor to the practice room, the elevator in the hallway opened. Emmeline O'Hanlon backed out of the elevator, rolling her enormous concert grand harp.

Ivan held the door for her.

"Thanks, Ivan."

"No problem."

Emmeline leaned against her harp. "I don't know why the brass section gets the first floor and we get the third. It's a pain to drag this harp up and down the floors."

"Get minions to help you."

"You're going to stand there, then?"

"I'm not your minion, Em."

"You're nobody's minion, Ivan."

What does she mean?

Emmeline tipped her eyes toward him. "You were amazing last night."

"Huh?"

"Paganini. Rimsky-Korsakov."

"Oh."

Emmeline smiled that sweet, ethereal, siren smile.

Ivan didn't return it. *Never return Emmeline's smiles.* He did it once eight or nine months ago. Next thing he knew they had ended up going out on and off for at least several months afterwards. Would he call that dating? Would she? Maybe it had something to do with their proximity in SISO. Oh yes, and that purely emotional kiss backstage after that giddily exuberant summer concert in Jacksonville.

Purely emotional.

That was what his two best friends had tried to warn him about.

Do I think a lot with my emotions?

Ivan shoved his hands into his pockets.

Emmeline had gone ahead, chatting with some cellists. Ivan didn't follow them as he made an abrupt turn into the men's restroom. He washed his hands and dried them thoroughly with paper towels. He did that so that he could have clean hands before he touched the violin, especially since it was borrowed. He treated the Vuillaume as if it were a Stradivarius. He might never be able to play a Strad again after the auction last night, but at least he could try to make the best of what he had been given.

Grandma Yun had taught him to be thankful to God.

He was thankful for Brinley too.

Are Matt and Seb right?

Well, the difference between those summer dates with Emmeline—who was a nice Christian girl—and the winter introduction to Brinley—who was nice but not a Christian by her own admission—was that he had felt nothing for Emmeline. It was just that. A platonic fling, if it had been such a thing. Nothing happened between him and Emmeline.

Well, nothing's happening between Brin and me, either, right?

Yeah. Except for two kisses and half a cookie.

Slowly, Ivan made his way to the practice room.

They had left the door open and he could hear them now, starting without him. A Christmas medley.

One good thing about the SISO Christmas concert series was that they almost always played the same carols and same classical arrangements everywhere they went. Conductor Petrocelli was smart enough to make a big deal about their annual themes. The only deviation from that was Zoe's birthday party, where she had made certain requests.

Speaking of Zoe, Ivan wondered how she and Quincy were doing in Paris. Ivan had been so preoccupied with SISO—and Brinley—that he hadn't had a chance to email or text Quincy to see how he was faring, preparing to be a new father.

Can't imagine being an uncle soon.

When he reached the practice room, he found Conductor Petrocelli standing there tapping his feet. Ivan nodded to him as he took off his backpack to get to his violin. Petrocelli motioned for him to follow him out of the room.

They turned down the hallway toward Petrocelli's office.

This can't be good.

Ivan prayed to God to protect him from whatever it was. His tardiness had done him in this time. He was sure of it. Warren Yamaguchi was going to take over as concertmaster. Ivan was going back to the second string. Forget ever trying for even the principal second string position. He'd better build up his music studio because SISO was coming to a close.

Ivan stopped at the door.

There was a man that he had never seen before in Petrocelli's office. Thick neck. Thick arms. Thick chest. And probably thick thighs. He was built like a linebacker all the way. Even his cropped blond hair looked intimidating. Ivan had bounced off a few of those walls of bricks on the football field years ago. The pain had always been his to bear.

Whassup?

"Sit down, Ivan." Petrocelli rounded the table to his side of the desk.

Ivan sat down at the only chair left in the office. The seat felt awfully hot.

Why am I sweating?

"This is Mr. Art," Petrocelli said.

Art? Is this a joke?

"Nice to meet you," Art said.

His hands were huge. Ivan almost didn't shake it. Wanted to tell Art that even though both his own hands were insured, he still had to protect them from getting hurt.

"Art is here on a special delivery and he'll be working with us for a while."

"A special delivery?"

Petrocelli had always been a calm man, Ivan thought, except when he was yelling at the brass and woodwind. He hardly ever yelled at the string section, being a violinist himself who had duetted with Itzhak Perlman. Now Petrocelli seemed to be trying to keep it all in instead of jumping around in great expressive animation as he sometimes did when he had exciting news.

For that reason, Ivan was sure the news was bad.

Like I'm going to be fired and this bouncer is escorting me off the island.

"The auction last night was a great success," Petrocelli began. "Netted millions of dollars for historic preservation."

Whew. I'm not fired.

Thank God for the Sea Islands Preservation Society.

"Sounds good, sir." Ivan calmed down, crossed his legs, and relaxed a bit.

"The new owner of the Schoenberg Strad has decided to loan it to SISO."

"Wow. How generous. Who is he?"

"Don't know. Only a patron of the arts who wants to remain anonymous."

It made sense. Ivan thought that anyone who had over five million dollars to throw into the ring for a Strad had the right to remain anonymous. Maybe out of embarrassment at being the "winner" in the bidding war.

"Now we have the Strad. Our first ever Strad. The stipulation is that only SISO's best violinist gets to play it."

"Warren?" Ivan cringed. *Aargh. Don't give the man ideas!*

Petrocelli laughed. Then just as quickly, his face returned to its normal sour disposition. "You, unfortunately."

"Me?"

Petrocelli pointed to the big guy. "Mr. Art here is the string—"

"String? What string?"

"String attached." Petrocelli frowned at Ivan the usual way. His eyebrows came together and his nose bridge wrinkled, his eyeglasses rising up. "Everywhere the Schoenberg Strad goes, Mr. Art goes."

I bet Art isn't even his real name.

"I hope you packed, Mr. Art." Ivan looked at his new escort. "We're going out of town for four days."

"I'm always packed."

Somehow Ivan suspected it was more than a suitcase full of clothes.

CHAPTER THIRTY

"What did Grandma tell you about me?" Ivan had to know. Here he was in his three-star hotel room in Savannah resting before tonight's concert thinking the whole world was well only to find out that his very own flesh-and-blood had tattled on his colorful childhood on St. Simon's Island.

"You'll have to talk to her about it."

He could hear Brinley snicker on her end of the phone. He didn't like it at all. He made a mental note to text Grandma to tell her to stop regaling Brinley with his past. He wanted Brinley to think the best of him.

"Maybe she shouldn't spend so much time at your house, Brin." In the distance he could hear Brinley telling Grandma that Ivan wanted her to go home. He heard the response. Something about "no fun."

"What did she say?" Ivan asked, stretching out on top of the covers on the double bed in the room he shared with another violinist.

Art had taken the Schoenberg Stradivarius to the hotel vault. He had no idea how Art could sleep at night with that five-point-four-million dollar burden on him.

"She said you're no fun and told me to hang up." There was amusement in Brinley's voice. "We have to go now. We're having dinner at the Brunswick Senior Living Community. By special invitation, no less."

"Let me guess. Hiram Jacobs."

"The very one."

"All right. I guess I'll let you go." *No, I don't want to let you go.* "It's good to hear your voice, Brin. I miss you."

"I miss you too. Did you sleep well last night?"

"My roommate snores in quarter-note *fortissimo.*"

"Sorry. Earplugs?"

"No help. They fall off." Ivan reached for his iPad. "We're going to post some photos of our events to the SISO website. I'll email you when they're up. Also various members will probably update their Facebook pages. Are we friends?"

"You mean on Facebook or in real life?"

"I'd like to think we're more than friends in real life."

"Do you, Ivan?"

"I mean, we've done more than just hold hands."

"You mean what happened at the pier?"

"And the lighthouse. I know we didn't make any commitments." Ivan could feel her lips on his. The memories were vivid. "When I get back to town, let's talk."

"I'm flying out to Vienna to join my parents after Christmas. I'm going back to Atlanta from there."

"When do you come back to St. Simon's?"

"Usually, a few times a year."

"Your next time back?" Ivan tried to keep his cool but he knew he was getting anxious inside.

"End of January."

"I'll be home on Saturday, and we have about a week before you leave."

"I'm afraid so, Ivan."

Ivan's heart sank. He wasn't sure if he wanted a long-distance relationship. He couldn't change his trajectory now, not even if he took Grandma with him. He was a rising star in SISO. It had taken six years to stabilize his music studio. He couldn't move to Atlanta just to see if there was something between him and Brinley.

Or could he?

Not with Grandma Yun in tow.

Maybe his friends from his Bible study were right. This seemed to be a dead-end relationship. Tragically, almost all his relationships in the last six years had led nowhere. He could count on three fingers how many girlfriends he'd had. The last one, Emmeline, had parted ways with him amicably. He had been too busy for her. Now that he thought he had more time, Brinley was too busy for him.

"What are you doing tomorrow?" Brinley asked.

"Charleston. We'll be there two nights. Then I'll be home for Christmas." He sang the end of his sentence.

"You can't carry a tune, Ivan."

"That's why I'm all instrumental. What are you doing the next few days?"

Brinley seemed to hesitate telling him. Then: "I'm buying a house on St. Simon's."

"A house? I'm confused. You said you don't come to—I mean, go to—St. Simon's much."

"For now. I can't keep staying at my parents' house whenever I come to town."

"What do you mean by *for now*?"

Brinley hesitated again. "I'll tell you later, okay? Family business and all that."

"Okay. You can trust me."

"Maybe."

"You don't trust me?"

"A million worker termites say I shouldn't."

Ivan groaned. "You're not going to let me live that down."

"Nope. Not until my dying day."

"We'll know each other that long?"

Silence.

"Brin?"

"I have to run," Brinley said. "Aunt Ella is getting into things. Mom's things."

Ivan laughed. "May I call you again tomorrow?"

"You can call me anytime."

The call over, Ivan looked out the window on the

fifth floor of the hotel to the overcast sky. Good thing they were playing indoors that night at City Hall. The next night they'd play at the Cathedral of St. John the Baptist. The two grand concerts in a collaboration with the Savannah City Orchestra should be fun. Word was that someone from ASO would be there, scouting for violinists.

If he did well, would Brinley be impressed?

Shouldn't I be trying to impress God?

Well, God already knew all about him. Brinley knew little about him. Music seemed to be their common language. Perhaps if they did more music together, they could get to know each other more.

It was too bad that the SISO schedule was packed through Saturday and he would be either too busy or too tired to finish writing "Pleasant Days."

Then there was that Bach composition he had promised Brinley he'd play for her on her lost Damaris Brooks Strad, but it hadn't been recovered. Would she be satisfied if he played it on the Schoenberg Strad instead? It wasn't the Damaris, but it was a Stradivarius, nonetheless. Surely Brinley would approve.

Why would I want her approval?

In fact, why would she want to have anything to do with me?

He had nothing to offer Brinley. He was struggling to make ends meet, and would probably continue to struggle the rest of his life if things remained the same as they were. Why would she want to date someone as poor as he was? Look at that guy at the Oglethorpe Charity Dinner Monday night. That was the sort of date more suitable for Brinley.

I have nothing to offer her.

Except these hands.

Still lying on the bed, Ivan lifted his hands above his head.

Give me a violin and I can play anything.

CHAPTER THIRTY-ONE

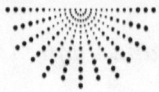

*W*hen Hiram Jacobs walked to the lectern in the Brunswick Senior Living Community cafeteria looking like the retired preacher that he was, Brinley was sure he was going to rain upon them a sermon of apocalyptic proportions. Perhaps even something rivaling that of Jonathan Edwards' fiery "Sinners in the Hands of an Angry God" that had caused a revival in 1741.

And then Hiram broke into an old folk song that everyone else attending the Wednesday evening service apparently knew, all except Brinley.

She sat there quietly taking in the words and the mishmash of voices by people who could carry a tune and also those who were clearly tone-deaf. As for her, her voice was silent. She neither knew the song nor wished to sing it. Instead, she wished to go home, for the song tugged at her heartstrings and beckoned her to see the woes of a poor wayfaring stranger waiting to cross over Jordan to see his Savior.

"How many of us don't have problems?" Hiram said when the off-key singing ended with gusto. "When we keep having chicken for dinner every week, I can tell you we have a problem!"

"We want steak!" someone shouted.

"You can't eat steak with dentures, Joe!" someone else lobbed back.

Hiram spread out his arms as if to part the Red Sea. "Listen, folks. We all have problems. Bills to pay. Illnesses. Kids who don't come to see us."

Brinley heard *amens* all around.

"Yet, our biggest problem isn't any of the above. Do you know what it is?"

Someone put up her hand.

"Yes, Sue?"

"You're taking too long, Hiram. Food's gonna get cold."

"Easy, Sue. Don't tempt him."

Brinley grinned at the banter among the seniors.

Hiram put up his arms again to calm the masses. Brinley could imagine a long stick, a la Moses, in his hand. "Glad you brought that up, Sue. Someday these bodies of ours are gonna get cold. Real cold. We'd better address the biggest problem our soul ever faces: sin. Sin separates us from God. Sin permeates every cell of our being and poisons us from the inside out."

Brinley wanted to shut him out but somehow Hiram reminded her of the way Grandpa Brooks talked. That Southern gentleman drawl. That lost language.

Hearing Hiram talk was like stepping back in time to her grandpa talk to the grandkids. If Grandpa Brooks were still alive he would've been Hiram's contemporary.

"What is sin?" Hiram asked to mumblings among his congregation. "I can name you three sins: lying, cheating, stealing. What's lying? The other day I heard someone say she was ninety. Truth be told, she was ninety-four and a few months more."

The mumblings lessened.

"Cheating. If you had an extra tile in the Scrabble game this afternoon but nobody noticed and you didn't say anything, better own up."

All quiet now.

"Anyone took a third hush puppy at the Seaside Chapel luncheon Saturday when all we were supposed to have were two? That's stealing food!"

Why couldn't they have all the hush puppies they wanted? Brinley wanted to just go out and buy these people food.

"So there. Our soul has a problem. The problem is sin." Hiram looked around the room. "But God has a solution. He sent a Savior. That Savior is Jesus Christ. Let me read Matthew 1:21."

With a deep voice that harkened to old-time revival preachers, probably like those circuit-riding preachers who had visited Brooks Plantations back in the antebellum South, Hiram read with such a reverence for the Bible that it put Brinley in awe.

And she will bring forth a Son, and you shall call
His name Jesus, for He will save His people from
their sins.

Throughout the entire sermon, Hiram hadn't looked at Brinley at all, for which she was grateful. She wondered if everybody else knew what sin was except her and whether Hiram was really preaching to the choir for the benefit of outsiders like Aunt Ella.

And me.

"Do you want peace with God? If you have Jesus, you have peace. He is the Prince of Peace, not only at Christmas, but all year long," Hiram concluded. "Let me tell you, folks. No matter what happens in this world, no matter how ravaging my cancer is every day or how painful my grief is over my sweet Camilla whom I'll see again soon in heaven, I have peace in my heart. Do you?"

Cancer? Hiram has cancer? He looks so... at peace.

The thought lingered in Brinley's mind throughout the turkey dinner and afterward when she drove Yun and Aunt Ella back to her parents' home on Seaside Island. She had to take one of Dad's SUVs since the Bugatti didn't have room for three people.

After sending her guests off to bed, Brinley found that she was thirsty. Too much sodium in the dishes at dinner? Minutes later she was downstairs in the kitchen, drinking a small bottle of San Pellegrino.

Looking around the chef's kitchen, Brinley knew her family had everything, and yet they had nothing.

They had nothing compared to Hiram and Yun. Even struggling Ivan had something she didn't have. Brinley knew she hadn't meant it completely when she made the deal with Ivan over his then termite-infested porch.

You tell me about the peace of God, and I help you with your peace on earth.

Had she dissimulated? Ivan hadn't known then that she didn't really want to know about the peace of God.

Tonight, though, she wondered.

Something about what Hiram said.

If you have Jesus, you have peace.

The ping of the elevator made Brinley turn to look. It was Yun McMillan.

"You thirsty too?" Brinley asked.

"No. I thought I should come downstairs."

"God told you?"

"Well, I would say God *led* me, not necessarily in an audible voice. You see, God and I have a relationship through Jesus."

Jesus.

Peace in my heart.

All year long.

"I want Jesus, Yun." Brinley put down her mineral water.

"Believe in the Lord Jesus Christ and you will be saved." Yun walked to the island where Brinley was still standing.

"That's all?"

"By believing in Jesus it means you acknowledge that Jesus died on the cross to save you from your sins and rose again from the grave to give you eternal life. By believing in Him it means you recognize Him as your personal Lord and Savior. Would you like to pray to accept Jesus into your heart?"

"Yes."

Divine timing was something unexplainable. Brinley echoed Yun in the simple prayer, asking Jesus to live in her heart, believing that He had died on the cross to save her from her sins, and that He had risen from the grave to give her eternal life.

Brinley thought that the heavens would send angels to carry her up and away, but alas, no such epiphany, though who knew if they were cheering her on at the moment.

All she knew was that for the first time in her life, her heart felt light, as if the burden of a thousand years had been lifted from her chest, the weight of it gone.

Gone!

A pure, unadulterated peace swept through her soul. And then she felt a whisper descend on her heart like a gentle feather. Three quiet words.

Pray for Ivan.

CHAPTER THIRTY-TWO

*C*lassically trained, Ivan had to fall back on his crossover days to pull off his string contributions to the collaboration between SISO and the Savannah City Orchestra, in the holiday pops concert Thursday night at the Cathedral of St. John the Baptist.

Fortunately, he didn't have to fall too far back in time as everything came back to him as if the last six years of detour had never happened. He was back again on the world stage, showing off his range as a concert violinist and ability to play in a large and loud orchestra. He could keep playing the old-time Christmas carols and traditional songs all night long, but alas, the concert was over in two hours.

Tomorrow morning, they'd pack up and go on the next leg of the SISO coastal tour. Up to Charleston for two evenings, then it would be Saturday and time to head home to St. Simon's Island, where he had left a big piece of his heart in the hands of a lady he had only gotten to know for a week but whom he wanted to love for a lifetime—

What did I just say?

"Yes, what did you just say?" Emmeline's voice cooed in his ears.

Ivan straightened up and tried to regain his bearings.

Oh, yes. Cathedral. Mingling. Meeting fans.

Not. They were waiting for the bus.

The crowd chattered around him in the center aisle and the old wooden pews of the tall cathedral. They might have been talking all this time, but he hadn't noticed. He wished Brinley were here, next to him. She would feel right at home in this glittery crowd and this old cathedral built on a cornerstone set in the late eighteenth century, probably when the Brooks family had lived in Savannah. Ivan thought that Brinley had an interesting family history.

Instead of Brinley, it was Emmeline O'Hanlon beside him, the harpist in a clingy black gown who had stuck to him like chewing gum on a shoe since he held that elevator door open for her to roll out her harp that Tuesday morning before they left St. Simon's. If she thought they were going to rekindle whatever it was they didn't quite have those six months they had been an item, she was sadly mistaken.

"Smile for the camera, Ivan."

The blinding flashes brought back memories of Jade Strings and their blitz through Europe and Asia.

They would have produced another CD if his life hadn't come to a grinding halt. Now six years trapped in time on an old island he hadn't expected to return to, six years of lost earnings and opportunities to make something of his career that could put him on the same plateau as Brinley.

Well, not exactly the same plateau, but it would get him into the doors of the rich and famous, that circle that Brinley was in.

Pipe dreams are for kids.

Emmeline was still posing up against him, her thin satin gown slithering up the outside of his left thigh as she leaned her torso against his chest. She looked like a puppy that rubbed its nose against someone's leg. It would be funny if people from church saw the pic—

Brin!

What if Brinley sees this?

Ivan stiffened up as if to shake off Emmeline. "Excuse me."

He hurried away before she could pull him back to the camera. Enervated from the two-hour concert, Ivan wanted out of here.

The central door went under the ornate pipes of the cathedral organ. Out there was the foyer and steps to where the bus was supposed to pick up SISO. He was at the door to the men's restroom when someone approached him.

"Ivan McMillan?" The fifty-something male with a bow tie and a female companion was shorter than Ivan, but he exuded authority.

"Yes, sir?"

"Bradley Whitfield. I spoke with Petrocelli about how much I enjoyed your solos."

"Thank you, sir." *Ah, another fan.*

"Such refreshing clarity. I particularly appreciated the precision of your double-stop trills and left-handed pizzicatos in the Christmas medley."

Ivan nodded. He wanted to say that any classically trained violinist could do that. Then again, he had a Stradivarius. That might have tipped it in his favor. And he had SISO to thank for it.

And God.

Note to self: Don't forget to thank God.

"I've heard many technical musicians, but these days it's hard to find up-and-coming violinists who have both mechanics and musicality."

Such effusing compliment. On what basis?

"It's nothing, sir." Ivan shrugged. "Christmas music. Well, I don't mean that Christmas music is nothing, but that it's not that difficult—"

"Oh, I didn't mean your musicality tonight. Someone emailed me the link to the Oglethorpe Charity Dinner videos on YouTube. I saw your execution of the 'Flight of the Bumblebee.' Mechanics is one thing, but mechanics plus musicality—you know what I mean."

Ivan nodded. In his mind he wondered. *Who is that someone who emailed this man the video links?*

"That didn't impress me as much as Paganini. I'm a big fan of Paganini. Your 'Caprice' tone—exquisite. Juilliard, right?"

"How did you know, sir?"

"A little bumblebee told me." The man pressed a business card in Ivan's hand. "Call me when your SISO season is over. Don't call me before then, as we obviously don't want to interrupt your season and make Petrocelli unhappy."

Ivan looked at the card.

Whoa! National Pops Orchestra!

He could hardly speak. Ivan whirled out of the cathedral foyer. All he could think about was that his career was finally taking off again.

"Hey, man." The straps to the backpack hanging off Art's shoulders fitted a bit tightly on the big man. "I see the harpist has a thing for you."

"Huh? What?"

"Focus, Ivan." Art popped a chewing gum into his mouth and offered Ivan some. "I was referring to the woman with you earlier. You know, the one in front of the camera inside such a sacred house of worship."

Ivan groaned. "You saw that too? We dated once. Briefly. She doesn't understand it's over."

"Tell her."

"I did. Plenty of times." Ivan went out the front door, where two short flights of steps would take them to the brick sidewalk. "You giving relationship advice now?"

"For a fee, I can give any advice. I'm heading back to the hotel. If you want, I can give you a ride in my rental. It has a nice sound system. And *fine* music."

"Unlike tonight's delicate numbers?" Ivan looked around. The tour bus was nowhere to be found. He could go back inside and wait for those introductions that hadn't come. He had thought that he might meet some ASO people after the concert. He had been hoping for some introductions. A few pats on the back about their performances.

Well, he did get a compliment from that representative of the National Pops Orchestra. That was big, wasn't it? Maybe. Maybe not. It wasn't Boston or London or Vienna.

I can't get my hopes up too high.

The other people who had run into him before and after the concert and during the intermission had mostly been SISO members and a few patrons who couldn't tell the difference between principal second violinist and first violin.

Ivan hadn't talked to Conductor Petrocelli since the concert ended. Ivan doubted if Petrocelli had him in mind if he ran into any ASO bigwigs.

"I need some sleep before we head out to Charleston tomorrow. Let's go." Ivan motioned. "Where are you parked?"

"On the other side of Lafayette Square. Only place I could find parking."

"Hope it doesn't rain harder."

It didn't. The drizzle dissipated as Ivan and Art crossed East Harris Street. It might've been quicker if they cut through Lafayette Square, but it was covered with trees. The streets had lights. Ivan followed Art down Abercorn and then he couldn't remember the streets beyond that. They climbed into Art's SUV and headed toward River Street.

"You know what's ironic?" Ivan asked.

"What?" Art was a tall man at the wheel. His head was nearly up against the roof of the SUV.

Ivan was tall but not that big. "SISO is not rich, yet every time we come to Savannah we stay in some swanky hotel on River Street. Know why?"

"Do I care?"

"Probably not, but I'll tell you anyway. Because one of the SISO patrons owns the hotel. SISO stays for half price."

"I was right. I don't care." Art cranked up the radio. He turned the dial until he found a jazz station. "You play jazz?"

"My brother Quincy is in a jazz band. Disbanded now that he's moved to Paris."

Art slammed on the brakes as a family van swerved out of an adjacent street and cut in front of him. "Tourists!"

Ivan saw that they were still on Abercorn, but now they were following a slow-moving van with stick figure decals on the back window and out-of-state license plate.

Art was unable to pass him. "Five or six minutes to the hotel, they say. No traffic, they say."

"You could cut across one of these streets here and get to Drayton one block over there," Ivan suggested.

"Thinking the same thing."

Coming up on Ivan's right was the old Colonial

Park Cemetery. Quiet and dark. He wondered if some of Brinley's ancestors had been buried here. He tried to remember what she had told him. A rich Charleston planter, heir to the Brooks family empire, had fallen in love with a poor, destitute, indentured servant girl from Sav—

The airbag exploded into Ivan's face and chest so fast, so quickly he didn't even realize it until he was already covered with the inflated bag. It took him a moment to reorientate. Then he heard a moan.

"Art, you there?"

No answer. Just more moans.

Ivan felt another impact, this time from behind the SUV. It felt like they were in a multi-car wreck.

Have to get out of here!

Was it safer for him to get out of the SUV or stay inside?

He tried to open the passenger-side door, but it was stuck. The SUV frame must have gone bonkers.

Ivan heard another groan. "Art?"

Then he heard the windshield shattering.

Doors opening. Chiming. Chiming.

As strong arms grabbed his tuxedo, Ivan reached for anything he could find, airbag, door, whatever his hands landed on, to prevent himself from being pulled out of the passenger seat.

In the shadow of the night, Ivan thought someone punctured the halfway deflated airbag and sliced through his seat belt before he was ripped out of the SUV and thrown down as if he were a bag of dirty laundry. He stretched out his arms to break his fall.

He body-smacked into the concrete pavement as he heard a sharp cracking sound like something snapped very close to his ears.

He screamed a million shards of agony as the sharp and mind-blowing pains shot up his left arm.

It wasn't over as leather gloves descended on him. As he heard metal against flesh and bones, he felt pain on his head, neck, and torso. His arms flew up in front of face to protect it.

In the cloudy night, he saw shadows of hoods and masks all around him coming in and out of visibility in the distant lights. The streetlights directly above him were apparently out.

Then shouts. Muffled screams. Gunshots.

Gunshots?

Ivan couldn't breathe. "Art!"

He couldn't get up. He felt his own flesh rip. He tried to get away, but something pressed him down like he was being sat on. The pain in his left arm increased.

In the racket of metal pipes beating up organic bones, Ivan's world faded to black.

CHAPTER THIRTY-THREE

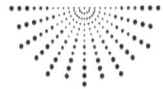

*S*titches went here and there on Ivan's forehead and cheeks. Where there were no stitches, Brinley saw swollen tissues and scrapes, as if the assailants had rubbed his face on the surface of the road. Bruises streaked his arms like broad brush strokes, blackish and reddish and looking painful, growing out of his hospital gown sleeves and down his arms. The bandages on his right arm were nothing compared to his left arm.

The full impact of what the doctor had told Yun earlier in front of Brinley hit her now as she stared at the cast on Ivan's left wrist that extended all the way to his elbow. The doctor had said that Ivan's wrist was broken in several places, muscles damaged, possibly tendons too.

The healing time? Months, possibly unknown. He'd still be feeling it more than a year from now.

His left wrist.

His livelihood.

Unless God worked a miracle, Ivan might never be able to play Paganini or Vivaldi ever again. What about his dreams of going back on the road, reviving his concert violinist career, or playing for ASO, or expanding his string studio?

From the hospital bed, Ivan's eyelids fluttered open. "Brin?"

"Hi, handsome," Brinley said.

Ivan chuckled then buckled. "Can't... breathe."

"Those ribs will heal," Brinley said. "At least there're no internal injuries."

Ivan nodded.

"See, getting better already." Brinley smiled.

Ivan reached up for her hand. Then he looked past her. "Grandma? Why... here?"

"To take you home, dear." Yun walked steadily with her walker toward Ivan's bed. "What else?"

Brinley thought Ivan's eyes were on her.

Sure enough. "Grandma—oww—shouldn't... here."

"Brinley is not to blame." Yun patted Ivan's foot through the hospital sheet. "I insisted on coming. I'd only worry if I was sitting at home waiting for you. It'll take more time to check you out of here than for us to drive home to St. Simon's."

"Ain't that"—Ivan cringed again—"truth."

"Shhh." Brinley squeezed his right hand gently. "Maybe you shouldn't talk."

"Dr. d'Almeida said you'll be fine in five or six

weeks," Yun said softly. She was holding on to the railings on the hospital bed.

"My... wrist. Elbow." He breathed slowly. "Tendons... Doc said—"

"Hush, Ivan. Rest." Brinley didn't let his hand go.

Yun tucked the hospital sheet around Ivan's legs. "Not to worry, dear. When we get home, Dr. Rao will take good care of you."

"Six months"—he flinched—"or more."

Brinley hushed him. "No more talking, okay? I'm glad you're alive."

Ivan nodded. "Art... okay? He... shot."

"Didn't I say stop talking?" Brinley laughed.

"Art?"

"If you must know, he's in surgery. Should be out soon. No worries, okay?" Brinley rubbed Ivan's hand. "We've prayed for him. He's covered."

"Prayed? Brin?" Ivan managed.

Brinley turned to Yun. "I guess we haven't told him."

"Told... what?" Ivan breathed out.

"Last night Brinley prayed to receive Christ, dear," Yun said.

Ivan nearly leapt out of the bed.

"That's grea—owww!" Ivan reached for his ribs. "Aaargggh."

"Maybe you should stay one more night," Brinley suggested.

"No. No." Ivan's eyes were closed. "Want... go home."

On the other side of the bed, Yun made a sound.

"Yun, would you like to sit down?" Brinley pointed to a chair by the window.

"I can't see him if I sit down in that low chair. I'll stand for now. Thank you, Brinley."

A nurse came in. "Dr. d'Almeida will be stopping by shortly. After that you can check out."

"I'll be right back." Brinley followed the nurse out to the nurses' station. "Whatever his insurance doesn't handle, bill me."

The nurse introduced her to a person behind the counter. "If you give her your info, she'll take care of it."

Brinley was doing that when the director of Brooks Security came up to her.

"Thanks again for driving us up here, Malik." Brinley walked with Malik Medcalf away from Ivan's hospital room.

"No problem. I'm glad nobody died."

"And for putting a couple of your guys to chaperone Aunt Ella while we're here."

"Don't want her wandering around again, collecting lawsuits."

"Pretty unbelievable," Brinley said. "Glad her meds are regulated now. Art okay?"

"Surgery went well, but his gut is all messed up. When he wakes up the SCMPD is going to talk to him."

"They might as well talk to everyone who attended the pops concert last night." Brinley was glad to hear that the Savannah-Chatham Metropolitan Police Department was on it.

"Everyone knew about the Schoenberg Strad from the auction. It was all over the news."

This is all my fault.

"It's not the first time a violinist has been attacked for carrying something expensive," Malik said. "That's why we hired Art."

"Are they going to keep him here for a few more days?"

Malik nodded.

"Anything he needs. Make sure he's taken care of." Brinley thought for a moment. "He lives alone?"

"He has a rental in Brunswick. I'm assuming he can recover there before he gets back on his feet."

"How long did you hire him for?"

"Just to keep an eye on the Schoenberg."

"Is there something else he can do for us?"

"I'll look into it."

"If he has to do paperwork or something for a while, so be it. Keep him on the payroll. If Dad or Diehl has a problem with it, talk to me. I don't want to let Art go. He took two bullets for Ivan. He can work for us, whatever he can do until he gets better and move on or stay. You know what to do."

"I'm sure he'll appreciate that, Miss Brinley."

Brinley spotted a small alcove where there was a vending machine. She stopped there and bought a bottled water. "Anything for you?"

"No, thanks."

Brinley sighed. "I can't believe this happened. I shouldn't have bought the Schoenberg."

"Pray, Miss Brinley."

"I'm doing that." For the most part Brinley followed Yun McMillan. That lady knew how to pray.

"Sorry I woke you up at three."

"I'm glad you did, Malik. You knew I would've wanted to know right away."

It had been no fun finding out that Ivan and Art had been attacked in an apparently staged traffic accident on their route back to their River Street hotel. Not only had they been beaten up pretty badly, Art had gunshot wounds in his stomach.

And Ivan.

Lord, I don't know how to pray for Ivan.

Broken wrist, cracked ribs, stitches up and down. Well, he'd walk out of here this afternoon. It was Art who would need more extensive surgery to repair his body.

All that for a 1721 Schoenberg Stradivarius. The violin wasn't worth more than four million dollars, but Brinley wanted Ivan to have it. She had told her telephone proxy to max out at six million. He came in close at five-point-four million. It was within budget, but as far as she was concerned, the Strad was probably worth no more than three million on the black market.

Now she had two Strads she owned not in her possession.

"Is Helen still in Vienna?" Brinley asked.

Helen Hu hadn't sent any more news for over a week. More than the Schoenberg, Brinley wanted the Damaris back in the Brooks family vault.

Now there was more work cut out for Hu Private Investigations, Inc.

"Budapest," Malik responded. "The informer said the thief moved the Damaris."

"I'm not paying for her European vacation."

"Yes, but she's sending someone here this afternoon to talk to the SCMPD. Try to see if there're any leads. Reps from the FBI Art Crime Team are also coming to town."

"It's all my fault." *Lord Jesus, help me fix this problem.*

"Can't go back, Miss Brinley. They say there's a reason God put eyes in front of our heads. Front. Forward. Onward."

"Still." Brinley glanced at the time on her iPhone. "Will they let me see Art even if he's not awake?"

"You want to see him?"

"I want many things, Malik. I want everything back to what it was. I want Ivan's wrist to be normal and not broken. I don't want anybody hurt—or killed —over a cheap Strad."

"Five million is not cheap to many people."

"But compared to a human life? Two human lives?" Brinley asked.

"I get it, ma'am. Still, the police and FBI are working hard to find the stolen violin."

Yet another one.

Brinley's thoughts were elsewhere. "Life is going to get harder here on out for Ivan and for Art. We better do whatever we can to help them. Why are you staring at me, Malik?"

"You're Ned's daughter all the way. If your brother were more like you and Ned, it might be a pleasure working for him also."

"Diehl? It'll never be a pleasure working for him. But someday he might come around."

"I've been praying for your brother's salvation."

"Thank you, Malik. Did you pray for me too before I got saved?"

"Everybody was praying for you, even the people in my church in Brunswick who don't know you."

I had no idea.

CHAPTER THIRTY-FOUR

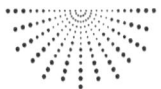

*I*t felt good to be pampered. Ivan padded out of the kitchen, full of pumpkin pie in his tummy. Who said he couldn't have pie for breakfast? There was plenty of it left. People from church had been bringing food every day since he came home from Savannah on Thursday. Their refrigerator was packed with food enough to last through Christmas and New Year's Day and beyond. So he could have another slice of pie if he wanted.

Four days into his healing, his ribs were feeling better. Maybe those extra kisses from Brinley did it.

I know better. God answers prayers.

He winced as he climbed the stairs to his bedroom to get ready for church, taking shallow breaths. The prescription painkillers helped some, but he'd rather be well, thank you very much.

There was something else worse that he was beginning to worry about, that sometimes throbbing, sometimes sharp pain in his left wrist. The dull pain, he could handle. If he didn't move his left wrist for a bit, then it'd be all right and he could handle the dull pain.

But the sharp pain was more severe. It extended from his wrist all the way to his elbow. He was scheduled to see Dr. Rao on Monday. He'd ask him about it. Meanwhile, he had some painkillers left from the Savannah hospital that could last him past Christmas.

To shower, Ivan tied a small trash bag around his left hand all the way to his elbow where the cast ended. He secured it with duct tape. A simple waterproofing solution. The hot shower relaxed his muscles that he hadn't known were tense.

Gingerly, he ran his fingers over the bruises on his ribs. At least there wasn't going to be any scarring there. Since he still had stitches on his face and right arm and legs, he didn't take a long shower.

He dabbed the areas of his stitches with a clean towel. He was grateful he could get them wet. On the first two days he had been home, he couldn't take a shower at all.

In the mirror, he peered at those stitches on his face.

Gonna have some scars.

Those stitches might be removed on Monday's visit to Dr. Rao's office. Those on his legs might stay there for a couple of weeks.

Ivan prayed that God would heal him quickly. Then he could get back to SISO, finish the season, and call that man from Boston. Whitfield something. Whatever his reason was for being in Savannah at that particular time when SISO was in town, Ivan was glad they had met. He still had the man's business card. It had been in his tuxedo pocket. At the Savannah hospital, his clothes had been salvaged and put into a plastic bag for him to take home.

Save for that business card, Ivan wanted to forget the entire Savannah episode. Fortunately, the attack had happened so fast and in such a dark area of the street—he had found out later that the assailants had shot out the streetlights—that he only remembered bits and pieces of it before he passed out. He prayed that what he remembered wasn't enough to cause him nightmares.

Some night it had been. After the assailants had thrown him onto the pavement, they didn't stop there. He had never been beaten up this badly before in his entire life, not even in high school, and not even when he was walking on backstreets and alleys to get around when he was at Juilliard in New York City.

He could still hear metal against flesh and bones from that Savannah night, feel the slashing pain on his head, neck, and torso, and remember how he had lifted his arms and injured wrist to protect his head.

Thank God I don't have a concussion.

Art had it worse. They had tried to kill him to get to the Stradivarius. He did his best, taking two bullets and getting bashed into the side of the SUV. Finally, to save his life and Ivan's, Art gave up the violin.

Good for you, Art.

Ivan found it a hassle to put his clothes on with one arm, and he couldn't get his cast into his usual oxford button-down church shirt. If only someone could help him dress. He found a turtleneck and a wool sweater, both with sleeves that could stretch over his cast.

He winced again.

Lord, I beg You. Please heal my wrist. I don't care about the other scars. But my entire career is in this wrist.

In about six weeks, the cast would come off. They told him he'd do some intensive physical therapy to get his old movement back. He had to recover a hundred percent mobility on his left wrist. He had to. If he didn't, Warren Yamaguchi would get his job. If he ended up being second violin, he'd quit SISO altogether.

Or should he?

Everyone knew he was a better violinist than Warren.

Yeah, but Warren doesn't have a broken wrist.

He picked up his iPad and went downstairs.

Grandma Yun was waiting for him in her usual rocker, talking to Brinley, who must've arrived while he had been in the shower. Otherwise, he would have heard her vehicle from his upstairs bedroom. Vehicles made a lot of noise on their gravel driveway. Someday when he had some money he'd pave that entire driveway with something nice. For now, it was dry enough, and Georgian rains hadn't washed away too much of it. It was functional. No one complained.

"My two most favorite ladies in the world!" Ivan declared as he entered the living room. "I'm ready to go whenever you are."

When Brinley got off the couch, Ivan hugged her as carefully as he could on his right side. Her lambswool sweater was soft and she smelled ethereal. He recalled the song he had written with her in mind.

Pleasant days indeed.

"If I stay on your right side, I'll be fine?" Brinley asked.

Ivan nodded. "My ribs will heal in a few weeks."

"Thank God they're cracked, not broken, and only two," Grandma Yun said from her rocker.

Ivan wrapped his right arm around Brinley's shoulder.

She looked up at his face. "When do they take those stitches out?"

"Monday, I think."

"That soon?"

"The rest, after Christmas."

"Do you need a ride to the doctor's?"

"Thanks for the offer, but Matt's taking me." Ivan couldn't thank Matt Garnett enough. In spite of his bluntness, his old friend was a true friend, always looking out for him.

Matt had been right. There was a better affinity between him and Brinley now that she knew the Lord as he did. Sure, Brinley still had a long way to go in terms of learning what it meant to be a Christian, but at least now they were on the same page.

Brinley touched his left arm. "I'm praying for you

that God will heal your wrist. I am so sorry about it all."

Sorry? He didn't get it, and Brinley didn't seem to want to explain. Oh well. "The docs said my cast can come off in about six weeks. Then we'll see. I hope to get back to normal quickly."

Back to normal?

Did he really believe that?

Somewhere at the back of his mind he knew that his life could never be smooth sailing. It had never been. Once upon a time he had thought he would spend a good number of years on the concert circuit. Then Grandpa Otto died, derailing his plans.

He had thought that with his Juilliard degree and world-stage experience, he could get hundreds of violin students. It had taken six years to get forty students.

He had thought that Brinley was the one for him. He wanted to play the violin for her the rest of his life. Now he couldn't play the violin at all for at least six weeks. After that came therapy and he wasn't even sure what that involved. His future was sort of fuzzy from here on out, but he wanted to get back to violin. *For sure.*

"I have news," Brinley said.

"Good, I hope?" Ivan teased.

"It could be bad, depending on how you look at it."

"Go on." Ivan had to know now.

Brinley looked at Ivan, then at Yun and then back to Ivan. "It's finalized. I'm quitting my sales job at

Dad's company, and I'm moving to St. Simon's permanently."

Ivan wondered about the implications of that decision.

"Say something," Brinley said.

"I think that's great news." Ivan wasn't sure what to think, really. Brinley in town every day? What was he going to do with her? He had nothing to offer her. No money to take her out to dinner. No money to buy her a ring—

What ring?

"We can be together more than once a month." Her eyes looked hopeful.

"I'd like that, Brin." Ivan leaned down and kissed her forehead.

"And I can have tea at least twice a week with Yun."

Grandma seemed to welcome that. Ivan watched her nod. Still, she was quieter than usual.

"What are you going to do on St. Simon's?" Ivan asked.

"I bought half of Dad's reno company."

"You did?"

"He would've sold me the whole business but he's such a control freak that it would kill him to be outside looking in. So he only sold me half of it."

"Sounds like a lot of work," Grandma said.

"Work is good. Besides, I'm working with some good people who know what they're doing, so I'm happy about my reno crews."

"What do you do with the houses you fix?" Grandma asked.

"I'm thinking we'd either sell or rent them out."

Grandma looked like she had another question but the clock chimed on the hour.

"Ladies, we'd better get going." Ivan helped Grandma to the door. "Don't want to be late for Sunday school or church."

~

*B*rinley sat on Ivan's good side at the edge of the pew. He didn't want anybody bumping his precious left wrist. Seaside Chapel was crowded with people attending one last Sunday morning service before they went out of town for the rest of the year. So all the pews were full.

The crowd looked different to Brinley now that she was saved. Her perception of people had changed. She saw individual faces as people and no longer as a collective mass. She saw each visage as he and she was, unique and brilliant. Each person made by God was individually loved by God. Wow.

And here was Ivan.

Brinley was sitting hip to hip with him with only room for an iPad sandwiched vertically between them. She found it amusing that Ivan was that modest. After all, they had kissed. And here they were in the sanctuary with an iPad between them. Maybe he was trying to be funny.

When they stood up to sing in church, Brinley

found that Ivan had a terrible singing voice. She was sure that God didn't count that against him. But wouldn't it be better for everyone if Ivan shut up or something? Was it a sin for her to even think such a thought?

I have much to learn about being a Christian.

After the congregational singing was over, Brinley sat down. She realized that Ivan had dispensed of his iPad. His right arm was over her shoulders now. Claiming her? She wasn't sure. She was glad he'd stopped singing his awful rendition of the otherwise soothing Christmas medley.

The soloist who went up front to sing turned out to be Pastor Gonzalez's wife, Olivia. After church today, Yun was going to introduce Brinley to her. Brinley was looking forward to telling someone other than Yun, Ivan, and Dad that she now believed in Jesus Christ. Dad was excited but Mom was leery.

What about Diehl? Well, Brinley would find out soon enough on Christmas Eve when her older brother would arrive in town.

Diehl had decided not to fly to Paris for Christmas, but spend Christmas Day on Seaside Island as he had done every year.

When Olivia Gonzalez sang "O Come, O Come Emmanuel," Brinley finally understood the words to the carol. It was like blinders had come off and she could see clearly without the fog.

The fog of sin.

It was only when Olivia was helped down the

podium that Brinley realized the *soprano leggero* could not see.

Brinley took some notes during Pastor Gonzalez's Christmas sermon centered on Matthew 1:21, which he had someone read aloud in its entirety.

> *And she will bring forth a Son, and you shall call His name Jesus, for He will save His people from their sins.*

Brinley's heart had never felt so loved.
My sins.
All forgiven.

CHAPTER THIRTY-FIVE

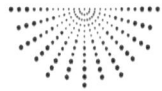

*C*hristmas Eve was here, and Ivan was ready. He slowly climbed out of the church van. "I'll be right back."

"Don't take too long," Matt said from the driver's seat. "Have a few more pickups to make before the service starts."

Ivan walked up the marble steps to the Brooks cottage on Seaside Island, pushed his sunglasses up above his head, and pressed the doorbell with his left thumb. It didn't hurt too much, but that might be because of the pain reliever he'd taken. That might be also why he didn't feel pain in his ribs when he breathed.

His right hand was in his barn jacket pocket, playing with a small gift box. A little surprise for Brinley. He had wrapped it himself. He hoped she liked it.

Nobody answered.

He pressed the doorbell again. *Lord, please give me patience.*

Now he was worried. Fortunately, before he could conjure up some silly ideas of the whys and wherefores, he heard the door click a couple of times and it opened.

"Merry Christmas Eve!" He stretched out his right hand. "You must be Brin's brother. I'm Ivan McMillan. Nice to meet you."

The man didn't shake his hand, as if Ivan were carrying some sort of infectious disease.

"Is Brinley in?" Ivan started getting a bit concerned.

"She's getting ready. I guess you can wait inside."

"Thank you very much. Are you Diehl Brooks?"

"Since birth."

"Whew. For a moment there I was wondering why a strange man was in Brin's house."

"Our parents' cottage," Diehl corrected him. He remained standing in the foyer surrounded by tall trees and an even taller staircase. "What do you want from my sister?"

"What do you mean?" Ivan felt the large foyer close in on him, the Christmas trees bending down and shaking their accusatory branches at him, contracting around his personal space.

"Don't play coy."

I should've waited in the van.

Ivan wanted to walk out of the inquisition, but his legs were stuck there, rooted to the marble floor with the Brooks logo right in the center of the foyer that now seemed more like a rotunda of a courthouse to him. His scruffy shoes seemed out of place. He was not in his element and he knew that Brinley's brother knew it.

He watched Diehl lean forward for the kill. "My sister and I are very different from each other."

And I love her.

Ivan caught himself. *What did I say?*

"Brinley wants a simple life. Is that what she's found in you? A simple man?"

"Uh, I—I don't know."

Wait a minute. What did he call me? A simple man? Or did he mean a simplistic man? Or a simpleton?

Ivan cleared his throat and prayed quickly. Brinley's smile filled his thoughts. "Well, when two people fall in love—"

"She's not in love with you, Jovan—Ivan—whatever your name is. She just thinks she is. She's been attracted to every musician she came in contact with since she inherited her music collection from Grandpa Brooks."

That can't be true. I can't believe that. None of her ex-boyfriends—

"But you're the first one outside the family who has ever played a Strad she owns. Which you promptly lost. Do you see how suspicious that is?"

"Excuse me?" Ivan protested. "I've never played any of her Strads."

"No? Art told me otherwise."

"Art?"

Art!

Ivan's jaw dropped as he realized who had bought the Schoenberg Strad at the auction. It was hard for him to believe that Brinley had paid over five million dollars for it. Why had she done it? Why?

"Art works for us," Diehl continued. "I suppose you knew that."

"I'm afraid this is the first time I've heard of it." Ivan felt defeated. *Why didn't Brinley say anything?*

"Brin wants to keep Art on the payroll in spite of his injuries. We're going to get to the bottom of this sooner or later. Our investigators are working with the FBI Art Crime Team. We're going to get the thieves who stole my sister's Strad. Let's hope you have nothing to do with it."

"Are you accusing me of something?"

"A five-point-four-million-dollar violin could come in handy for debt reduction."

"What? Wait a minute! You're pushing it, man." Ivan stepped forward, then thought better of it. He was in someone else's house. The last thing he needed was to be arrested for assault.

"My investigators tell me you're deep in debt," Diehl went on. "Near bankruptcy."

"That's none of your business." Ivan flinched and his left hand instinctively reached for his left ribs, thumping them with the cast. *Ouch.*

He took short, quick breaths.

"It's my business if you're going out with my sister. What happens to her inheritance affects me."

Now Ivan was mad. "Oh, and you think that

this"—he held up his cast—"is part of my nefarious plan?"

"A violinist with a broken left wrist. You're useless."

"Pretty much." Ivan perked up. "See, we agree on something."

Diehl raised his eyebrows.

"Does it make sense for me to damage my own future?" Ivan sighed. "I may never play again. The violin is all I know. This is how I make my living."

"So you need my sister to live on."

Many thoughts jumbled up in Ivan's head, but he couldn't get a single word out. He realized that no matter what he said, there'd always be a divide between him and Diehl.

And maybe also between Brinley and me.

"I think I better go." Ivan tried to rein in his anger.

"You'd better."

"Better what?" Brinley was at the top of the stairs looking down. "Hi, Ivan. I see you've met Diehl, the best brother in the world."

Ivan nearly gagged.

Brinley glided down the stairs in a simple pair of boot-cut jeans and a Christmas sweater.

She stopped where Diehl was. "Are you sure you don't want to come with us to the Christmas Eve service? Lots of room in the church van."

"I'm sure, Brin." Diehl eyed Ivan. "I'll see you and Aunt Ella back here at six forty-five and we can have dinner out."

"Our annual Christmas dinner with only the three of us." Brinley turned to Ivan. "Maybe you and Yun can join us?"

"Oh, no. We have our own Tiny Tim dinner and are kinda busy." Ivan smirked.

Brinley looked at Ivan, amused. "Are you all right?"

"Never been better. Would you like to go now?"

~

Everything seemed different about Ivan at the Christmas Eve service at Seaside Chapel. Brinley wondered what had caused him to change. She sat beside him throughout the evening, but whenever she reached for his hand, he would react by picking up his iPad or the hymnal or putting his right hand over the other hand as if to hold his cast. Clearly he did not want to touch her nor did he want her to touch him. His tone had changed so abruptly from last Sunday morning when he was all lovey-dovey.

What is going on?

Brinley felt the subtle rejection. Whatever Diehl had said—

Oh.

Diehl was all about money.

It had to be the reason for this change of tone.

Now it began to affect Brinley and she couldn't pay attention to the rest of the service.

Lord Jesus, forgive me.

Pastor Gonzalez didn't preach this evening. The program called for a rotation among three other pastors, one from some years before Gonzalez became pastor of Seaside, one from among the current pastoral staff, and one guy fresh out of seminary. Past, present, future? Each had fifteen minutes to talk about the Christ of Christmas.

At every interval, Brinley was praying for focus.

Further distracting her was Ivan himself. She tried her best to adjust to his still untrained voice throughout all the Christmas carols and sacred hymns, but at the end of the service, she prayed a somewhat selfish prayer that God would heal Ivan's wrist as soon as was miraculously possible so that he could play the violin again and, thereby, spare everyone from his lack of vocal facility.

CHAPTER THIRTY-SIX

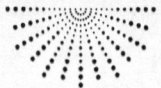

"*Y*ou tell Ethan Dad wants to talk to him. Go on, Elisa." A pause. "What do you mean he doesn't want to? Tell him it's Dad."

Brinley stepped into the sunroom. She didn't smile, didn't give away what was on her mind. There was no way she could imagine that there could be any truth to Diehl's accusation. In the two weeks she had been close to Ivan—oh dear, had it only been two weeks?—she didn't think he could be a thief.

His broken wrist proves it.

Why would any violinist destroy his own career like that?

Diehl shrugged at Brinley. She said nothing. It was sad that Diehl had kids and then couldn't be with them, for reasons too complex to disassemble.

"Whatever. Tell Ethan Dad loves him. What?

Yeah, next week. I'll pick you up next week." Diehl nodded into his phone. "Dad loves you too, Elisa."

He hung up. "I don't know what Isobel's been telling the kids. Ethan doesn't want to speak with me. Not even at Christmas."

"Growing pains?" Brinley asked, leaning against the doorframe like she usually liked to do.

"Poison is more like it." Diehl pocketed the phone. On the coffee table was a wine bottle and a glass. He raised the bottle toward Brinley.

"No, thanks," Brinley said.

"You don't drink anymore?" He filled half the glass. "You're getting a little weird, sis. Found religion?"

"I met Jesus and He changed my life."

Diehl laughed. He got up and stood at the tall windows. It was dusk outside. "This is about Phinn, isn't it? He drinks too much. You're reacting to his— shall we say, weakness?"

"Phinn? We broke up. I don't make decisions based on him." *Anymore.*

"I had lunch with him before I flew here."

"I thought he's in Courchevel."

"He's back in Atlanta. His parents kicked him out of the Alps."

"For?"

"Overspending. He's blitzing through his trust fund."

"I suppose on booze and women."

"You don't know that, Brin." Diehl finished off one glass, then another. "That one's for you."

Brinley was unperturbed.

"Phinn wants me to tell you he's sorry. He has a Christmas present for you. I put it under the tree in the living room. You can open it tomorrow."

Brinley's fingers instinctively went to the violin brooch. She touched it, as if to make sure it was still there. "You shouldn't have brought anything from Phinn. It's over."

"He's a friend." Diehl pulled out a pack of Dunhill cigarettes. "He's a very good friend of mine."

Brinley frowned. "You can't smoke in here."

"Dad's not here. Neither is Mom." He lit it. "So why not Phinn?"

"You knew we broke up in the summer. He's history."

"What's wrong with him, Brin?"

"Everything. Phinn and I fought all the time."

"You get used to it."

"Like you and Isobel?" Brinley asked.

Diehl didn't reply to that. "Phinn is one of us, Brin."

"One of us? And *who* isn't one of us? Is that what you're driving at, Diehl?"

"Figure it out if you know what's good for you."

Brinley shook his head. "I never expected you to be Phinn's surrogate, Diehl. You're my brother. You're supposed to protect me."

"I am."

"No. You're protecting your own interests. Marriage is not a business transaction. You know who said that to me? Our baby sister, Zoe."

Brinley wasn't sure any longer if she wanted to have Christmas dinner with her brother. She wanted to be as far away as possible from him.

Brinley remembered visiting a sobbing Isobel the months before the divorce had been finalized. She had spent the entire afternoon listening to her sister-in-law lament about having to give up a lucrative career to mold her life around Diehl's. Diehl was a crazy workaholic, she had said. Isobel, depressed and lonely, had wished her children had a father who was with them. Ethan had missed camping with his dad in the summer. Elisa missed sitting on Diehl's lap as he read them stories. Neither of them cared that Diehl put money into their bank accounts so they could do whatever they wanted. They'd rather have his presence even if he had brought them nothing but himself.

They'd rather have him.

That could never be. Diehl was married to his work first and foremost.

Perhaps Diehl shouldn't have come to Seaside Island. Perhaps he should've gone to Hawaii to see his kids.

Instead, he had chosen to be here with Brinley only to have her find out that he had come to ask her to reconcile with Phinn. What did Diehl know about love? What was in it for Diehl if Brinley were to get back together with Phinn?

"I'm leaving Brooks Investments, so you don't need to fight me anymore about making decisions," Brinley said. "Isn't that enough?"

"What are you talking about?"

"There must be a connection between Brooks Investments and your coming here to tell me to get back with Phinn."

"Must there always be a connection?"

"With you it's mandatory. So what is it, Diehl?" Brinley sat down on one of the armchair arms.

Diehl lit another cigarette. "Phinn wants a job at Brooks."

"You can't trust him. He's a spendthrift."

"But you can trust Ivan McMillan, the near-bankrupt violinist with the three mortgages and hundreds of thousands of dollars in credit card debts?"

Brinley sprang off the armchair. "Where did you get that information?"

She couldn't believe Ivan was in such a bad situation. *Yun is going to lose her house.*

"Helen Hu. Who else? With that broken wrist he's going to be unemployed soon."

Oh no. Lord Jesus, how do I respond?

"Ivan is not working for Brooks, so you needn't be concerned about him," Brinley said. "In fact, he's not even asking for money."

"No? Then how do you explain Plumb Good bills?"

"That's out-of-pocket, Diehl." Brinley didn't back away. The way to deal with Diehl was to face him front and center. He liked a good fight. The dirtier the better. But now that Brinley believed in Jesus, she didn't like Diehl's dirty fights anymore.

She had been reading her Bible every day, and there was this verse she had read in the last few days about overcoming evil with good. Diehl wasn't necessarily evil, but his tactics were not necessarily good either.

"You fixed his commode." Diehl laughed.

"It was more for his grandmother. She's ninety-seven years old. She's on a walker. I fixed it so she didn't have to walk all the way to the back of the house. Indict me if you will. For the record, Ivan reimbursed me for it."

With a home-cooked meal, but Brinley didn't have to tell Diehl the details.

Diehl was silent. Then: "You've always had a heart for needy people."

Brinley knew he wasn't going to apologize.

"So I'm needy, Brinley. Help me out. Tell you the truth, I don't want you to leave Brooks Investments. Since Parker died..." His voice choked up.

"I miss Parker too." Brinley had invited his widow to join them for Christmas Eve dinner, but Riley and her two children were visiting her parents in Houston through the new year.

Diehl regained his composure. "Maybe you can help me transition your position to a new sales VP."

"How long do you think that'll take?"

"I'm thinking a month."

"Kanisha already knows what I do."

"I'm not sure I want to keep her."

"For the record, Diehl, I do recommend her." Brinley realized then for the first time that she had always pronounced the first syllable in her brother's name the same way she pronounced "deal." True to form, Diehl was always about making deals. Kanisha would get along fine with him. "When do you go back to Atlanta?"

"Tomorrow morning."

Brinley was sad that her family had grown apart. Over the years, people moved away, lives changed, schedules differed. She prayed that someday when she had a family of her own that she and her husband would be able to start and keep a tradition of yearly family reunions with their children and grandchildren. *Lord willing.*

"Could you take Phinn's present back to him?" Brinley asked as calmly as she could. "I'm not opening it."

"Sure, sis, but I think—"

"Do I tell you what to do with Isobel?"

"No."

"Then let me handle my own personal life, Diehl."

"All right. It's just—"

"Diehl."

"Okay." Diehl got up. "Now that we've had our little heart-to-heart talk, let's go eat."

Well, it is Christmas Eve, after all.

Besides, maybe she could tell him about the Christ of Christmas. Possibly.

Or not.

Yun had said people had to decide for themselves whether to choose God.

"Is Aunt Ella back?" Brinley asked.

"She's meeting us at The Priory."

"Someone dropping her off?"

"She's there with Herbert or Hopper or somebody."

"Hiram."

"That's it. Hiram. Apparently Aunt Ella has news for us."

"News? What news?"

CHAPTER THIRTY-SEVEN

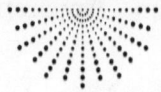

*B*rinley was sad to see her brother go home right after breakfast on Christmas Day. But she was glad that he agreed to return that gift from Phinn, whatever it was. It was a small box of something and Brinley could guess he wanted to resuscitate their dead relationship.

And she was glad that Mom and Dad had called from Paris to wish them a merry Christmas though she didn't feel that it had been necessary for them to apologize to Diehl for taking the family jet. It was Dad's BBJ, and he could fly that plane wherever and whenever he wanted.

After dropping Diehl off at the Brunswick Golden Isles Airport, Brinley drove Aunt Ella to Brunswick Senior Living Community for lunch with Hiram and his friends. Her news last night could've been alarming. Brinley was thankful to God that Aunt Ella hadn't pulled a Zoe. It was a relief to her that all Aunt Ella had announced was that she was moving into the Brunswith Senior Living Community the day after Christmas.

Whew. At least Aunt Ella hadn't said she was moving in with Hiram, though they would, technically, be in the same building.

Aunt Ella's one packed suitcase was at the back of the SUV together with a couple of gifts that Brinley had purchased for the McMillans.

"I still can't believe they expedited your application to live here." Brinley pulled up to the community gate.

"It does help when you offer to buy up lands on both sides of the property."

"You what?" Brinley nearly slammed on her brakes.

"To expand BSLC so more retirees can live here. Make it a resort." Aunt Ella placed a warm hand on Brinley's arm. "They're going to give me a nurse on call around the clock, three meals a day and all the snacks I want, plus friends. That alone is worth it, dear."

Brinley could barely look at her.

"I hope you'll come to visit me often, Brinley. You're the only family who does."

"I will, Aunt Ella. I will."

"Thank you for my Bible," Aunt Ella said as Brinley drove toward the BSLC cafeteria entrance.

"Did you download it?"

"Yes. Hiram helped me put it on my smartphone. He's very techno-savvy."

Techno-savvy? "Where did you pick up that word?"

"Don't underestimate us seniors, child."

Before Brinley could figure out how to get Aunt Ella into the building and park the car, Aunt Ella was shrieking in delight.

"Look, Hiram's over there." Aunt Ella pressed a spindly finger to her heaving chest.

Brinley slowed down the SUV in case any overly excited senior walked into her path. She parked the vehicle right in front of Aunt Ella's welcoming party, which included Hiram leading the pack and the people whom Brinley recognized had given Hiram a hard time during his Wednesday night sermon.

That very night Brinley accepted Jesus Christ as her personal Lord and Savior.

It was still sinking in.

Brinley was glad that she hadn't missed the opportunity to thank Hiram for the sermon when he joined them for Christmas Eve dinner at The Priory the evening before. It had been interesting for Brinley to see Diehl's shocked and disappointed reaction as Hiram explained to him what Brinley had done.

Seeing Aunt Ella so happy with her new friends in the latter years of her life made Brinley resolve that she would enjoy life on earth, however short or long it was, and to know God more, the God who had come down to earth to save her soul.

What Christmas is about.

∽

One more stop for Brinley. She pulled up to the McMillans' house to find the whole place decorated for Christmas. There were icicles hanging off the porch railings, and even a plastic tree next to the two cheap plastic chairs. Before she could reach the front door, Ivan and Yun burst out shouting, "Merry Christmas!" to her as Ivan began to sing "Go Tell It on the Mountain."

Brinley tried to keep her face set to "grin and bear it," but every time she clapped for it to be over, Ivan went through the refrain again. And again.

By the time they got inside, Brinley thought her ears were going to pop.

How could such a handsome dude have such a lousy voice?

God sure has a sense of humor.

"Look what arrived yesterday." Yun pointed to the motorized wheelchair. She hugged Brinley. "You shouldn't have."

Brinley realized that maybe she shouldn't have. With Ivan's left wrist out of commission, who was going to help Yun carry the wheelchair to and from places in their truck? Perhaps people from church could help. But when they got home? Then what?

"Thinking too much again?" Ivan whispered in her ear as he ran his good arm around her waist. "I talked to Matt. Sundays and whenever we go to church, he's picking us up with his van. It has plenty of room for the wheelchair. It's taken care of."

Brinley nodded.

God provides for His own.

"Look what Ivan got me." Brinley pointed to her violin brooch that Ivan had dropped into her palm after dinner the night before. "Charleston. 1812. You know I love old things."

Yun gave Ivan two thumbs up. "I have something for you too, Brinley."

Brinley looked to where Yun pointed. She stepped over to the tree to pick up a gift bag. She pulled out the red and green tissues to find another box inside. It was a Bible. She opened it to read the inscription from Yun. "Thank you. This is sweet."

"Sorry it's large print," Yun said. "Only way I could see the verses I underlined for you."

"You took the trouble?" Brinley flipped through the pages. Here and there, Yun had carefully under-lined with a straight ruler some key verses. "This is too much, Yun."

"Not too much to get you a jumpstart on your Christian walk with the Lord."

"I will read these."

"I hope so, Brinley."

Brinley put the Bible back into the gift bag and placed it by the door so she didn't forget to take it with her on her way out. "Oh, and in the merriment, I forgot to give Ivan his Christmas present."

"No more, Brin. No more. You've given me too much."

"Just one more thing."

"Let it be under five dollars." Ivan shook his head.

"Could be." Brinley whipped out an envelope from her goose-down jacket pocket. "Merry Christmas, Ivan."

She watched Ivan open the envelope. She was happy to see that Ivan could move his left fingers extending out of his cast. She waited as Ivan read the Christmas card and the tear-off bookmark.

"Trust God. I like that."

"Proverbs 3:5-6. It's the verse that Dad told me about. Said it's pretty common, but that I should memorize it."

"That's good, Brin." He turned the bookmark over. Brinley watched his reaction. "Free hugs and kisses for a year."

"Does that qualify as 'under five dollars' for you?"

"No, Brin. This is priceless." He stepped toward Brinley. "May I claim one now?"

Brinley wrapped her arms around Ivan's neck, pulled him toward her, and kissed him gently. Once.

Then she whispered in his ear. "Feel free to claim a kiss for every scar."

Ivan looked stunned.

"I smell gingerbread cookies." Brinley turned to Yun. "May I have some?"

"All you can eat, dear."

Brinley left Ivan standing there in the family room as she headed for the kitchen with a chuckling Yun in her motorized scooter.

CHAPTER THIRTY-EIGHT

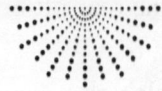

*N*ew Year's Eve was rainy and wet. Ivan decided to stay at home with Grandma instead of attending the SISO concert at the Old City Hall in downtown Brunswick. The event was indoors, but the pain in his left wrist bothered him. In a few days he'd be back at the doctor's office for them to take a look at the cast. It felt a bit tight in places.

I can't wait to get it off.

Four more weeks.

At the back of his mind Ivan knew that he was counting more than just the days when his cast would be removed. He was counting the days until he would see Brinley again. He was happy that she could fly out to Paris to spend a couple of days with her parents and sister. He hadn't heard from Quincy lately, but he assumed he was fine. Busy with his pregnant Zoe, he supposed.

It was almost eight o'clock at night. It would be in the middle of the night in Vienna. Wrong time to call Brinley. He decided to text Art a "Happy New Year!" message.

Instead of texting back, Art called. "Hey, man. Happy New Year."

"You sound good, Art." Ivan sat down on the old recliner. He couldn't get the footrest to work. "They repaired you well, I gather."

"I'm home now in my condo. This is the life, Ivan. My employer sent me a housekeeper and a cook."

"Is that right?" Ivan wondered whether Brinley's money would run out. All these charitable deeds she was doing. Why? Even before she had been saved, she'd been a very charitable person. Now that she was saved, she was even more generous with her money.

Maybe she needs to stop and let people work for something.

"This is my reward for doing my job, Ivan."

Oh. That too.

"How's your wrist?" Art asked.

"I'm feeling the pain, but it's not too bad."

"Your ribs?"

"Healing nicely. I can breathe now after a couple of weeks. Need time to heal, is all."

"Don't overdo the painkillers. You can't get off it easily. Ask me how I know."

Ivan laughed.

"When do you get back to work?"

"I don't know, Art. This cast comes off four weeks from now. After that I have to do some therapy. Not sure what to expect. But I want to get back to work. My entire career depends on my wrist."

In Ivan's heart, he feared that Conductor Petrocelli had already decided on his replacement, Warren Yamaguchi, his very capable assistant concertmaster.

"That bad, huh? Well, I can tell you my entire career doesn't depend on my guts though I should've listened to my gut feelings. Shouldn't have parked that far away from the cathedral."

The pain in his ribs stopped Ivan from laughing too hard.

"What's so funny, man?" Art asked.

"Gut? Gut feelings?"

"I don't know what kind of person would make a joke out of life and death."

Ivan knew he was kidding. "I'm sorry. You cracked me up. Get it? Cracked?"

"I told you, man. Lay off the painkillers." Art was beside himself. Then he calmed down. "You and I need to ask the Lord for help, Ivan."

"He may not answer my prayers." Ivan recalled all those prayers that God had denied him thus far. Being debt-free, going back on tour, reconciling with his sister.

"God always answers prayers, Ivan, though it might not be the *yes* you're looking for."

"Good point." Ivan figured he had to either keep

praying or change his prayers to match God's will for his life.

But what was God's will for him right now? His entire career was in limbo until the cast was off and the prognosis was in. Until then he had to sit tight and wait.

Or should he figure out a Plan B?

No. He decided he didn't want Plan B. All he ever wanted was to play the violin and that was it. God would have to give it back to him or else he had nothing left.

Or do I?

"Well, I need to get my beauty sleep. Take care, Ivan. Maybe we'll see each other around. I'm still on St. Simon's."

"You are? Great. Would you like to come to our Seaside Chapel men's Bible study group sometime?"

"Sure. When I feel better I'll give you a call."

~

*B*y Wednesday the mass student exodus from McMillan Studio was unmissable. Out of Ivan's forty students only three stayed and only because they decided to switch from violin to piano. The rest of them—students and their parents—assured him that they would *consider* coming back to him when his wrist healed and he was able to play again.

What good was a violin teacher who could not show the students how anything was done? Besides, there was an unwritten guideline among music teachers that one didn't steal other teachers' students. As far as Ivan was concerned, once his students were gone, they might never return to his studio.

Sitting there at the waiting area of Rao Family Physicians, he wondered if he could even pay for this doctor's visit. They hadn't called him yet. He could still get up and walk out.

Several more email pings later, and Ivan snapped shut his phone, tired of reading all those "we're sorry we have to go to another violin teacher" emails.

Two-thirds of his income came from his string studio. The other third came from SISO. Disability checks were one thing but his hourly income kept the three mortgages afloat. If nothing happened by the end of January, the bank could demand the loan balance. After all, they were already a month behind. He was surprised the bank hadn't called.

How did this happen? What was he going to say to Grandma?

He had been intercepting the mail so Grandma didn't see the inevitable. How long was that going to last? She'd find out eventually that they couldn't make the payments, if she didn't already know.

Maybe he was doing this upside down. Maybe he should have paid the primary mortgage first instead of the liens.

Maybe he should talk to an accountant. Well, accountants cost money. Maybe he could talk to Matt Garnett. Matt knew how to manage money. He could help him figure this out. Well, it meant Ivan had to show Matt his royal mess and live with the pain of embarrassment at his poor money skills. Or he could take one of those financial management classes at Seaside Chapel. They had them from time to time.

He looked around the waiting area, wondering how worse off everyone else was. He almost stood up to leave, but an interior door swung open, and a nurse called his name.

Oh well.

He and Grandma usually saw intern Tristan Rao, the son of Dr. Andrew Rao who ran the practice. Tristan attended Seaside Chapel and had started to go to the same Sunday school class as Ivan. He wasn't in today because he was visiting his extended family in India. Other doctors and nurse practitioners were.

Ivan didn't need to see Tristan personally. He was here to get his wrist X-rayed to see how his bones were healing and to get his cast checked. He was pretty sure he'd kept it dry, so he wasn't worried about that.

Lord, heal me, please.

He hoped that God would answer that prayer here on earth. Of course, people were healed when they arrived in heaven, but he wasn't ready to go there yet. He had a long bucket list to get to after he paid off all these debts he had.

His wrist cast would be off soon. He knew that Grandma Yun was praying for him too. Perhaps more intensively than he ever knew how to pray.

He also knew that Brinley was praying for him. She was still in Paris. She had texted earlier saying that she had missed him, but also that she would be spending the rest of January in Atlanta, transitioning her position in her dad's company to someone else.

By the time Brinley returned to St. Simon's Island, his cast would be off. Then he could get back to playing the violin, right?

Thank You, Lord.

CHAPTER THIRTY-NINE

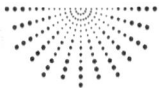

"*T*he McMillans fall in love fast and deeply, I think." Zoe was lying prone on the nineteenth-century settee that Mom had bought for her Paris apartment.

Across from her on the other side of the Persian carpet, Brinley wondered what Zoe had meant. She didn't ask. Zoe was like Mom, and like Mom she would explain, given the chance. So Brinley waited while she looked in Zoe's direction. Behind Zoe, tall windows opened to the Parisian skyline. In the distance, the Eiffel Tower was changing into its night colors of glitter and lights.

"Otto and Yun met on a blind date, and were engaged a week later. Their daughter, Jade, had birthed three children by two different fathers by the time she was twenty-three. Quincy and I were an item two months after we met. You and Ivan... What's going on between you two?"

"I don't know, Zoe. We're still getting to know each other."

"And?"

"I think we're close."

"And?"

"I think we're serious about each other. I didn't think we'd last past Christmas, but here we are."

"See what I mean? Quincy kissed me on our first date. He was very passionate."

Ivan almost kissed me before we went on a date. What did that say about him?

"I think Quincy is bored with me now, Brin." Zoe's eyes turned red.

"Hush, Zoe. Watch out for those hormones."

"Maybe that's it. You might be right."

Or I might be wrong.

"Quincy has been antsy. If I didn't know any better, I'd say he doesn't like Paris."

"Well, some people like to visit, some like to stay. It varies, as with any city." Brinley folded her legs under her and leaned against one side of the wing-back bergère.

"What a diplomatic answer." Zoe sprang up. "Hold that thought!"

She ran past Brinley, heading in the direction of the bathroom. Seconds later, Brinley heard her retch.

Brinley felt sorry for her sister. This morning sickness had been why Zoe and Quincy had canceled their trip to Vienna with the rest of the family. Mom and Dad had gone anyway, even though they didn't get any tickets for the New Year's Day concert by the

Vienna Philharmonic. Brinley was sure they'd find their way into some other smaller orchestral celebrations, and maybe even throw in an opera or two.

Zoe returned to her settee, looking rather sick.

"May I get you something?" Brinley asked.

"I can hardly eat. I'm sorry we had to cancel lunch at Le Meurice twice."

Brinley didn't mind. She would rather eat at home. But Zoe loved that restaurant, where dinner for the two of them would have cost more than a thousand dollars. "How about some soup?"

"I'll heat up something later if I get hungry. Right now nothing is staying down, you know. Don't get pregnant. It's miserable."

Brinley laughed. "I don't think that's going to happen anytime soon."

"Why not?"

"For one thing, I have to keep that vow with Grandpa. For another, Ivan... I mean, he's a devout Christian."

"And you became a Christian too, Dad said."

Brinley nodded. "We're going to have this sweet and clean relationship."

"Until you get married."

"That's not even in the horizon."

"That's probably what we should've done. Then I wouldn't be second-guessing my marriage now."

Brinley sat up. "Zoe."

"Quincy snores. He slurps his soup. And puts his foot in his mouth all the time."

"That's all?" Brinley asked. "I'm sure there're

worse things than that. Like infidelity, drugs, serial killing, whatever."

"I guess if you put it that way, it puts things in perspective. He is crazy about me or he seems to be."

"The McMillan passion, huh?" Brinley wondered. "It lasted for seventy years for Otto and Yun."

"Good point." Zoe had to get up again to go throw up. "I think I'm going to bed afterward."

"Feel better. I'll be praying for you."

"Thanks, sis!"

Brinley checked the time on her iPhone. Almost six o'clock Paris time. That would be about noon on the Georgia coast. She wondered what Ivan was doing. They had texted and called each other almost every day. She thought that Ivan was very interested in her. She thought he wanted to explore their relationship further.

But after talking with Zoe, she had to make sure.

Three weeks.

That wasn't nearly enough time for Brinley and Ivan to know each other, was it? They were attracted to each other, but was it love?

What was love?

What did real love look like?

Then again, they had talked to each other almost every day. Three full weeks of communication. More than some couples did all year long.

Brinley texted Ivan. "You there?"

He texted back right away. "Didn't want you to

think I wanted to call you all the time, but I do. Did I say all the time?"

Brinley was still processing what Ivan had texted when her iPhone chirped.

"Hey."

One word and it made Brinley's heart flutter. She wished Ivan had an iPhone but he didn't. So to talk with him they had to Skype. She turned on the app. "You look like you just came out of the shower."

"I did."

"How's the wrist?"

"Still painful. I won't know the full extent of the damage until I get out of this cast."

"It's the second of January today. Hey, only three and a half weeks left before they saw that thing off. Hang in there."

"I know. The twenty-eighth can't come soon enough. You'll be back the following week, right? On the third of February?"

"That's the plan. If Diehl needs me to stay in town a bit longer, that's the way it goes. I want a smooth transition so they won't call me back." Brinley had a feeling it shouldn't be a problem, but one never knew with Diehl.

"I hear you. Whenever you get back here, we'll celebrate. I'm taking you out to dinner."

"I prefer a home-cooked meal."

"I know, but I miss you and I want us to go out and eat dinner at someplace special. Just the two of us."

"That'll be nice." *Don't overdo it.*

"Do you want to pick a place?"

"Surprise me, Ivan."

"I will, then. Maybe somewhere cozy where we can talk."

Brinley laughed. "We always talk."

"That's how we get to know each other. Say, why does your dad call you Brinley Brin?"

"Better than Bratty Brin."

Ivan laughed. "Sure. I can't believe you were a brat."

"Oh, I was the perfect child."

"I can't believe that either."

"Neither can I. Seriously, I was the obscure middle child. I neither excelled nor failed. I was middle of the road, plain Jane, ordinary."

"You're not ordinary nor obscure, Brin. Every time I think of you my wrist hurts less."

"God is healing you." Brinley moved to the window. She adjusted the iPhone to catch a view of the Eiffel Tower. "Look at that."

"Cool. You're going up there sometime?"

"Nope. It's too crowded. Like Vienna this time of year."

On screen, Ivan sat back in his plastic chair. "Nice of you to stay behind with your sister instead of going to Vienna."

"I'm glad to spend time with my sister."

"How's my brother doing?"

"I see him now and then. He's not here. He's taking a conversational French class this evening."

"Immersion is the best way to learn. Sounds like they might be staying in Paris for good."

Brinley sat down on the settee by the window so that her backdrop was the night city. "Like that view?"

"Like you better."

Brinley prayed silently for the right words to say.

"Uh-oh. Whassup?" Ivan leaned toward his laptop camera. "Having second thoughts about us?"

"I'm not sure if we had any first thoughts. Are we moving too fast?"

"Come see me and let me kiss those doubts away, Brin."

"That sounds like a commitment."

Brinley heard some extra noises coming from Ivan's side.

"Grandma is calling me about something," Ivan said. "I have to go. Take it easy and think of me."

"And God. Don't forget God."

"That's a given, Brin."

"Okay. Just want to be sure."

∼

The long walk down the gravel path between the trees to the mailbox by the roadside gave Ivan time to think about the conversation he had with Brinley only moments ago. Things Brinley had said here and there now gnawed at him, things like:

Are we moving too fast?

What did she mean by that? Warning bells from his friends at the Seaside Chapel men's Bible study group rang in his head, what Matt and Sebastian had suggested at their last meeting in December.

Maybe she's waiting for a better offer later and you're available now.

Ivan wondered if Brinley had met someone new in Paris. Surely in her rich circles it would be easier to meet eligible bachelors than not. They might not even be bachelors as long as they were single, divorced, or available.

How am I going to compete with those rich guys?

The mailbox was stuffed. Ivan could barely get the mail out. There were what looked like belated Christmas cards with foreign postmarks. Some were from Grandma's missionary friends, and some were from her relatives in Seoul.

Then there were bills, bills, bills. He could feel the pressure in his chest. The pressure to pay up.

Then there was his box of checks. *Better not write any of those. They'd bounce.*

A few envelopes slipped out of his hands. He reached down to pick them up. Told himself he should've brought a plastic bag to carry all of these back to the house. Propping the stack of mail between one good hand and one in a cast, he started his walk back to the house.

To the right and left of him, the green space on the property extended quite a way off. Grandma and Grandpa had bought the house back in the fifties when land on St. Simon's Island had been cheap.

This land would eventually belong to him, Quincy, and Willow. Grandma had wanted to split it three ways.

He wondered now if he could talk to Quincy and Willow into selling two-thirds of it to some of those developers. The sale of the land might be enough to pay off all these debts, the bulk of which he had been handling

Until my wrist broke.

"Lord, when are You going to heal me?" Ivan shook his head and then felt bad. It was as if he were shaking his fist at God.

God would heal him when He healed him. Ivan was at God's mercy, not the other way around. He couldn't make God do anything.

Usually, after he had checked the mailbox, Ivan would sit on the porch to go through the bills. However, it was way too cold today.

Grandma was waiting for him in the living room. "Any bills?"

It was a longstanding joke between them.

"Enough to build a bonfire." Ivan dropped the pile onto one end of the couch, sat down, and began to sort through the envelopes.

He spotted several envelopes from credit card companies. Funny how it went. The more debt he was in, the more invitations he received to open new credit card accounts and to take out new loans. Well, he could use the new loans to pay off the old loans.

Use new debts to pay off old debts.

Not sure how one gets out of a hole by digging some more.

"Are we making payments on the house?" Grandma asked quietly.

"Working on it."

"What does that mean, Ivan?"

It means we have no money. "I'm moving money around so we can make the house payments. I have no income right now, so it's going to be tough for a while."

"Moving money around?" Grandma stopped rocking. "How long before they take the house?"

"If we miss the *next* payment." *Yeah, the next payment after this month's.*

"Tell me the truth, Ivan."

Ivan knew Grandma would see through it. Carefully, he worded it. "We're broke, Grandma. I am so sorry I wasn't able to get us out of debt. We've missed a payment in December, and we're going to miss another one this month. One more in February, and we're out on the streets."

Ivan expected Grandma to be upset, but she didn't show it. All she said was: "God has a solution."

"I wish He'd fixed it already."

"Patience, Ivan."

"Time has run out and God hasn't come through."

"Don't speak like that about the God who saved your soul."

"Time has run out."

"And whose fault is that?"

"My fault." *Might as well give in.*

"No, Ivan. We're all at fault. From Otto's crazy business ideas to our lack of financial sense. None of us McMillans ever knew how to manage money. I remember Otto's parents living through the Great Depression. Things aren't as bad today as they were back then, but life has always been hard for our family. If only we learned how to manage what little we have, we wouldn't be shaming God now."

Ivan wanted to sink into the couch. He felt that he was the man of the family now that Grandpa Otto was dead and Quincy was out of the country. But he had failed to be the head of the household.

"Ivan, look at me."

"Yes, Grandma?" Ivan's shoulders sagged.

"Our real home is in heaven. If we have to sell this dump, then sell this dump."

"It's not a dump, Grandma. We grew up here."

"Those times will always be in our memories, but there comes a time when we have to move on. Beatrice at church told me about this place in Brunswick. Low rent. Low utilities."

"Beatrice lives in a trailer park, Grandma."

"So what? It's a roof over our heads. Maybe that's how God is providing for us." Grandma rocked again in her well-oiled rocker. "Sometimes we have incorrect expectations of how we want God to provide for us when perhaps He has already provided."

"Don't forget to think of God," Ivan said. "That's what Brinley said to me on the phone just now."

"She did?" Grandma smiled. "I'm glad to hear

that. She's growing as a Christian. Something we need to be thankful for."

Yeah, sure. But that doesn't solve our financial mess.

Ivan wondered how he was going to keep his promise to take Brinley out to a nice dinner. He couldn't even afford cheap hot dogs on sale now, let alone take her to Saffron on Jekyll, which he had in mind. Saffron would be the type of restaurant that Brinley was used to. He wanted to show her that he could live that kind of lifestyle too. Eat in that kind of restaurant.

But where was he going to get the money to pay for even that one dinner with Brinley? He regretted the impulsive invitation.

Sigh.

Ivan gathered up some mail and passed them on to Grandma. "Probably Christmas cards."

"I guess it takes a while for airmail to get here." Grandma placed the stack on her lap and began to cut open the envelopes with a letter opener she always kept in her pencil stand on the table where her Bible was.

Ivan went back to the rest of the mail. He pushed the box of checks to one side. He stacked the bills one on top of another to one side of the couch. They were about three inches tall. He started to rip up some of the junk mail, but it hurt his left hand to even hold it for his right hand to tear up the envelopes. So he tossed the pieces one by one to another part of the couch. Store flyers, cable service deals, postcards from dentists and churches he had never even heard of, credit card offers—

Credit card offers.

Maybe that was how he could take Brinley out to dinner. Well, not just dinner but also to make partial house payments and pay off some bills.

Don't forget God.

Brinley's words came to mind, but—

It's just for one dinner.

Right?

CHAPTER FORTY

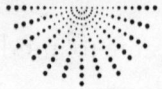

*O*n Monday morning, two days after Brinley had arrived home in Atlanta, she was back in the city, going to work at Brooks Investments for the last time.

Peachtree Street was honking loud and its Midtown sidewalks crowded with pedestrians going here and there, completely oblivious to Brinley and the thousand things filing through her head as she rehearsed for her meeting with Diehl and Dad. She had prepared for this, and Dad had agreed to meet after his European trip. Now she had to remember what she wanted to say to them.

Starbucks in her own travel mug in one hand and her laptop tote in the other arm, Brinley left the chilly January sunshine and entered Brooks Tower, a glassy twenty-one-floor salute to opulence and all that Ivan and Yun would be uncomfortable with, the bubble that lords of the manor were in and the peasants needed not apply.

Yet Brinley saw things differently than before. Now everyone was equal at the foot of the cross of Christ, where wealth and birthright didn't mean a more prominent place at the table.

That birthday suit we all came in is the same suit we all go out in.

Brinley didn't remember who had said that, but it reminded her that her life had to count. Her Bible reading had gone well, but Yun had reminded her that she would learn more as a new Christian if she were in a teaching church and a good Bible study regularly.

Atlanta had many churches, and Seaside Chapel pastor's wife, Olivia Gonzalez, had made some suggestions for her. For instance, Midtown Chapel was a sister church to Seaside Chapel. Maybe she'd check it out soon. Then again, Brinley wanted to be back on St. Simon's Island as soon as possible.

The elevator opened and disgorged Brinley on the penthouse level, where Diehl had staked his office claim. The hallway was rich with old burled walnut walls that Dad had salvaged from somewhere, a reminder of the past and things of old. Brinley passed by Mom's touches to the decor, urns and pitchers and vessels.

Above her, Dvořák's "Humoresque in G-Flat Major" played through the speakers, its undertone a reminder of Ivan. When his wrist healed, could he play this? If not, then what was he going to do? Ivan's entire career, and possibly life, was wrapped up in his violin.

If she were in his shoes, what would she do? Would she be so attached to an instrument, a job, a career, that if it were taken away from her, she would be dysfunctional?

Brinley found her brother in his throne room flanked by walls of glass. Outside were other tall office complexes and hotels, a veritable jungle of deals and transactions and sales and gold and money. Things that Brinley no longer found as important as they used to be when she was jetting around the world cutting deals for Brooks Investments. Been there, done that. To be sure, she'd been thinking it since before she met Jesus in December, but more so now that her perspective had changed.

She studied Diehl.

He was busy at his iPad, not looking up. But that's Diehl for you. Always working, always pushing for that last sales figure. He had worked harder since Dad semi-retired to Seaside Island, but all that could change with this meeting. It probably wouldn't help Diehl make more time for his own kids, but perhaps it could remind him—ha!—that there was life outside of the family business.

Life, like Ivan. For me.

Brinley inched toward the custom glass table through which she could see Diehl's shoeless feet in his favorite wool socks. She waved in front of Diehl. "Hey, Diehl Brooks."

"Did you see Jared a few weeks ago?" Diehl still didn't look up. "Jared Urquhart?"

"Has it been that long? Let me see." Brinley checked her iPhone. "Oglethorpe Charity Dinner. December fifteenth. Why?"

"He wants Brooks Investments to invest in some new properties on St. Croix."

"So?"

"He asked for you specifically. Could you go down there to assess what he's got and see if we can be a part of it?"

"No."

Diehl looked up. "You're still working here through January."

"I'm transitioning out, remember?" Brinley sat down in one of the plush armchairs.

"Fly there for a day of business, a day of R&R."

"No, Diehl. Why don't you send Kanisha? She's taking over my position. Give the account to her."

Diehl sighed. "I guess you don't get it that I don't want you to leave."

"Well, I don't want her to leave either." Dad walked in. Took the other armchair. "But what you think is best might not be best for your sister."

Brinley greeted Dad and found herself staring at a new painting on the wall behind the chair he sat on. Another Picasso, Diehl's favorite—

The *Dora Maar Au Chat?*

No way.

"How much did you pay for that?" Brinley

pointed to the unlikeness of Pablo Picasso's mistress in vivid geometric blocks and curves.

"A hundred. Why?"

"A hundred million dollars?" *How many Stradivarius violins can I buy with that?*

How many senior citizens can I feed and clothe and provide houses to stay in with that?

"One of a kind."

"So you work yourself to death for stuff that will all burn up one day."

"I'm a collector like you, sis. Only I don't collect white trash."

"You take that back, Diehl. Ivan is not trash." Brinley was on the verge of tears. She composed herself. Next to her, Dad said nothing.

Diehl leaned back. "What's your problem, Brin? Out with it. I don't have all day. I have a company to run."

"That's exactly it, Diehl. You have a company to run. And you roll over everyone in your way. You don't care who you hurt, whose lives you destroy, where they end up, whatever, as long as you get what you want."

Diehl stared at her.

"I don't know everything that you said to Ivan on Christmas Eve, but I can pretty much guess."

"What might I have said to him?"

"You threw him down. Stepped on him. Spat at him. You think that if Ivan and I somehow end up together, he'll take all my money and prevent me from selling my shares to you."

Diehl kept his poker face. "I'm trying to protect you, sis."

"Protect me or protect your interests in Brooks Investments?"

"She has a good point there." Dad sounded amused. "If I could give you the entire company, Diehl, I would, but I've already written the will and such as it is, your mother would pitch a fit if I give your sisters less than your shares. Brinley here probably doesn't mind, but Zoe has a lot of expenses."

"You want my third of the company, Diehl?" Brinley asked. "It's only money."

She saw the flicker in Diehl's eyes. "You would give up nine billion dollars for that piece of garbage?"

"It takes one to know one," Brinley snapped.

Dad raised an arm. "Children."

Brinley sighed. "I'm sorry, Diehl. I didn't mean to call you trash."

"You thought it."

Brinley's shoulders slumped. "I wish Parker were here. He was always the peacemaker between us."

"We all miss him," Dad said.

Diehl's voice was low. "Now it's just you and me, Brin, duking it out."

"I don't want us to fight." Brinley padded around the executive desk and hugged her only living brother. "I love you, you pain in the neck."

Diehl patted her arms. "I love you too, sis."

CHAPTER FORTY-ONE

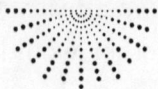

"You have a low tolerance for pain," Vittorio, the occupational therapist, said to Ivan one hour after a chainsaw-toting nurse practitioner from Rao Family Physicians ripped off the cast from his left arm and sent him down the street to his next stop of the day. "Have a seat."

Ivan sat across from him at the small table. He rubbed his swollen wrist gently, as if it were a puppy. That really, really hurt. Those exercises they did a minute ago—

Oh boy.

"Tolerate?" Ivan blurted, cringing at the lingering pain in his wrist. But this! This was so much more severe than his cracked ribs that had all but healed in the previous six weeks. "My wrist is swollen. When is this going to heal? I have to get back to work or someone else will take my job."

"They'll understand. It takes time."

Time I don't have.

Ivan stared at his wrist and willed it to turn. He couldn't do it. The wrist was stiff.

"We'll have to let the new bones get stronger, right?"

"Right away," Ivan snapped. "I can't believe this."

"Let's get an ice pack on that wrist. Get the swelling down. Then we'll work on your mobility." Vittorio waved to an orderly.

"Then? Like when?" Ivan was breathing heavily now. *Have. To. Get. Back. To. Work.*

"Tomorrow if you can come in. We'll do it daily until—"

"Daily? For how long? This was supposed to be my big day. Got the cast removed."

This was the last Wednesday in January he had been waiting for since the week before Christmas.

And now this?

Ivan had thanked God profusely on his drive to the doctor's this morning. He had told Grandma not to wait for him at lunch because he would go from Dr. Rao's office to the occupational therapy center for a few hours to get his mobility back.

One hour after the cast had been removed, Ivan wasn't thanking God anymore.

Lord, why are You allowing this to happen to me?

Vittorio looked at Ivan calmly. "It's normal for you to feel like you can't do anything right now, but work with me, and we'll get you back to functionality in no time."

"Functionality? That's not good enough. I need to get my wrist back to a hundred percent or my career is over."

Vittorio didn't reply. He seemed to be waiting for Ivan to calm down.

"I have to be able to play my violin again." *Whatever my violin is. The Strad is gone. The Vuillaume is also gone.*

"This is my livelihood." Ivan tried again. "How long will it be before I can have a full range of motion in my wrist?"

"You play in SISO?"

"Yeah. First violin. Concertmaster." *Was.*

Vittorio didn't seem impressed. "I think I've heard SISO play before sometime in the summer. Outdoor concert at Neptune Park?"

"Yeah, I was there."

"You guys were pretty good."

Pretty good? Put us up against ASO any day. "Thank you. Now, how long will it be?"

Vittorio swiped through Ivan's records on his Galaxy tablet and pressed a few things that Ivan couldn't see. "Not going to lie to you, Ivan. In your case, maybe two to six months, four if you work hard."

"Four months!"

"If you work very hard. No one can guarantee you complete recovery, not even God." Vittorio picked up a printout from the printer nearby and placed it on the table in front of Ivan. "This is our schedule for the next two weeks. We're going to take it one session at a time. Baby steps."

Ivan stared at the schedule. *Lord Jesus, help me.*

"Do you have something you can work toward?" Vittorio asked.

"Like what?"

"A more defined goal. I know you want to get back to work, but is there something specific you want so badly that you'll do anything to get better so you can pick up that violin again?"

All Ivan could see was Brinley's face.

I want to play Air *for Brin again even if she never recovers her 1698 Strad.*

"Think about that carrot on a stick, and make your way toward it." Vittorio stood up from his desk.

Ivan folded the schedule of death and pocketed it in his barn jacket.

"I'll see you in the morning, Ivan." Vittorio stood up. "Keep that splint on there so nobody touches your wrist."

"I will. Say, don't I have a thirty-dollar copay?" Ivan wasn't sure if he should ask, but it was done.

"Nope. All taken care of. We'll bill your insurance. You're good to go."

"All right. Fair enough." Yet it bothered him as he walked out of the East Beach Therapy Center where the cold January bit down on his head under an overcast sky.

All taken care of.

Again.

~

*a*gainst his better judgment, Ivan called Brinley when he got into his truck. He knew that his heart and mind were not in equilibrium right now, but he needed to hear her voice. He cranked up the Chevy.

Outside his window, he could see the parking meter. He had ten minutes before he had to put more quarters in, but that wasn't going to happen. He had no more coins in his pocket.

"Four months, huh?" Brinley said on the phone.

"Yeah. Long road ahead."

"We'll do it together, Ivan."

"This pain is mine alone to bear."

"Not true. I'll be back soon, and I'll go with you to therapy."

"What can you do?" Ivan backed the truck out of the parking spot.

"I'll pray. Keep you company."

Ivan would like that but... "I don't want you to see me in therapy."

"That bad, huh?"

"Pain all the way. Dr. Rao said the new bones are in, but the OT gave me some exercises and it about killed me. And we haven't even started. Torture begins at seven o'clock tomorrow morning."

Ivan drove through the green light.

"Get some rest," Brinley suggested. "Prepare yourself."

"Why are you always positive?" Ivan asked.

"Why are you always negative?" Brinley shot back.

"We make quite a pair."

"We may never reconcile our differences, Ivan."

Ivan didn't want to hear that. "Tell me that's a joke, Brin. I can't take any more bad news."

"Bad news? I look forward to seeing you again. That's good news, isn't it?"

"Yeah. What are you doing now?"

"Packing."

"I wish I were there to help you pack." Ivan turned onto Ocean Boulevard.

"Well, nothing to it," Brinley said. "I've been living out of suitcases the last few years. I pack light. The movers are going to handle everything else."

"Is your new house move-in ready?"

"Not really. Next week I'll call Toby about it. See where they're at. Give them a push if I have to. I think they're painting now."

"I haven't seen it."

"You will. But it's merely a house, Ivan. A roof over our head. Nothing like heaven."

Nothing like heaven.

"By the way, can you wait a few extra days?" Brinley paused. "I have to go to Savannah for a few days with my VP-in-training."

"Sorry to hear that. I was looking forward to seeing you."

"Me too. So I'll see you in February?"

"Just in time for Valentine's Day." Ivan began

planning in his head. What could he give Brinley that she didn't already have?

"Oh, I have to go. The movers are here. Call me anytime. See you soon."

"All right, Brin. Thank you for talking with me. I *love* hearing your voice."

Did I say love?

CHAPTER FORTY-TWO

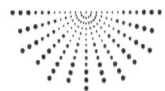

"What about a left-hand violin?"

Ivan couldn't answer Vittorio the torturer. Ivan the victim was writhing in pain, thank you very much. His left wrist hurt with searing bolts of acute pain zipping back and forth between his elbow and his left radius and ulna bones, then leaping to his thumb and a few fingers. It happened every time he flexed his wrist or contracted his fingers.

"Don't they have violins that you can put on your right shoulder?" the physical therapist asked again.

"Yeah, but not the Strad—aaarrrggghhh!" He couldn't lift his left arm, couldn't turn his hand, couldn't clench his fingers, couldn't do much of anything Vittorio tried to help him with.

His mobility was zilch. Almost.

Perhaps seven on a Monday morning was way too early for therapy.

Perhaps he should've taken more painkillers before he left the house.

Just cut off my wrist already!

"We're a nonviolent facility, Ivan." Vittorio's facial muscles didn't contort.

"I didn't say that out loud."

"You did too. It's going to be hard for a couple of weeks and then it'll get better, I assure you."

"You can't promise."

"The variable is you, Ivan." Vittorio raised an eyebrow. "Did you do the exercises I told you to do yesterday?"

Ivan barely nodded. Well, okay. He had done the exercises, but stopped when it became tearfully painful.

"Did you put an icepack on your wrist?" Vittorio asked.

"Yeah."

Vittorio rubbed his arm to get some circulation going. Ivan felt better. He closed his eyes. "Good news for you, Ivan."

"Is there any?"

"Since you didn't have any surgery, your healing should be pretty standard."

"Standard?"

"Let's do more exercises on your entire arm." Vittorio went looking for balls.

Ivan tried to sneak away.

"Mr. McMillan!"

He crawled back to the treatment table.

"Do you want to get better or not?" Vittoria asked.

"Want—aaarrrggghhh!"

And so it went on until the session was up. He could barely remember all that they had done except that once again, Ivan didn't have to pay a dime. He was feeling a bit suspicious of this free healthcare he was getting. Vittorio could not disclose any information to him.

He left the OT center in near tears. He hoped nobody saw him.

Lord, heal me!

Something Vittorio had said made Ivan think.

A left-handed violin.

He had seen some renowned violinists play it that way. The chin rest, strings, everything would be a mirror image of the right-hand violin where he held the bow with his right hand. He'd have to contact a luthier to see if he could get a left-handed violin where he could control the strings with his right hand, which didn't have a broken wrist.

Could he make a living that way? At least until his left wrist healed?

He'd be the only violinist on the wrong side of the string section. Would he have to sit away from the other violinists or risk poking their eyes out with his bow? Would any orchestra even accept him into their staff?

Premature!

Vittorio had mentioned in passing that it would

take baby steps to get back to his old form. Ivan decided to make a mental list of the basic functionalities he needed: turn his wrist, hold the fingerboard, play both arm and wrist vibrato, handle the portamento—

Whew.

Ivan expelled a breath into the cold Atlantic air.

Beneath the splint, his left wrist throbbed staccatos to an invisible metronome.

He called Brinley again, but she didn't pick up. He texted her, giving her the lowdown on Vittorio from an obviously skewed perspective. But it made him feel better to complain to someone, to let it out, to say it.

More phone calls and apologies from his students' parents came. His music studio might as well close with only one student left. He knew that kid; she wasn't really interested in music at all. Her mother had made her do it so she could perform on stage vicariously through the poor daughter, who'd rather be a cheerleader. She had both violin and piano lessons. With violin lessons out of the question for another four months, Ivan had offered her a discount.

But one student does not a music studio make.

～

At the end of a grueling week, Ivan saw enough improvement for him to brave dropping in at the SISO studios at rehearsal time. He entered the rehearsal room quietly and found a wooden stool in a corner, on which he sat and watched SISO go through its repertoire for the upcoming music festivals in Jacksonville and Miami.

He knew the numbers by heart, knew exactly when the arpeggios, chords, slurs, and time signature changes would occur. He counted through the rests, and nearly picked up his invisible bow when the string section began the next movement.

For a moment music was Ivan's therapy. For a moment the worst was over this Thursday. Vittorio was done breaking him up and he had the rest of the day off.

The orchestra stopped abruptly.

"No, no, no!" Conductor Petrocelli repeated it several times, a string of no's followed by Italian expletives lost in translation.

Ivan might be a Christian man, but he even missed Petrocelli's rant on the lack of maintenance, passion, or something or other that every single Sea Islands Symphony Orchestra member had been accused of during the last year Ivan had been in it.

Scold me now! I miss being scolded!

A ping in his wrist jolted him out of his memory walk. The clock on the wall registered a good thirty minutes past the time for him to take more over-the-counter pain meds. He wondered if he could possibly not take any at all and survive Vittorio and his physical therapist's torture chamber.

Maybe not.

He kept telling himself that once his wrist had full mobility, he'd be back playing vibrato, both arm and wrist. If he couldn't vibrate the strings with his left hand, then he was done.

SISO started up again. This time Ivan was impressed with Warren Yamaguchi's rendition of César Franck in the string and piano duet. He knew Warren had the technical skills, having been a product of the Suzuki Method back when he was in San Diego. He was here in SISO because his retired parents now lived on Hilton Head, and he wanted to be close to them. Ivan knew what that was like.

At the next break, the entire string section came to wish Ivan well. He felt loved.

"Good job there, Warren," Ivan said when Warren passed by.

"Thanks, man. Sorry about your wrist. I hope you get well soon." Warren stepped closer.

"Me too."

"Too bad you'll miss the Jax Festival next week but take it as an opportunity to get well."

"That's a good way to look at it," Ivan said.

"Then you'll be ready to play again when the SISO Hall opens in October."

"They moved the date back?" *Nice.* That gave Ivan three extra months to get well.

Warren nodded. "Funding issue or something. When the hall is built, we'll all be salaried."

"Nice."

"I hear there's a delay too with the museum. It won't open until next year."

Ivan thought that the Sea Islands Museum of Musical Instruments had a nicer ring to it than the

Coastal Georgia Music Museum. And it would have some of the Brooks violins on display unless Brinley changed her mind.

Brinley again.

Something inside Ivan gnawed at him, making that visceral connection between his feelings and his wrist. If he didn't get back his old form, his violin career would be over, and he wouldn't be able to support her, let alone a family.

Why am I thinking that?

"How's that wrist?" Emmeline strutted toward them. Warren took the opportunity to leave. "Our women's Bible study group is praying for you."

"Thanks, Em."

"I heard that Brinley Brooks accepted Jesus. Have you asked her to join our women's Bible study?"

"I'm sure that the pastor's wife is on it."

"You could still ask her, anyway."

"I don't want to pressure her, you know. She just got saved."

Emmeline still stood there. "You two are serious?"

"We're dating." Ivan didn't want to say more. There had been disputes between him and Emmeline about the meaning of "dating" when they had spent time with each other the summer before.

"I heard she bought the Strad for you. Kind of ironic, isn't it, that you can't play any violin now?"

Emmeline's words stung like those hornets he had run into playing in the backyard when he was a kid. "It was for charity to benefit historical preservation. People bid on many things. Last year it was an antique cabinet or something. This year it happened to be a musical instrument."

"An instrument that happened to be a Stradivarius violin. Wonder who put it up for auction."

"Em, I don't care." Ivan did remember that Brinley wasn't the previous owner. That was good enough for him.

She wasn't even supposed to be at the Oglethorpe Charity Dinner that December evening when she dropped over five million dollars on an old Stradivarius violin. She had only gone to the dinner on the behalf of her dad who had been out of the country at that time.

"You don't have to defend her, Ivan. It is what it is. If you didn't have the Strad, you wouldn't have been robbed."

"Are you saying that every violinist who owns a Strad will be robbed?"

"The probability is higher, don't you think, than say a Guadagnini or your old Vuillaume or Suzuki or some cheap violin that the rest of us can afford, not that I need one since I play the harp." Emmeline leaned on one leg. Her tight—very tight—pants showed all her curves.

Too bad her beauty is offset by that tongue.

"Enough, Em." Ivan got off the stool.

"Hey, I'm just trying to help."

"Help?"

Emmeline sidled up to Ivan. "I think you should know. Your name is no longer on the SISO list."

"I'm on the disabled list." *Yeah, of a small regional orchestra that pays per rehearsal and per performance.*

"If you can't play, you don't get paid, Ivan. Duh."

Ivan tried to remain calm, but inside he did not like the reminder at all. "I was told SISO is going to let me sit out for four months until my wrist heals."

Emmeline chuckled. "This week, two violinists came in for auditions."

"Musicians come and go all the time."

"Well, you're going, Ivan. The one who is joining us in Jax is an assistant concertmaster." Emmeline grinned. "You don't believe me? Ask Petrocelli. When was the last time you spoke with him?"

Three days ago. One day before the audition with those new violinists.

If there was anything happening, Petrocelli had not let on, but Emmeline might have a point. Ivan decided he'd need to make an appointment with Petrocelli and get this cleared up.

"In light of all this, it's good for you to have a benefactor, don't you think, Ivan?"

Benefactor?

Ivan tensed up. He clammed up before he said something he'd regret later. "I have to run."

He walked away to find Conductor Petrocelli, but heard Emmeline lob a final dart at his back. He was sure others heard it too.

"Tell me, did you play for her anytime she wanted?"

∼

George Frideric Handel greeted Ivan at the porch, a mellifluous "The Arrival of the Queen of Sheba" from the *Solomon* oratorio broadcasting everywhere as Ivan unlocked the front door. The key was stuck. He jiggled the key in the lock and turned it with his good hand. The key came out but only after a considerable effort on Ivan's part.

I'll get the WD-40 later.

His left wrist was hidden inside the barn jacket sleeve, but the pain had returned. It was time to take more acetaminophen. He slogged through the foyer and put the stack of mail on a narrow side table. There used to be a mirror above the side table, but it had broken.

"Well, SISO seems to be doing fine without me." Ivan stepped into the family room, where he knew he'd always find Grandma.

"I'm not worried about them. How did your therapy go, dear?" Grandma asked.

"Like my arm's going to fall off." Vittorio's boot camp might be good for him in the end—way in the future—but getting there could kill Ivan.

"That bad, huh?"

Ivan noticed that Grandma was knitting a rose-colored scarf of some sort. "Who is that for?"

"A special person."

"Meaning you have no idea."

Grandma chuckled. "I make them in case

someone has a birthday or something. When's Brinley's birthday?"

"In the summer sometime." Ivan rounded the coffee table and stretched out on the couch, one foot above an armrest and the other foot hanging over the couch. He looked up at the old paint on the ceiling.

"I can't turn my wrist." He lifted his left wrist above his head. "I can't put my fingers in a supine position. Forget sliding on the strings."

"Soon, Ivan. Soon. It has only been a week. You remember when I broke my hip? I had to get used to a titanium hip."

How could I forget? "You have a higher tolerance for pain than I do, Grandma."

"I was determined to walk again."

"I guess my determination is—uh, nonexistent. I'm tired of this."

"Patience, Ivan."

Ivan glanced at his watch. "Don't you have tea with someone today?"

"Peggy came down with the stomach flu."

"Hope she feels better."

"It's harder when you're past eighty and get sick," Grandma said quietly. "Did you bring in the mail?"

"Yeah. Mostly bills. I didn't look at them, but I think any day now the mortgage is due again." Ivan closed his eyes. He had never felt this exhausted in his life. That was some workout Vittorio had inflicted on him. So many different ways to spell pain. "This is going to go on for four more months."

"If you work hard, it'll be over sooner than later,

dear." *Knit. Purl.* "When you don't see the results, it's hard for you to keep going. But until you believe, you can't get to the results."

"I'm tired, Grandma. I see nothing at all."

"This is when faith comes in, Ivan. When you walk by faith, you're not walking by sight."

"Sight at this unsightly splint? A grim reminder of my doom."

"We can thank God that He healed your ribs."

"Yes. Thank You, Lord." Ivan sighed. "You know the three students I had left? Well, they all canceled but one. And she probably won't make it past summer."

"When you get better, you can get new students. At least SISO is keeping you on."

"About that..." Ivan expelled a deep breath. "I talked to Petrocelli this morning before I left the studio."

Grandma put down her knitting needles.

"I don't get paid if I don't play, and I'm going to be out of work for four months. With my music studio all but closed, I'll have to cancel our healthcare plan. We have no savings. Three mortgages and no savings. How did we get here?"

Grandma thought for a minute. "We'll pray and ask God to provide. He has never failed us or forsaken us."

"I have some disability insurance. It should hold us over for a while, Grandma." Ivan didn't say that most of that would go to doctor visits and therapy sessions. Then there was food, electricity, gas, water, and the truck. He couldn't cycle at this time because he couldn't hold the handlebar properly with his left hand. Those three mortgages might have to be put on hold.

"My social security checks can help," Grandma offered.

Ivan didn't say that their quarter-million-dollar debt would eat up any social security checks and then some.

"We can't borrow any more money." Grandma resumed knitting.

"No one would loan us anything, not even Matt. He knows I can't pay him back." Ivan heaved a deep sigh. "Maybe I can get a job that doesn't require my left hand. It's only until I reopen my music studio and get back to SISO."

All his training had been in music. He wondered what he could do if he weren't a violinist. "I'll call Argo Perry and Matt Garnett. They have stores. Maybe they have something I can do."

"We could sell the house," Grandma suggested, but Ivan noted that her eyes were on her Steinway Victorian upright piano.

"I hope it doesn't come to that." They'd survived this long. Ivan wanted Grandma to be confident they would overcome this even though in his heart he knew it was a losing battle. "I hope to keep this house for your grandchildren and their children."

"Our real home is in heaven, Ivan. Don't hold on too tightly to things on earth."

CHAPTER FORTY-THREE

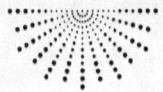

"*D*ad, you're losing your edge," Brinley said as she took Dad's rook and ambushed his queen. By the look on his face, Brinley knew he hadn't seen it coming.

"I fold."

"Giving up so easily?" Brinley leaned back and stretched in the reclining leather seat. Outside the Boeing Business Jet windows, puffy clouds belied the southern winter they were in, an ode to summer and sunshine and warmth.

"We're landing soon. Let's do a rematch when we get to the cottage."

Brinley nodded. Across the Napoleon chessboard, Dad looked worn out. He was only fifty-eight, but he looked past sixty. The lines on his face had deepened since the stroke, as if everything he did required more effort now. His walking stick would remind him of shortening years and of his future heavenly home, but the silver shaft would always be a Post-it note of his enormous wealth that he couldn't take with him to the afterlife.

"How's your house reno coming along?" Dad asked.

"I'm hoping it'll be done in two weeks."

"Toby and Megan still fighting?"

"All the time. Disagree on everything from cabinets to colors to who to hire and when to fire."

"That's going to delay the reno."

"I'll threaten them tomorrow."

"Slap them with cold, hard cash. Always works." Dad laughed. Then: "I'm thinking of retiring."

"Again?"

"Diehl's doing well with Brooks Investments in Atlanta. I'm confident you'll take Brooks Renovations to new heights."

"We still need you, Dad."

"I know, but I want to spend more time with your mom. She's going to stay in Paris for a while since Zoe's got that morning sickness."

That was nice that Dad missed Mom. Forty years of wedded bliss. Sure, they had fought, but they always made up and moved on.

"I guess you can tell me what you want done with Brooks Reno and I'll take care of it from here."

"That's it, Brinley Brin. I don't want to bother with all this stuff anymore."

"You're saying you want me to buy you out of Brooks Reno?" Brinley had already bought half.

They'd signed the papers only two weeks before back in Atlanta.

"Well, if I died, you'd inherit the company. This way I get some spending money. Make me an offer, Brin."

"I'm going to be out of money if you keep selling me stuff, Dad."

"At least you're paying for it in cash."

"Like you always said, never buy what you can't afford. No point getting into debt." *I've seen what it does to people. To Yun. To Ivan.*

"So what's the hang-up, Brinley Brin?"

Brinley wasn't sure what to tell Dad about the purchase-on-a-whim. *Well, just say it.* "You know where Riley's art gallery is on Mallery?"

"What about it?"

"Think one street over. Pelican Road."

"I've heard of that area. Some vandalism over the summer."

"Well, kids were out of school. Nothing better to do."

"You think that's it?"

"Yeah. I talked to some city council members. They think if we revitalize the area, it'll bring up the property values."

"So? What does that have to do with you?"

"I bought that warehouse in the corner."

"You didn't."

"I did. When I bought my new house, I asked my agent to check into that property. The owner is desperate. Short sale. Half price."

"Still a bad move. It's over a hundred years old. I know you like old things, but that's... You should've asked me, Brin, *before* you bought it."

"I don't have to ask you about everything, Dad. I think Brooks Reno can turn that entire block into a mix-used development."

"Work and play? Like Seaside on the Gulf, or Avalon in Alpharetta?" Dad logged into his laptop to look at a map.

Brinley watched him check out the satellite images.

Dad didn't look up. "Not a bad idea. Go on."

"The property next door to the warehouse is now available." Brinley pointed on Dad's laptop screen. "Would you like to invest in it?"

"With the money you pay me for the rest of Brooks Reno?"

"We could preserve the history of the area. Restore it. Get rid of vandalism. Give kids a place to go in the summer. All at the same time."

"A daughter after her dad's own heart." Dad laughed. "Tell me. How did you end up with the warehouse in the first place?"

Brinley wasn't sure how to say it. It had begun with Johann Sebastian Bach, threaded through whale-watching and a view from the St. Simon's Lighthouse. And what Ivan had said when he pointed out that warehouse from the crow's nest.

Maybe someday I could rent space in that building for a music studio.

Ivan's left wrist might have been damaged but

he'd get it back, wouldn't he? Even if he couldn't play in concerts, he could still teach, or at least run a music studio. There had to be something he could do. Maybe even help musicians with injuries. Teach music to special needs students. Music therapy. It was endless what could be done.

Then again, nothing might come of it.

"It's all my fault, Dad. I bought him the Strad. That's why he was attacked."

"We're talking about Ivan McMillan?" Dad asked.

Brinley nodded.

"Helen Hu and the FBI are all over it. Don't worry, Brin."

"I shouldn't have bought him the Strad."

"Now you're trying to make up for it by buying a run-down warehouse? I don't see the connection."

"Ivan dreamed of a music studio in that warehouse."

"You bought it for him."

"Well, to revitalize the city block."

"No, Brin. To pay a penance for your sins. And if he never plays violin again? Wouldn't that warehouse remind him of what he couldn't have?"

Now Brinley didn't say anything.

"Brinley Brin, look at me." Dad scooted forward in his recliner. "You're a believer now. When Jesus died on the cross He paid for all your sins. You cannot pay enough penance to make up for what you thought were errors in judgment or whatnot."

"What do I do now, Dad?"

"You ask God to forgive you for what you thought was your mistake, and ask Him to make things right in His way and His timing. You can't *fix* things yourself. You're not God. Fixing things is God's business, unless of course, He wants you to be part of the solution, such as if you had to make restitution. Then do it, but in God's way, not yours, and only if you're sure it's what God wants you to do. Got it?"

"Clear as mud."

"In other words, trust God, not yourself. Wait for God to show you the way. Don't jump the gun."

"Okay. Simple enough."

"You remember the verse I gave you?"

"Proverbs 3:5-6?" The same one Brinley had jotted down on the bookmark she had given to Ivan for Christmas. Boy, was he surprised that was all she had given him, though he might never know all the other things she had been doing for him.

"Yes. 'Trust in the Lord with all your heart, and lean not on your own understanding; in all your ways acknowledge Him, and He shall direct your paths.' That verse." Dad recited from memory. "You never go wrong trusting God. Until you see the big picture, don't make a judgment call."

"You think I made a mistake buying the warehouse?"

"We don't know yet, do we? Things are still unfolding. Until we see the end of the story, we're still right in the middle of it." Dad paused. "Having said that, I love the mixed-use idea. All right. I'm in."

"Thanks, Dad. I won't let you down." Brinley's

voice shook. "This retirement thing. Are you going to move to Paris, then?"

"We'll shuttle between our chateau and the Seaside Island cottage, yes."

"How often will I see you and Mom?"

"As often as you want. We'll be back on Seaside Island every other month or so. If we're over there in Europe somewhere, call and I'll send the BBJ to pick you up."

"You don't have to, Dad. I'll fly commercial." Brinley felt better. "When do you leave for this trip?"

"In a couple of weeks. I might see Helen Hu. Say, why don't you let me handle the Damaris hunt and you focus on Brooks Reno?"

"Why?"

"I need something to do. Maybe your mom and I can go on an adventure."

"A treasure hunt?"

"We used to do that, you know. Hop, skip, jump all over Europe looking for antiquities."

"Uh-huh. That's how Diehl came about."

Dad cleared his throat. "Has it been thirty-five years ago?"

"All right, Dad. I'll buy you out of Brooks Reno. You invest in Pelican Road. It's a win-win."

"Yep. I'll take care of the Strad. You take care of your labor of love."

Love?

CHAPTER FORTY-FOUR

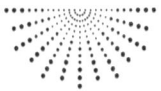

The moment Ivan saw the menu, he knew he would have a full stomach tonight. He glanced across the table. Brinley placed her menu down.

"Decided already?" Ivan asked.

"I'm not very hungry tonight. I'm going to have some salad."

Ivan couldn't read her face. Was she dissimulating? What did she mean by not being hungry? Salad was one of the cheapest items on the menu. Was she insulting him? Didn't want him to pay too much for their first formal night out?

"You look nice this evening," he said instead, straining a smile.

Brinley did dress well. On the drive here, Brinley had explained to him that her fabric was called a jacquard. The rose colors on her dress reminded him yet again of the "Pleasant Days" composition he should finish sometime.

For her.

"Thank you," Brinley said quietly. "You look nice too. I like that cord jacket. Black looks good on you."

"You sound a bit tired."

"A little bit. I'm glad the transition is done, though it took more than a month." Brinley sipped water.

"How's Brooks Renovations coming along?" *Not that you have to do any work.*

"I miss having Dad looking over my shoulder, but it's nice to have veto power."

"I suppose there's a lot of work to buy, fix, and sell houses."

"Or rent them out. Yep." Brinley nodded. "I'm not working alone, to be sure. I thank God for a good crew."

"It still sounds harder than playing music."

"You think so?"

"Yep. I'm not much into construction and renovations."

"I agree."

"What's that supposed to mean?" Ivan folded his arms.

"Well, you let your house fall apart—oh, I didn't mean to bring that up."

"No, let's." Ivan liked a challenge. "I was going to fix things. You stepped in front of me."

Brinley leaned forward. "Are we fighting? Is this our first fight?"

"Actually, no. This is our second fight. The first one was over the subterranean termites, remember?"

Brinley smiled. "Well, considering the termites had been eating your porch posts, I think they were no longer subterranean."

"No worries, Brin. Now they're no longer anywhere."

The server came to take their orders without a notepad. It amazed Ivan. *I mean, is he going to remember everything we're ordering? Even some fast food places use an iPad to take orders.*

Ivan decided to go for one of the most expensive items on the menu, some sort of lobster and scallops combo, and a couple of extra sides. And soup to boot. He ordered dessert while he was at it. If there was anything left over, he could take them home for a midnight snack. He roughly calculated the cost. As long as he stayed within two hundred dollars it should be fine.

Brinley pointed to the wash of sunset in the sky. "Some view."

"We should've timed it better. We could have gone upstairs to see the sunset before we were seated. Next time I'll make a later reservation."

"It's all right, Ivan." She had a glow about her in the late afternoon light of the Atlantic. The sun was setting on the other side of the restaurant, but the pastel colors spread over the sky, darkening bit by bit as they sat there looking out.

"My friend Sebastian said he had to pay a premium price for this view," Ivan said.

"I bet. It's nice that he'll make it all back with his award-winning restaurant."

"Yeah. Back then he was the youngest chef in the Southeast. A lot of pressure there." Ivan wondered whether Sebastian Langston was working tonight. If he was, maybe Ivan could introduce Brinley to him.

It kind of made Ivan feel important to rub shoulders with *titled* people. The James Beard chef-owner of Saffron, for instance.

"Pressure can be tough. I know that from having been in sales," Brinley offered. "Then again, he should be able to handle it, right, since he has God?"

It seemed like an innocent newbie Christian question, so Ivan tried to answer it. "Sometimes it feels hard going through the pressure, but if we keep in mind that God is always with us, He makes it more bearable."

"But we still have to go through it sometimes."

"More often than not." Ivan stared into the distance.

Outside the cantilevered dining room, beyond the wintering sea oats, the sands of Jekyll Island stretched toward the Atlantic Ocean. The sea and sky and God's creation carried on, oblivious to his dilemma. Dusk was setting in, but tomorrow, another day would cycle in.

Ah, try to think of something pleasant.

"We should come out here and have breakfast on the rooftop balcony someday."

"Or we could walk on the beach to see the sunrise for free."

Free? Ivan knotted his eyebrows. "Why do you say that?"

"A lot of things in life don't cost money. You know that. God's love is free, for example. His salvation is free. His creation here is also free."

"Don't turn philosophical on me, Brin."

"Sorry."

"No need to apologize. I would love to walk on the beach at sunrise with you." *Every day for the rest of my life.*

Ivan reached for his soda to regroup his emotions.

"That was a lot of stuff you ordered," Brinley said. "You must be famished."

"I ate lunch, if you must know. This is a feast to celebrate us." He reached across the table with his right hand and held Brinley's left.

Someday I'll put a ring on that finger. "I can't stop thinking of you."

"I hope—never mind."

"What, Brin?"

"Bad timing."

"Say it."

"Well, okay. Was going to say that I hope you think of God more."

"Of course I do." Ivan frowned. He was irritated at this new Brinley.

Pious. Questioning his every move.

Can't a man just enjoy the evening without being reminded of anything serious?

"Sorry. I'm learning to be thankful for everything God has given me, for life, salvation, my family, you."

"Good to know." Ivan rubbed the back of Brinley's hand gently. She had such smooth skin. No scars anywhere that he could see. "I'm surprised at how soft your hand is considering you do house renovations."

"I don't do them myself most of the time. I have Toby to do all the work for me."

"Toby?"

"Tobias Vega. He's my GC—general contractor." Brinley chuckled. "He hates me now. He's having a hard time getting along with my interior designer."

"If they don't get along, why put them together?"

"They have to get along. They're the best people I have. I'm sure they'll figure it out. I want to move into my new house ASAP."

Ivan sat back as the soup came. Brinley had opted to have her salad served at the same time as Ivan's main course. They said a blessing for the food and then Brinley told Ivan not to wait for the soup to get cold.

"Want some of this?" Ivan's spoon was in midair across the table. *Hope this isn't breaching any table manners.*

Brinley leaned forward over the small table and sipped. "That's pretty good."

"More?" Ivan asked, somehow remembering the cookie pieces that Brinley had fed him in his basement not long ago.

"No, thanks." Brinley dabbed her lips.

"Maybe you can show me your new house," Ivan said, enjoying another spoonful of delicious soup.

"Yes, as soon as it looks like a real house inside. It's sort of partly gutted right now. If you want to see what a war zone looks like, we can see it as it is."

"No hurry. I'd like to see it when it's done, though. I'm visual that way."

Their main courses came and then it was all about eating as Ivan made a big show of eating his lobster sans shell, like he was swallowing gold foil, which incidentally was sitting on top of the intricately plated dish. He decided to save the gold foil to remember this evening by. No need to mess up his digestive system.

"Don't make me choke, Ivan." Brinley was trying to hold it all in as she munched through her beef steak salad.

When Ivan saw the dessert he offered part of it to Brinley. "I didn't say half, okay? I said *part*."

They ate the whole dessert with nothing to spare.

"I'm going to pop this dress," Brinley whispered.

"Next time wear a stretchable one."

"Good idea."

When the guest check came, Ivan nearly fell off the chair onto the shiny, polished floor. Even the speck of dirt he spotted on the floor by the table where the server had passed must've been expensive.

The numbers were unmistakable. They were three figures long and twice as much as he had expected to fork out tonight on the new credit card. He had been using that credit card to pay his bills for this month. He was sure there was a couple of hundred dollars left on there, enough for this meal and the tips.

Maybe he shouldn't have ordered that lobster dish. He couldn't return the gold foil now. Who put gold foil on dishes, anyway?

Maybe it'll just go through.

I'll deal with the overdrawn charge tomorrow.

Maybe he could call his friend, Sebastian, and get an IOU. Ivan retrieved his disposable phone and texted Sebastian.

I'm at your restaurant with my girlfriend. Short of money. Can I get an IOU? Pay you back.

No immediate reply.

He peeked into his old wallet with black duct tape at the bottom. He kept that part away from Brinley so she couldn't see that there was a rip in the wallet that he had repaired some months before. There were no other credit cards he could use. They were all maxed out. As for his debit card, forget about it. Nothing there.

He was quite sure that he was short. Not sure by how much since he hadn't worked on his finances in a few days. He had thought he had set aside a couple of hundred dollars for this dinner. Only now the bill said he owed Saffron over three hundred dollars, not including tips. A bowl of soup, salad, two main dishes, two extra side dishes, one dessert, soda, water, taxes. That was all. He peered at the check again.

Oh, my gold foil lobster thingy was $265.

Not $26.50.

Yikes.

Well, he'd never been to a restaurant where they didn't put dollar signs in front of the prices nor decimal points at the end of them. He had assumed—

The bill shook in Ivan's hand.

He started to panic.

~

"*A*re you okay?" Brinley asked.

Across the table, Ivan was sweating.

"Fine. Fine." He tugged at his neckline. His tie skewed sideways. If she didn't know any better, she'd say that his right hand—his good hand—was shaking holding that guest check.

Brinley watched him place what looked like a brand new unscratched credit card into the guest check folder. The server came and took it away.

Ivan checked his phone again.

"Expecting a call?" Brinley wondered who he had texted earlier.

"Uh, my friend Sebastian. Maybe he'll come out here to meet you."

"That'll be nice."

Then he pushed back his chair. It creaked. Several other customers glanced his way. "I'll be right back."

He was gone a long time.

Brinley finished her mineral water. The server was back before Ivan returned. He refused to put the check down.

"May I see it?" Brinley asked.

"I'm afraid I need to speak with the gentleman."

"He's probably in the men's room. Anything I can convey to him when he gets back?"

"Not sure if he wants you to know..."

"Know what?"

"That his card was declined."

Brinley remained calm. Ivan needed a budget. If they were to go further in this relationship, she was going to require him to get on a budget. "Let me see the bill."

Yikes. Ivan's done it this time.

Brinley couldn't believe how much it had cost either. She reached for her purse and retrieved four one-hundred-dollar bills. "Keep the change."

"Yes, ma'am."

As soon as the server left, Ivan was back looking distressed.

"Everything okay?" Brinley asked. "You're not getting sick, are you?"

"No. I'm fine. I was trying to get ahold of Sebastian, but he's not available."

"Well, are we ready to go?" It was dark outside and pushing nine o'clock. Brinley wanted to go home and go to bed. Tomorrow morning she would get back on the treadmill.

Before Ivan could answer, the maître d' came to the table. "Miss Brooks, Mr. McMillan, I hope you've had a pleasant evening."

"Beautiful view, great food, excellent service," Brinley said. "What more could we ask?"

"That you come back soon, perhaps?" he said.

"Your mother and sister frequently stop by for lunch when they're in town. Perhaps you'll join them sometime."

"Of course. I will, Rémy."

"Thank you and have a wonderful night."

Ivan cleared his throat. "The check?"

"It's taken care of, Mr. McMillan." Rémy's voice was suddenly cold, Brinley thought.

"That's great." Ivan sat up straighter. "I guess Sebastian got my message. Well, Brin, let's go home."

CHAPTER FORTY-FIVE

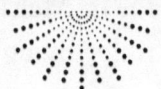

*T*he old curtains held together by duct tape
fluttered a little when the heater revved to
life. Next to it and under an old desk, Ivan stretched
out his legs to catch the heat through the socks on his
feet.

It was late, pushing three o'clock in the morning.
But he had to stay up. The bills weren't going to pay
themselves.

He had spent hours moving dollar amounts on
paper to try to pay all the bills. Water, gas, and electricity came right after food. Grandma Yun's medications and vitamins would be out-of-pocket as his
music studio health insurance wasn't going to cover
any of it. Ivan's own prescriptions would be taken
care of by the disability insurance. *We hope.*

Then there was gas for the truck. He couldn't
ride his bicycle until his left hand had enough
strength to grip the handlebar. Until then he had to

drive the truck to find work. The truck could take him far in case he found work on Jekyll or somewhere off St. Simon's Island. He could sell the truck and buy a cheaper car, but who'd want a poorly maintained 1945 Chevy truck?

Ivan went down the list. Tens of thousands of dollars of unpaid credit card debt he couldn't possibly pay now. Nearly two hundred thousand dollars of house mortgages spread over three loans, one primary and two liens. He wondered how long it would take to pay all that off.

He dared not ask God to rescue him because part of the debt was his own doing. Then again, God could solve this problem.

Lord, fix my finances. Help me get out of debt. Help me never to get into debt again.

This was a new month, and almost everything was due or overdue. Ivan stared down at the lists of income and expenses. Without his students, his music studio income had been zero dollars since January. He would have to miss a third house payment or pay partial amounts to all three mortgages. Perhaps he shouldn't have tried to pay off the liens back in November. It had caused him to skip a house payment.

What in the world had he done?

Now they were in trouble. According to Matt, Georgia law said that three missed payments would trigger the bank's foreclosure proceedings on Grandma Yun. The house was in her name though Ivan paid all the bills.

How could I do this to her?

Instinctively, his right hand gripped his left wrist as the twisty, seizing pain ripped up his wrist. His thumb pulsated and so did several of his fingers. The swelling had gone down after two weeks of therapy, but the pain inside the wrist was still there.

Ivan feared he had more damage than the doctor and X-rays could tell.

The vent in the old house quieted. Ivan started to feel cold again. In the middle of winter, the only way Ivan knew to keep the heating costs down was to wear more clothes at night. Sweatshirts and sweatpants were not nearly enough. Ivan pulled the old blanket from his high school days, folded it in half, and hung it over his shoulders.

There. He was warm now. Barely.

He wondered if Grandma was as cold as he was. Perhaps she needed more blankets and quilts. He didn't want to go downstairs to check on her. She was a light sleeper and his walking around looking for blankets in the linen closet in her bedroom would wake her up. He decided that if she was cold, she could get the blanket herself.

He went back to the pieces of paper scattered on his table. He had printed out some sort of chart. His old laptop was whirring on its last legs. He entered those expenses into his accounting software, and found that he was short on everything except his occupational therapy sessions.

Those were somehow taken care of.

Hmmm...

He had assumed it was his disability insurance, but he doubted it paid for everything. He jotted down a note to himself to call the therapy center to find out who had been footing his bills.

Ivan moved numbers around to no avail. He couldn't make the house payment if they were to have money for food. Without income sources other than Grandma's social security checks, they would have to live off credit cards again for the second month. He had already maxed out two of those credit cards. It made no sense at all for him to write checks off one credit card to pay off another. But desperate people didn't always do common sense things.

I have to find a new job.

Or sell the house.

Or both.

Where would they go if they sold the house? There were a couple of trailer parks they might be able to rent in. Or they could move to Atlanta to live with Ivan's sister, Willow. Willow might be mad at Ivan, but surely she wouldn't turn away her own grandma who had raised her. Maybe as Ivan regained his strength he could help teach piano or sub for Willow in her studio.

What kind of other music work could a one-armed violinist do? Ivan wasn't sure. SISO could use a better music librarian, but that position was also part-time. What Ivan needed was a full-time job, even if at minimum wage. Something that had health-care for him and Grandma.

Ivan opened up a spiral-bound notebook and

began jotting down his job jar for the next day, which would be here in a few hours when the sun rose. First thing he should do was call Matt Garnett. Matt owned two businesses next to each other, one an antique store and the other a thrift shop. Ivan figured he could try to get work there to hold them over for four months until he could play and teach violin again.

Ivan leaned back against the rickety yard sale chair. He rubbed his temples. A headache started from one side of his head and shot to the other side.

"How did we end up this low?"

They had been struggling, but had managed to make ends meet and pay the mortgages. He loved his music studio and SISO experiences. What changed all that? Wh—

Brinley Brooks.

Everything had turned upside down since Brinley showed up. Sure, she had done some good things for the McMillans. Grandma owned a new motorized wheelchair now to get around at home and at church. The commode had been fixed. The termite problem under the porch had been exterminated.

Then Brinley had gone and done the unthinkable. She had bought the 1721 Schoenberg Stradivarius violin in a fundraising auction, and loaned it to SISO, who then let Ivan use it.

And here we are.

One missing violin, several broken bones, and

two lost jobs later, Ivan could see clearly whose fault it was.

He had been blind; he didn't see it coming. Rich people were nothing but trouble for poor people. It would've been better had the two worlds kept to themselves.

Ivan groaned.

How had it happened? How had he fallen in love with someone like her standing there at the pier watching right whale migration? What in the world made him kiss her a second time at the top of the lighthouse? And to reveal to her his dream of opening a music studio in that warehouse building in the Pier Village district?

Could it be possible that God had brought Brinley into his life and that they hadn't bumped into each other? Why would God do that?

Ivan tightened the ratty blanket around his shoulders, and rolled onto his old creaking bed. Would God have brought Brinley into his life to bless him and Grandma?

Nah. We've never been that blessed.

~

*I*van woke up with a kink in his neck and his cell phone chirping in his ears. He hadn't planned on answering it, but his finger didn't get the memo. By the time Ivan realized it, he was turning over on his bed and saying hello in a raspy, just-woke-up voice.

"Hey, man. You rang?"

Sebastian Langston. *I should thank him.*

Ivan cleared his throat. "Hey, Seb."

"Sorry I missed your call. I'm in Miami at the food festival here. I ran out of juice on the phone."

"Not a problem. I appreciate your taking care of the situation last night."

"What situation?"

"At your restaurant." Ivan wondered how to say it without showing shame. Shame that he had no handle on his finances. Shame that he had taken Brinley out without enough money on his credit card. Shame that he had no money in the bank to even withdraw enough cash at a teller to cover the dinner.

"What about it? You said something about IOU?"

Ivan detected some tentativeness in Sebastian's voice.

"Yeah. I'm sorry, Sebastian. I had no idea the dinner was going to cost that much, and I had no idea my collectors cashed my payments, so I am eternally grateful, friend, that you gave me that grace and mercy about my insufficient funds. I'll pay you back whatever I owe you, all right?"

There. I said it.

It was true that the collectors had cashed the checks he had written against the credit cards, those checks that had come in the mail together with the temporary credit cards that he had activated to pay the bills. Unfortunately, they had all arrived in the same week, depleting his credit card. His new credit card. He had lost count how many new credit cards he'd had in the last twelve months juggling payments.

"Seb, you there?"

"I'm here. Let me check on something and call you back, Ivan."

"Okay." Ivan put his cell phone on the stack of bills on the table and traipsed to the bathroom to brush his teeth as quickly as he could in case Sebastian called back.

He wanted to make good on this IOU. He was probably about a hundred dollars short, so if he sold something, he might be able to get the money to pay Sebastian back. He looked around his bedroom for something he could sell. Grandpa Otto's World War II medals were probably not worth much. The old nineteenth-century McMillan family Bible was too precious to sell. He wandered into his closet, pushed here and there.

He saw his box of music manuscripts.

When he had been touring the world trying to establish Jade Strings as the go-to ensemble, he would stop at old music shops across Europe and pick up old violin music sheets, some in ink, some pencil, and all handwritten. He could ask Matt if his antique store would like to have them. He could get an estimate and give Matt a discount. It would still be a better deal than what he could get from the pawn shop in Brunswick.

He dived for his cell phone at the first ring. "Yeah?"

As expected, it was Sebastian. "Hey, I called

Rémy, my maître d', and he said that it's all been taken care of."

"That's what I'm saying, Seb. Whew. You rescued me from embarrassing myself in front of Brinley." It was bad enough that he had no money. It was worse if Brinley saw him in his poverty. Not that she hadn't already figured it out. But a man had his dignity.

"I didn't do anything, Ivan. I told you."

Oh no.

"My phone had no battery," Sebastian said. "I got it charged up this morning, and heard your message for the first time ten minutes ago."

This is bad.

"So who paid for my dinner last night?" Ivan asked, fearing the answer.

"Well... Rémy said the lady paid in cash."

The lady paid in cash.

Brinley.

Now my shame is complete.

Ivan couldn't remember the rest of the conversation with Sebastian, but he hurriedly said goodbye and hung up.

"Who am I kidding?" he asked himself. "I can't even go to a restaurant like rich people, eat like they do, and pay like they can."

They're the lords and ladies of the manor, and I'm just a poor serf.

"Note to self! We live in two different worlds. There can't be a middle ground." Ivan ran that thought through his mind as he got more upset by the minute. "I'll always be the hired entertainer. Nothing more."

Not a hired entertainer, but a bottom feeder.

Yeah. Once a bottom feeder, always a bottom feeder.

"How can a bottom feeder date a lady of the manor?" Ivan knew then that he and Brinley were never meant to be. In the scheme of life, she was the one who had everything, and he, the one who had nothing.

We live in two different worlds. There is no middle ground.

What about their kisses at the pier and lighthouse?

I'm sure the kisses were a stupid mistake.

CHAPTER FORTY-SIX

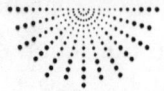

"*H*e won't come out." At the bottom of the stairs, Yun McMillan tried to mask her pensiveness. "Maybe it's the painkillers."

"You think that's making him sleep this much?" Brinley counted to ten and then knocked on the door again. "Ivan? It's me."

"Maybe we shouldn't wake him up."

"That's what you said Thursday when I called, Yun." Today was Saturday and Ivan still didn't want to see Brinley. She wondered what was going on. What was making Ivan lock himself away from the world?

"I'm sure he's not starving," Yun offered.

"Yeah, you mentioned the food wrappers in the trash can at night."

Yun shifted in her electric wheelchair. She looked older now than the week before. Brinley couldn't believe that Ivan could be this heartless, letting his grandmother fend for herself. She made a mental note to get Yun some help.

For now, this minute, she had a bigger problem. An oversized child was ensconced behind that old wooden door, and the only way to break in was to destroy part of the old oak panels, circa 1900, and she couldn't do that if the integrity of this historical home were to be preserved.

I don't have time for this.

It had been a mentally exhausting week for Brinley. She had spent the entire week dealing with a squabbling contractor and designer rushing to complete her new house. Add to that the paperwork required to purchase Brooks Renovations, stocks and all, from Dad. As nice and as generous as Dad was, he wasn't about to give away his pet company for next to nothing. The multimillion-dollar deal went through in the end, even though Brinley knew the bills from her business attorneys would be tremendous.

Still, Dad could now continue to support Mom's expensive buying habits with those extra millions. Market value of the company.

Thank God it's done now.

All she had wanted was to kick back and relax, but that wasn't meant to be the moment she received Yun's text this morning.

Brinley banged on the door again. "Ivan! Lunch is getting cold."

A muffled noise. Then: "I'll eat later."

"He's alive." Brinley sighed. She went downstairs. "When do they ever grow up?"

"Men in general or musicians?" Yun chuckled.

"Is that an indictment of yourself?"

"Brin, there is always a child in us, that carefree spirit of wanting everything to be beautiful and nice and lovely. Life is not always that way. Ivan is handling his pain and difficulty badly, but I hope you don't think all Christians behave this way."

"We all have different stages of spiritual maturity. I get that. What I don't get is this. Why on earth, with God's power, do we wallow in misery, thinking the world has ended?"

"The world as Ivan knew it has ended. Violin is all he knows since he was four."

"I'm sure he's more than just a violinist."

"You and I know that. But does he?" Yun wheeled toward the kitchen. "We'll need patience with him."

"And prayer." Brinley followed Yun. At the island, she unpacked the Southern Soul Barbecue boxes.

"Indeed. Lots of patience and prayer." Yun headed for her CD player on the counter next to her old refrigerator. "And maybe a slap upside the head."

"For sure." Brinley laughed.

Yun tried to swap out a CD from her player, but the buttons didn't work. Brinley stopped divvying up the beef brisket and Brunswick stew to go help her.

"Looks like it's broken." Brinley read the CD cover. Hymns. "Okay. Let's eat while it's hot and I'll play some of these songs for you on the piano. How does that sound?"

"You don't have the sheet music."

"Not yet. I'll buy them on my iPad." Brinley finished plating their lunch, saving some for Ivan in a container. She labeled it with his name and a smiley face on it, and put it as close to the front as possible on a prominent shelf in the refrigerator so he could see it right away the next time he opened the door.

Yun said the blessing, a long one, longer than her usual mini prayers.

Brinley listened intently, wondering why it'd taken her this long to kneel at the foot of the cross when all the riches of the universe were right there in the palm of God's hand. How much of God's blessings had she missed in her twenty-six years of life?

Or perhaps she hadn't missed any. God had blessed her anyway because His love was great that way.

"Amen." Yun dug in.

Brinley ate slowly. Everything from Southern Soul Barbecue was delicious, from the hickory-smoked beef to the plain white bread. They talked about nothing in particular. Yun wasn't preachy today. Something seemed to be on her mind, Brinley could tell. The nonagenarian ate very little, as if she had to save it for more than one meal.

"That hit the spot." Yun placed a wrinkly hand on Brinley's arm. "Thank you. You didn't have to do this."

"Happy to, Yun. Now. About the hymns. I take

requests." Brinley reached for her tote bag and the iPad inside.

"I like everything on that CD. Pick any one you like."

"I can do that."

They adjourned to the family room.

Soon, sheet music downloaded, Brinley sat down at the old Victorian piano, all eighty-eight keys still intact, but in need of a tuning. Brinley managed as best she could without being distracted by some of the voiceless keys.

Yun's voicing the lyrics more than made up for the poorly tuned piano. Brinley continued playing, a silly smile pasted on her face. Her heart was full and she was at peace. This was one of the simple things in life she'd craved. And now she had it.

All to Jesus I surrender...

Brinley wasn't sure when Judson Wheeler Van de Venter had written the lyrics or when Winfield Scott Weeden had put it to music, but she had heard it at Seaside Chapel more than once when Grandpa Brooks had taken her to church back in her teenage years.

So much time had passed since then. But the old hymn remained.

I will ever love and trust Him...

In His presence daily live...

Brinley continued sight-reading as Yun's voice rose to finish the song with gusto. Her eyes sparkled when she finished singing.

Brinley swiped the iPad to get to the next song.

"Oh, this one is Ivan's favorite," Yun said.

"Is it?" Brinley wasn't here to play it for Ivan. It was for Yun, to help her feel better about her grandson's plight, and perhaps to make her own self feel better too. But hymns and spiritual songs weren't to make people feel better, were they? Brinley knew these were offerings of praise and adoration to God.

So. I will play this next song for You, Lord Jesus. And only You.

The iPad screen blurred the words of Fanny Crosby's old hymn. Brinley dried her eyes and reached for the black and white keys, adding to the notes on her iPad as she went on. She couldn't hear Yun singing along, but it didn't matter. She was playing "Blessed Assurance" for the Lord. And only Him.

This is my story, this is my song...

Praising my Savior all the day long...

In her mind, Fanny Crosby had nailed it. That hymn had summarized all that Brinley had found in Christ. She hung on to the last note.

"Can you remember your improvisation?"

The whisper in her ear startled her.

Brinley spun around and came face to face with Ivan. He straightened up. She left her bench and almost hugged him. But she didn't because of his cracked ribs.

"Your ribs?" she asked.

"They're fine."

Brinley pointed to his left wrist in a splint. "Does it hurt?"

He didn't reply.

"How long have you been standing there?" she finally asked, trying to appear insouciant about her memories, but failing.

"Long enough to see that you transposed the key."

She hadn't even realized it. He had somehow sneaked up on her near enough to compare the notes on screen with the notes on the piano.

"Does that mean you're back?" Brinley asked.

"Back where, Brin?"

"Back to music." *Back to me?*

"I'm done with music."

"What are you—"

"We need to talk, Brin. See me in my studio?"

~

"*Y*ou can't come here anymore, Brin." Ivan tried to remain impassioned, but he felt uneasiness in his heart at having to tell Brinley these things.

"Shouldn't we let Yun determine that since it's her house?"

It wouldn't be her house for long once it's fore-closed. "I need to get my life back in order."

"It's out of order?"

"It's been a mess since you and I started dating each other." Ivan didn't want to blame her, but the words came out that way.

"So it's my fault?"

Ivan sighed. "You're a distraction."

"I'm a distraction."

"Stop echoing me, Brin."

"I don't get what you're saying, Ivan. I thought we had something special. You kissed me twice."

"Mistakes. They won't happen again."

The pain in Brinley's face was too much to bear. Ivan turned away.

"You're taking it out on me because your wrist is broken." Brinley's voice was tearful.

"My career is over."

"But not your life." Brinley frowned.

"My career supports my life."

"I thought your life is in Christ."

She talks like Grandma now. "Of course."

"Then why are you looking to yourself to solve your own problems? With God's help, we can go through this difficult time. Together."

"There's no *together*, Brin. Please go on with your life and let me be."

I can't believe I'm breaking up with her. For a moment, Ivan was no longer sure this was what he should do.

He prayed again. And again, God was silent. One thing he knew, though. He and Brin were never meant to be.

And yet...

Brinley seemed to sense what Ivan was struggling with because she reacted. She reached for Ivan again, her hands on his arms. The fragrance of that light perfume invoked the song he had started writing for her back in December.

She came closer, and lifted her chin toward his face.

Ivan turned his lips out of reach.

Just out of reach.

He stepped back. From now on their lives would bifurcate. "We live in two different circles, Brin. Circles that don't intersect. They collide."

"Then our circles are too small."

Our circles.

It was like her to be inclusive, Ivan thought. She'd always been kind, generous, considerate. And he'd played her like a fiddle. Now he was casting her aside.

Dear Lord, forgive me for sinning against this woman.

But he knew he had to let her go. Free her to live her new life.

I have to protect her from me.

"I wish it could be different," Brinley said. "I wish that we didn't have barriers between us."

"Barriers we were born with, Brin. Nothing we can do about that."

"I disagree."

"See? We can't even agree on basic things."

"This is not basic, Ivan. This is your misconception about our relationship, and possibly about God."

"You got saved, what, a month ago, and now you're all spiritual and know all things?"

"Not what I'm saying."

"What could you possibly know about God? You're such a new Christian."

"I am still learning about Him, but I do know one thing." Brinley pointed to Ivan's wrist. "I know that nothing is impossible with God. He can heal you in so many different ways."

Sounds like something Grandma would say.

And yet...

"He can choose not to heal me."

"That's possible, but if that's the case then He has something better in store for you, Ivan. From the pit a concerto rises."

"From the pit a concerto rises?"

"Stop echoing me, Ivan."

And yet...

All his life Ivan had wanted to be a concert violinist. What if that wasn't what God wanted him to do? The thought scared him. As if on cue, his left wrist twitched and a sharp pain shot up his arm to his elbow. He winced.

"Your wrist is not your life, Ivan."

Ivan knew she was right.

And yet...

"Please don't come here anymore, Brin. What we had was in the past. It's over. Go on with your life. Find someone who can take care of you better than I ever can."

"Who's telling who what to do now?"

"I want you to have a great life, Brin. But it's not with me."

"And you've determined that because you broke your wrist."

"I've had time to think about it." His wrist wasn't healing. It had been three weeks since the cast came off. He couldn't do anything with his violin.

"You're thinking with your emotions, Ivan."

"Emotions? What can I say? I'm a passionate man."

"Mozart had emotions too, Ivan. And he died in poverty because he couldn't manage his rich life."

Mozart? She's insulting me with Mozart? He had no comeback for that.

"If you're in pain, this is not the time to make life-changing decisions—"

"Change? Everything has changed, Brin." He raised his left wrist in protest. "My concert career? Over. SISO? I've been replaced. My auditions with ASO? Canceled. My hope to play in Boston? Forget it. My music studio? Closed. My bills? Mounting up."

This broken wrist is the death of me.

The more he thought of it, the more his anger rose. "All because of your stupid Strad. I want my life back!"

"It's my fault now?" Tears welled up in Brinley's eyes. "I thought you wanted the Strad. Didn't you?"

"Don't you get it? You ruined my career, my life, everything!"

Ivan couldn't believe he said that. He'd taken it out on Brinley. He wished he could take back the words. He was about to pull her toward him, kiss away the tears, and tell her everything was going to be fine.

But he'd be lying. Here on out, nothing was going to be the same again.

And yet...

No. It has to end right now or my life will spiral further down.

"So let me give it to you plainly. Goodbye, Brinley Brooks. Close the door on your way out."

CHAPTER FORTY-SEVEN

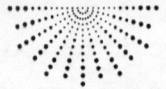

*T*hat night Brinley dreamed that she was a little girl sitting on Jesus' lap in a wide open field. All around them, fluffy white flakes fell from the sky, covering the ground in a sea of creamy white. Before the question reached her lips, the answer came to her heart.

Manna.

Brinley woke up so full she wasn't hungry for breakfast.

Manna.

God will provide.

Over a cup of coffee in her parents' sunroom against a backdrop of distant ocean waves and gulls, Brinley replayed the entire conversation with Ivan in his studio the day before.

His words burned in her ears. His censure of her was confusing. All she could think of was what Yun had said to her.

We'll need patience with him.

Lots of patience and prayer.

She opened the Bible Yun had given her. Yun had suggested she start reading the New Testament and she had tried to do so almost every day. She wanted to develop the habit of daily Bible reading.

Yun had also suggested that Brinley join the Seaside Chapel women's Bible study group. Even though they met Tuesday evenings at the pastor's house and Pastor Gonzalez's wife usually taught, Brinley didn't have to be a church member at Seaside Chapel to attend the Bible study. Good to know. In fact, she was hoping to get some more information at church this morning.

She glanced at her iPhone. It was only eight o'clock. Sunday school didn't start until ten, and the service until eleven. She had an hour or so to putter around. Next week she would move into her new home, only two blocks from Seaside Chapel. She could walk on the beach to church if she wanted to.

Ping!

Startled, she checked her messages. Yun McMillan had texted her, wanting to meet her at church at 9:45 a.m. to introduce her to the different Sunday school classes she could go to. Yun told her that Ivan wasn't feeling well and he was skipping church that morning. The way Yun phrased it made Brinley wonder what was happening in Ivan's mind and heart. It was as if he was playing truant from God. Brinley texted Yun back to arrange a place inside the church to meet.

Well, at least she wasn't going to be alone at church.

It dawned on Brinley that perhaps one reason God had saved her at this time was to provide her a shield before her budding relationship with Ivan collapsed. In the deep recess of her heart, she was surprised and glad to be at rest. Her rest baffled her a bit. She began to understand what Paul meant by incomprehensible, unexplainable peace.

I have it now.

The peace of God I've been looking for all my life.

Without a boyfriend. Without a fiancé.

She'd be lying to herself if she said Ivan's rejection didn't affect her even a little bit. After she had left Yun's house the afternoon before, the rest of her Saturday was ruined. She had been too numb to eat supper, and she'd gone to bed early.

And woke up full of the comfort of God.

I have to forgive Ivan.

Brinley blinked away the sting in her eyes, turned to the book of John and began reading the next chapter.

~

*B*rinley stepped into the quiet hallway, cold and old, a grim reminder of Grandpa Brooks's failed lifetime attempt to recover his family's Damaris Brooks Stradivarius. A short walk led her to a locked steel door. She placed her hands on the biometrics panel, stared into the retina scanner, and punched in the ten-digit code she had memorized and changed every year.

The steel door opened to a lost world of woe. There were twelve of them here, various instruments hand-crafted by the luthier Antonio Stradivari himself. Not by his students, but by his own hands. From the 1700 guitar hidden away in a Tuscany farmhouse for three hundred years, undocumented until it had ended up at Christie's auction house before Grandpa whisked it away to be reburied here, to the violas and cellos that Grandpa had spent an enormous fortune securing, the entire collection was a silent tomb.

No music filled the air except the ping of the elevator door outside the vault, and only when Brinley came down here.

All stringed instruments, all silent voices never to be heard again unless Brinley did something about it. Standing there in her silk pajamas, she wondered what she could do to speed up the opening of the SISO Museum of Musical Instruments. Like Ivan had said, these Stradivari-made instruments were meant to be seen, displayed, exhibited, shared.

Brinley moved among dustless glass cases toward a wall that held a row of Stradivarius violins. Right in the middle was an empty case. Hung on the wall, it had been empty since 1972 when Grandpa Brooks started this underground private museum. Nailed to the wall next to the case were the words, "1698 Damaris Brooks."

Brinley held up her iPhone and snapped a photo

of it. She forwarded it to Helen Hu with the message, "To let you know your effort will not go to waste."

The private investigator had been close to tracking down the stolen Strad with Interpol, and yet in the last week, no more word from her. Last Brinley had heard, Helen was in Brussels. Sure, Dad was taking over the Brooks' side of the investigation, but Brinley still wanted to know what was happening. This was her Strad, after all, her Strad that she wanted—

Forget him.

Even if Ivan could play the violin again, their relationship had abruptly ended because he couldn't handle a broken wrist. It was a sad commentary on human nature.

Five Strad displays away was another empty case. For two days it had housed the 1721 Schoenberg Stradivarius, two days before Brinley lost five-point-four million dollars in investments. Now all she could do was wait for her insurance claim to be paid. She hoped the violin would be recovered undamaged soon.

Brinley made her rounds through the room. She remembered being in this room with Grandpa in his last days. Remembered the promise she had made. In spite of the odd vow that Grandpa had made her take, it all made sense now. God had used the strange request to protect her and save her for her future husband.

Whoever he will be.

Here in this room were representations of the Brooks family wealth. This Stradivari collection had only been Grandpa's hobby, just as Dad purchased homes on at least two continents because he could, and Mom bought furniture everywhere to fill those houses because she must buy what she saw. Money seemed to ever flow every which way.

Brinley knew she had everything but love until God's love came. She wished she could now share the love of God with Ivan.

Ivan?

Forget him.

A sound from her iPhone broke Brinley's muse. Time to go to church.

~

*B*rinley held her Bible tightly against her chest and walked into Seaside Chapel to meet Yun, who had gotten a ride in the church van earlier in the morning. The rotunda was crowded with people milling about, but she found Yun by the sanctuary door in her motorized wheelchair chatting with a woman whom Yun introduced as Skye Langston. A hello and a hug later, Brinley went with Skye downstairs to the basement, where most of the Sunday school classrooms were.

"I saw you with Ivan on the Sunday before Christmas," Skye said. "I had to be someplace after the service, so I couldn't stop to say hello."

"Well, nice to meet you now," Brinley said.

"Yun said that Ivan's struggling with his wrist recovery."

"He needs a lot of prayer."

"Tell him we're praying for him."

Brinley wasn't sure how to respond, but straight up was probably best. Casual-like. "Oh, we're not together anymore as of yesterday."

"I'm sorry to hear that. I bet it's his fault." Skye rolled her eyes. "He can be kind of rude like that."

Rude? "I don't know. I'm still processing it all."

"Well, this could be awkward, but he's in this Sunday school class I'm taking you to, although he's not here today—according to Yun."

Do I want to be in Ivan's Sunday school class?

Should she? What if Ivan showed up one day? He had been attending that Sunday school class long before Brinley was saved. She was the newcomer. If anything, she had to be the one to leave. Then again, why should she? Wasn't Seaside Chapel big enough for both of them?

"It should be okay for today," Brinley said. "Maybe next week I'll find another class to attend."

"I don't see why you two can't sit on opposite ends. It's not like you have to talk with each other. Besides, Sunday school is only forty-five minutes long. And Ivan doesn't own the place."

They arrived at an open door where laughter and chatter spilled into the hallway. Brinley followed Skye to an empty seat in a large circle of chairs, maybe a dozen or more.

"We sit this way so we can see one another," Skye explained. "I prefer this to staring at the back of people's heads."

Brinley didn't care either way. This was her first time in Sunday school in a long time. When Grandpa Brooks had been alive, they had all been active in church.

Skye introduced Brinley to a couple of people around them. One of them was Emmeline O'Hanlon. Brinley tried not to react visibly to someone who had dated Ivan the year before.

"Ivan told me a lot about you," Emmeline said.

"Has he?" Really, Brinley was skeptical.

"He and I traveled a lot together. I play harp in SISO."

Her emphasis of *together* bothered Brinley. Then she reminded herself that she and Ivan weren't an item anymore, their erstwhile closeness notwithstanding. "I like harp music."

"But you like violin better," Emmeline said.

Whatever. Brinley turned to the other person standing there. "And you are?"

"Tristan Rao. Geriatrics." He seemed to have startled himself with his own words and started to mumble.

"We're not at a medical convention, Tristan." Skye laughed. To Brinley, she said, "He gets nervous in front of beautiful women."

"You're very pretty." Tristan then backtracked. "Sorry. Did it again. Foot in mouth."

Before he made any announcements, the Sunday

school teacher for this twenty- and thirty-something class introduced himself to newcomers as Benicio Ketteridge. He asked Skye to tell everyone about their visitor.

"Thanks, Ben. This is Brinley Brooks. She's a new believer. Yun McMillan led her to Christ about two months ago, right?" Skye turned to Brinley.

Brinley noticed now that Skye spoke with her hands, and she had some burn marks at the base of her palm. The shape looked like the handle of a pot. Poor girl. What happened there?

"Yes. The week before Christmas." The night before Ivan broke his wrist that changed his life and ended their relationship.

"Are you attending any Bible study?" Benicio asked.

"Olivia Gonzalez invited me to her Tuesday night's."

"I hear she's got a good group going. Several ladies here are in that group, including Skye."

"Good to know. I'll try to go as soon as I get settled."

Benicio raised an eyebrow. "Settled into town?"

Brinley nodded. "I'm moving to St. Simon's from Atlanta. I have family here."

"Nice. Let us know if you need help in any way. We'll pray for safety and a smooth transition."

"Thank you. I want everything to go well." Was that too much to ask for? All Brinley wanted was a miracle from God to make her general contractor, Tobias, stop fighting with her interior designer and rental manager, Megan Zimmerman. Then the house would be renovated on time for her to move in next week.

Next week!

"Since Brinley is new here, let's go around the room and introduce ourselves." Benicio waved his pen in the air. "That way we won't be strangers to her when we see her at church."

There was Matt Garnett, whom Brinley had met on Christmas Eve when he went with Ivan to pick her up in the church van for the evening service. He looked tired and his long-sleeved shirt was all wrinkled. He sat next to Sebastian Langston, who looked like a hunky male model. Turned out he was Skye's older brother and chef-owner of that expensive Saffron restaurant on Jekyll Island that had been the last straw for Ivan.

It also turned out that Sebastian was very needy. He had many prayer requests for his girlfriend whose name Brinley couldn't remember, but should have since he had mentioned it umpteen times in the same sentence.

When Benicio started to teach, Skye helped Brinley find Ephesians in her Bible. She could have searched for it on her iPhone, but she wanted to read it out of a printed book today. And so she did. After Sunday school, she made a note to herself to read that passage again because Benicio had said way more than she could process.

Something about God instructing the husband to love his wife.

Love.

Benicio said that if the husband didn't love his wife, he was sinning against God. Thus, Brinley reasoned, a man shouldn't marry a woman he didn't love. Brinley mulled over that as several people in the Sunday school class walked together to the sanctuary for the service.

Clearly Ivan doesn't love me.

"Brinley."

She heard it twice before she turned to see who had called her. It was Matt Garnett from Sunday school.

"Matt Garnett," he said.

"I know. You said that in Sunday school."

"In case you don't remember."

"I might not tomorrow, but right now I do."

"Well, that's why I'm going to give you my business card." Matt handed Brinley a crumpled card, a corner torn. "If you need any antique furniture to decorate your new house, give me a call. I own Garnett Antique Shop at the Village."

"I've seen the store. Haven't had time to go in. Maybe I'll do that next week."

"Great. I'll be in town next week. I also own the thrift shop next door. If you want some bargains, call me."

"Love a good bargain."

Leaning down, Matt whispered, "Be patient with Ivan. He's an idiot."

Brinley laughed so hard she began to choke. "We were just going out. Nothing to it."

"No? My friend is crazy in love with you."

So why did he dump me?

"He'll come around. For now, he thinks he has to be a certain somebody for you to love him."

Oh.

CHAPTER FORTY-EIGHT

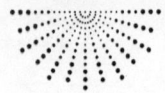

"*I* want to move in this Saturday, Toby. Where is my countertop?" Brinley stood in her incomplete gourmet kitchen with both hands on her hips.

Dust and debris and delays were everywhere. The cabinets had no doors, the faucet had no sink, and the counters had no granite tops.

Outside it was raining heavily, so heavy she couldn't hear the ocean anymore. All she could hear were thunder strikes and sheets of rain coming down. It had been raining for two days, but eventually it would let up. She hoped her house wouldn't wash away into the ocean, it being this close to it and all.

"Ask her." Tobias pointed to Megan who had been fuming since Brinley walked into her new house through the back porch door.

Megan sighed. "We had a miscommunication—"

"*You* had a miscommunication," Tobias snapped.

"I didn't. I told you my installers have another job this week. So the granite countertop needed to arrive by last Friday or it won't be in until next week."

"Who placed the order?" Brinley asked.

"I did." Megan leaned back against the topless island. "They told me Friday. They had a delivery mess-up. The countertops arrived this morning, but Toby's guys are not here."

"When can they come back?" Brinley asked Tobias.

"Next Tuesday."

Megan stepped forward. "He has another crew in Savannah, but he won't send them here. They could install this in the next two days."

"It's Megan's fault. Why should I cover for her?" Tobias asked.

Brinley looked back and forth at the two of them. "I think it's my fault."

"Yours?" Tobias and Megan said in unison.

"Yep. I made a mistake." Brinley swiped her iPhone and looked up her contacts. "I put both of you in charge of my reno. Equal footing and all that. Now we're late by two weeks as it is, and you're telling me we could be late again. Problem is, we need one head, and not two heads butting each other."

Tobias and Megan both nodded.

"So let me call Alonzo, and you can take orders from him tomorrow onwards." Brinley found the number. "Then you can get everything done by Saturday."

"Wait a minute." Tobias put up his hand. "Did you say Alonzo? My grandpa?"

"Uh-huh." Brinley's iPhone was at her ear.

"You don't want Grandpa in charge, Brinley."

"You can do better?"

"Yeah."

"Then why haven't you, Toby?"

Megan laughed.

"You too." Brinley put down her iPhone. "It's not like you two are going to marry each other. I'm only asking you to work together for the next four days, get my countertops in, repaint the sunroom walls in the right color, get the light fixtures installed, clear my driveway so I can move in this weekend. Is that too difficult for you or do I need to hire your competitors?"

"I don't appreciate the threat." Tobias frowned.

"Here's the threat, Toby. I need a place to stay. Rent me a place or get this house done."

Megan turned to Tobias. "You can't afford to rent her a place, Mr. Vega."

"No. I don't think so." To Brinley, Tobias said, "Okay. But don't pull the *grandpa* card on me again."

"Maybe I'll put him on the payroll for insurance." Brinley chuckled.

Tobias rolled his eyes. "See what I have to put up with, Megan?"

"She gets things done, for sure," Megan said.

"Now that we're all lovey-dovey, could you do me a favor?" Brinley asked. "Hug and make up."

"What?" Megan said. "I'm not touching him."

"Alonzo or hug?"

Tobias moaned something unintelligible and made the first step toward Megan.

Brinley watched them hug and then glanced at her watch. She had to leave now if she were to make it to the Seaside Chapel women's Bible study group. "Hey, I said hug and make up, not hug and make out."

Tobias stepped away from Megan.

"Four days," Brinley warned them. "You have four days."

～

*B*rinley left Tobias and Megan in some sort of unspoken truce as she headed down the road toward Seaside Chapel. Olivia Gonzalez lived across the street from the church. The rain hadn't subsided when Brinley arrived. She wished she could park closer, but there were cars in the driveway and up and down the street.

Four houses away on the narrow street, she got out of Dad's nondescript SUV and reminded herself to buy her own car next, although Dad did say he didn't mind her using his car perpetually. Thing was, he had meant his Bugatti. The last thing she dared to do was to park a two-million-dollar car in a garage that didn't have the same level of security as the Brooks estate. *No, thank you.*

Since she had returned to St. Simon's, she had been driving this SUV, which Malik, Mr. Security, said was the safest for her with its ballistic wind-shield. The reinforced SUV door was super heavy. She had to put her entire weight on it to get it closed. That was why Malik had insisted she used this SUV above all the other vehicles Dad had.

Seriously, I need my own car.

The irony of getting out of a secure vehicle only to walk about unescorted at dusk wasn't lost on her.

With a Publix apple pie in one arm, an umbrella in the other, and her tote bag with Bible and iPad hanging off a shoulder, Brinley arrived at Pastor Gonzalez's house and was greeted by his two teenage daughters. They took the pie from her and showed her to the family room where about ten or so women had gathered. Brinley didn't think she was late at all. Apparently some of the women had come earlier to gab.

Skye Langston waved to her and patted an empty spot on the couch. It seemed to Brinley that she had saved that spot for her. Nice. As Brinley sat down, a little teacup dog came up and brushed past her jeans.

"Good to see you," Skye said.

"Good to see you too." Brinley saw the Band-Aid on Skye's palm. "What happened to you?"

Skye brushed it off. "Cooking accident. Hot handle. Happens sometimes."

"You cook a lot?"

"I'm a personal chef."

Brinley's eyebrow rose up. "Really?"

"Have to put my Le Cordon Bleu training to good use."

"I could use a personal chef." Anyone would be better than Mom's personal chefs who had come and gone.

Around them, more people arrived and looked for seats.

"Let's talk. One of my clients canceled and I do need a new client. What's your email?" Skye typed it into her tablet. "When do you want me to call you?"

"How about next week? I'm moving into a new house this weekend. Kinda busy. Do you usually cook and bring or come and cook?"

"I do both."

"You might like my new kitchen." Brinley looked past Skye. Where Olivia Gonzalez was sitting, Brinley saw one of her daughters whisper in her mother's ear. Olivia perked up.

"I hear that everyone is here. So let's pray," Olivia said. "For those who are just joining us, we usually do our Bible study and then we eat dinner. That way we can chat all evening after having put God first."

Put God first.

Brinley thought that was a sermon in itself. After praying, Olivia asked someone to read aloud Luke 10:27. A volunteer did. Brinley followed along in her Bible from Yun, which had a slightly different translation.

> *So he answered and said, "'You shall love the Lord your God with all your heart, with all your soul, with all your strength, and with all your mind,' and 'your neighbor as yourself.'"*

Emmeline sat down after she finished reading from her Bible. Brinley thought she had a clear and pretty voice.

"Love God first," Olivia said. "That's not to be confused with serving God in a church or ministry or on the mission field. Those can come as a result of your loving God. But when you love someone, you think of that person almost all the time, don't you? Loving God with all our soul, strength, and might means thinking of Him first, putting Him first above all others. In your heart, God has first place. Is He number one in your life? Better yet, is He your life?"

Putting God first above all others.

Above Ivan.

Brinley prayed for God to show her how to focus on God and not on how Ivan had treated her after all that she had done for him.

"Love God first," Olivia said. "Then love your neighbors as yourself."

Love God first.

Then love Ivan.

When Brinley saw that other women were taking notes, she did too. Olivia kept on making her points in a calm manner in spite of the loud thunder and rain outside the cozy little house.

By the time they ate dinner, Brinley was famished. They scattered all over the house and ate everywhere there was seating. Brinley went back to her corner of the sofa, where she had left her tote bag.

The mushroom risotto was delicious. She ate quietly as she looked around the room, wondering how people could hold a plate in one hand and a fork in another while standing up, eating and talking at the same time.

Her gaze veered to Olivia sitting in the dining room. A slither of light coming from the chandelier shone down on her. So calm. So peaceful in spite of her not being able to see. She wondered how long Olivia had been blind.

Next thing Brinley knew, she had walked into the dining room. "Is this chair taken?"

"Sit down wherever there is an empty seat," Olivia said. "Whoever left it can sit somewhere else. It's okay."

Brinley sat down across from the pastor's wife. "I'm Brinley Brooks."

"I recognize your voice."

"I enjoyed your Bible study. I learned a lot this evening."

Olivia smiled as her fingers groped her plate for a dinner roll. "God's word is inexhaustible."

Inexhaustible. "I'll remember that."

"In my life, I've learned to trust that God will always be an answer to any problem I face, especially when it comes to people. People are messy."

"I agree." Brinley polished off the risotto and wanted more. "Would you like me to get you anything? Another drink? Seconds?"

"Thanks, but this is all I can eat."

When Olivia couldn't find her fork which had fallen off her dinner plate onto the plastic tablecloth, Brinley recovered it for her.

"Thank you, Brinley. I usually don't lose my fork." Olivia smiled. "Someday when I get to heaven I can see all these."

"How long have you... I mean..."

"Since I was a little girl. I was ill and then I couldn't see anymore."

Brinley blinked. "Was that before or after you met Jesus, may I ask?"

"Before." Olivia paused. "It's better to be physically blind than to be spiritually blind, you know?"

Brinley nodded, but she knew Olivia couldn't see that. "I know."

"Spiritual blindness is harder to cure. Sometimes it's forever."

"That would be bad." Brinley glanced past Olivia to the wall behind her. Was it her imagination or was something crawling down the wall? It was smooth and shiny in the light. Like sheer sheets of—

Water.

"Uh, Olivia?" Brinley walked around the table toward the wall and lifted her eyes. There were several wet spots on the ceiling where it met the sheetrock wall.

"Yes, Brinley?"

"Is your roof leaking?"

"Oh, it leaks from time to time. Why?"

"Water is coming down the wall here."

"Is it? Like a waterfall?"

"Like a waterfall." *Unbelievable.*

"I suppose that's bad."

"Very. I think we better get out of the dining

room. The ceiling could collapse." Brinley picked up Olivia's plate, leaving her own, and helped her out of the dining room. "I know a good roofing company. Would you like me to call them?"

"Well..."

"I work with these people all the time," Brinley added.

"Give me the number, then. I know my husband has been talking to some volunteers at church, but I don't know where the discussion is at, so let me talk with him first so we'll be on the same page." Olivia called for her daughters.

"Fair enough."

Be on the same page.

The thought wasn't lost on Brinley that when she married—someday, maybe—she would like to be on the same page as her husband. She could name nobody in her family who was on the same page as their spouses. Dad and Mom were usually on Mom's page. Diehl and Isobel—oh well. They'd been divorced two years. Definitely not on the same page. She hoped and prayed that Zoe and her new husband, Quincy, were on the same page for the baby's sake.

Somehow Quincy reminded her of Ivan.

Though their relationship had been short, having begun in December and ended in February, it had been a mixed bag, Brinley thought. Some days she and Ivan had been on the same page on things. Some other days, not.

Lord, help me let Ivan go.

CHAPTER FORTY-NINE

*I*t ticked off Brinley to no end that in spite of her pep talk, Tobias and Megan were still late in finishing up her new house on the beach. The rain that had lasted three or four days didn't help, though she thought that was an excuse for the conspiring pair to get away with it. Brinley thought she might threaten to yank the Pelican Road project from them, but reno people she could trust were hard to find.

She decided that after they were done with the house, she'd invite the two over for a debriefing dinner. Surely they could evaluate the situation and find ways to improve on timely delivery in the next project. After all, she owned Brooks Renovations now, all of it, and the last thing she needed was to fail Dad.

And possibly God.

No one was at home this Valentine's Day at the

Brooks family cottage. Mom and Dad were now traveling through Italy celebrating love. Zoe and Quincy were in Paris with *their* morning sickness.

Diehl was at work in Atlanta. Diehl was always at work. Someday he'd burn out and crash. *Wait and see.*

She prayed she didn't have to step in to cover for him in Brooks Investments. She was busy with her own company.

Lunch was a simple bowl of organic salad with slices of grilled beef on top. Brinley thought she could cook the beef herself if someone showed her. Maybe she should learn to cook. Or maybe she should call Skye, the personal chef. That'd be the easy route. Skye would probably love her new gourmet kitchen.

As soon as Toby installs my countertops.

Then I can move in.

Sigh.

Sitting on her favorite barstool at her parents' kitchen island, Brinley studied the music sheet she had placed across the island. She was going to learn this piece today. She had played it a couple of times since she had bought it at a music store in Paris, but had lost interest in it after Ivan had dismissed her abruptly.

Well, Mr. McMillan, you don't own Bach.

She adjourned to the foyer, mercifully cleared of Christmas pine trees. Instead, a soft wash of faux suede taupe treatment covered the walls surrounding the Steinway concert grand. Brinley propped up the piano lid before she sat down on the piano bench.

She lifted the fallboard and spread the music sheets across the rack, put her iPhone next to it where she could see—so she couldn't accidentally sit on it and crack the screen—and began to play.

Falteringly at first.

Then it all came back to her. Those years and years of piano lessons that Mom and Dad had paid for her. She had been the only one who had taken piano lessons through high school. Diehl had stopped at eighth grade, having been more interested in football and girls than piano auditions and recitals. As for their sister, Zoe, she had always been into woodwind instead.

After getting the bass clef notes down, Brinley sight-read the treble clef notes until she could play the entire *Air on the G String* from memory. That didn't take too long because it was such a simple piece.

Over and over she played it, remembering that December evening at Zoe's birthday party when Ivan had played it solo.

Our song.

What was happening with Ivan? Wasn't he supposed to be a Christian example to her? Why had he fallen apart when the bottom dropped out? Did real Christians do that? What about trusting God?

Pray for Ivan.

Those were the same words she felt in her heart the day she accepted Jesus.

"How do I pray for him, Lord Jesus?" Brinley asked aloud. "What do I pray about?"

Her iPhone leaning on the music rack chirped, and Brinley jumped off the piano bench yay high.

She swiped the screen. "Yes, Malik?"

"The answer to your question, Miss Brinley, is yes. I do know a decent Honda dealer. He has some new models in this weekend. I told him to expect you."

Brinley sat back down on the edge of the piano bench. "Thanks. Appreciate it. How late are they open?"

"Only until midnight. You don't have a lot of time."

"Funny, Malik."

"Do you need a ride over there? I'm free this afternoon."

"It's Valentine's Day. Don't you have a date or something?"

"No, I don't."

He didn't say more. Brinley was in no position to suggest that the widower change his status. Malik had his reasons for deciding not to remarry, and there was nothing Brinley could do about the war wounds and angst he still carried from his Special Forces days in Afghanistan nor about his lovely wife who had died of a brain aneurism a few days after their first wedding anniversary. Some things were best left buried.

"I'm busy running Brooks Security." Somehow Malik felt the need to explain. "There's no time for frills."

Perhaps he was rationalizing his life to himself,

Brinley thought. "Frills, Malik? All right. No need to explain."

"I was thinking that if you wanted to drive a hybrid crossover—or whatever you said you wanted—off the lot today, I could drop you off. Save you a trip."

"And maybe hang around to make sure they don't mess with me?"

"That too."

"Okay, Malik. I accept. Pick me up anytime."

"How about now? I'm outside."

The security office was in the guesthouse next door, but surely someone else had the weekend shifts. "Tell me you didn't work today."

"I gave some of my people the day off so they could spend it with their sweethearts."

"How thoughtful. You need a raise, Malik. I'll see to it."

"Why, thank you, Miss Brinley. I should hang out with you more often."

"Give me five minutes to be decent."

"I'll be right here."

It didn't take five minutes. Brinley ran upstairs two steps at a time, grabbed her purse from her bedroom, threw on a winter coat, and she was outside locking up the front door before Malik could finish his fries.

"Want some?" Malik pointed the cup of fries in Brinley's direction.

"Sure. I don't think it's good for us, though."

"Speak for yourself, Miss Brinley. I've had fries since I was a little kid."

The drive to the Brunswick dealership was greasy. Brinley wiped her fingers off on a paper napkin as best she could. "Any word from Helen about my Strads?"

"I talked to her last week. She's still tracking it. I don't know why she can't do it from over here. Costly for her to be over there in person, don't you think?"

"Sure was, but now that Mom and Dad have decided to join her, I'd rather she be with them than someone else. You never know what sort of things my parents will get into."

"Ain't that the truth. Tell me, is it true Ned used to be some sort of amateur sleuth?"

"In their twenties, before they had Parker, he and Mom roamed the world, solving crimes. Not sure if they were paid, but Grandpa Brooks used to say that they spent a fortune living the high life." Too much money in the family. Too little to do after college.

"How romantic."

"Getting into trouble was more like it. I wouldn't be surprised if Dad tracks down the Damaris soon. All he needs is one lead. After so many years, he has it now."

"And so much money spent on recovering one old violin." Malik didn't say anymore.

Brinley could guess what was going through his mind. "You're thinking there are hungry people in the world and all that money could be spent feeding them."

"Something like that."

"Well, we do feed the hungry and clothe the poor too. Grandpa's foundation has contributed close to a billion dollars to that over the years."

"I know and that's good."

"Glad you approve, Malik. I do agree, though. Maybe we can do more. Show more of God's love." Help people at church and in the community. There were poor people on St. Simon's Island too, people in poverty—

Ivan.

Why won't he let me help him?

CHAPTER FIFTY

*A*ll Ivan thought about as Matt Garnett drove him and Grandma to church in his van was that he was going to lose his health insurance in about a week. There went his wrist recovery.

Any day now, Grandma's house would go into foreclosure. No job. No income. He might as well go into bankruptcy.

"You remember my cashier who's supposed to go on maternity leave for a few months?" Matt asked as they turned into the Seaside Chapel parking lot.

"Yeah." Ivan felt bad that he had been slow in filling out the job application form.

"She just quit yesterday. So I need someone almost immediately. Maybe you could fill in for her? It's light work. No heavy lifting."

Ivan said nothing. Could this be a solution from God?

God?

God has abandoned me.

Or has He?

The battle in his mind and heart confused him. He didn't know what to think, what to feel, what to do. All he knew was that he was in a big financial mess and that because he was ashamed of it all, he had broken up with Brinley so she didn't see him this way.

"It's minimum wage, if you must know. But if you work full-time you get healthcare," Matt continued.

"That's very generous of you," Grandma Yun said from the seat behind them.

"That's what friends are for."

Ivan thought for a bit. Anything to hold them over would work. "After church today I'll get the forms filled out and email you."

"You do that." Matt parked his van.

"You have some sort of on-the-job training?"

"Part of the package." Matt exited the van.

"Thank you, Matt." Ivan followed him out.

Matt turned around. "Thank God, Ivan."

Yes, thank God.

It stuck in Ivan's mind as he helped Grandma out of the van and into her motorized wheelchair, which Brinley had bought for her at Christmas. She knew exactly what they had needed. His mind ran through some of their events together. The commode. The termites. The wheelchair.

Ivan wondered if Brinley still had—

Never mind.

He couldn't believe she was now his ex-girl-friend. How did that happen?

What have I done?

He walked into the Sunday school class and almost made a U-turn to get out of there.

Matt didn't say anything about Brinley in our class!

Sebastian Langston and his sister, Skye, blocked the exit.

"Hey, man! Good to see you back in Sunday school." Sebastian slapped Ivan's good arm. "Doing all right?"

"Yeah. Getting better every day."

"Excellent!"

Next thing Ivan knew he was sitting down and half-listening to Sebastian chattering. That guy could talk. Ivan was uncomfortably aware that he was across the circle from Brinley. They could see each other eye to eye.

Brinley didn't seem to pay him any attention, which bothered him. She was talking to several people—men. That bothered him more. When Tristan Rao stood closer to Brinley—

We broke up.

Ivan tried to keep an "I couldn't care less" face on, hiding behind his growing beard that was becoming itchier and itchier by the minute.

Benicio Ketteridge began to speak. "Hope everyone had a good week."

Nods and amens and positive replies went around the room.

Ivan felt that he was the odd one out. It had been a miserable week. His wrist had hurt most at night. OTC pain tablets hadn't helped much. It didn't help his wrist, and it didn't help his life.

He was acutely aware that he was now penniless, although Matt had come to the rescue with a job offer.

His elderly grandmother praying quietly with tears streaming down her face reminded him over and over that he was a failure in life.

A failure!

No. I didn't have a good week.

Benicio looked directly at Ivan. "Glad to have Ivan back with us. How's that wrist?"

At the corner of his eye, he saw Brinley look his way.

"Slow going, but getting better." It was one of those things. When people asked him how life was, he'd always say, "Fine." It was an outright lie.

Was his wrist getting better? No idea. Only God knew. And God, the One who had made him and saved him, seemed to be silent right now.

Why, God? Why don't You heal me right away?

"We will keep you on the prayer list," Benicio said. "These things don't heal overnight."

It may never heal.

Benicio looked around the room. "Major praise report, people. You remember the heavy rain this week? Pastor Gonzalez's roof leaked, and the roof almost came down on some sweet ladies during the women's Bible study."

"I was there," Skye said. "And so was Brinley and Emmeline. We all saw it. Water coming down the wall like sheets. It was crazy."

Brinley and Emmeline at the same place? Ivan couldn't imagine what they could have said to each other.

"Not to worry," Benicio continued. "They have a new roof now, and the wall has been repaired."

"Insurance took care of it?" Matt asked.

"After the deductible."

"Do they need help with that?" Matt asked again. "We can all give some."

"No worries. An anonymous donor took care of it. They're getting their entire house repainted inside and out. God provides. That's what we're going to study this morning if we get going here." Benicio opened his Bible. "Turn with me to Philippians 4:19, please."

Ivan knew the verse by heart. He followed along as Benicio read it aloud. "'And my God shall supply all your need according to His riches in glory by Christ Jesus.'"

Need? Needs?

Yet something else that Benicio had said vied for his focus.

An anonymous donor.

He glanced at Brinley. She was reading the Bible on her lap. That Bible looked like the one Grandma had given her. She looked so sweet, so pretty sitting there with her Bible. Grandma had said that her newfound faith was genuine.

Good for her.

~

Ivan was the first person out of Sunday school right after closing prayer. He wanted to go outside and stand for a few minutes to catch his breath, but the February weather was still cold out there and it would bother his wrist.

Stupid wrist! Heal!

After splashing water on his face in the men's restroom, he realized he looked pretty bad wearing that scraggly beard. But he didn't feel like shaving it off. In fact, he didn't feel like doing anything right now, not even attending the church service. He wanted to go home and lock himself up again.

Vanish from the world. Hide in a cave.

Grandma is probably disappointed in me.

Well, it was going to get worse when they were both thrown out in the streets. He had called his sister, Willow, in Atlanta with whatever minutes he had left on his cheap disposable cell phone, and asked if she could take them both in.

Willow had said she had a new roommate taking up the other bedroom, but if Grandma didn't mind sleeping in her bedroom, and if Ivan didn't mind the futon in the living room, they could make it work. It pained Ivan to think that his poor sister would have to sleep on the floor indefinitely.

Poor sister.

Poor.

Ivan spoke to nobody as he dragged himself to the back pew. When he was a little kid, he liked sitting in the back row because nobody told him not to suck his thumb or sit up straight. Everyone's back was turned toward him. He and Quincy would sit there pinching each other to see who could handle the pain the longest without shrieking and getting slapped by Grandpa Otto's big hand.

Quincy had always won.

Ivan had known then, as Vittorio had found out, that he had a low tolerance for pain.

Matt sat down next to him. "Easy to find when you're sitting in the back row."

His friend handed a piece of folded pink paper to Ivan. "Read it."

"Why?"

"I want to know what it says."

"You read it, then." Ivan handed the paper back to Matt. "Who is it from, anyway?"

Matt handed it back. "I think you'd better read it. Go on. Service is starting."

Up ahead the choir was filing in.

Not knowing what to expect, Ivan unfolded the paper. There was a fragrance. A familiar fragrance. *Pleasant days.*

He held his breath and began to read.

I'm sorry I ruined your life. Please forgive me.

It was unsigned, but Ivan knew exactly who had written it. It was the same handwriting on the *Trust*

God bookmark he had ripped up and thrown into the trash can, and then picked up and taped back together using packing tape, shortly after freeing Brinley from his sorry life.

And yet.

A tenderness touched his heart, the same feeling he had the day they had walked on the pier and climbed the lighthouse. Yet, as quickly as it had come, he dismissed it.

Just a silly emotion.

Must've been some strong emotion because Ivan then fought it all the way through the church service, on the drive home, and the rest of the Sunday afternoon, evening, and night. And it spilled over to the next day, culminating in a big, bad headache.

He picked up the note and read it again.

Oh, Brin. I wish I could tell you I love y—

No.

He tore the note to shreds.

CHAPTER FIFTY-ONE

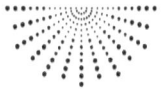

*M*onday couldn't get here fast enough for Brinley. She was at her new house bright and early to wait for the movers to get her truckloads of furniture from the storage compound in Brunswick all the way to her new oceanfront retreat.

She had given Tobias and Megan four days to finish up and yet they were still late by two days due to various "unforeseen" circumstances. As promised, she had called Alonzo Vega to supervise the bickering duo, more to keep her word and irritate Tobias at the same time than to get any work accomplished.

She knew Tobias was going to hate her for a while, but eventually, he was going to thank her for making his dad feel useful and for giving them father-son time that Tobias had been lacking.

See, I know my old friend more than he thinks.

Before she could unlock the front door, it swung open.

"Morning." Tobias looked like what the cat dragged in. Red bloodshot eyes, tousled hair, crumpled plaid flannel shirt with a button missing, jeans with paint all over them.

"Just morning? Not *good* morning?"

"Technically, it's not a good morning. Didn't want to give you the wrong impression."

Brinley tipped her coffee mug at him. "I'd offer you coffee, but I don't share cups."

"I've had too much." Tobias limped away, his leather tool belt dangling around his hips.

"Why are you limping, Toby?"

"Tobias."

"Tobias, old friend, why are you limping?" Brinley followed him up the stairs. A sonorous and reverberant snoring cacophony increased as she climbed.

There, inside the door of her guest bedroom, Alonzo Vega was sleeping on the hardwood floor, a corner of the drop cloth as his blanket.

"When your dad wakes up, tell him he's fired for sleeping on the job." Brinley sipped coffee.

Tobias laughed so hard he dropped the roller from his hand. Fortunately it was clean. He caught it before it hit the floor, though.

"Good catch, Toby. Might have a career in baseball after all."

"That ended in high school with a torn ACL, Brin."

Brinley nodded. "I know. Is it bothering you now? Is that why you're limping?"

"Nah. A hammer fell on my foot this morning. Last night. Whenever." He opened a can of paint.

Brinley stopped him. "Toby, look at me."

"Got work to do." He was about to pour the paint into a tray.

"Stop, Toby. Now."

Tobias looked up. "Don't tell me it's the wrong color. I'm not repainting the wall again!"

"Toby." Brinley took the can of paint from him. It was pretty heavy. She replaced the lid. "I want you to go home. Get some sleep. Nobody is going to stay in this guest room for who knows how long. Maybe my brother will stop by, but it won't be in the next few weeks or even months. So go home, get some sleep, and come back tomorrow."

"I'm not going to get fired?"

"Not today." As the sun shone in, Brinley thought that the white tones on the wall had a warm and soothing feel to it. "If you take your dad with you."

"I told you hiring him was a mistake." Tobias arranged the paint rollers, brushes, and paint cans against the wall.

"What mistake?" Alonzo's voice was raspy and came from behind them. He was sitting up.

"We're calling it a day and going home, Dad. Hey Brinley, you need any help later today with the move or something?"

"Megan and the movers should be here, and she'll tell them where I want everything to go. It's going to be just the way I had it in my Atlanta house."

Megan had started out in Atlanta before exhaustion caused her to move out of the busy metropolis to the more laid-back Georgia coast. Somehow Dad had found her, and she revived her interior design business. Doubling up as a property manager gave her the income she needed to feed her workaholism.

"Same design, huh? You don't like changes, do you?" Tobias asked.

"I do too." Brinley waved her arms at the sea blue wainscoting and the white frames of the transom windows. "I changed some colors."

"But they're essentially what you had before. In your old house."

"Which does have a nautical theme."

"In the city." Tobias helped his dad to his feet.

"Nothing wrong with living in the city," Brinley said.

"It's landlocked."

"What's landlocked?" It was Megan's voice coming from the door.

"You're ready to go to work, aren't you?" Brinley took in her sneakers, jeans, and pretty blouse. From the corner of her eye, she saw Tobias looking in the same direction she had been.

Megan ignored Tobias. "Movers are outside, Brinley."

Brinley waved to Tobias and his dad as she went downstairs. She liked her open floor plan. The kitchen flowed to the dining room to one side and to the family room on the other side, connected by a salvaged wide-paneled oak floor, which Brinley had bought at a local antique auction years ago just waiting for a house to put them in. Dating all the way to the early nineteenth century, the old oak floor had come from an old church in Darien that had been razed for development.

Beyond the oak floor in the currently empty living room, the new French doors beckoned Brinley to check out their shiny brass knobs and clean shatterproof panes. One never knew when a hurricane would strike.

Pretty soon my furniture will fill up this family room.

To those furniture pieces, she'd add small little finds here and there on her travels, unlike those expensive and large period pieces that Mom would buy.

She knew exactly where her piano was going to be. Right next to the piano she'd have a music stand. An antique music stand Mom had found in Vienna and was going to give to her. A music stand for—

Why am I thinking of him?

Brinley knew she had to let him go.

But how, Lord?

She was still ruminating on what to do when the movers backed their tractor-trailer onto her driveway. All her belongings from her house in Buckhead, except for her grand piano, had fitted into that semi. She might have to buy new furniture to cover the rest of the space in this new house.

Her iPhone chirped.

It was Yun McMillan. Brinley quickly answered it. "Is everything all right?"

"Yes, I'm fine. Thank you for asking."

Brinley waited.

"Would you like to continue our Tea for Two?" Yun asked. Brinley thought her voice sounded tentative.

"Of course. You know Ivan doesn't want me to go to your house, but you're most welcome here at my new home if you don't mind all the boxes and dust."

"Congratulations, Brinley. I'm happy for you. No, I don't mind dust at all. How about tomorrow?"

Nervous voice. So unlike the Yun she had met in December.

What have you done to your grandmother, Ivan?

CHAPTER FIFTY-TWO

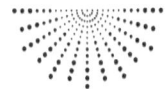

"*P*eter asked the Lord about forgiveness. He said, 'Lord, how often shall my brother sin against me, and I forgive him? Up to seven times?' We find that in Matthew 8:21." Yun's voice was clear.

Brinley wasn't sure if she wanted to hear that. She wanted to be mad at Ivan.

"It's not natural for us humans to forgive. But it's supernatural for us to do so," Yun added. "If we are in Christ, God gives us the grace to forgive."

"I want to slap him."

"Me too, Brinley. Me too. That boy needs a spanking."

Boy? Ivan was thirty. "Sure behaves like he does."

"You and I know that, but he has to learn it the hard way. Give him time."

How much time? Brinley sighed. "More tea?"

"Yes, please."

Brinley poured more chai. "I'm glad we can continue to have our tea time."

"I hate sneaking around Ivan, but it's the only way to get here."

"I can send Cara to pick you up anytime, you know," Brinley said. "No need to get a ride from someone else."

"Oh, they're happy to do it. Don't worry." Yun sipped tea with delicate hands on the china cup.

Brinley was enjoying her chai too. They were sitting in her newly painted heated sunroom where the winter sun shone in but the cold stayed out. Outside the sunroom, the day was bright and the sky a swath of blue and white. The distant surf sounded muffled this afternoon.

Inside the room, boxes were everywhere. The furniture pieces had arrived from her Atlanta home, and some were still sitting in the trailer parked outside the house. For now, Brinley had an armchair and a love seat, the latter of which she had offered to Yun.

"I'm thinking of selling my Victorian upright," Yun announced.

"Are you serious? Why?"

"I'm going to be ninety-eight next month." Yun brushed invisible lint off her wool dress. "I've had the piano long enough. It's someone else's turn to play it now."

Brinley knew there were more reasons than that. Perhaps Ivan's being out of work had something to do with it. And the mortgages Yun had accidentally mentioned back in December. The situation was terrible, but there was nothing she could do about it without stepping on Ivan's dignity in the whole matter.

Yeah, and then she went and destroyed his entire livelihood by giving him what she had thought he wanted: a Stradivarius.

"Do you happen to know someone who might want to buy it?" Yun asked earnestly.

Me! Me! I like old things, remember?

"Well, how much are you selling it for?" Nonchalant-like.

"The last appraisal said it was worth twenty-six thousand. I'll sell it for twenty if I can get a quick sale."

"Let me ask an appraiser friend of mine to see if he can give you better numbers." Brinley picked up her iPhone and went to work.

Yun sat there, waiting patiently.

Brinley wasn't sure what was going through Yun's mind. Had she even talked to Ivan about this? What did Ivan think about the family heirloom being sold?

Her piano appraiser friend texted back. He wasn't in Savannah. He was out of town for his winter break, and wouldn't be able to get back to the Georgia coast right away.

No matter. Either way Brinley knew she wanted the Steinway. It would add to her collection of musical things in the vault—

You know, musical instruments are meant to be seen and played, not locked in vaults.

Ivan's words came back to her.

She frowned.

"What's wrong?" Yun asked.

"Bummer. The appraiser is on vacation and won't be back until after I've gone home to Atlanta," Brinley said. "How about this? I'll give you twenty-six thousand dollars now for the Steinway. After the new appraisal, I will pay you the balance of what it's worth."

Yun's eyes were wide. "You think it's worth more than that?"

"A lot more. My guess is it'll top thirty. But its history is priceless. It would be an honor to keep the Steinway for you so we won't forget its history."

Yun was visibly moved. "Thank you, Brinley."

"I can transfer the money now to your bank account. Or would you rather I write you a check?"

"A check. I'm old school. I don't know much about electronic bank transfers."

But you know what it is. "Or would you rather I give you cold hard cash in unmarked bills?"

Yun laughed so hard her cup was rattling on the saucer.

Brinley glanced at her iPhone. "It's not nearly three o'clock. The bank is still open. What say you if I write you a check and we go to the bank now and you deposit it?"

"Now? Right now?"

Brinley smiled. *It's just spending money.*

Besides, the old piano was cheaper than any other musical instrument in her collection. And way cheaper than what Ivan had called the "stupid Strad" that was still unrecovered. While Ivan was all huffing and puffing about the five-point-four-million-dollar Strad, Brinley was more concerned about recovering the other family heirloom. She'd pay a whole lot more to get the 1698 Damaris Brooks Stradivarius back into Brooks family ownership. In fact, she'd pay whatever the private collector would ask.

And I mean whatever.

If she had to sell some of her stocks at Brooks Investments, so be it. Grandpa Brooks had spent his entire life looking for that violin. And now she and her parents were very close to completing his quest.

"Yes, before you change your mind," Brinley told Yun.

"I'm not going to change my mind. I know you'll take good care of the piano."

"I will. When the SISO Museum of Musical Instruments opens up, perhaps I'll loan your Steinway to it along with the rest of my string collection."

"A collection? How many instruments do you have?"

"Not many. They belonged to Grandpa Brooks. He gave it to me before he died. But it was missing his great-great-whatever-grandma's violin."

"Yes, you mentioned the Strad at Zoe's birthday party."

It had only been a couple of months, but it seemed so far away.

How could she ever forget that *Air?* The way he had looked at her when he played it?

Our song.

The pain in her chest intensified. She breathed in and out gingerly.

I can't forget him. Help me, Lord.

The sooner she went back to work, the better. "If you don't mind, I'd like to move the piano today."

"You don't waste time, do you, Brinley?"

Brinley called the piano movers. Yes, they could do it today, but it would cost double. She put them on hold. "What time do you want them to go to your house?"

"If we do it today, we need to do it before five. That's when Ivan gets home from the doctor."

Oh. Ivan again.

"What did he say about your selling the Steinway?"

"He doesn't get to decide. It's my piano. My decision."

Ivan doesn't know. Uh-oh.

And Brinley didn't want him to stop the sale.

Yun seemed to sense that. "Let me tell you the truth, Brinley. Ivan isn't going to get his SISO job back anytime soon. His music studio is shut down for the foreseeable future. It looks like we're going to lose the house. I don't want to lose the piano too. I'd rather keep it in the family, but seeing the situation as it is, my guess is that the piano will be sold later as part of my estate sale or something. I'd rather know where it's going to go before I go."

"Please don't talk like that. You're not going anywhere, Yun. Have more tea."

Yun shook her head. "Someday if the piano makes its way back to my family, that will be fine. But for now I think it'll be safe with you."

"I'll take care of it. I promise." Brinley sighed.

Yun raised an eyebrow, waiting.

"I don't get it, Yun." It was a puzzle Brinley couldn't unravel. "Isn't Ivan a Christian?"

"Since he was six years old. You're asking what's happening with him? If God is so good, why is Ivan a mess right now?"

"Yes."

"God's goodness is independent of us."

"Why is Ivan miserable?"

"He is walking by sight and not by faith right now. He needs to get down on his knees and repent, but he's a stubborn boy. We need to wait for God to work in his heart on this."

"You're a patient lady, Yun."

"It says in Isaiah 55 that God's thoughts and ways are higher than ours. He sees more than we do. He does more than we can."

Brinley realized then that Yun was the only person she had ever known who seemed to have a Bible verse for every need.

"Pray for Ivan, Brinley. He needs all the prayers he can get." Yun put down her cup and saucer on the side table. "Now let's go before the bank closes."

Brinley helped Yun off the love seat and into her motorized wheelchair. Yun seemed to be getting proficient with that thing. She whirred it around to get her coat slung over the backrest of the love seat.

On the phone Brinley told the piano movers to meet them at Yun's address at four o'clock. She pocketed her iPhone and helped Yun put on her coat. The garage was near her new kitchen, but she had a ramp put in for accessibility in case she decided to sell her house later.

Yun was a pro with her new wheelchair. "I like my new wheels. Thank you for my Christmas present."

"You're more than welcome. Just don't get a speeding ticket." Brinley held the door as Yun puttered into the garage. "If you had a ramp like this you wouldn't need to climb those porch stairs."

Yun shook her head. "I need the exercise."

And it would cost money that Ivan didn't have, Brinley didn't say. *That stubborn dude!* If only he'd let her accountant help him sort out his bank account. He'd have a proper plan to get out of debt by now. But no. He had to learn it the hard way.

But he wasn't her problem, was he?

Then why is he still on my mind?

Brinley couldn't shake off the thought.

CHAPTER FIFTY-THREE

"What did the therapist say, dear?" Grandma Yun was at the screen door when Ivan trudged up the front porch steps.

Behind him, Matt backed away his van, its wheels crunching gravel on the way out. The sun came down on Ivan's back, but the winter wind blew away any warmth from his neck.

"Long road ahead, Grandma." Ivan's voice was low. He closed the door and bolted it.

"At least your bones are healed."

Ivan nodded. His ribs didn't hurt as much anymore. He could move his wrist some. He still couldn't lift heavy things, but he was getting there. He wished that Brinley could come over and massage his arm and kiss him and make him feel all better.

But she's history.

When Ivan turned around, Grandma was shuffling off on her walker. Was it his imagination or was she walking slower than she ever did?

"It might take less energy to use the motorized wheelchair, Grandma."

"I need the exercise." She went in the direction of the kitchen, and Ivan followed her.

"Four months will be here before we know it." It was a soft voice, but Ivan heard her.

"Grandma." He had to tell her the truth.

"What, dear?" She turned around.

"We don't have four months."

Grandma didn't move.

"We're way behind on our house payment." Any day now the house could be foreclosed on.

"I know. Then?"

"We'll go on an adventure and move in with Willow."

"She'll get tired of us after a few weeks."

"Hopefully my wrist will heal and I'll be back in business."

Do I believe that myself?

Ivan leaned against the doorframe and took in the sight of the old kitchen where Grandma Yun had taught him to scramble eggs when he was a kid missing his mother. His grandparents had kept the two boys and a girl occupied so they didn't think about how their mother had abandoned them to run off with some guy to who knew where. To this day Ivan had no idea where his parents were, whether they were still alive, or what they were up to.

"We have to keep praying."

Ivan could barely hear her.

"Yes, Grandma. Appreciate every prayer." He choked out the words.

"Thank God the tendons are not broken. Thank God we have insurance."

"Disability." Not enough, but somehow things were covered. He'd figure all that out later. "Don't worry, Grandma. I'll be functional. Maybe even play violin again. I won't be able to play Paganini or anything fast for some time to come."

Or have a crossover concert career.

"But you'll live." Grandma waved her hands. "Want something to eat?"

"What do we have here?" He walked toward the island. It was worn out, the Formica chipped and part of the side glue had come off, baring the stained plywood underneath it. Grandma had tried to keep it clean and that was the best they could do.

Grandma pushed the brown paper bag toward him. "Chinese takeout. Like we used to do on Thursday nights with Grandpa Otto. Remember?"

Ivan remembered. "We'd watch reruns on TV."

Maybe not.

He'd sold the TV yesterday morning to the kid down the street. A hundred dollars out of that. They could buy food for a couple of weeks.

If we watch our spending! So what is this takeout food I see?

"Where did you get the money, Grandma?"

"God always provides, dear." Grandma tried to

get a plate out of the cabinet, but she seemed to have lost strength.

Ivan quickly went around the island and helped her get a couple of dinner plates. They were chipped too, like everything else. He put the plates down. He helped Grandma to their rickety folding kitchen table and seated her.

Then he went back to the island and ripped the paper bag to get the boxes of takeout. As he was doing that he noticed the receipt. Including delivery charges, it was—

"Are you kidding me? Fifty dollars!"

"It'll be fine, dear. We won't have to cook for a few days."

"Yeah. It's a feast." Ivan bit down on his lips. He didn't want to scare Grandma with the news of the two checks that had bounced this week. Water and electric. Good thing the antique Chevy was paid for. He'd have to save gas by cycling more. But his wrist hurt badly when he held the handlebar. He'd have to get a ride from Matt. Matt said he didn't mind, but Ivan didn't want to impose on his old friend.

"So what's the occasion?" Ivan asked.

"Celebrating life."

"That's all?" Ivan placed a full plate of food in front of Grandma. There were almond chicken and beef and lots of onions and Grandma's favorite, shrimp fried rice.

Grandma Yun's eyes lit up. "I don't know if I can eat all this."

"I know you can." Ivan chuckled. "There's more, besides. Who wants to say grace?"

"You do it."

Ivan sat down. He'd make it brief. Thank God quickly and dig in. But as he opened his mouth to call out to God, he found that he couldn't speak. He'd been so mad at God that he found it hard to come now before Him, the Creator and Ruler of the universe, to thank Him for this food bought with money that would have to come out of their maxed-out credit card.

Why did God allow their life to be this hard? It was maddening.

Maybe he should talk to an accountant to get their finances straightened out. Well, wasn't that what Brinley had told him to do?

Brinley.

I can't get her out of my mind, Lord!

"Are you going to say a blessing or not?" Grandma asked.

"You say it."

Slowly, Grandma spoke. "Thank you, Lord, for who You are, for the many blessings You have given us over the years, for my Otto, who is in heaven now and whom I will see again soon, for my two wonderful grandsons, Quincy and Ivan, and my lovely granddaughter, Willow, in Atlanta, and the new great-grandchild to come, whatever his or her name will be."

As she paused to catch her breath, Ivan wondered when Grandma's prayer would ever end.

"And for dear Brinley, so sweet, so caring, so kind, who now knows You. Thank You, Lord, for saving her soul."

Why did she have to bring up Brinley?

"Her salvation means so much to me and might have been why You kept me on earth this long. Thank You for letting me share Your Gospel with her, for her listening ear and her desire to grow in grace day by day. So many blessings, Lord. Forever I will give You praise and honor and glory. And now for this food..."

Grandma went silent.

Ivan opened his eyes. She was wiping tears off her face. Her eyes were still closed and she continued praying. Ivan bowed his head again.

"And for this food, Lord, thank You. Thank You. In Jesus' name I pray. Amen."

Ivan dug in. It was just dinner. What had overcome Grandma?

"We're going to be all right, Grandma," Ivan said between spoonfuls of rice. "My wrists are insured and I'll try to see if we can get some sort of money to hold us over until I can work again."

"The studio?"

"When I get better I'll reopen it."

"You sound positive." Grandma managed a smile. "That's good."

They said nothing for a while.

"I'm sorry you had to hear the argument between Brinley and me the other day. I forgot voices carry from the studio."

"She didn't ruin your career or your life."

"Well, if she hadn't given me the Strad—"

"If you hadn't accepted it..."

"You have a point there. It's too late now. We've moved on."

"We can't move on past the point of our last error, Ivan." Grandma speared a shrimp with her fork. "And if we don't learn from our mistakes, we will be stuck in the roundabout for a while."

A roundabout. "I should write a book with all your sayings in it, Grandma."

"I have them all written down in the margin of my Bible next to the verses that inspired me, if you want to get started."

Ivan laughed. "You know, that's what I like about you, Grandma. Always looking forward. Never looking back."

"Oh, I do look back. All the milestones we have, dear, are our Ebenezers, memorials to the faithfulness of God. Never forget that God is always faithful no matter what happens to us."

"Since He is sovereign, He knew this was going to happen to us. Yet He let it."

"You know this is a fallen world, Ivan. Since Adam's sin, the whole world is cursed and tainted by sin. Pain and suffering and death are a part of our life on earth. But someday, when we get to heaven, it'll be perfect. Just you wait. And I'll see my Otto again."

"I miss him too, Grandma."

"He was a dear man, my Otto, although he had

no head for figures. I'm afraid you might have inherited some of that."

"I'm trying to get us out of debt and then we'll be fine."

"God can get us out of debt. Trust Him, Ivan."

Proverbs 3:5-6.

That verse that Brinley had been memorizing.

Ivan ate quietly. When he finished his plate, he placed a hand on his stomach. "That hits the spot. Thank you, Grandma."

He cleared the table. "Why don't you go rest while I clean up the kitchen?"

"I think I'm going to go lie down." Grandma Yun seemed to have difficulty getting out of the chair.

"Are you all right? You're not getting sick, are you?" Ivan helped her to her walker. Then he walked with her to her bedroom at the back of the small house.

"I forgot my Bi—never mind. I'll read it in the morning."

"I'll get your Bible for you, Grandma. Did you put it in the usual spot?"

"No!"

Ivan was taken aback. *What is going on?*

"No, Ivan. Tonight I am going to recite some verses I already know by heart."

"Sounds good to me, Grandma." *No need to be uptight.*

Ivan helped her get to the bathroom where she brushed her teeth and combed her hair. Then he put her favorite nightgown on the bed, and left Grandma in her bedroom.

He returned to the kitchen and put away the leftovers in the refrigerator.

I can't believe that cost fifty dollars.

~

*T*he house was quiet save for the water from the faucet and clinking dishes in the sink and his memories of Brinley drying plates in December. He remembered how she had disarmed his concerns and allayed his fears of being looked down upon as poor. Sure, but what had she really thought?

Forget her.

It could never be.

He wished the dishwasher wasn't broken. It was hard to wash everything by hand, but the latex gloves kept his hands dry. He tried not to use his left hand as much but he had no choice. His wrist throbbed as the soapy water sloshed over the plates and silverware. If he turned it the wrong way—this and that—a sharp pain in the wrist made him wince.

He tried to get his mind off the pain by thinking of something else. He thought of the things that Grandma had said to him this evening. She had always been a teacher. Even now at such a grand age, she had not stopped teaching her grandchildren.

Never forget that God is always faithful no matter what happens to us.

Had he forgotten God?

In his recent unfortunate circumstances, in his horrifying fear that he could never turn his wrist to reach the strings on the fingerboard again, in his anger over the potential loss of income doing what he loved best, in his inability to see any good in this tragedy, had he forgotten God?

Not in the sense that he had abandoned his faith, but that he was upset that God let all these bad things happen to his life and that somehow he had to fix things himself as if he were taking God's place over these problems?

Had he *forgotten* God?

As he dried the dishes and put them away in the cabinets, the coin flipped in his mind. *Has God forgotten him?*

Grandma Yun would object to that, but at the bottom of a hole with no way out, Ivan wondered about it. Had God just plain old abandoned him and his family?

Grandma Yun had always been a strong and faithful Christian. Why didn't God reward her? Why did God allow her life to be so bad and their living conditions so poor?

Sure, Grandma would say their lives were not all that *bad*. Someday they'd all go to heaven and things would be perfect.

Yeah. In heaven.

But they were here on earth. Next week, the house payment was due. They had no money to make the payments. All his income from SISO had been used to pay their multiple mortgages. At the back of his mind he wondered if they should have consolidated the mortgages or perhaps paid off the first before the second or third.

I'm a musician, not an accountant.

A headache formed at the top of his head and spread to all sides. He'd better get some sleep and think about this in the morning. A few days from now, he would start his first day of work at Matt's thrift shop. However, he wouldn't get paid until the following Friday. And minimum wage wasn't going to keep the house. It was too little, too late.

It seemed silly to get a performance degree from Juilliard and tour the world only to come to such a bitter end with his music career. Why did God allow this? Had God not given him the gift of music? Why take it all away? He was only thirty years old. What was he going to do the next sixty years if he lived that long? He had no other skills except music.

Sure. He could teach piano. But his first love was the violin.

First love?

Shouldn't my first love be God?

He felt ashamed as the verse from Revelation 2:4 filled his mind.

Nevertheless I have this against you, that you have left your first love.

That was one problem with living with Grandma Yun. She had made him and Quincy memorize so many verses that they were all coming back to spank and pinch him now.

Ivan wiped the counters and the island, wrung out the dish towel, hung it over the old faucet, and then turned on the nightlight so Grandma could see in case she came out to the kitchen in the middle of the night for some reason. He stood at the kitchen door. He could see himself and Brinley again, standing against the sink doing dishes that Sunday afternoon. He could hear her, hear what she had said to him.

So trust your God. Wait it out. It will turn out better than you thought.

Well, it hasn't, Brin. And maybe it never will.

Still, in his heart, Ivan knew Brinley had been right. Shortly after that, she had accepted Jesus Christ as her Lord and Savior. And then he had dumped her because he didn't want her to see him mired in his shaken faith. She had been growing exponentially as a new believer, whereas he had hit a slump in his spiritual growth. He didn't want her to see him like this.

A failure.

Perhaps someday when he had climbed out of this pit they could reconnect—

No. It's best for us to part ways. I'm no good for her.

"But is that what God would have wanted?" Ivan asked aloud to no one.

I'm not jealous of her spiritual growth and ashamed of my own spiritual collapse, am I?

He heard an owl or two hooting from the small grove of live oak trees behind the house. Somewhere in the distance a dog barked. A truck revved. Usual sounds of the night.

There you go. Life goes on.

Ivan was heading upstairs to brush his teeth and go to bed when he remembered that he hadn't checked the doors and windows and made sure he had turned off the lights. Saving electricity had been something that Grandpa Otto had harped on, and that he hadn't forgotten.

He had locked the front door earlier, but he headed there to it again. The living room was dark so he turned on the light to get to the windows and side doors.

Hmmm. When did we paint that wall green—

He froze.

Where's Grandma's piano?

CHAPTER FIFTY-FOUR

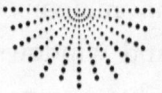

The next morning, Grandma Yun didn't wake up this side of life.

Ivan had gotten up early to get to the Seaside Chapel men's Bible study group meeting at the Scrolls bookstore. Running late, he had left the house without any breakfast and without knocking on Grandma's bedroom door. He didn't give it another thought the entire time he was at the Bible study and at Vittorio's therapy session.

By the time he had gotten home around nine or ten in the morning, rigor mortis had set in. Ivan called 911. The coroner estimated that Grandma had died sometime in the night.

His entire life with Grandma Yun flashed before his eyes when Ivan wept as they carried her body out of the house to the coroner's office to determine how she died. He could see Grandma playing the piano accompaniment as his younger self practiced his violin. He glanced at the empty wall where that old Victorian once stood.

Grandma had sold the piano three days ago so that they could pay part of the mortgage. It was all for nought because it wasn't enough. Nonetheless, Ivan hoped the museum that Grandma said the piano would eventually go to would take good care of their memory piece.

The next three days leading up to the memorial service and graveside funeral were busy days for Ivan. Quincy flew home from Paris to help with the funeral arrangements. Willow would be arriving soon from Atlanta to attend the funeral. They were all the family whom Grandma had close to her.

Ivan half-wished Brinley could be there, but she wasn't family, and he didn't want her to do anything more for him. She'd caused enough damage to his life as it was.

"Is there anything else you need?" Matt asked as they sat on the front steps of the porch under an overcast sky.

Ivan wiped his eyes with the base of his palm. He couldn't believe Grandma was gone, that she'd never walk across this rickety porch again, use her walker, tell him she was praying for him, and put up with him.

"No. You've done plenty, Matt. I appreciate it more than words. You're a good friend. No, a terrific friend."

A great friend.

Matt Garnett had donated a pine casket. He had

mobilized their entire church to chip in to pay for a burial plot. Almost every family at Seaside Chapel had contributed, even if it was a dollar here or there. Numerous ladies cooked dishes for the after-funeral reception at church. He had even made the musical and speaking arrangements for the memorial service.

It was all coming together because Matt was the ultimate organizer. He even bought Grandma's mobility scooter at a fair price so that Ivan wouldn't go broke from the funeral expenses.

"I'm praying for you, Ivan."

"Thanks, Matt." Tears streamed down Ivan's face. "It's my fault."

"She's a couple of years to a hundred years old. When it's time to go, it's time to go."

"She would still be alive if I hadn't stressed her out."

"You can't know that, Ivan."

"I wish I had managed our finances better. Then we wouldn't be behind in our mortgages, she wouldn't have to sell her piano, and we'd be living happily."

"If you want to use that line of reasoning, then how about this? If your grandpa had managed his finances better, his widow and grandchildren wouldn't be in this financial mess."

Slowly, Ivan he lifted his left wrist in the air.

"Put that down," Matt said. "I don't attend pity parties."

Slowly, Ivan put his wrist down.

Matt glanced at his watch. "Funeral's in a couple of hours. Why don't you ride with me?"

"Sure thing." Ivan felt this heavy pall all around him, closing in, strangling him. He didn't want to be alone in this house. Grandma had always been there waiting for him when he came home from work, and waving goodbye to him when he ran off to SISO practice or somewhere.

He expected Grandma to open the creaky porch door any moment now to ask him if he wanted spaghetti for dinner.

Life is going to change.

Ivan's left wrist twitched a searing pain up his forearm again. Somehow it wasn't as bad as the grief in his heart. He closed his puffy eyes.

The crunch of gravel made him look down the meandering driveway to where a small Toyota was coming in their direction.

Willow.

Ivan hadn't seen his sister, Willow, in several years. She had called at Christmas, but didn't show up in person. One would think that five hours wasn't too long to drive from Atlanta to the Georgia coast, but she almost always had an excuse even when school was out.

Granted, she barely eked out a living running a piano studio and going to graduate school. Every Christmas season she was paid to play piano at parties, dinners, church plays, and so forth. Many times the regulars were on holiday, and she substituted for them. It paid well; she charged three-figure amounts for one or two hours of repeatedly playing Christmas carols and hymns.

Ivan stepped off the porch as Willow coasted her Toyota to a stop. The door flung open, and Willow came running out, tears on her face.

"I'm too late!" She wept into Ivan's barn jacket. "If I hadn't taken that extra gig, I could've been here at Christmas. It would've been our last Christmas together as a family."

"Shhhh..." All Ivan could do was pat her shoulders. He prayed silently for her. For spilt milk never returning to the bottle. What was done was done—

Done.

Like what had happened between him and Brinley?

Ivan wished he could retract everything he had said to Brinley earlier in the month when they had broken up. Yet dignity forbade such yielding. It would be admitting that he had been wrong to send Brinley away. She could use it against him. She could have wanted her money back. Compensation for plumbing costs. Restitution for the stolen Strad.

"Grandma is in heaven now." Ivan pushed back a lock of hair on Willow's face. "She's with Grandpa. That's what she had wanted for a long time, to see Grandpa."

Willow nodded. Two years younger than Ivan, they had been close through high school and then college at Juilliard. Their relationship had splintered after Grandpa Otto died. Lately it had improved as the brother and sister grew older and hopefully, wiser and more mature than their younger twenty-something days.

"Would you like to rest a bit, freshen up before we go to church? Matt can take us both in his van so you won't need to drive."

Willow nodded again.

As Ivan helped Willow up the porch steps, he heard thunder in the distance. They had chosen the wrong day to have the funeral. It had been clear skies Thursday when they had the viewing at the funeral home. And clear skies the day before that too. However, today, the forecasters said it would rain through the weekend.

Matt waved to Willow. "Praise the Lord that Yun is saved. She's not grieving now. We are."

"It's hard." Willow broke down again.

Ivan took her inside, then came out again to speak with Matt.

"Zoe and Quincy texted. They're meeting us at the church." Matt hesitated. "Brinley is with them."

Ivan said nothing.

"She is devastated."

So am I.

"Zoe says Brinley is having a hard time," Matt said. "I think she needs you."

"What am I to do about it? We broke up." Ivan clenched his fists. His left wrist hurt when he did that, but he didn't care. It wasn't Matt's place to give him relationship advice at this time.

All Ivan wanted was for the funeral to be over.

Grandma was already in heaven. She didn't care how short her funeral was.

"I don't know, dude. Pray about how to handle her. At least be nice to her when you see her."

"I suppose I can do that."

"You'd better. I don't think your grandma would've wanted it any other way."

~

*B*rinley used to hate funerals, their unremitting obsequies, sea of red eyes, and awful cacophony of sobs. She used to think that there was nothing happy about people dead and gone, family bereaved and left behind. Nothing happy about the cold, dark spaces of loss, a past that could not be recovered and a present sapped of verve, a heavenly future notwithstanding. Things to come were, well, things to come.

Today some of those feelings were still in her as she entered the Seaside Chapel sanctuary to see Yun's closed casket. The open casket viewing had been the day before, but she had chosen not to go to the funeral home because she knew she'd come face to face with Ivan. Something in her was still raw from his rejection of her that she could not bring herself to show up even though she had considered Yun a friend.

Brinley decided not to sit with the McMillan family in the front. Being Yun's granddaughter-in-law's sister didn't qualify her as close family. Having been rejected by Ivan in his self-focused spell had further widened the chasm. The front rows were filled with not only McMillans, but also representatives from the Park family, who'd flown all the way from San Francisco, Vancouver, and Seoul for this sad day.

Brinley thought that Ivan must've favored his father for he looked like none of his cousins from overseas.

She found the corner of the back-row pew insulating. She sat silently, spoke to no one, sobbed alone, and thought of Yun and how it was too late for words, too final for eventualities.

What sliced at Brinley was not the act of saying goodbye to Yun, but the fact that the last time they had gotten together, Yun had been downtrodden. Such a strong spiritual woman brought down by a wayward grandson who should be slapping himself awake to see the reality of the situation.

His actions, his failed plans—if there had been any—had left his grandmother no choice, but to sell her beloved Steinway Victorian upright piano. While Brinley had added a generous amount to the appraised value of the piano, it was obvious that if Ivan had paid more attention to his finances, Yun wouldn't have had to hawk off a family heirloom. Even with that piano sold, they still didn't have enough to pay off the McMillan family home.

I blame Ivan.

Some people came to sit down beside her. It wasn't until someone squeezed her hand that she realized it was Tobias and his grandfather, Alonzo. Alonzo's eyes were red and he was barely keeping it together.

Tobias held Brinley's hand, like he had used to do when helping her cross the roads back when she was six and he was older.

"Gonna be okay, all right?" he whispered.

Brinley nodded.

Many times, she had wished Tobias was really her older brother.

A haunting violin began to play "Amazing Grace." Brinley didn't care who was playing. She was too busy keeping her head down, to be alone in her grief. She stared at the wood pews in front of her, wood that every now and then resembled the panels on the sides of a casket.

Yun McMillan had been a good friend.

A dear friend.

Gone.

Before Brinley met Jesus, she had thought that Christians were overtly religious by nature, but Yun had been the least condescending of all. Preachy she might have been, but Yun had meant well. At their last tea time together, Yun had pleaded with her to forgive Ivan.

Forgive him?

A group of senior adults gathered on the platform and sang some of Yun's favorite old-time hymns. When they reached "Blessed Assurance," Brinley recalled that bittersweet day when she had sight-read that hymn for Yun, minutes before Ivan kicked her out of their house in a dismissive way that confused her to this day.

Forgive him.

One by one, Yun's singing friends came forward to tell a joke or a story about Yun. When an elderly gentleman in a wheelchair finished the story about the time he tried to cozy up to Yun at the ice cream social, there was not a dry eye in the sanctuary amidst the laughter. And the missionary trips overseas that Yun and her husband Otto had taken in her lifetime! Brinley had no idea she had traveled that much. The time she had to eat green caterpillars in Papua New Guinea or taste fried grubs in Botswana...

Pastor Gonzalez went up to speak.

"She is not here," he announced, and the entire crowd leaped to their feet and cheered, breaking into an a cappella "O Happy Day."

This is how Grandpa Brooks's funeral should've been.

While his, ten years before, had focused on death and the past, Yun's funeral focused on life and the future. Brinley choked up when Pastor Gonzalez spoke of nothing except the love of Christ, the hope of Christ, the heaven of Christ, culminating in the cross of Christ, which he preached as the bridge to heaven.

"Yun McMillan crossed that bridge. She is now experiencing eternal life. Yun had hope. Do you? Yun is alive. Are you?"

The funeral service ended with the pallbearers carrying Yun McMillan's coffin out to the hearse.

Sitting in the back, Brinley saw Ivan for the first time since their last conversation some thirteen days ago. He walked alongside six pallbearers, three on each side, Quincy among them. Ivan himself did not carry the coffin. Brinley figured he was still recovering from his injuries.

As soon as the casket was out of the sanctuary, Tobias told his dad they should leave. Alonzo nodded.

"Take it easy," Tobias said to Brinley. "See you at work later."

Brinley nodded.

Zoe came up to Brinley in her Valentino black, the maternity dress concealing her three-month pouch. "Let's go, Brinley."

"I'm not sure if I should go. You know how I feel about cemeteries." The last time Brinley went to a graveside service was in Charleston when they had buried Grandpa Brooks in the family mausoleum.

"Come for Grandma Yun's sake. You're practically family."

Brinley sucked in her tears.

"It's unbearable for me too, but I have to go for Quincy's sake." Zoe dabbed her eyes.

Brinley didn't tell Zoe that there would be no closure here. Life was a continuum, and Yun simply adjourned to heaven. Someday Brinley would see Yun again. That comforted her. The certainty she had about it was unmistakable, a confirmation that she was really a believer now. The course of her eternal destiny had changed.

"You'll be fine, Zoe." Brinley patted her sister's shoulder. "I'll come if you want me to."

"I do."

Brinley held Zoe's arm as they made their way to an awaiting car. Silently, the funeral procession went up Frederica Road.

~

*A*s Grandma's casket was lowered into the ground, all Ivan could think of was, "What now?"

For six years he had been singularly focused on providing for Grandma Yun. They had managed to survive, so he wasn't altogether a failure at that. Now that Grandma was dead, everything she had owned was in the grandchildren's name, but it still had three mortgages, and with three payments behind on the primary loan, he knew it was a matter of days before the McMillan family home went into foreclosure.

Willow had no money.

Quincy—never mind. He was living off Zoe.

I'm sure that says a lot about us to Brinley. What an embarrassment to the McMillan name.

To Ivan's left was Quincy, looking either stunned or stoic. Ivan couldn't tell. Next to him, Zoe was crying quietly. She had hardly known Grandma, but perhaps her pregnancy made her a bit more emotional than usual. The rest of the McMillan and Park family members were around them with Grandma's only surviving sibling, a younger brother, in the front, face sullen. The oldest living relative now.

As Pastor Gonzalez read passages from the Holy Bible, Ivan kept thinking that Brinley should be standing next to them.

Where is she?

He had seen her get out of the car with Zoe earlier as they crossed the lawn to the gravesite. He had wanted to go to her, kiss away the tears from her eyes, and tell her everything was going to be all right.

But it wasn't his place.

It was over between them. *But who was that guy sitting next to her in the last row back at Seaside Chapel?*

When the graveside service was all over, Ivan backed out of the crowd to look for Brinley, against his better judgment. He wanted to see her. Make sure she was okay. Make sure she could go on.

That's all.

Ivan found her at the back of the crowd, dabbing her eyes on a wad of tissue soaked all the way through. She didn't seem to realize he was walking toward her. Didn't even look up when he folded her into his arms, his splint pressing against her back through her black sweater. He felt her snuggle against him inside his coat as if she knew who he was without even looking.

They stayed that way for a while, silently grieving for Grandma Yun.

Ivan didn't want to let her go.

What have I done to this poor thing?

Poor?

It is I who am poor in all manner of it.

Ivan rubbed Brinley's back. She spoke not a word.

He leaned down and kissed her forehead. He didn't know why he did that. He sure didn't want to send her mixed signals. It was over between them. This was a final goodbye.

Or was it?

Brinley pulled her arms from around his waist. Without a word, she walked away.

CHAPTER FIFTY-FIVE

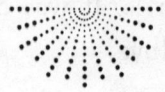

*I*van locked the front door and stepped into the living room. Matt, Quincy, and Willow had left after dropping him off. They had offered to stay a while longer, but he had told them not to worry. He wanted to show them he could move on, but really, he wasn't sure how.

Everywhere he turned, memories of Grandma Yun swept through his mind in droves like a slideshow from the past. There was his baseball in a shadow box by the wall from when he was twelve years old. Grandma had saved it for him. Someday he'd give it to his children, she had said.

Here was the braided rag rug that Grandma had made years ago. There was her old Bible still sitting on that scratched old oak table next to the run-down rocker she had always sat in. He could see Grandma rocking and telling him to read his Bible every day.

Now the rocker was still. Cold and still.

Ivan made a beeline for the Bible on the side table. He opened the Bible to Grandma's last bookmark. It fell on Isaiah 30:19.

For the people shall dwell in Zion at Jerusalem;
    You shall weep no more.
    He will be very gracious to you at the sound of
your cry;
    When He hears it, He will answer you.

"Weep no more." Ivan barely voiced it.

His chest hurt badly.

He sank into the sorry couch, Grandma Yun's Bible still in his hands. Tears fell onto the old pages, and he couldn't wipe them off fast enough.

Hate to ruin Grandma's Bible.

No words came out of his mouth, only guttural sounds. There was an agony so deep within his chest that Ivan felt like he was going to implode. The pain was too much to bear, and he couldn't get it out.

Lord, I've failed.

All his careful planning to work hard and pay off the house so Grandma Yun could live in a house that she finally owned. All his dreams of fixing up the house so that Grandma could have a nice, lovely home to read her Bible in. Maybe great-grandchildren to sit on her lap and listen to her stories of Grandpa Otto.

All that was gone.

Could never happen.

Yeah, I know Grandma is in heaven with Grandpa, and they don't care about this house anymore.

But it was his hope, his prayers, his wishes.

Unanswered.

Ivan wiped bitter tears on his cheap oxford shirt he had bought off the bargain rack at Matt's thrift shop.

Poor! I'm always poor!

Why, Lord?

Just like that the words came to him: Rich in Christ.

Yeah, but I'm going to lose this house. You knew that, Lord! Why didn't You stop it?

Ivan sat there for a while. Then slowly, his chest still constricting, he eased off the torn couch and placed the Bible carefully back on the table where it had always belonged. But when he lifted his hands off the Bible, he felt a sharp pain inside his left wrist under the brace. That tendon again.

This too, Lord! Can things get any worse?

The funeral this morning was a blur. Truly, he should not have parted ways with Brinley after the graveside ceremony because they could have kept each other company. But he didn't want her to see him grieve. Besides, he had broken up with her and keeping her company could be misconstrued as an apology. He didn't want to apologize. He wanted her to see him strong.

And he wanted her to see him back in form.

A façade?

Ivan knew he wasn't as strong as he wanted to portray to Brinley. How could he when he couldn't even pay off Grandma's debts? If he'd been a concert violinist, he could have, but that career had been cut off before it ever began when Grandpa Otto had died, and Ivan had to come home to take care of Grandma. All his hopes of launching the rest of his life off of his Juilliard degree had been dashed.

He'd worked long and hard to build up his music studio, but to what end? St. Simon's Island was a small place with very few students. If his music studio had been in Savannah or, better yet, Atlanta or even Boston, he might have more students and more income since they'd pay more in bigger cities. The music studio and his hourly wages at SISO were barely enough to pay off the debts. Grandma said she'd go with him to Atlanta if it meant he could get a better job, but Ivan knew she'd rather stay on the island.

And truth be told, he did too. He never liked big cities.

Then again, the first thing he had to do was get out of debt. He should sell this house. That would be the end of it. It'd been in the McMillan family since 1902. But some old things were never meant to be kept.

But.

Maybe if his wrist healed, he could be a concert violinist now that Grandma Yun was dead. Maybe he could earn enough to save the house. Maybe there was still time to keep the bank at bay if he worked out a payment plan.

Or maybe he needed an accountant like Brinley had said.

Okay. I admit it now. I'm no good with this.

But maybe if he could borrow some money—

No, wait.

Brinley had alluded to him that he shouldn't borrow any more money.

Aarrgh. But what does she know about poverty?

Her words from earlier this month came back to him. She'd called him Mozart. Not the prodigy Mozart, but the thirty-something has-been on the throes of death scribbling scraps of music manuscripts to pay for mediocre medicine to keep him alive for another day. Yeah, that one who died anyway and was buried in a pauper's grave. That musician.

Nope. Not gonna be like that.

I'll prove you wrong, Brin.

Ivan nearly ran down the stairs to his basement studio. Using his right hand that still worked, he snapped open the lid to his violin from high school. Gingerly, he unwrapped his left wrist splint. He flexed his fingers slowly, then a bit more forcefully. The pain was still there.

Lord, help me.

He adjusted the tuning pegs on the violin with his right hand. Found the bow.

He turned his left wrist upward for his fingers to reach the strings. A bit of pain there, but he could bear it. But before his fingers could reach full supination, a searing pain stung his wrist and shot up his forearm. He yelped and nearly dropped the violin.

He knew then.

It was over.

CHAPTER FIFTY-SIX

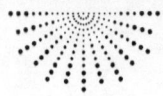

"*W*hat's wrong with men?" Brinley tapped the top of the interior door panel where her right arm rested. Outside the pickup it was blustery. She could see the choppy waves as they passed by Massengale Park on Ocean Boulevard. They were dropping off some equipment at another one of Tobias Vega's job sites before heading to the Village.

"Is that a question, or are you exclaiming?" Tobias didn't look at her from the driver's seat.

"Don't know. Both, I guess." Brinley listened to the blinker.

Simple quadruple time signature. Blink, blink, blink, blink.

Must everything remind her of Ivan?

"I shouldn't answer the question, don't you think?"

"Toby, you can be objective," Brinley said. "Ask

me about women. I'll tell you." *Uh, maybe. We're all different.*

"You can't tell me beans about why my girlfriend left me." He parked the truck.

"Sure can. Two words: your mom."

Tobias laughed. "You might be onto something."

"No offense. I love your mom. But if your girlfriend can't cook better than your mom, it's over."

"So I need to date a chef."

"That's all there is to it, Toby. Problem solved. I'll send you the bill." Brinley stayed in the truck. She watched Tobias call out to a couple of his construction guys from the two-story Victorian with a tarp on its roof. They came over and hauled off the pressure washer from the truck bed.

Tobias climbed back into the pickup and backed it out of the driveway. "I don't know this guy you're referring to, but I can tell you, if he's anything like I am, it's going to be hard not to be able to work, especially doing what you love. You know what I mean?"

"Uh-huh."

"Take my grandpa, for example. He's been a plumber forever. Now he's retired and he still thinks he's in charge."

"He's still in charge. Your little brother needs too much on-the-job training." Brinley remembered that episode when Felipe refused to send someone to fix a toilet and almost lost that job at Yun's house.

Yun's house.

"Say, Toby? Could we—uh, could we go down a

couple of streets? I want to drive by Yun's house one more time. To say goodbye, you know?"

"Sure thing. My grandpa's cut up about Yun's passing."

"Lots of people are. I'm one of them. I enjoyed having tea with her." *Someday I'll see Yun again and we can have another cup of tea.*

"Grandpa thought they had something going."

"She was so stunning he froze at the door."

"Really?"

"You know what Alonzo said to Yun? 'If you'd just show me the offending commode, I will resolve the issue for you.'"

"That sounds like something he'd say. He's quite a character. That's why Grandma married him." Toby turned pensive. "I wish—never mind."

"You wish your grandparents never broke up."

"How could she walk away from Grandpa? He's such a great guy." Tobias shook his head. "The divorce was bad on my brothers and me, but I think it took a toll on my parents too. Nobody believed a seventy-year-old woman would walk away after decades of marriage. Grandpa complained that he shouldn't have married someone twenty years his junior. Wandering eyes or something like that."

"You do have an interesting family," Brinley said. "My brother Diehl has been through a divorce. One time too many."

"It's a silly game, I think. Grandpa still comes over to Grandma's house when we have birthdays and such because nobody cooks like Grandma, and he knows it."

"I'll pray for your grandparents." Brinley meant it.

"Pray? You're sounding religious, Brin."

They slowed down behind some traffic.

"It's not religion, Toby. It's a relationship with God through Jesus Christ."

"God. Jesus. Religion. Case closed."

"Got to believe in something, Toby."

"Myself. I believe in myself. I am my own god."

"Your choice."

"Yep. My choice." Toby slowed down. "Tell me where to go."

"Beyond those trees—"

Brinley gasped. In front of Yun's house was a *For Sale* sign. In the yard were boxes, full trash bags, old lamp shades, broken shoe racks, and general garbage waiting to be picked up.

"Pull up, Toby." On her iPhone now, she called her real estate agent. She got out of the truck as Tobias parked, all the time talking on the phone. "Foreclosed? Do you have a courthouse date? Uh-huh. Find out if there are other bids. Call me back pronto."

In Georgia, a foreclosure meant the McMillans had missed three months of house payments. It could be a quick sale if the lender wanted to get rid of it.

Brinley knew that if she had to bid for it, she would. She didn't care how much it would cost. She almost always won bids.

But at a high price.

Look what happened when I bought the Schoenberg Strad.

Brinley went up the front porch. She rang the doorbell. Nobody answered. She peered through a window. The entire floor was bare.

Ivan had lost Yun's house.

~

"*L*et me get this straight." Tobias frowned as he looked up and down the building façade. "You want this entire warehouse gutted and then nothing?"

Brinley knew it looked bad. Dirty and grimy with age. Abandoned. Broken windows patched up. No one had dared to touch it with a hundred-foot pole.

"Right. Fix any structural or foundation problems." Brinley stepped on the cracked cement driveway to get to her general contractor. Right there in front of them the entire bottom part of the brick exterior wall was covered with graffiti. Nice street art if the building hadn't been devalued by vandalism. One block down from Mallery Street and the landscape had surely changed.

"If you let this building sit too long, you're going to lose money." There was strain in Tobias's voice.

"Patience, friend. There're no bids. You get the rest of it."

"I'm not worried about that. I have plenty of work to do around town. I'm thinking about you, Brinley.

You're buying up this entire block. It could be a royal flop."

"You'll still get paid."

Tobias raised his palm. "Don't look at me as your GC right now. Look at me as an old friend. If this entire project fails, you're going to lose a lot of money."

"I hear you, Toby."

"You mentioned something the other day I didn't catch on to until now when we're standing here looking at this space with all its acoustics."

"I said a lot of things."

"You said that this warehouse could be a centrally located music studio. A music studio for whom?"

Brinley didn't want to say.

"Don't get your hopes too high up, sister. Sometimes people move on and they never come back."

"I'm going to rent out this warehouse and Yun's house—if I get it—one way or another. If things don't work out, I'll flip the properties," Brinley decided. "You know me, Toby. You know I'm not attached to a building, only the history of it."

"For what it's worth, I've said my piece." Tobias rolled his eyes. "I think you should raze this warehouse and rebuild."

"Then it won't be old, Toby."

"We can keep a few of these old bricks. Whatever we can salvage."

"No. I want the warehouse the way they had it a hundred or more years ago. If you have to reinforce it to keep the exterior bricks, do it. For that matter, I want this entire block preserved, if at all possible."

"Anything you want, Brinley. It's your money. As long as I don't have to work with Megan. Find another designer, Brinley."

"You like Megan. You guys work so well together." Brinley walked around the building.

Tobias was right beside her. "Haha. Did you know she tore up my favorite flannel shirt in your new house when we hung the chandelier?"

"I don't want to know. I'm glad my house is done now." Brinley headed for the other building next door, the one that Dad had agreed to invest in. She took a few photos on her iPhone.

"Have you thought of a name yet for this development?"

"Pelican Road after that street out front."

"You're going to name this multimillion-dollar investment after a bird?"

"Better Pelican than Crow."

"Good point. Pelican." Tobias seemed to be mulling it over. "I'm liking it more and more. You sure you don't want to go inside?"

"Not until they reinforce everything with steel."

"You're afraid the building will collapse on you."

"The inspectors said everything is fine."

"Maybe you shouldn't have bought this place, Brinley. Tell me you didn't buy this building on a whim and then work everything around it."

"The house I'm living in now, I knew I wanted it the day I saw it. You remember?"

"Yeah. That morning you binged on doughnuts."

"Uh-huh. Insult me, why don't you?" Brinley snapped a few more photos before she looked back at the warehouse again.

Tobias might be right. It would probably be cheaper to tear down this building—and the entire block—and start over.

Start over.

Was that what she had to do now without Ivan?

"You still don't take long to make decisions, do you?" Tobias asked.

"If I know what I want."

"And if you know how to get it."

"Well, the difference now is that I pray about it first before I decide."

"What does your God say about moving on?" Tobias unlocked his truck doors.

Brinley climbed into the work truck. "Huh?"

"When to move on from the past. What does your God say about that?"

"I don't know, but He knows I like old things."

"Sister, this is a wake-up call. Sometimes old things don't like you."

CHAPTER FIFTY-SEVEN

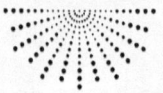

"*I* know you don't want to be here."

Ivan listened to his sister say those words and watched her dish out some sort of shrimp fried rice onto his plate. It didn't look too great, but considering the circumstances, Ivan could eat anything.

He also knew that free dinner came with a price.

In many ways, Willow reminded him of Grandma Yun, who had never missed an opportunity to get down to business.

"I know you don't want me here, either," Ivan said. "I'm sorry I'm imposing on you."

"It's not that, Ivan." She scraped the bottom of the pan.

Ivan sat down at the folding table in the kitchen that was even smaller than Grandma's on St. Simon's Island. Willow's little rented house in DeKalb was only minutes from Emory, where she went to music school to get her master's degree. To supplement her scholarship and student loans, she taught piano when she wasn't in class and on weekends.

Willow had gotten a roommate to sublet the second room in the house. That cut her rent in half. But it had left Ivan nowhere to sleep except on the futon in the living room. He had felt uncomfortable all week long with two women walking around him in bath towels.

He had to get out of here.

But where could he go?

He was bankrupt.

Homeless.

Penniless.

The money from Grandma's piano hadn't been enough to pay of the mortgage. The bank took the money and foreclosed on his house anyway. He had been too far behind.

He had sold his violin to someone Willow knew for two thousand dollars. That was all he had to live on, possibly for the rest of the year. Willow had taken pity on him and had not made him pay for his food and lodging at her house, but he knew she was stretching her own finances. He didn't want her to get into debt on account of him.

Now he wished he had stayed on St. Simon's and worked for Matt. However, he couldn't bear to be where Grandma had once been only six days before. The grief was still too fresh, too raw. He had to get away.

Willow sat down across from Ivan. The table was small.

Ivan scooted back in his chair, and bumped it against the side of the refrigerator. "Sorry."

Willow asked Ivan to say a blessing for their food. Ivan didn't feel thankful at all. He made his prayer quick and short and practically meaningless. His heart wasn't in it. It wasn't that he was mad at God, but—

Well, was he mad at God?

Shouldn't he be mad at himself?

"None of this would've happened if Grandpa Otto hadn't taken out a second mortgage, and Grandma broke her hip and I had to take out third mortgage, and if Brin hadn't bought me a Strad that caused me to get beaten up and end up with a broken wrist."

"Listen to what you just said."

"What?" Ivan raised an eyebrow.

"You just blamed everyone else but yourself."

"I'm just a victim of—"

"Uh-huh."

Ivan cringed. "I see what you mean. I'm sorry. I shouldn't dishonor our grandparents' memories."

"Tell me more about this Brin." Willow seemed amused.

"Brinley Brooks. She is—was—my girlfriend. Well, sort of. We only went out for about a month and a half. So maybe I shouldn't say girlfriend."

"Was she at the funeral?"

Ivan nodded. *I should have held her by my side throughout the funeral. She cried alone.*

"I think I saw her," Willow said.

"Well, it doesn't matter now. But for a couple of months it seemed we had known each other all our lives and were meant to be together."

"How long have you known her?"

"I've seen her at various SISO events on and off for about a year before we started going out. We would say hello and no more. She had always been with someone." Ivan himself was dating Emmeline at that time. "We met up again in December when she came alone to her sister's birthday party."

"Something happened?"

"We clicked over Bach." Ivan regretted it now. He should've had more self-control.

"Clicked?"

"We were clearly attracted to each other." Ivan recalled that Thursday night when he had almost kissed Brinley when he walked her home. "Love came later."

"How much later?"

Ivan shrugged. "She kept coming over to have tea with Grandma and it just happened."

"What just happened?"

Walks. Talks. Kisses. Hugs. More kisses.

"I wrote her a song. She didn't—doesn't—know it's for her."

"That serious, huh? Does she know that if you wrote her a song you're in too deep? You didn't write a song for Gemma."

"Gemma? She's ancient history, Will."

"Six or seven years ago. Not too long."

Gemma was Ivan's last serious girlfriend. Anyone he had dated between Gemma and Brinley hadn't been serious prospects. Not even Emmeline, his on-and-off casual girlfriend, whatever that meant.

"Brin—Brinley is—was—different."

"I'm sorry." Willow drank some water.

"Sorry? For what?"

"Your tenses, Ivan. You can't decide if she's in the past or still in the present. You can't decide if you should call her Brin or Brinley."

"I guess she's Brinley now. Only her close family members call her Brin." Ivan ate silently. Then: "I love her, Will."

"Have you told her?"

"I can't."

"Because?"

"I can't afford to love her." He knew Willow was studying him, thinking about what to tell him. She'd always been like that. Maybe she had something to say he should hear. He waited.

"Is she high maintenance?" Willow asked. "Help me understand who this woman is."

"She's an heiress. Billions to her name." Ivan got up and cleared the table. He loaded the dishwasher with his right hand. *Thank God for dishwashers.*

"Oh, I see. To her, a five-million-dollar Strad is pocket change. Something like that?"

"Five-point-four."

"Even worse."

"Well, she has at least several Strads she inherited from her grandfather. So yes, stuff like that doesn't matter to her, I don't think."

"What matters to her?"

"People, I think, even before she was saved. More so after. She kept doing things for Grandma and me, buying us stuff, taking care of things. I'm thinking they were all primarily for me. She seemed genuinely happy to be with me and do all that stuff for us."

"Why didn't she pay off the house then if she kept pouring money on you?"

Ivan stopped what he was doing. "If I hadn't broken up with her, she might have."

"You're a fool, big brother."

"I'm not a beggar."

"You could've saved Grandma's house from being foreclosed on."

"I don't like handouts."

"What are you doing now?"

"I told you I sold my last violin. I could help with groceries and such."

Willow got up, hugged her brother. "No need. I wasn't trying to be mean. I was only trying to help you think through this."

"I appreciate that, Will. But truth be told, I don't want Brinley's money." Ivan grimaced. "I want to be my own man, you know. But I can't afford her. I can't even get a job with my injury now, let alone marry and feed a family."

"Marry? I thought you were just going out."

"I wanted more, but I can't have more. Look at

me. I don't have health insurance. I can't even pay for therapy. My wrist will probably never heal right. This injury ended my career and any hope of making it with Brin—Brinley."

"Let me go get my violin."

"You don't play the violin, Will."

"Never mind. Inside joke." Then she said, "Do we have a focus problem, Ivan? Did Brinley fall in love with your violin or the man behind the violin?"

"She deserves better than me." Ivan sighed. "Such is my life, Will. You know that. It seems like I'm always a bottom feeder."

"Why do you question everything God gives you, Ivan?" Willow opened the refrigerator to get a can of soda. She offered Ivan one, but he refused. He didn't want to put her out.

"I don't deserve anything." Ivan walked around the folding kitchen table and plopped down on the futon in the living room. It sagged in the middle and was nubbly here and there.

"Yes, you do." Willow came out of the kitchen after him and sat down beside him. That was the only seating in the entire living room not counting a couple of mismatched barstools next to an upright Kimball piano by the wall.

Willow had an apple on a paper plate and a knife in her hand. "You deserve death and eternal separation from God. You know that."

She cut up a slice of apple and offered it to Ivan. He took it, grateful for the healthy dessert.

"Yet He sent His only Son, Jesus, to die for you

and take your place," Willow said. "So be thankful and stop questioning God."

"It's not that, Will."

"You're not questioning God? Seems to me like you have some sort of trust issue."

"Trust issue? What are you saying?" Ivan chewed the apple carefully. Had to make it last. Savor every bit of it.

"All our lives, it's been hard. You had it the hardest when Quincy moved out and it was just our grandparents, you, and me. You felt like you had to step in and keep an eye on the family. Life was hard for us, and you got so used to everything being difficult all the time, things not working out, things going wrong, things being messy and all that good stuff. So when things get better you can't tell. Can't see it."

"Maybe."

"You know I'm right, Ivan. I've had six years to think about it." Willow offered Ivan another slice of apple. He took it. He hadn't realized how delicious Granny Smith could be.

"When you learn to trust God, things improve, but in ways that sometimes don't match your preconceived expectations. When they don't, you, Ivan Benjamin McMillan, reject it as coming from God because you think you know better."

"I don't know better."

"Exactly. But you think you do when you walk by sight and not by faith in our Mighty God, who provides in ways that are beyond our expectations.

Drop your low-level expectations and trust high-level God."

"That's easy to say, Will."

"What are you showing Brinley about your faith, Ivan?"

"She moved on."

"On her own volition or did you push her away?"

"I spared her."

"From what? From seeing that your faith is weak and your peace is fake?"

"Well, when you lose everything—"

"You haven't lost God. You never lose God." Willow rubbed her brother's shoulder. "God is still here for you."

"I know. That's in my head, but my heart is hurting. It's messy with Grandma gone."

"I know." Willow began to cry softly.

Ivan put an arm around his sister's shoulders. He didn't say a word.

After a while, Willow started to sing "Count Your Blessings."

"You remember how we used to sing that?" she asked.

"First song we sang in children's choir when we moved in with Grandma and Grandpa." *So long ago now.*

"We went to church a lot. Sometimes four or five times a week."

"Just following Grandma around as she directed this and that choir."

"Children's choir was my favorite part of those

years." Willow blew her nose. "No idea why Grandma made 'Count Your Blessings' our theme song."

"How easily we forget," Ivan added, heart heavy. Maybe he wasn't praying right or asking God the right questions. Instinctively, he flexed his left hand. The pain was still there, but not as bad as a month ago. *Thank You, God.*

It would take time, but step by step—

That's it.

Step by step. That was how he had to trust God.

In his entire life, God had provided through good times and bad. When his parents abandoned him and his siblings, God provided his grandparents to take them in and raise them. When it was time to go to college, God provided him a full scholarship to not just any music school, but that prestigious, world-renowned Juilliard. The word *full* was not lost on him.

Full.

God hadn't done things halfway, had He?

What about his left wrist? He lifted it into the air and felt it with his right hand.

Willow must've noticed his action. "Hey, you still have your wrist. That's one more blessing to count."

A realization dawned on Ivan. "That's right. It's still here."

"And you have all your fingers on both hands. They still work, don't they?"

"Yeah." He had been googling for some freebie wrist exercises he could do that didn't require a therapist. Whether they were any good or not remained to be seen, but he could thank God that his wrist was slowly coming back to form, though what form, he had no idea at this time.

Functionally, he could move his fingers, yes. So all was not totally lost, was it?

His sister stopped humming. "Want to teach some piano while you're here? Sub for me while I study? I have an exam coming up in two weeks. Will you still be here?"

Ivan thought for a moment. "Maybe, if you don't kick me out of the house by then."

"We're getting along all right now. Maybe we've grown up." She smiled. "Sub for me and you don't have to pay rent."

"Deal. But you know I won't stay long. I just need a place to sort things out."

"A pit stop? That's okay too. But if you go negative on me, moan and complain, you're out of here." Willow got off the futon. "By the way, how long are you going to keep that beard?"

Ivan's fingers scratched under his chin.

"You think your girlfriend would like it?"

"Not sure..."

Ivan stopped and wondered about his own words. He should have said, "I don't have a girlfriend." But what had come out of his mouth said otherwise. How could he consider Brinley still his girlfriend if they had broken up?

"Yep, you were right. You're still in love with her." Willow waltzed away.

CHAPTER FIFTY-EIGHT

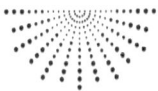

The Garnett Antique Shop façade with old world letterings on its glass doors and windows deceived Brinley into thinking that Matt's store was small. The store might be narrow in the front, but once she stepped inside, Brinley realized that it was wider in the back and went up two floors.

Above the stairs up against the right wall were two signs with arrows pointing up. One said "Books & Music" and the other said "Watch Your Steps."

Brinley wondered what Yun McMillan would've said about that second sign had she been alive. Perhaps she might have questioned whether it should have said "step" instead of "steps."

Oh well. She would never know.

"Hello!" Matt was walking up to her. "Glad you stopped by."

"Mom, this is Matt Garnett. He owns the store."

When there was no reply, Brinley looked around. "Mom?"

Matt chuckled.

"She was right behind me when I came in," Brinley explained. "She's probably somewhere in the store. She'll want a tour."

Just then Mom appeared from around a step-back cupboard that was taller than she was. Before Brinley could introduce them, Mom had taken care of it herself before getting down to business.

"Is this poplar?" Mom pointed to the cupboard in distressed red.

"Poplar and cherry, ma'am. Got it out of Charleston," Matt said.

"Charleston. That's where my husband's family was from."

"Let me tell you when it was made. There's a signature in one of the drawers..."

Brinley walked away before she could hear the rest of the conversation. She wandered around the store, overwhelmed by so many old things that she didn't know where to begin. Her focus the last ten years had been on musical instruments, but today she was looking for something to fill that wall next to her panoramic window in her new bedroom. She was thinking of a secretary.

She saw a stack of painted boxes from the eighteenth century. Rhode Island. Next to the boxes was an old child's high chair. Nineteenth-century Savannah. Funny how the design hadn't changed.

Somehow she was drawn to the high chair, but she didn't know why.

Thinking of Zoe, maybe.

Past the dining and kitchen stuff, she saw a plain, walnut plantation desk. She looked at the year it was made.

"1853." Antebellum Georgia. *This will go nicely with my ergonomic chair.*

The price looked about right too.

After browsing a bit more, she went upstairs. She was walking around when she heard footsteps coming up.

"I want to show you something." Matt led Brinley to some old music manuscripts in a box on a table. The price per sheet was scribbled on the box.

Brinley picked up a sheet music. Then another. Violin. Solos. Duets. Some with accompaniments. Some not.

"I think there are about five hundred sheets in here. I've sold a few of the pieces already, but they're so old, so brittle, and some of them were handwritten."

"I see." Brinley put the sheet music in her hand back into the box. "You're telling me this because...?"

"The idiot who sold me these was getting out of town fast. He needed the money, so he sold it to me for what I think is a fraction of the value."

"He? Do I know him?" Brinley asked.

"I just gave a clue."

"You did?"

"Yes, he's the village idiot."

Brinley bristled. "I don't want to hear that said of him."

"You still have feelings for him." Matt lifted a music sheet. "Some of these are originals from the 1700s and should be in museums. Stacked up in a box is a bad place for them to be."

"They need to be in a temperature-controlled room."

"Exactly. I don't have that here. But if you want the entire collection I'll give you a thirty percent discount."

"Is that his price or your retail after your markup?"

Matt looked offended. "It's not off the markup price. I want his collection to go to a good home."

"Someday he'll want all these back."

"Right."

"I'll take it if you throw in a thirty percent discount on a certain plantation desk I saw downstairs."

Brinley thought Matt was giving her some sort of "you're crazy" look. She held her ground. "Thirty percent off both and I'll take them off your hands."

"I can't operate this shop at that big a discount."

"Yes, you can, Matt, because my mother and I are here. We shop."

That gave Matt something to think about. "Well... I might be able to do ten percent."

"Ten? That's measly, Matt. My mother could buy your entire store."

"Well..."

"Tell you what, Matt. Twenty-five percent across the board for both Mom and me, and we have a deal."

"But I've got to stay in business."

"Want to bet that my mom will ask to see what else you have in your warehouse? Tell me you have a warehouse somewhere."

"Got one in Brunswick."

"There you go, Matt. Do we have a deal?"

Matt sighed. "You're quite a bargain hunter."

"Would you be so kind as to help me take that box downstairs? I have to watch my many steps."

As they went downstairs, Brinley took the opportunity to ask about Ivan.

"Still at his sister's house. Said he's subbing for his sister in her piano studio."

"Good to know he's doing something."

"Not much he can do, really. No healthcare, no insurance, no therapy."

Brinley stopped in her tracks. "Seriously?"

"I told him he'd have to find a way to get into therapy for that wrist or it's going to lock up for good. He'll never play violin again."

"You can't make him do it. We can only pray that God will reach him."

"Yep. He's a stubborn fool as far as I'm concerned. I've known him a very long time, but I've never seen him fall this low. I offered him a job next door, he took it, but when his grandma died, he upped and left town. I had to scramble to find someone else."

At the foot of the stairs, Brinley saw Mom flitting

from table to table, armoire to armoire. She floated past Brinley. "I think I'm going to start collecting American now. Kind of tired of European antiques."

Tired of collecting? I doubt it.

Brinley followed Matt to the checkout counter, where he placed the box of violin music.

"Show me the plantation desk you want," Matt said.

Brinley did.

"Nice one. It was in an old house in Beaufort for a long time. The owner died and the house was sold with everything in it. I found some other stuff there too if you might be interested."

"Like?"

And so it went for another hour. By the time Brinley drove Mom home to Seaside Island in Dad's Bugatti, Mom had bought enough rococo chairs and a sofa to redo her upstairs library. And somewhere in the house, Mom would find a place to stuff the step-back cupboard that didn't go with anything else she had.

CHAPTER FIFTY-NINE

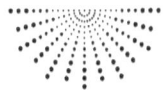

*T*eaching Bastien on the piano to kindergarteners was super easy for Ivan. While he was a classically trained violinist, he'd spent some of his time maintaining his piano skills for music composition, especially the accompaniment.

If he kept his left wrist steady and only moved his fingers, he could handle those big notes in the primer music book. To show the students how the notes were played on the piano, he used his right hand, even if the notes were on the bass clef.

It had been a month since he'd been here trying to sort out his life and providing relief for his overworked sister. Willow had classes at Emory at various hours of the day, and when she wasn't on campus, she was here in her house teaching piano to little kids. Most of them were children of faculty members or people in the area. The lessons were only twenty to thirty minutes long and he didn't have to sub too many times each week. Besides, Willow handled the more advanced students, those who required one-hour lessons.

Not like the four or five hours of violins he had to hear every day in his own strings studio back on St. Simon's.

Back on St. Simon's.

Ivan was getting homesick, and he knew it. He missed Brinley something fierce and shouldn't have dumped her. He cringed.

Dump was such a strong word. He saw it now. He couldn't handle his own mess and he'd taken it out on Brinley.

Would she be able to forgive me?

She may never take me back.

Ivan was dusting the piano and closing the cover on that old Kimball when the front door opened and slammed shut.

Willow dropped her tote bag on the floor and slid down onto the futon. "I pray to God I graduate in May. I don't want to stay another semester."

"That bad, huh?"

"Not *bad* bad. Just tired, you know."

"I'm sorry I'm no help." Ivan walked toward Willow. "Your dreams of our resurrecting Jade Strings might be over, at least with me in it."

"I'm not sure if I want to travel all over the world anymore. I like teaching piano, and I might do that for a while."

"I like teaching your beginner students. They're cutie pies."

"Aren't they? Those little fingers trying to reach the keyboard. I worry sometimes that they'll fall off the bench."

"I like it that you let their moms sit in so they know what their kids need to practice all week. My students' moms ran for dear life as soon as the lessons started."

"You're making it sound worse than it really is."

Ivan sat on the piano bench. "Piano is easier for anyone to pick up, I think. You should hear my new violin students. It takes them a while to get it right. Maybe as long as a year or two—some take three and never get it at all—before they stop sounding like screeching banshees."

Willow rubbed her temples. "I can't handle too much of that sort of cacophony."

"Of course, they'll all even out and then it's on to whether they can really play the instrument, whichever it may be. I've heard some difficult piano pieces and also some difficult violin pieces."

"Does your Brinley play any instruments?"

My Brinley? Ivan kept a poker face. "She plays the piano."

"Really? I'd like to meet her someday if you two ever get back together again. Maybe she and I can play a duet."

"Not gonna happen."

"Oh, you're such a pessimist." Willow got off the futon.

Ivan thought his sister was always on the go, never sitting down too long in one place.

"You can thank me now, Ivan."

"What for?"

"For showing you that violin isn't the only instrument you can teach. That life, as you know it, hasn't ended."

Ivan cleared his throat. "It only tells me that I should consider offering piano lessons in my own, uh, music studio. That is, if I ever rebuild it." Ivan adjusted the Velcro on his wrist splint. "Although..."

Willow smiled. "Why don't we trust God to heal that wrist in a way that's best for you from here on out?"

"I want a hundred percent. I'm not getting it."

"Trust God that He has something better for you than the 'Flight of the Bumblebee.' File that under 'been there, done that,' and move on to better things."

"Might be easy for you to say."

"You know as well as I do that violin is not your life, Ivan."

"Jesus Christ is." He knew, and yet in the fog of pain, he had forgotten.

"You got it. Take away the violin and you haven't lost everything. Take away Christ and you have absolutely nothing."

"I can't believe my little sister is reminding me of things I should know already."

"You know how it goes. The fog of war and all that. Cheer up. Remember how God saved you?"

Ivan could see Grandma Yun ushering him and Quincy down the church aisle, past the pews, to stand among all the other little kids as they belted out a medley of hymns in front of the congregation, hymns sung out of tune as every little pair of preschooler eyes were on Grandma Yun directing the kids, who could barely stand still let along focus on singing. Ivan and Quincy had always stood in the back, straight and tall, singing to the best of their vocal abilities and meaning every word of that one hymn.

Jesus loves me, this I know...

That afternoon twenty-four years ago he had given his little heart to Jesus, desiring to love God and trust Him for the rest of his life. And now, why did he find it hard to trust God? Why did he doubt God? Why did he forget God?

You have some sort of trust issue.

Willow hadn't minced her words.

She was right. Ivan had questioned everything God had provided for him the last four months.

God had sustained him since Grandma Yun's passing, but he wondered what his future would be.

God had been healing his wrist inside out, but he complained it wasn't healing fast enough. God had kept his hands intact, but he complained about not being able to get back to violin.

God had given him a place to stay at Willow's house, but he wondered when he would overstay her welcome.

God had brought him to Willow's studio to show him the possibility of teaching piano, but he had balked at it even if it were only for a short season in his life.

Questioning God showed his lack of trust in his perfect God.

Ivan admitted now that he had been putting stock in his own abilities, his talents, his gifts, his hands, his fingers, his violin. If Grandma Yun were alive today, she'd be sad. Perhaps she had been and it had killed her.

Quietly in his heart, Ivan began to pray.

Forgive me, Lord, for not trusting You.

Ivan knew then what he had to do.

CHAPTER SIXTY

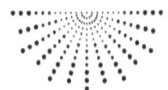

*I*van knew he was right. There would be food here. At six-thirty every Friday morning at the Seaside Chapel men's Bible study group meeting house at the Scrolls bookstore, the bagels and cream cheese spread appeared, looking like a million dollars right now to his empty stomach.

Oh boy, was he ever glad for free food. He hadn't eaten on the five-hour Greyhound bus ride from Atlanta to St. Simon's Island because he had slept on the trip, but he also hadn't eaten the night before, skipping dinner to avoid imposing on Willow.

Rock bottom.

His one-month sojourn at Willow's house had been good for his soul. He'd had lots of time to think about his life and what to do next. He still wasn't sure about everything, but one thing he knew to do. He had to get back to St. Simon's Island and ask Brinley to forgive him before he could move on to the rest of his life.

With the money he'd saved from the sale of his last violin—he had refused any payment for teaching Willow's students—Ivan knew that he could buy a one-way bus ticket to St. Simon's and have enough leftover to get food and a job.

Maybe Matt had another job available for him at the thrift shop. Matt, his most patient friend. A true brother in Christ.

For a place to stay, he could camp out at a campground somewhere.

"Don't eat it all!" Sebastian Langston slapped Ivan's back. "Good to see you, man. Has it been a month since you've been gone?"

"Yeah."

"How's that wrist?"

"It's healing." Somewhat. He needed to get back into therapy quickly.

"We've been praying for you, Ivan. Every week. Matt reminds us if we forget."

Ivan glanced over at his old friend. "He's a good friend."

"We all are. If you need anything, holler. Do you need a place to stay?"

"Well, I do, but..." Ivan was trying to figure out how to say it without appearing needy or desperate, which he was, when Matt yelled at them.

"Take a number, Seb. Ivan's staying at my house."

"I guess I do have a place to stay," Ivan said to

Sebastian. He'd have to save the campground for later.

Sebastian wiped cream cheese off his chin. "When can you play in SISO again?"

"I don't know."

"Surely they want you back. You're their star." Sebastian motioned for him to sit down next to him in the circle of folding chairs. Sometimes Ivan wondered if Matt purposefully let them sit on these uncomfortable chairs to keep the Bible study down to an hour flat.

"They have a new concertmaster." Ivan settled down and wondered if it would look bad if he went back for a third bagel.

Sebastian shrugged. "I've heard that Warren guy play. I like you better."

"Thanks, Seb."

"We'll keep praying for you until you can get back in shape."

The door chime jiggled. Ivan looked up. Tristan Rao from Rao Family Physicians.

"Tristan." Ivan shook Tristan's hands. "Didn't know you're attending this Bible study now."

"Matt here is very persuasive," Tristan said. "I'm sorry about your grandmother. She was a wonderful woman."

"In heaven now with Grandpa."

"Our consolation and comfort." Tristan pointed to Ivan's wrist. "How's your therapy coming along?"

"Really tough." *Painful.*

"I bet. Getting full mobility is going to take a lot of time. How long have you been at it?"

"Roughly two months."

"You have four to six months to go. Take it easy."

Ivan nodded, sipping coffee. It was hot and delicious. He downed it, then placed the empty cup on the floor. When he lifted his head, Tristan was opening his Bible and a bookmark fell out. It looked exactly like the bookmark that Brinley had given Ivan—

Why does everything have to remind me of her!

"Who's teaching today?" Ivan asked, breaking his own muse.

"I am." Sebastian raised his hand. "We're going to go over what Pastor Gonzalez preached on Sunday and discuss how we've applied it to our lives this week. First, let's pray to ask God to help us understand His Word."

Ivan thought that Sebastian's prayer was short and succinct. Then Sebastian handed Ivan an extra printout of the sermon notes from Sunday. Ivan was at Willow's church in Atlanta the Sunday before, but he couldn't remember what was preached.

All he knew was that he missed Seaside Chapel and wished there was something like that near Willow. She didn't want to drive more than five or ten minutes, so Midtown Chapel was out of the question, since he had to carpool with her. Willow's church was around the corner from her house. The congregational singing was passable, but the pastor's sermons had put him to sleep every Sunday.

Yeah, I miss Seaside Chapel.

Sebastian swiped his iPad and found the Bible verse. "Mark 8:36 says, 'For what will it profit a man if he gains the whole world, and loses his own soul?' Is that something we consider in our daily life?"

Ivan had since sold his iPad. He held his three-dollar paperback Bible open as he scanned the sermon outline in his hands. Pastor Gonzalez had taken apart the verse, but it all boiled down to the last point on the printout.

Nothing in this world could compare to what a Christian had in Christ.

Yes, Ivan had the basic intangibles in Christ—salvation, eternal life—but he didn't have the peace and joy that he should have.

"It's funny how we sometimes think of the verse as it pertains to an unsaved person losing a soul while gaining the world, and while that is true, for a saved person, our souls are secure in heaven forever and we can never lose them."

"No one can pluck us out of God's hand." Tristan flicked that bookmark in his fingers and for some reason it annoyed Ivan. It fell on the floor.

Ivan quickly reached it, and flipped it over, but there was no writing there.

What am I thinking?

He gave the bookmark back to Tristan, who muttered *thanks*.

"I don't know about you, but I'd rather not have anything in this world and have my soul be right with God." Sebastian looked around the room. "Truth is, that's a struggle for me. My girlfriend wants things. Things, you know."

"Mine's the opposite." Tristan shrugged. "She keeps giving things away. I mean—huh?"

Sebastian was clearing his throat and mumbling something.

"Pardon?" Tristan turned an ear toward Sebastian. "You said something?"

Sebastian cleared his throat again. "Let's see if we can memorize this verse and we'll take it through another week. It's important for us to think about this long and hard."

Whassup? Ivan looked from Tristan to Sebastian.

"Okay. Thanks, Seb." Matt uncapped his pen, ready to write on a clipboard. "So any prayer requests?"

"I need a job," Ivan admitted.

"Got a few new positions you can apply for," Matt said. "My cashier had her baby, but she's not coming back. There's that and a few backroom jobs."

"I'll do it. Do you need me to reapply?"

"Nope." Matt gave Ivan two thumbs up.

They went around the room adding prayer requests to their list. Only four guys here today. Sparse. Everyone jotted down the prayer request. They moved on to the next. And the next.

It's good to be home.

Ivan finished his coffee as he listened. Sick people needed healing. Career people needed directions.

"You know, that's what I like about our group," Ivan said before they began praying. "We pray for one another, care for one another, help one another."

"Brothers in Christ, Ivan." Matt slapped Ivan on his shoulder. "Brothers in Christ."

CHAPTER SIXTY-ONE

"*M*an, you still have pictures of your ex-wife all over the place." Ivan put down his duffle bag on the floor and picked up an antique silver frame off an old console table near the door to the balcony overlooking the playground and pier.

Matt Garnett didn't answer.

"That was a beautiful wedding, Matt." Ivan remembered because he was Matt's best man.

"Yeah. The most important day of my life before I got saved."

Ivan stood at the window. Outside was cloudy. Beyond the live oaks and the playground, he could see the lighthouse where he and Brinley had—

He turned away. "Hey, Matt. Just want to thank you again for letting me stay here for a bit."

"It's not all freebie. You know you need to put in some good hours at my shop."

"For sure."

"Where's your violin?"

"My what?"

Matt was standing there at Ivan's duffle. "Violin, dude. Where is your violin?"

"I'm not playing it anymore." Ivan didn't want to tell him that he sold his last violin to pay for food and to keep up with the minimum payments on his bills. He'd have to declare bankruptcy soon, but he wanted to hold out as long as he could. No need to disgrace the memories of his grandparents, who had raised him better than this.

"That's the stupidest thing I've ever heard, Ivan."

Ivan lifted up his braced left wrist as if to prove his point.

"You're such a whiner, Ivan. Remember when I beat you at track in tenth grade and you cried?"

"I did not!"

"Yeah. Sure. You said a bug flew into your eye. Like anyone's going to believe it."

"It did! A gnat of some sort!"

"Your ego flew into your eye, Ivan." Matt elbowed him on the way to the small galley kitchen. "Want a sandwich?"

"What you got?"

"PBJ. Not grape, though. Ran out. Apricot is what I have. On sale."

"Anything. I don't care." Ivan glanced at the distant lighthouse one more time.

He wondered how Brinley was doing. Where she was, who she was going out with. But he told himself it was a passing interest, these thoughts of his. Brinley and Christmas were over.

The month or so he had spent at Willow's house in Atlanta had been therapeutic. He didn't know anybody at her church, so they didn't ask him questions he didn't want to answer. For the most part, he kept to himself and was even able to sub for Willow a couple of times in her piano studio in exchange for room and board. Teaching little kids piano was easy and he didn't have to turn his wrist, so it all worked out. He did his own physical therapy since he had no health insurance, and he could flex his wrist more now.

All in all, he was getting better.

Thank You, God. And I'm sorry I was such a pain in the neck.

Willow's piano studio in Atlanta was smaller than his violin studio. He wondered if they might come together to expand their music studios, but he really didn't want to move to Atlanta. He didn't care for the traffic and people and noise and city life and all. If he went further and further out into Atlanta's suburbia, the number of students would be fewer.

Yet somehow on St. Simon's Island he managed to end up with forty students before his violin studio shut down due to his injury. He didn't want to open a piano studio even though he could play it. He wasn't as interested in piano as he was in violin. But now that his violin career was over, perhaps piano was as good a Plan B as any other.

Meanwhile, Matt had offered him a job at his

thrift shop. Maybe he could get some discounts on summer clothes. He should replace his faded cargo shorts.

Matt handed him a triple-decker peanut butter and apricot jam sandwich.

They bowed to say grace. Ivan dug in. He hadn't realized he was hungry again. Well, the bagels this morning only lasted so long.

"So what made you come back here, Ivan?"

"St. Simon's is home." And yet he wondered. With Grandma Yun gone and the house lost, was the island still home?

"You know that girl of yours—"

"Emmeline?"

"No, stupid."

"Stop calling me stupid."

"Anybody who dumped Brinley is stupid." Matt laughed. "Anyway, are you coming to church Sunday?"

"Yes. Why?"

"Just wondering. Brinley has joined our church."

"So?" Ivan took a deep breath. "I don't care, Matt."

"Really, dude?" Matt closed the peanut butter jar and put it away in the refrigerator. "Funny. Brinley got saved. Her spiritual life is going way up. You've been saved a long time. Your spiritual life is going way down. Who is learning more about God and life and such?"

"And why does it matter to you?"

"Because I'm your friend. And a brother in Christ."

Ivan didn't reply. Didn't want to continue talking. He had to sort it out.

With God.

And with Brinley.

"I need to get back to the shops," Matt said. "You can come with me if you want, or hang out here. I'm waiting for a new shipment of music manuscripts. Nineteenth century. You might be interested."

"Not anymore. But I'm sure someone will buy them from you."

"Yes. Someone is. You know, the one who likes old things."

Only one person he knew liked old things. "Brinley?"

"She bought all your violin music, you know. Said someday you'll want them back."

"She did?"

"No. I made that up. Of course, she did. That woman's in love with you."

I don't want to hear that.

"You don't want to hear that," Matt said.

"You know me too well."

"Bro, I can hear you when you think aloud." Matt shook his head as he unhooked a key from a nail on the wall. "Here's the extra key to the house. Come and go as you please, but no pets. And I expect you to start paying rent soon."

"Not to worry, Matt. I won't be here long. I

appreciate the work at your thrift shop, but sooner or later I'm going to have to get back to music."

"You can always teach violin. Oh, wait, the wrist. Bummer." Matt shook his head. "I think that's a cop-out, Ivan. You *can* teach. You just won't find a way. Violin is not the only instrument you play."

True, but I don't want to hear that either.

"I can hear you." Matt was at the door and Ivan was right behind him.

Ivan was going with him to the shops after all. He decided he didn't want to mope about in Matt's apartment for the next four or five hours. Better do something to take his mind off his penniless life.

"You can teach piano, right?" Matt asked. "You said you subbed for your sister."

"Only for about a month."

"Music is music, right?"

"There's a big difference between violin and piano."

"Really? All I know is that if you can't play violin, find another instrument or do something else alto-gether. Life goes on. You know that, but you won't humble yourself before God to ask for His help to enable you to move on."

"I've asked for His help countless times. Silence is all I get."

"Could it be because you don't want answers that don't match up with your preconceived plans?"

"My plans? Not working so far."

"Exactly! You forgot Proverbs 3:5-6, the verse Pastor Gonzalez had everyone at church memorize last year, and which you expanded on in our Bible study back in December. So how about an action plan, dude? Like, maybe: surrender all your plans to God and let Him clean up your mess?"

Ivan didn't reply. *Everywhere I go that verse pops up!*

They filed into Matt's dented and scratched cargo van. He had furniture in the back, but Ivan knew he couldn't help him unload those with his bad wrist.

His bad wrist.

I've got to stop focusing on my bad wrist.

Ivan fastened his safety belt and noticed a three-by-five card duct-taped to the door of the glove compartment. It was Proverbs 16:3.

Matt seemed to have noticed. "Let's think about that verse. 'Commit your works to the Lord, and your thoughts will be established.' I got it memorized because I need it myself."

Ivan caught two words: works and thoughts.

And began to get it.

If he committed his *works* to God, then God would help line up his thoughts so he could accomplish those works, those plans, those goals.

All right. Something for him to think about.

But first, he had to get a job that matched his skills. Working in Matt's shop was only temporary.

Oh. There it is again: work.

Silently, Ivan prayed in his heart and surrendered his career to God.

CHAPTER SIXTY-TWO

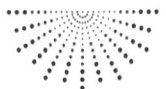

"Good to see you back!" Pastor Tom Gonzalez pumped Ivan's hand vigorously. His handshake was firm and purposeful.

Ivan had no idea how Pastor Gonzalez had found him after church. He must've seen him enter the sanctuary with Matt Garnett at the start of the service. The Seaside Chapel pastor missed nothing. At all.

Once again, his sermon was apropos. Ivan hoped Brinley was paying attention, if she were at church today.

Why does everything make me think of her?

After church, Ivan found a dark and obscure corner of the lobby to stand and wait for Matt to finish chatting with the ladies. He, on the other hand, had no intention of talking to anyone, no plans to explain why he was back in town though he doubted if anyone cared, and hoped nobody came to talk to him, especially Brinley. Well, she might have left through another door because he hadn't seen her at all.

And yet.

Yet here, in a dark corner of the old church, his pastor had found him.

"How's the wrist?" Pastor Gonzalez asked. The fifty-something man towered over Ivan's six feet. An imposing figure at the pulpit.

"It's healing, Pastor. Not a hundred percent, but getting there."

"Fractures take time to heal. I remember when my son fell off his bike and broke both wrists. We had to baby him. It was more painful for his mother than it was for him."

Ivan chuckled. "It's no fun being down."

"Certainly. How long has it been for you? A few months?"

"Yes. Two more months to go and I should be able to use my wrist again." *I hope.* "There's a bit of tendon damage, so it's touch and go."

"Keep up the therapy."

"Painful therapy."

Pastor Gonzalez laughed. "If it were easy, it wouldn't be called *physical* therapy."

"Good point."

"We've been praying for you. We'll keep praying until God completely heals you however He chooses to."

However God chooses to?

Ivan could take that in many ways. How God

chose to heal him hadn't been revealed. Ivan prayed it was what he wanted: to be able to play the violin again.

"The most important healing, though, is never physical," Pastor Gonzalez continued. "My son Lance had to learn patience. What's God teaching you through this?"

Ivan wasn't sure how to deal with the pop quiz.

"I think I'm learning to trust God more," he finally said. "That was a good sermon this morning. It helped me."

"Glad to hear that," Pastor Gonzalez said. "As Christians, we know we have the basics in Christ such as salvation and eternal life in heaven. But speaking for myself, I sometimes miss out on the other intangibles such as peace and joy and the rest of the fruit of the Spirit when I let the tangibles, my corporeal needs, my physical problems, whatever, overwhelm me."

"You too?"

"Yep. Me too. Like when that hurricane took out the roof of the church a few years back. You remember that?"

"Oh yeah. The whole church was soaked."

"Just the building. No one died. No soul perished."

"Thank God for that."

"Yes. We had to meet outdoors on the beach on Sunday mornings, and in the YMCA when it rained. Quite an ordeal."

"I kinda liked having church on the beach."

"Well, that's the thing. That entire episode began our Fire Pit Services, and we have one Wednesday night, as you saw in the bulletin."

Ivan nodded.

"You coming to that?"

"I might."

"I want to see you there." Pastor Gonzalez slapped Ivan's shoulder. "Want to have lunch with us?"

"What are we having?" Ivan already knew.

"The usual. My daughters only know how to cook one thing."

"I know. Enchilada." Ivan figured almost every member of Seaside Chapel had had lunch at the pastor's home after church on Sundays at one time or another. Some might have gone over there more than once. They lived across the street from the church and their doors were never closed.

Ivan wondered why he hadn't spoken to Pastor Gonzalez about his problems. He might have given him some good pointers. Maybe Ivan could have suffered less and endured more. Or something.

This morning's sermon was yet another one of Pastor Gonzalez's convicting messages. Straight from God and one more thing Ivan needed to hear. If he lined up all the verses that he had heard since December, they all really boiled down to one thing. And he'd better learn it fast if he wanted to get out of his mental slump.

Trust God.

Pastor Gonzalez waved to his son down a hallway, motioning to him that it was time to go. To Ivan, he said, "We can walk to my house, and then you can come back and get your car."

"I rode in with Matt. Let me tell him." There was Matt over there, surrounded by what looked like a growing audience.

That was Matt. The popular one. People around him were roaring with laughter. Ivan didn't want to interrupt the flow of adulation.

"Invite Matt too if he wants to come. I have to go get my wife now. I'll see you at the house."

"Okay, Pastor."

As Ivan crossed the lobby to get to Matt, he spotted Brinley walking down another hallway. She was wearing a long floral skirt and a matching lavender blouse. Her hair had grown longer past her shoulders, but it was still as straight as sawgrass.

Oops. I don't think she'd want me to compare her hair to sawgrass.

She was alone, and somehow that made Ivan happy. Not that she was *alone*, but that she wasn't with some guy other than her father. As he was thinking that, he saw Brinley stop at the glass doors leading to the parking lot. She stood to one side, as if waiting. *For her father?*

Ivan wondered whether he should go up to her to talk to her. Or whether he should leave her alone.

But his feet didn't move.

Just then Brinley looked his way. She didn't smile. Didn't wave. Maybe she didn't even see him.

I'm here!

He wanted to shout, but shame filled him. He remembered clearly how badly he had handled his misfortunes, how he had told Brinley to get lost and get out of his life. His exact words at the studio were what he could not forgive himself for.

Don't you get it? You ruined my career, my life, everything!

He didn't mean it. But he couldn't take every word back now. Maybe he could ask her to forgive him.

She was still standing there under the Exit sign. People walked past her. She didn't move. She was still looking in his direction.

Was she waiting for him to make the first move?

This was a showdown. Someone had to blink first. Ivan decided he was the one who had to do it. He had handled his own tragedies poorly. Now he had to be the first one to go to Brinley and ask her to forgive him.

As Ivan was thinking about his next step, some guy showed up to open the door for Brinley.

Dr. Tristan Rao.

Maybe they were at the door at the same time. A coincidence. That thought went out the door when Ivan saw Tristan put his hand on Brinley's waist.

I'm too late!

CHAPTER SIXTY-THREE

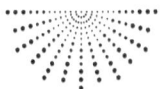

*T*hat was Ivan. As clear as day, it was Ivan.

Brinley couldn't focus on what Tristan Rao was rambling about as he drove them to lunch. Something about a duet. No, she didn't want to do a duet with Tristan when her heart belonged to someone else.

Someone who is now back on St. Simon's Island.

It should be a happy day, but Brinley didn't feel it. Why did Ivan stand there down the hallway? Why didn't he come to her and say hello? He was still wearing something on his left wrist. Probably a brace.

Thank You, God.

Ivan would never know that she had been praying every day the last three months for his wrist to heal. Sometimes she'd been in tears that it had been her fault, but God had comforted her through His Word.

So much she had yet to learn. She wished Yun

McMillan were still alive to guide her through the Bible, but she had been enjoying Pastor Gonzalez's wife's weekly Seaside Chapel women's Bible study group. Olivia Gonzalez had been quite insistent that the Holy Spirit of God was her real teacher.

So all was not lost.

Not that lost, anyway.

She could picture Yun in heaven now without her walker or her titanium hip. She would be carefree and loving life with Jesus. She could just see the Lord Jesus telling Yun, "Well done, good and faithful servant. Here are your rewards."

Brinley thought of her salvation as Demere Road came into view. People cycled on the sidewalks under green trees. The McKinnon St. Simon's Island Airport was to the left. Small planes were landing and taking off.

The sky was clear and blue. It was a perfect spring morning. Easter was next Sunday, and it would be Yun's first Easter in heaven. It would be so much more perfect than this.

Southern Soul Barbecue was packed as usual. Brinley remembered getting takeout from here that day so long ago after Ivan's wrist accident on the day he told her to get lost and never come back to that house.

How ironic it was that she had bought that house when it went into foreclosure to save it from being razed for rampant oceanfront development. She had rescued the house for future McMillans. No matter who Ivan eventually married, she could only wish him God's blessings.

She could not bring herself to hate him in spite of all that he'd spewed at her that day.

You ruined my career, my life, everything!

"Quiet, aren't you?" Tristan said after they ordered and as they waited for an empty table. His hands were in his pockets.

"I saw someone at church after the service today."

"Someone from your past?"

Well, Brinley wasn't sure if he was still in the past. Ivan and she had some unfinished business and until that was resolved, neither could move on.

"The man who broke my heart."

"You still won't tell me his name."

"It doesn't matter."

"We want to be transparent with each other if there is to be the possibility of *us*."

"There is no *us*, Tristan. We're only going out to lunch." They had met in Sunday school, the one that Ivan had been in until he left town.

As if on cue, Brinley's iPhone pinged, saving her from further talk about being an item with Tristan. "It's Helen. I've been waiting for this."

"Good news, I hope."

Brinley was still texting when she followed Tristan to a table vacated by customers. They waited for the server to wipe the table before they sat down. Their food came soon afterward. Beef briskets for her and whatever it was for Tristan. He said the blessing and they dug in.

"What did Helen say?" Tristan asked in between bites.

"They're still in Vienna, but they couldn't find the you-know-what." Brinley didn't want to say it aloud. The place was crowded. Not just walls, but people had ears. Considering she had refused any security personnel around her—much to Dad's protest—it was best if she stayed low key wherever she went on St. Simon's Island.

"You mean the Stra—"

"Yeah." *Sigh.*

"Now what?" Tristan tore off a piece of white bread.

"Now I pay to get it back."

"Sounds expensive."

Not much more than what Grandpa Brooks had spent in his lifetime to find it. The 1698 Damaris Brooks Stradivarius violin must return to the Brooks collection. And Brinley would do everything she could and pay any amount to get it back.

And Ivan will play Air *on it for me. He promised.*

Ivan again.

"What are you going to do the afternoon before the Fire Pit Service Wednesday night?" Tristan asked.

Brinley checked her calendar. Meeting with Tobias Vega over another renovation job. An elderly couple couldn't afford to fix up the home they had been staying in since they were married in the fifties.

Brooks Renovations would do it for charity. She hoped the meeting would be over by five. The church event didn't start until the sun went down.

"Since we're not helping with the food, we don't have to be there until six o'clock, right?" she asked.

"I want to get there early in case there's something I can help with."

"Good for you." Brinley forked more beef, but knew she had to take the rest to go. The portions were enormous. She would be eating more delicious beef brisket for dinner tonight.

"Do you want me to pick you up at five forty-five then?"

"I don't know, Tristan. I'm not sure when my meeting will end. I think it's five but I never know with Toby's schedule. I'll let you know."

Tristan seemed satisfied with the explanation. He looked nervous and then slowly began to speak again. "Brinley?"

"Yeah?" Brinley was sipping unsweetened tea.

"This is the third lunch we've had together," Tristan said.

"Uh-huh."

"I do enjoy your company, Brinley."

Uh-oh.

"I know you agreed to go out with me. I hope it's not because I'm safe."

It's exactly because you're safe. "Look, Tristan. We're not dating."

"We could be."

"I'm still recovering from my last relationship,

and from what I've learned over the past years, it's a bad idea to start a new relationship on the rebound."

"I hear you."

"The thing is that I am not sure if we're right for each other."

"We aren't?" He looked shocked.

"I am seeking God's perfect will for my life, and I need to focus on Him."

"I see." Tristan was visibly uncomfortable. "So you think maybe we should stop having lunches with each other?"

"Alone, yes. Your prospective dates would think you're taken."

"But I want to be taken."

Brinley smiled. "You're a hoot, Tristan. Funny, clever, brilliant, helpful, handsome—"

"I get it. Parting shots."

"Don't look at it that way." Brinley asked the server for a to-go box. "Look at it from God's perspective. He has someone special in store for you. When you see that person, you'll know. You have no doubt in your mind and heart whatsoever that she's the one who will share your life with you, have your kids, and love you until her dying day. And someday, she will realize it too if she hasn't already. Don't let me get in the way of your personal bliss, Tristan. It's not worth it."

"Wow. Sounds like you speak from experience."

Silence.

Tristan cleared his throat. "Whoever he is, he was an idiot to let you go."

CHAPTER SIXTY-FOUR

*T*van's hopes went up a sixteenth note when he saw that Brinley wasn't sitting next to Tristan at the Fire Pit Service on Wednesday evening. Perhaps it was because she was over there surrounded by other women.

He was a bit alarmed when he saw Emmeline O'Hanlon in the group. Skye Langston, he wasn't worried about, but Em? It could be bad if she and Brinley had talked about him—

Lighten up. Not everyone talks about you all the time.

To be sure, Ivan paid closer attention to Tristan Rao. He was chatting with some other church members now and wasn't even looking in Brinley's direction. Good news?

Ivan spotted some other church people in the crowd of twenty or thirty. Thin group tonight. According to Matt, some people were going to visit family for Easter this coming Sunday, so they didn't expect many regulars to show up tonight if they had to finish up work before heading out of town for their long weekend.

The people in attendance tonight were scattered about in the church pavilion and on the sand with their beach chairs, waiting for the sun to set and the fire to rise from the fire-pit. He sure missed these outdoor services since he'd been on his self-imposed exile in Atlanta.

Good to be back. Or is it?

"What are you feeding off?" Pastor Gonzalez spoke without a microphone tonight.

That made Ivan straighten up on his thrift shop beach chair, one of his very few worldly possessions these days.

"Are you feeding off what people say or what God says? Are you feeding off my sermons or God's Word?"

Pastor Gonzalez made his "I'm watching you" rounds with his eyes. He was strolling around the fire-pit, his voice lifting above the Atlantic waves some thirty feet away from where Ivan was sitting in a dark corner, where he had hoped to gather his thoughts before confronting Brinley later.

Inevitably, Pastor Gonzalez stopped in front of Ivan. Said nothing. Then moved on.

Thank God.

"I challenge you to study God's Word for yourself, to discover the unfathomable riches in Christ that all of us believers are privy to. Don't be a bottom feeder, eating crumbs off the table like dogs. Sit at the table with the Master, Jesus Christ Himself, and learn from Him."

That's me.

Ivan's mind played back his entire bottom-feeding life, from being abandoned by his parents as a little kid to losing the McMillan family home to foreclosure to sustaining a career-ending wrist injury.

Yeah. Eating crumbs.

Pastor Gonzalez was standing on the other side of the blazing fire now. In the firelight, sparks rose up and danced in the coastal wind.

"Everything that has happened to me in the past is a stepping stone to my future," he said. "I try not to underestimate the power of God over my own stupidity and failures. If you ask Olivia, she can tell you my horror stories."

"A tell-all memoir is in the works," Olivia quipped from her camp chair. She was surrounded by her two older stepdaughters, who had come home to visit, and her youngest daughter, Bryanna, who was still in high school. Her college-aged son, Lance, was somewhere in the vicinity, home for spring break. Ivan had seen him earlier.

Everyone laughed. Pastor Gonzalez went to his wife and held her hand. Ivan thought that was touching.

Wish I could hold Brin's hand too. Like that.

"Ask yourself a simple question when you wake up every morning." Pastor Gonzalez seemed to be wrapping up his sermonette. "Are you more spiritually mature today than yesterday? Than last week? Last month? Last year? A decade ago? I hope so. Grow spiritually in the Lord, and see what amazing things He'll do for you, in you, and through you. That's all I have for you tonight."

Pastor Gonzalez closed with a short prayer for good fellowship the rest of the evening.

When Ivan opened his eyes, Matt Garnett and a couple of other Seaside Chapel church members were standing up with their guitars. They played a medley of quiet hymns, the music from their guitars interspersing with the crackling of the fire and the crashing of the ocean waves.

The hymns of old calmed his spirit and soothed his soul.

On the other side of the fire-pit, Brinley wasn't talking with Skye and Emmeline anymore. She was just sitting there, a paper plate on her lap.

Here goes.

Ivan got up and went around the back of the circle toward Brinley. She didn't seem to notice him because other people were walking about too. Somewhere in the undulating human voices, someone started to play guitar again.

"May I throw that out for you?" Ivan pointed to her plate and fork.

Brinley lifted her chin. "Thank you."

Something shimmered in her eyes.

"Would you like me to get you something else?" Ivan asked.

"Nothing. Thanks."

Nothing from me?

No! That can't be what she means.

As Ivan walked across the sand to the nearest trash can, he cautioned himself not to read too much into what Brinley said. They had been separated since the week before Valentine's Day. He had broken her heart. She had every right to think nothing of him.

I have nothing to give her.

Nothing—

A realization hit him, the same way the other epiphany slapped him in the face in Atlanta when he had his heart-to-heart talk with Willow when she reminded him that in spite of his woe-is-me whining, his bad wrist was still attached to him. The broken wrist was temporary. He had mourned it like he had lost his wrist permanently.

I have nothing to give Brin.

Nothing but the love of God.

He doubled back to Brinley. She was getting up to go. "Brin, wait."

Brinley looked back.

"We need to talk." Ivan's words came out in spurts, totally asynchronous to the backdrop of ocean waves. *Only a musician would have noticed that.* "Walk with me?"

∾

"*I* lied, Brin. You didn't ruin my life," Ivan said as they settled onto the wooden stairs of some beachfront hotel behind them.

Brinley kept her eyes on the ocean. Under the full moon, the Atlantic waves were shimmering silver and blue interspersed with dark and foreboding waters. Above the roar of ocean and the distant laughter and singing outside Seaside Chapel's pavilion, Ivan's words echoed in her head.

You didn't ruin my life.

"I don't hate you. In fact, I fell in love with you halfway through Bach that evening at your sister's birthday party. Do you remember that?"

Of course.

But Brinley couldn't speak. Something in her chest or throat or whatever—she didn't know—had reminded her of her feelings on that Thursday evening when Ivan had walked her back to her parents' cottage.

The memories slammed into her equipoise or what was left of it—before Ivan had shredded it to bits.

"I'm sorry I've been stupid," Ivan tried again. "Forgive me?"

Brinley said nothing.

"We may never get together again, but I want to walk away knowing you have forgiven me." Ivan touched her hand, but she pulled away. "Okay, then. This is going to be hard for both of us."

"You think?" Brinley glared.

"She speaks." Ivan chuckled.

"Be serious, Ivan. Do you know how long you've inflicted your personal issues on me?"

"You counted?"

"Roughly forty-two days."

"I'm so sorry."

He seemed to genuinely mean it, but Brinley had had it with people's recurring apologies—

Seventy times seven.

The last verse that Yun McMillan had read to her three days before she passed away was Matthew 18:21. It stuck in Brinley's mind, but she hadn't expected to be reminded of it now.

Not now, God. I'm trying to be upset with Ivan here. Gimme a moment.

Still the words were clear. She could recite every word from the Bible that Yun had used.

> *Then Peter came to Him and said, "Lord, how often shall my brother sin against me, and I forgive him? Up to seven times?"*

But—

"I pray that someday you will forgive me, Brin. I can see I've hurt you."

"More than you can *see*."

"I know. Again, I'm very sorry. I would spend the rest of my life making it up to you if I could, but considering this is the end of the road for us, I guess you'll have to settle with the fact that I have tried to make peace with you."

"You talk a lot."

"I'm trying to apologize here." The wind ruffled Ivan's hair. He looked cute as he tried to fix his hair so it didn't come down his forehead and into his eyes.

Cute?

Brinley glanced away.

"Even though we're going separate ways, we're going to run into each other every now and then, and I'd rather not have this hostility between us."

Brinley zipped up her hooded cardigan. "I thought you live in Atlanta now."

"Well, I was until I felt convicted to come home to make amends with you."

Home? He considers St. Simon's Island his home?

Brinley might be upset, but she was also inherently curious. *This I have to hear.* "Did your sister kick you out of the house?"

"Strangely enough, not this time. Grandma's death has reconciled us."

"Glad to hear that."

"However, I do believe that had I stayed another month, I would have worn out my welcome."

Brinley laughed.

"Made you laugh."

"And made me weep too, Ivan." *Oh, so many times she had lost count.*

"I know." He lifted a strand of hair away from Brinley's face. "I don't know how many times I've said I'm sorry, Brin."

"I forgive you."

"I'm glad I got through to you."

"You didn't. Jesus got through to me. All I know is that He has forgiven me for my sins, so it would be wrong of me to withhold forgiveness from you."

"Sounds like something Grandma would say."

Brinley placed her head on Ivan's shoulder. "I miss Yun very much."

He wrapped his arms around her, drawing her close. "I miss her too."

"Now will you forgive me?" Brinley asked.

"Of course, but for what?"

"Fixing your commode. Giving you a Strad. General interfering." She then realized there were more things she'd spent money on that she wasn't prepared to tell him about at this time. Too much for her to explain, too little time to do it properly.

"Don't worry about it. I should've said *thank you* instead of making a big stink out of everything you were trying to do for me, everything God was trying to bless Grandma and me with."

"We're all learning," Brinley said. "How is your wrist, if I may ask?"

"You may. I'm still in pain about every day, but I'm handling it. My fingers can slide down the strings now, but I still can't do the vibrato. I can't play the—uh, any Bach, really."

"Sounds like you need to give it time."

"It's not happening."

"Patience, Ivan. Want me to kiss it and make it all better?" Brinley teased.

"Maybe." He seemed serious. "I still have the coupon you gave me at Christmas for free hugs and kisses for a year. I must confess that when I got mad at you, I tore up the bookmark, but I repaired it. Does it still count if it's taped together with packing tape?"

"Well, considering your behavior the last two months, I'm not sure if you're hug-worthy."

"Point taken. I'm sorry that I handled things poorly."

"I did too. Not just you." Brinley shrugged. "Are you back in town for good?"

"I'll try to stay out of your way, but I do like going to our church."

Our church?

"No need to find a new church, Ivan. Seaside Chapel is big enough for the both of us."

"I'll go to a different Sunday school class so we don't have to run into each other."

Brinley thought about it. "That could work."

They sat in silence, watching the night, listening to the ocean. In the distance, the singing around the fire-pit was dying down.

"I may never play violin again," Ivan finally said.

"It's not the end of the world."

"I tried teaching voice, but my vocal cords are wretched."

Why is he so negative? "You can always teach piano."

"I now work in Matt's thrift shop."

"At least you have a job."

"I only earn minimum wage."

"Income is income." Brinley thought Ivan could do better, but it was a good start.

"And I'm homeless."

"You're what?" Brinley recoiled away from Ivan.

"For now. Actually, I'm bunking with Matt temporarily. Once I earn enough income I can rent my own place."

Brinley shifted on the steps. "As you know, I'm in the real estate investment business. Just so happens I have a house for rent." One of many, but there was one particular house she had in mind.

"A house?" Ivan shook his head. "I can't afford to rent a house. A trailer, maybe."

"I'll rent you *one room* in the house. I'll even throw in a complimentary stove. Two hundred a month." Brinley would have to foot the remaining monthly payment amount herself, but it was nothing if it meant that Ivan had a place to stay.

"Two hundred dollars for one room? That's cheap. But why?"

"I don't want to see you living under a bridge."

"So you do care. For the record, I've never lived under a bridge, at least not yet."

Brinley dug up her iPhone from her jacket pocket and swiped it a few times. "I'll have my rental manager call you. How can she contact you?"

"I don't have a phone."

"That bad, huh?" Brinley wanted to say that reloadable disposable cell phones were cheap these days, but she didn't want him to think she was telling him what to do. He'd rather learn it by himself.

"Have her call Matt's shop."

"That'll work." Brinley studied him. "Are you ever going back to music?"

"Maybe someday."

"God has given you a gift, Ivan. I can't imagine His letting it go to waste. He began a good work and He'll complete it. Trust God."

"Yes, I'm learning that."

"I've heard very few people play the violin like you do. Well, there's—never mind. You're better looking."

"Haha."

"And if you need a job in a music studio—"

He lifted a hand. "You've helped me enough, Brinley. Let me figure out my career on my own."

"Just trying to help."

"I know. Thank you."

"You going back to therapy?" Brinley asked.

Ivan nodded feebly.

"You have to if that wrist is going to get back into shape."

"I know. I'll find a way."

Brinley prayed that he would. She decided to make sure he did. East Beach Therapy Center was in the phonebook. If her memory served her right, she had seen its CEO at some of the historical functions in town. A generous grant for a rehabilitation program for injured musicians would move his mountains. Seriously, she didn't have to go that far to get Ivan back into therapy, but it would help many more musicians than Ivan alone.

The wind picked up. It might be early April, but the night air was still cool.

"There's a reason for the fire-pit, Ivan. We're too far away to stay warm. And don't tell me we have each other." Brinley got up, brushed the sand off the back of her jeans, and faced Ivan.

"Your fifteen minutes are up, Ivan. I'm glad we had our little talk. I wish you God's perfect will for your life."

Ivan frowned at Brinley's outstretched hand. "You want me to shake your hand?"

"Friends, right?"

Ivan's eyes widened. He looked confused. "I'm not sure if I want to be just friends."

His hand warmed up Brinley's and disinterred images of their weeks together that seemed to stretch forever. She had kept it all in throughout their little talk, trying to remain as objective as she could about his apologies and his being back in town.

Ivan didn't let go of Brinley's hand. Instead he stood up and drew her close.

"I thought we had a good thing going." She put her face against his flannel shirt. She loved the warmth of his chest and the sound of his heartbeats. "What happened to us, Ivan?"

"I had too much on my plate."

"We could've been there for each other."

"I know, Brin. I've done many regrettable things in my life, and that's one of the worst ones."

"That's a reason we have family, friends, community."

"Maybe I've been alone so long that I didn't know how to not do it on my own." Ivan rubbed her shoulders. "I wish you were with me through my dark days. I wasn't there when you grieved over my grandma. I blamed you for everything when deep inside I wanted you so badly. I didn't think I could be good enough to be your h—uh..."

"Husband?" Brinley asked.

Silence.

"Why didn't you fight for us, Ivan?"

Silence.

"What is wrong with you and me together?" Brinley asked.

"I guess I couldn't get past myself. But now I have."

"I got saved, Ivan. I'm attending church. Going to a Bible study. Aren't you happy for me?"

"I am. I started praying for you that night you came home to Seaside Island."

She remembered that night. "I appreciate your prayers."

"It was all going swimmingly until I broke my wrist. I failed that faith test. I lost my fellowship with God. I lost you."

"You haven't lost God or me, Ivan."

"I don't deserve you."

"Nor I you. And neither of us deserves God. Yet He chose to give us life and salvation out of His own love."

Ivan stared at her.

"What, Ivan?"

"Your spiritual growth is amazing."

"And it's because of you. Because you dumped me—"

Ivan winced. "Don't remind me."

"Truly, I needed time away from you to grow in the Lord as a new Christian. If you were around, I wouldn't have been sure whether I believed in Jesus because you did. Since you weren't around, I knew without a doubt that my salvation is genuine."

"Yeah. I would've been in the way." Ivan kissed her forehead, accepting, welcoming.

"God worked it all out for our good."

"Romans 8:28." Ivan held her hand. "Would you like to have lunch with me tomorrow? I have about an hour between shifts."

"Hang on." Brinley checked her calendar on her iPhone. "My schedule is packed all day Thursday. Maybe you can take the time to talk to my rental manager. How about lunch on Friday?"

"Friday lunch it is. Noon okay with you?"

"Sure. Name the place."

"Meet me at the foot of the lighthouse."

CHAPTER SIXTY-FIVE

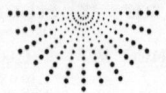

*I*van McMillan stood there. Just stood there.

He couldn't believe what he was seeing. The yard was immaculate. The grass cut, the bushes trimmed. The live oak trees with their Spanish moss hung lower and looked fuller in the afternoon sun.

And was it his imagination or had Grandma Yun's house expanded?

The carport was gone, replaced by a two-car garage with carriage doors. The roofline extended all the way over two new windows above the garage. Ivan walked around the garage and came face to face with a garden that Grandma Yun had spoken about, but no one had the wherewithal to execute. Butterflies were everywhere on various bushes, and the air smelled of gardenias. He faced the back of the house. Walls of windows were everywhere overlooking the garden.

He wished Grandma Yun could see all this. Under the two o'clock afternoon sun, the entire property brightened in natural light on this sunny, rainless Thursday.

Too bad Grandma is not here to see this beauty.

Then again, heaven is even more exquisite.

Ivan heard a vehicle door slam and he made his way to the front of the house. Parked right behind the car he had borrowed from Matt was a big SUV. A well-dressed lady tumbled out of it.

"Hello! You must be Ivan McMillan. I'm Megan Zimmerman." The rental manager with the name tag and a thick folder shook his hands. "Did you have any difficulty finding this place?"

"No. I used to live here." Ivan followed her up the steps to the porch. The pine boards looked brand new. Stained and silent as he stepped on them.

She fixed them.

"No wonder the owner is letting you rent this place for dirt cheap."

Dirt cheap.

Somehow those words didn't sit well with Ivan. Maybe it was a mindset. He'd have to fix that sort of thinking. Pastor Gonzalez said on Sunday that his confidence needed to be in Christ and not in his circumstances.

When Megan opened the front door, Ivan didn't hear a thing. The door no longer creaked. He followed her into the house.

And just stared.

The entire interior had been renovated, but every room was empty.

"Empty, this house rents for two thousand a month, but you can get it fully furnished for four if you like."

"Who would rent it fully furnished?"

"Usually corporate executives on retreats or long-term vacationers. People come and go all the time." The rental manager stepped farther into the house. "I can't believe you're getting this place for one-tenth the cost. Are you a family friend?"

"Something like that." Technically he was only renting a room, but that was a joke. He'd get the whole house. The living room was bright and airy and overlooked the butterfly garden. He could envision Grandma Yun sitting in her rocker reading her Bible by the window.

Tears welled in his eyes, but he knew better than to weep over the past. Grandma Yun was with her Otto now in heaven, where the splendor and the glory of God were above and beyond anything they could ever have on earth.

And his grandparents were both well now. No walkers, no weak hearts, no titanium hips. Just pleasant days in the sunshine of God's eternal and unlimited love.

Pleasant days.

Ivan's thoughts went to his old studio downstairs. What had Brinley done to the basement space, he wondered? He'd have to find that out later as Megan led him to the kitchen.

The kitchen. Wow. Ivan couldn't believe his eyes. The back wall had been pushed out and this was a huge kitchen with shiny appliances. Right in the middle of it was a kitchen island the size of a small car. He could envision a family utilizing this space.

A family?

Mine.

Would Brinley want to live here? He felt inadequate all of a sudden. Renting would have to do for now, but someday he wanted to own his own house.

Sure, it was a steal at a couple of hundred dollars a month, but a warning niggled his mind. He would be renting from Brinley. He hated that dependency, especially after what her brother had said to him.

He hated owing anyone anything. Well, anyone but God.

Trust God.

Was he trusting God now?

"Do you want to see the rest of the house?" Megan asked. The many keys jangled in her hands.

"Yes." This wasn't Grandma's house anymore, not the way it had been.

Brinley must have gotten this house when it had gone into foreclosure. Or perhaps she had bought it directly from the bank. He hadn't known who had bought the house because the bank had taken over at that time and he was out of the equation.

He wondered why Brinley had bought the house.

Was it her memories of spending time here? She liked old things. So maybe she was keeping history alive.

Megan's phone rang. "Why don't you look around on your own? I'll be on the porch."

"Sounds good." Ivan wandered to the back of the house. Standing at the doorframe to what used to be Grandma Yun's room but bigger, he realized it was now a library or another sitting room. Through the tall windows he could see the grove of live oaks behind the house. They seemed closer to him now as if the entire back of the house had been pushed out.

He stood at the window for a moment, remembering his childhood days of playing with wooden swords and towels for capes among the live oaks and running in and out of the fort that would've been over there in a small clearing.

Sunrays peeked through overhanging oak branches, making shifting designs on the green grass in that space where he and his siblings had spent many seasons.

Maybe I'll build a fort again.

For my kids.

Our kids.

Brinley filled his mind and a warmth filled his heart. Full of love and peace and joy. "Lord, why are You so good to me?"

Yet those warning signs still fired off in his mind. He was about to go downstairs to the basement studio when Megan returned to the foyer.

"Ready to sign the rental papers?" She had a silver pen with her.

"Would you give me a minute? I'm going to take a look at the basement."

"Sure thing. It's finished." Megan began texting as Ivan dashed to the door at the top of the stairs.

The empty basement had been repainted. All the walls were cream and the window frames were white. The glass panes looked new and sunshine came in. The old, stained carpet was no more. In its place was stone flooring of some sort, looking nice and clean in the late morning sun.

Ivan could still remember where he had stood when he played most of "Pleasant Days" for Brinley right after she had brazenly fed him with half a cookie. It seemed long ago now, but it had only been last Christmas.

He remembered finishing the composition. It was still in his laptop, untouched these four months. He couldn't have played it with a broken wrist. In the last four months, he hadn't lifted a violin or a bow to test his wrist again since the day he buried Grandma Yun.

That chapter of his life was over.

Or is it?

He flexed his left hand under the brace. It wasn't hurting as much as it used to. Vittorio, the therapist, had said before that his wrist needed time to heal. The broken bones had fused and his wrist was some-what functional now. The tendons no longer twitched, but he still couldn't turn his wrist with its original range of motions, and still couldn't play as much music as he'd like.

Forget Paganini and Rimsky-Korsakov and Vivaldi.

I'm done.

Or am I?

After all, Brinley had said she didn't care if he never played the violin again. Still, there was that promise he'd made her. Well, we'll cross that bridge if she ever got her 1698 Damaris Brooks Stradivarius violin back. Somehow he doubted that would ever happen.

For now he had a new job at Matt's thrift shop. He appreciated Matt letting him off work an hour early today so he could come here. But it might be all for naught.

A couple of knocks on the door at the top of the stairs echoed down to him. "Mr. McMillan, I have another appointment to go to. Have you decided?"

Lord, she wants to know now. Should I rent this house or not?

Until he heard from God clearly, Ivan knew he'd better not make any rash decisions. He had learned his lesson. What had Grandma Yun told him growing up?

Don't do anything until you're sure you've heard from God.

Radio silence right now. Ivan knew it wasn't necessarily a big old *no* from God. It could be that this wasn't the time for him to make this decision. But two hundred dollars a month was only one-tenth of a way smaller apartment. What if this was his halfway house? What if this was God's provision for him at this time in his life?

At peace, Ivan knew what he had to do. He

reached the top of the stairs, where Megan was waiting, clicking her pen. "What kind of rental agreement did Brin—uh, the owner—say I can look at?"

Megan smiled. "Brinley has told me to expect the unexpected."

"She has?"

"We have three different rental options. You can rent it monthly, biannually, or yearly. She told me to bring all options."

She knows me well.

"Let's take it one month at a time," Ivan said. He wasn't sure where he'd be six months from now. He hoped that Brinley would still be in the picture, but he wouldn't be able to tell until they met for lunch Friday.

"She said that's probably what you'd want."

Ivan was amused. "What else did Brin say?"

"She said to make sure you know there's a brand-new dishwasher in the kitchen."

"Is there?" How could he forget her drying the plates and silverware after church one Sunday in December? Brinley had probably never done dishes before in her entire life. Yet she had helped him without complaining.

What a sweet spirit she had even before she met Jesus.

I have wronged her, Lord. How can I ever forgive myself?

Just like that the answer came to his heart.

Because Christ has forgiven you at the cross so long ago.

Those were based on Grandma Yun's words, her tireless years of trying to impart Biblical truth to her grandchildren.

A rebuke. A reproach. A gentle reminder.

Go and sin no more.

CHAPTER SIXTY-SIX

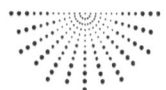

*A*t exactly noon, Ivan had been sitting for five minutes on the steps of the gazebo on the grassy grounds of St. Simon's Lighthouse, waiting for Brinley to show up. She was late and he was beginning to worry though Matt had given him until half past one o'clock for lunch. Tourists milled about, oblivious to the pitter-patter in his chest, the twinge in his left wrist, and the quiet tumbling of the antique store find in his pocket.

He flexed his left hand, stretching and retracting his fingers. The pain in his wrist had decreased, but slowly. He thanked God for his health insurance from his new job at the thrift shop. He could be working there a while.

Twice this week he'd gone to duke it out with Vittorio, his physical therapist. He was glad to have his reluctant patient back even though he had complained that a whole month of self-therapy didn't cut it. He made sure that Ivan knew it by making his wrist work harder than usual.

Ironically, Ivan had welcomed the new regimen. Motivated to get well, to be able to return to functional life, to be two-handed again, he pushed himself harder and harder through the exercises all week. Every day. Several times a day. To the point that his left hand was now able to—

"Hi."

Ivan had no idea how long she had been standing there.

"Are you thinking what I'm thinking?" Brinley sat down next to Ivan on the steps.

It was the same question he had asked her at the after-party that December evening.

Has it been that long?

"Scales," Ivan said. "I was thinking of being able to play scales now. Thank God."

"See, God is healing you."

"Yes."

"And slides?" Brinley looked into his eyes.

He had caught her staring at him like that a few times back when they were together.

It seemed she liked to search his eyes. Not sure what she was seeing now. It was a partly cloudy day with no sun in his eyes.

"Portamento? I need more time to work on that, but I'm getting there." Ivan wrapped his arms around Brinley. He didn't care that there were people around them, walking about, taking pictures at the water's edge and around the St. Simon's Lighthouse in front of them. He was comfortable here with Brinley.

Too comfortable to move.

"Once my fingers can curl and slide, then we can work on the rest of it." Ivan wasn't going to tell her now, but his carrot on a stick was that "Air on the G String." Bach would be pleased that his little number was therapeutic.

But what Ivan did want to tell her today would take a whole lot of courage. He prayed quickly for God to infuse him with the right words to say.

"I'm happy that you're working your way back to the violin." Brinley sat closer.

"With God's help, I'm going to try my best and see where it goes. If I can play the violin again, I'll do it. If not, then God's will be done."

"Yun had said that God's will is best for us."

"She was right." Ivan breathed evenly. "I've stopped complaining. It was a bad testimony to show you, my friends, the people at church, even the PT, and the world."

"Yeah. When the bottom falls out, the Christian freaks out."

"That was me, but not anymore." He mustered up his courage. *Here goes.* "I love you, Brinley Brooks. Will you marry me?"

The pause was too long. Then he heard a sigh.

"No."

This is bad. "Why not?"

"You're exasperating," Brinley said.

"I'm in love."

"Your life is upside down."

"I'm in love." He kissed her cheek.

"Your faith is very weak."

"My love is strong."

"I don't think so. You ran away and hid, Ivan."

"I've learned my lesson." He kissed her earlobe. "So marry me? For better or for worse? For richer or poorer?"

Brinley didn't respond.

"In sickness and in health?"

Brinley still didn't say a word.

"Forsaking all others? Just the two of us, Brin, for the rest of our lives. Marry me?" He paused and expelled a breath. "I asked three times. At some point you have to say yes or no so we can move on, you know?"

He waited.

And waited.

"If it makes you feel any better, I'll call a law firm tomorrow and have them draw up a prenup." Ivan seemed resigned. "I don't want your money. I want you."

"That complication never crossed my mind," Brinley said.

"What then?"

"I need an affirmation that God wants us to be together."

"You want to flip the fleece this way and that? Better not test God too much. I think it's pretty clear He brought us together." Ivan held Brinley's hands. "Would you believe that I knew it was you the night we walked from the guesthouse to your parents' cottage, but I fought it?"

"I knew it was you too, but not that night. Maybe later. Is that our affirmation from God? That we both know we're meant for each other?"

"Brin, I have nothing to give you but my love."

"Before I was saved, I had everything but love. Now I have God's love. Yours would be icing on the cake."

"We love because He first loved us." Ivan had never been surer. "I love you. I want to spend the rest of my life with you. I want to wake up every morning hugging you and seeing your smile. I know you love me too."

Ivan worried a tad when Brinley didn't respond. He decided to keep on talking.

"You show your love by giving me stuff and doing things for me. Don't think for a second that I didn't know you paid my medical bills, bought back all the music manuscripts I thought I had to sell, kept in touch with Matt to make sure I was okay, and prayed for me, not to mention all the other stuff you've done for me and Grandma when she was alive, from driving her home from the party and all the other good deeds, too many to enumerate."

"God is good, Ivan."

"Indeed He is." He patted her hand.

Brinley rubbed his left arm. "I love you more than you'll ever know."

"I figured!" Ivan's heart warmed.

Gently, he cupped her face with both hands, slid

his right hand around her neck, fingers going through her hair. He leaned toward her, forehead touching hers. "Brin, marry me. Make me the happiest man alive."

"Yes, but..."

Ivan's jaw dropped. "Yes, but what?"

"Promise me you'll live on a budget the rest of your life."

What in the world? I'm trying to get engaged and she wants me to do what?

"I'm below the poverty line."

"So what, Ivan? Everybody needs a budget. As you earn more, your budget gets bigger. Do you want me to help you with it?"

"No. No. My friend Matt is pretty good at these things. I'll ask him."

"Fair enough. You promise?"

"All right. I promise to budget and live on it, so help me God. Marry me?"

"Yes."

"Yes?" Ivan couldn't believe his ears.

"It has been yes, but you knew that." Brinley lifted her lips to find his.

Ivan didn't want to let go, but the rumbling in his stomach was a wake-up call.

Brinley pulled back from the embrace. "Let's eat before you die of starvation."

Ivan dug into the brown bag next to him and pulled out a sandwich with the letter 'R' on the wrapper. "Your Reuben. Shall we say grace?"

Brinley nodded and they bowed their heads.

"Dear Lord, thank You for this food You have provided for the nourishment of our bodies," Ivan prayed. "Thank You for not letting us go hungry. Thank You for Brinley, who can share this lunch hour with me. May our conversation bring glory to You and edify us both. In Jesus' name I pray. Amen."

"Amen." Brinley started eating her Reuben.

Next to her, Ivan dug into his Cuban sandwich. "Want some of this?"

"No, thanks." Brinley wiped her lips with a paper napkin.

"Oh, I forgot something." Ivan put down his sandwich, wiped his hands carefully, and dug around in his pocket for the ring. At first he couldn't find it, and then he touched it at the bottom of the pocket.

Thank God.

Boy, was he glad he had patched up that hole in there.

Fingers tremulous, Ivan nervously placed the sapphire ring on Brinley's ring finger. He had bought it for a rock-bottom price at the thrift shop. A natural blue sapphire cabochon set on a silver ring. It looked like the work of a hobbyist, someone with a lapidary wheel. Maybe a rockhound, maybe a gem collector. Only God knew. The history of it was lost since it had arrived in a box of old things anonymously at the thrift shop drop-off door.

"A bit loose. We can get it adjusted," Ivan said.

"No worries. I love it." Brinley stretched her fingers in the sun. The noonday sunlight bounced off the sapphire. "In the eighteenth century, they used sapphires and emeralds more than diamonds for engagement rings."

"I didn't know that."

"This is very pretty. Love the sapphire. Love this blue."

"I do too." Ivan thought the ring looked understated on Brinley's finger, but then it wouldn't draw attention. He waited to see if Brinley would ask where he had gotten it. He'd tell her if she did. Well, she didn't.

"If you must know, I paid cash for it out of my first paycheck today." Those words seemed to carry away his burden. He didn't want Brinley to think that he had gotten into debt to buy her an antique engagement ring.

"I like debt-free purchases."

"It's a natural sapphire."

"Nice."

"It was on sale."

"Wonderful."

"Matt helped me choose it. After all, he'd been married before, so he sort of knew what he was talking about. At least, I hope he—What?"

"Hush, Ivan. Didn't I say that I love it?"

"I wasn't sure..."

"Be sure of this. God is good. Trust God. God provides. Thank God."

"Wow. You really are growing spiritually, Brin." Ivan finished his sandwich and scrunched up the paper wrapper.

"I love my ring, but I love you more. Remember I said *yes* before you gave me the ring."

She loves me. "Good point."

Brinley pulled his good arm and got him up on his feet. "Now let's get you back to work before you get fired."

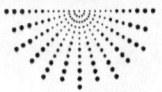

CHAPTER SIXTY-SEVEN

*B*rinley stepped up to the porch and crossed the floorboards. "No more creaks. Great!"

She was about to ring the doorbell when the door flung open. And there he was. All smiles. Brinley knew he wasn't like his brother, Quincy, rushing to Zoe, lifting her off her feet, spinning her around, and kissing her until she passed out.

Nope.

Ivan simply stood there. He reached for her hand, gently held it, and tugged her toward him. All slow and quiet-like.

"How's the wrist?" Brinley asked. She always asked, even if she had asked a few hours before when she called to see if she could come over this beautiful Saturday morning. He said he had to work at the thrift shop from noon to nine, but she could come over before he left the house.

"It's healing."

Brinley felt Ivan had more to say, but didn't. She wanted the details. How was it healing? What did the doctor say? What did the therapist do?

"I go back to the doctor on Tuesday." It was all Ivan offered.

"Good. I'll keep praying."

"Thank you." Ivan didn't let go. "Why are you sad? I'm not dying."

"Helen Hu still can't find your mother. We may never find her."

"Trust God, Brin. My mother will come home when she's ready. If she's not ready, no one can make her. So all we can do is pray." Ivan rubbed her chin. "Now cheer up. Come see the house."

Brinley stepped over the threshold and looked around. "Wow. This whole place is still empty."

"Not all empty." Ivan pointed toward the living room. "I have chairs now. Two bucks each."

"What a deal." Brinley stared at the flimsy plastic folding chairs. *Well, chairs are chairs.*

"Yeah. And I found two barstools—slightly scratched, but who cares, right?—for the kitchen island. One for you and one for me."

Thoughtful. Brinley smiled as Ivan led her to the covered porch outside the living room.

"Grandma would've loved this space," Ivan said.

"I tried to remember what she wanted." And she did try. Every detail of her conversations with Yun as much as she could remember when she discussed the renovation and expansion of the property with Tobias Vega.

"This is exactly what she'd been talking about for years."

"Do you think she can see this from heaven?" Brinley asked.

"I don't know. If she's in the crowd of witnesses, maybe?"

"Maybe." Brinley leaned against Ivan, breathing in the coastal April breeze. To her left, the live oak grove swayed in the bright sun rising up into the sky. To her right, the driveway meandered toward the road. In front of her was green grass leading to the marshes, where herons and egrets flew in and out.

Ivan kissed her forehead. "I'm so glad you gave me a second chance with this house."

Brinley shrugged. "It was empty, anyway."

"Oh, and here I was thinking you saved it for me."

"That too." Brinley spotted a railing with a missed paint spot, but she decided to worry about it later. Tobias needed a break from her pushing him to get this house renovated. This house had been a mess with its cracked foundation, but it had all been taken care of. And she had rewarded Tobias's hard work with the warehouse project. No complaints from the general contractor.

"Let's sit out here a while?" Ivan asked. "I'll go get the folding chairs."

Just then the doorbell rang.

"Who could that be?" Ivan asked.

"Oh, that's probably my housewarming gift."

Ivan's eyebrows shot up. "You brought me a housewarming gift? As if renting this house to me at one-tenth the price isn't enough?"

Brinley walked past him and reached the door before Ivan did. She greeted the two men.

"Where do you want it, ma'am?"

"Get it into the house and let him decide where to put it." Brinley pointed to Ivan, who looked perplexed.

"Is there a bigger door than this and maybe not so many steps?" one of the men asked.

"There's a handicap ramp in the garage," Ivan said. "It leads to the foyer. The garage door is open. I was airing out some things."

"That'll do, sir."

Brinley stepped out onto the porch, and Ivan followed her. He looked out into the driveway. Brinley watched him stare at the plain moving van. She was sure he couldn't figure it out. It was a good thing their regular van with the company name stenciled across the side wasn't available today.

"You're getting me furniture?" Ivan scratched his head.

Brinley bit back tears as Ivan's jaw dropped when he saw what rolled out of the back of the van. Then she laughed out loud as he practically jumped off the porch to greet Yun's Steinway Victorian upright piano, which Brinley had ordered tuned and polished after she had taken it out of the vault.

The piano movers rolled the piano into the

garage next to Matt's car—which he had let Ivan borrow—and up the ramp and into the house.

"Where do you want this?" one of the guys asked Ivan.

"Right there." Ivan stepped toward the same wall where the Steinway had stood for decades.

After the movers left, Ivan was still staring at his grandma's piano. His back was to Brinley.

Brinley gave him time. She stood to the side and waited.

Finally, Ivan turned around. "Grandma sold the piano to *you*."

"I thought you knew that."

"No, I didn't. She said it was going into a museum."

"Yes. The SISO Museum of Musical Instruments, but it's not built yet, as you know. And what else did she say?"

"That maybe someday the piano might make its way back to the McMillan family." Ivan stepped closer to Brinley. "Just like someday the Damaris Brooks Strad might return to your family."

"I guess your *someday* is happening sooner than mine."

"Trust God, Brin." Ivan stroked her shoulders.

Brinley cheered up. "Better not let your new piano students touch this antique."

"No. I'm buying two pianos from a small church in Darien. They're closing and they have a few old pianos in their Sunday school classrooms that need to go. Matt's helping me transport them here."

"Thinking of adding teachers already?"

"Got a great deal on the pianos I couldn't pass up. I brought Matt with me and he's the ultimate negotiator. He bought all the oak pews and stained-glass windows from the church and asked them to throw in a couple of pianos. Want to see my flyers?"

Like an excited entrepreneur, Ivan led Brinley to the kitchen. On the island table, a small, old beat-up laptop whirred to life when Ivan pressed a key. He sat on the barstool and scooted closer to the screen. He tapped a few times, then slid the laptop toward Brinley.

"I'm putting these flyers all over the place." Ivan's eyes lit up. "Listen. 'Always wanted to learn the piano, but never had the chance? Or second time around at the piano? Choose thirty– or sixty-minute lessons. Babysitting provided.' What do you think?"

"You're paying a babysitter?"

"Yeah. I lined up some teens who need after-school jobs."

"Okay."

"Why? What's wrong, Brin?"

"These are all piano lessons."

"Yes." Ivan's warm right hand went around her waist as he pulled her toward him. "I don't have to turn my left wrist at the piano."

Brinley had to concur. "I keep my wrists straight and sturdy at the piano keys."

"Right. It doesn't hurt as much when I do that."

"You remember the Fire Pit Service when I said I don't care whether you'd ever play the violin again?"

"Yes, I do remember. And I appreciate that."

"I'm okay with whatever God has in store for you —for us—but I want you to be at peace with that yourself."

"Don't worry." Ivan rubbed her chin. "I'm trusting God, Brin. My entire life is in God's hands."

Brinley nodded. "While we're talking about trusting God..."

"Yes?" Ivan knitted his eyebrows together.

"About the prenup."

"Your lawyer hates it."

Brinley shook her head. "She loves it. But I'm not signing it."

"Why not? What's wrong with it?"

"Both your grandma and my sister reminded me that a marriage is not a business, Ivan." Brinley leaned against the island. "In a marriage, what's yours is mine and what's mine is yours."

"I have nothing to give you, Brin."

"God has provided for us everything."

"But financially, I'm starting over with this music studio. I'm working at a thrift shop to pay my bills."

"At least you're working. Someday your music studio will grow, Ivan."

"I hope so."

"Someday you could move it to the warehouse in the Village, you know, in case you want to use Yun's house to raise a family instead."

Ivan studied her face. "The warehouse? You still remember it."

"Can't forget stuff like that." *Not when I paid cash for that building.*

"It was only a dream, Brin. I have nothing."

"Nothing? You have the love of God, Ivan. That's more than all the treasures of the world. 'For where your treasure is, there your heart will be also.' Remember that verse?"

"Yes. Luke 12:34."

Nodding, Brinley closed the gap between them. "You know that our focus should be God, not money. Regardless of what our incomes are, you are the spiritual leader in our family or else our marriage is doomed before it begins."

"I guess I'd better step up. Thank you for the vote of confidence. I'll do my best not to let you down." He turned serious. "Brin?"

"What?"

"I can't get over what you've done for me."

"No big deal."

"No? You salvaged Grandma's house. Kept her piano. Kept McMillan memories alive."

Brinley decided to save the warehouse news for later. He'd find out soon enough.

"Most of all, you waited for me to come around."

"Yun said to be patient with you." Yun had said so much more that Brinley could never thank her for now that she was gone.

"I'm glad you didn't give up on me." Ivan wept into her hair. "I thank God for you, Brin."

They held each other for a while until Brinley

pointed to her wristwatch. "Aren't you supposed to be at work at noon?"

"There's time." Ivan seemed to study her. "Want to grab an early lunch and walk on the pier a bit?"

"With the smell of fish bait wafting in the air?"

"Oh, I forgot. Saturday. Lots of people fishing there today."

"I'm just teasing." Brinley still remembered that Saturday at the pier. "I don't care, Ivan, as long as I'm with you."

"I'm glad you're easy to please. Lunch is on me." Ivan slung his messenger bag over his shoulder. "We'll have to take two vehicles. I'll be working late tonight. Stocking and all that."

"Don't forget church tomorrow morning." Brinley fished for her car keys.

"I'll pick you up at eight. Just have a big old pot of coffee ready and I'll be good to go to Sunday school."

Brinley thanked God that they were going to the same Sunday school class and the same church. That way they could be on the same page about their beliefs and be of equal yoke as Olivia Gonzalez said in the women's Bible study. Her only regret was that Yun couldn't see this development in Brinley's life with Ivan, their engagement and upcoming wedding, and the return of her Victorian Steinway to the McMillan family home.

Someday they would all be in heaven together again and they could then reminisce about this life and all these times.

For now, life had to go on here on earth without

those who had gone on ahead of them, and Brinley was thankful to God that she could share it with Ivan.

~

"A prenup?" Dad took Brinley's pawn. "What kind of prenup?"

"It's a vow of poverty." Brinley frowned, trying to anticipate Dad's next move on his Napoleon chessboard, which was now back in the family room at the Brooks cottage on Seaside Island. Dad was in town for a few weeks, but then he'd be off again to join Mom in Europe.

"No kidding." Dad laughed.

"Not funny, Dad. He wants me to agree not to bail him out at any time in our marriage. He wants us to have equal shares of stuff. Like if we bought a TV, we each pay half. I can't surprise him with a whole TV."

"Even if you could buy its manufacturer and parent company."

"Uh-huh. I've already sent it over to Annette."

"Her law firm will laugh this all the way into the blooper reels."

"Be serious, Dad. This is the rest of my life we're talking about." She took his queen. "Your future grandchildren hang in the balance."

"I *am* serious. I think that Ivan is a keeper. And I can't believe you beat me again."

"What you taught me, Dad."

"We should play chess more often. Remember we used to play when you were little?"

"In this very room." Brinley looked around. The family room hadn't changed a bit, except for the furniture that Mom cycled out every year or so. Outside, April was bright and lovely and warming up. Pretty soon it would be time to go swimming. "Time, isn't it, Dad? Always time."

Dad pushed back from the chessboard. "I'm beginning to like this Ivan."

"Why? He's stubborn."

"He's self-made."

"Who in the world would turn down a chance to share nine billion dollars?" Brinley knew the answer before the entire question left her mouth. Ivan. Ivan would if only because he wanted to play his violin. Someone else could worry about the finances.

"And a half, Brin. Stocks went up yesterday."

Brinley threw up her arms. "See what I mean?"

"He's going to have to learn it the hard way. Did you show him the warehouse?"

"Not yet. If I did, then this prenup might make sense."

"Would it?"

Brinley shrugged. "He wants to show me that he can hold his own."

"Take care of it, Brinley Brin."

"I will, Dad. I'm not signing it."

"Nine billion dollars say you should, Brin."

"It's a marriage, not a business."

"It could be his dignity we're talking about."

"He's been working on a budget. I've told him we're not setting a wedding date until he gets his finances in order."

"Brin."

"What, Dad?"

"What does that say about your love for him if you hold your wedding day hostage?"

Brinley paused. "I don't want our marriage to start off with unpaid debts from day one. What will we teach our children?"

"Even if he sets up a budget, he still needs to follow through."

"Right. His friend Matt is helping him."

"Good friends are hard to find."

"What does Pastor Gonzalez say about this budget prerequisite?"

"He was amused, but thought it's a very practical idea."

"I do too, Brin. If this plan of yours ends up getting the wedding day moved, your mom would be thrilled to death. In fact, you know she'd like nothing better than for you to postpone your wedding until after Zoe's baby is born. She can only handle one thing at a time, you know."

Brinley smiled. "That's why we're going to get married as soon as possible, Dad."

"Is that right?"

"It doesn't take long to set up a budget considering how little money Ivan has. But what will get him is working out a payment plan with the creditors. He doesn't want me to see his mess, and for his sake, I won't unless I have to. Anyway, once that's done, we can move on to the wedding."

"My checklist daughter."

"The wedding's easy, Dad. Ivan and I have decided to make it a small beach wedding. Keeping it simple. Low budget. Not making a big deal. Not requiring a whole year to plan. Since Mom's busy with Zoe and her future grandchild, I think we can sneak a small, short, and sweet wedding by her."

"Ha. I doubt it. Better put your foot down ASAP, Brinley Brin."

"I am."

"I'll back you up as long as I get to walk you down the aisle."

"I wouldn't have anyone else do that." Brinley picked up her purse. "How's Mom doing these days?"

"Your mom thinks she has to bid in person at the Christie's auction next week. She has her eye on a fifteenth-century cradle."

"Yikes, Dad. I don't think that's up to code."

Brinley found her keys. She glanced around the sunroom. *Sure miss this place now that I have my own house.*

"Time for me to go. I have a meeting with Toby and Megan to sort out their differences so they can be productive at Pelican Road."

"Like herding cats."

CHAPTER SIXTY-EIGHT

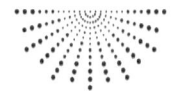

*I*van was stocking the media shelves in Matt's thrift shop when he spotted Ned Brooks walking toward him with security in tow. Ivan put the VHS cassette on the bottom rack right next to the row of vinyls he'd arranged earlier with his right hand.

His future father-in-law had called him a week before to ask him to meet him for lunch, and what could he have said? At first Ivan wasn't sure about talking to Brinley's dad at all, but then a man had to eat. Who'd turn down a free lunch? It wasn't going to cost that much at Barbara Jean's. So he said okay.

"Who views that stuff anymore?" Ned pointed to the VHS shelves with his polished walking stick.

"You'd be surprised. Ninety-nine cents each if you're looking for one." Ivan stood up and shook Ned's hand. "You're early, Mr. Brooks."

"Ned."

"Ned." Ivan wasn't sure he wanted to be on a first-name basis with Brinley's dad, Ned Brooks, only the richest man he knew.

Okay, just on earth. God in heaven is the richest of all. I get it, Lord. Thank You for the reminder.

"You finish up. I can wait." Ned looked around.

"Have you been here before?" Ivan asked, lining up more VHS cassettes.

"Not this store," Ned said. "But I've been to thrift shops in my lifetime, yes."

"You have?" Ivan didn't believe him.

Ned seemed to study him up and down. Ivan felt uncomfortable to be so scrutinized, but the green employee vest hid most of the faded secondhand T-shirt he had on, so he knew he looked somewhat decent. And yes, the twill cargo shorts he had on cost only four dollars on the deep discount rack, but it was Eddie Bauer. It would have cost him at least fifty bucks at the mall.

He had shaven this morning and trimmed his sideburns, so Ivan was confident he passed the test.

"There's a lot about me you don't know, Ivan."

I bet. Ivan pushed the empty shopping cart to the side. A shopper passed by with an armful of clothes on hangers. "You can have this cart, ma'am."

She thanked him and dumped her finds into the cart and took off.

Ivan glanced at the clock on the wall. He was a bit embarrassed he didn't have his own watch. But he held his head up. *I'm rich in Christ.*

He chided himself for comparing statuses. That

hadn't been what Grandma Yun had taught him. What was that verse again? The one about each person minding his or her own business? He'd look it up later on his iPad.

Oh. He'd sold his iPad.

Never mind.

"Looks like it's almost twelve o'clock," Ivan said. "Let me clock out and we can go."

"Sounds good, son."

Son.

Ivan tried not to read too much into it, but that three-letter word warmed his heart. It didn't help his concern about the reason for the lunch. It was too soon after the prenuptial agreement that a lawyer from church had helped him draw up pro bono.

He had to do it. Had to prove to Brinley that he wasn't marrying her for her money. They might struggle a bit in the first year of their marriage, but he was confident that Brinley would eventually see that love was all they needed.

As he hung his store vest onto the rolling coat rack, he wondered whether Brinley would mind living in a trailer park if that was all they could afford. Maybe it was a dumb idea to do the fifty-fifty expense agreement. Too late now. He'd signed it and he was waiting for Brinley to return the agreement as is.

When he came out to the floor, Ned was examining the wheels of a nineteenth-century curricle in the shop window by some wrought-iron fences and bistro chairs.

"That actually belongs to Matt's antique store next door, but he didn't have room." Ivan went up to Ned.

"Matt Garnett?"

"Yes."

"My wife bought a bunch of stuff from his antique store."

"He's a picker too, sir."

"A picker? I need to talk to him. Maybe he can help me find some old auto parts."

"You like old things too?" Ivan chuckled.

"I liked old things first. Brinley got it from me, young man. Not the other way around." Ned straightened up. "What's the price tag on this curricle?"

"Well, let's see..." Ivan walked to the front and then around the two-wheeled two-seater until he saw a dangling tag.

Whoa. Lots of numbers.

Calmly he told Ned. "And it's dated 1850, if it helps."

"Might be one of the last ones. I'm surprised it's still intact."

"What do you mean?" All the while Ivan was wondering if they would ever make it to lunch before he had to return to work.

"You know anything about curricles, son?"

"Sorry, no. I only know music history."

"The curricle was the sports car of its time. It was fast and furious. Lots of wrecks and all that."

"Those poor horses." It was all Ivan could say.

Ned stepped back to take a photo of the curricle.

The default sound on Ned's iPhone told Ivan that he probably had just sent the photo to someone. An appraiser, perhaps?

"There was also the phaeton, but it was heavier," Ned continued. "Later on, about a century later, convertible coupes were all the rage. Same idea."

"And you have one of those in your collection."

"I have a 1935 Duesenberg, yes. Maybe I'll take you for a spin someday."

Maybe.

Ivan could have reciprocated if his 1945 Chevrolet truck wasn't a pile of rust in Matt's junk-yard in Brunswick.

Ned's iPhone pinged. Ned read the message and smiled. "I want to talk to your friend Matt about this curricle. I can't believe it's in here."

"It looks restored."

"I agree. How long has it been here?"

Ivan shrugged. "It was here when I started work last Friday. You'll have to ask Matt. Unfortunately, he's picking in South Carolina today. He'll be back tomorrow morning as far as I know."

"Whereabouts in South Carolina?"

"Charleston and Port Royale. He goes there a lot. I wouldn't be surprised if this curricle was in some-one's basement all this time." Ivan went to the checkout counter to get a business card. He handed it to Ned. "Looks like it's the store number on there. I used to have his number when I had a cell... Uh..."

"Why don't you put a Sold sticker on that

curricle so nobody else takes it?" Ned asked, handing Ivan a credit card. "I'm sure Matt also lists this online."

"I'm sure he does." Ivan couldn't believe it. He made a sale in the thrift shop to Brinley's dad, of all people. He gulped as he swiped the card. The string of digits when he rang it up made him a bit dizzy. What made him dizzier was then he put the receipt on the counter for Ned to sign, looked up and saw that it was nearly one o'clock. He'd missed his lunch hour and it was the end of it.

Ned must've noticed his eyes on the wall clock. "How about you come over to the house for dinner tonight?"

"Uh..."

"It'll just be you and me. Brin won't be there. My wife's in Paris." Ned pocketed his wallet. "We have a lot to talk about. When do you get off work?"

All Ivan heard was: *We have a lot to talk about.*

That couldn't be all good. Did Ned have a problem with the prenup? It wasn't that bad, was it?

"Tonight I'm working late, sir. I work late every night except Wednesday nights when I have church. And Sundays. We close on Sundays."

"We'll have to do lunch another time. How about tomorrow? Same time?"

"We can do that, sir."

"For today, sorry we had to cancel lunch," Ned said. "I'll have Chaz here go get you a sandwich or something for lunch and you can eat it on your break. How does that sound?"

"Thank you, but no need. I'll be fine."

"I'll see you tomorrow at noon. Barbara Jean's."

"Yes, sir. How about I meet you there, sir?"

Ned laughed. "So that I don't come here to buy up the store?"

Ivan didn't know what to say about that. "Well, the antique store next door might have more stuff you might like to see. I've gotten some old music manuscripts there myself. Nineteenth century."

"Possibly from Charleston too?"

"I wouldn't be surprised. Matt's raiding history there, but that's not the only place he goes."

"All right, son. Sorry our lunch is a bust."

"But you made it out okay. You're not going to ride that curricle, are you?"

"Nope. It's a museum piece. Goes into my vault."

Another vault. "Have you ever thought of opening up a museum so everyone can see your old cars?"

"There's a reason it's called a *private* collection."

"But history is meant to be shared."

Ned seemed to be mulling it over. "Just like the musical instruments you talked Brin into loaning to the future MOMI."

How did the SISO Museum of Musical Instruments get into the conversation?

"Does she tell you everything?" Ivan blurted, but it was too late to retract his thoughts. Somehow he felt comfortable with Ned. Too comfortable. There should be a distance between him and his future father-in-law.

"Not everything, but we're close."

"Glad to hear that, sir. My dad and I weren't—uh, I haven't heard from my dad in years. I don't even know where my mother is. Brinley is very fortunate to have you and Mrs. Brooks around."

Ned looked visibly moved. "Well, son, I'd better let you get back to work. See you tomorrow. Noon. Don't be late. Bring a starving stomach."

"Yes, sir." Ivan watched Ned and his one-man security walk out of the thrift shop. He had a new respect for Ned, the gulf between them notwithstanding. He thought Ned was rather down-to-earth.

Brinley must've gotten that from him.

CHAPTER SIXTY-NINE

*A*t 11:45 a.m. Ivan crossed the street and walked briskly. One block down and Barbara Jean's came into his view at the corner of Mallery and Beachview. Friday traffic was always heavy in this part of St. Simon's Island with camera-ready tourists and locals going about their business.

He had more than an hour for lunch and he had Ned Brooks to thank for that. The sold curricle had made Ivan's boss and friend a very happy store owner. Matt kept saying that Ivan was a natural salesman and all that blah, but Ivan knew the truth. Ned saw an old thing he wanted and he bought it. That was all there was to it.

Ivan thought he'd be the first one there, but once again, his future father-in-law was early. Sitting in the booth looking out the window, watching people passing by as if he had no care in the world, Ned seemed genuinely glad to see Ivan greet him.

One table away, Ned's bodyguard had already begun eating. Ivan thought that it must've been one of the most restrictive jobs in the world to guard the rich and famous because someone else's agenda, twenty-four seven, became theirs.

Then Ivan remembered Art-with-no-last-name who had guarded that 1721 Schoenberg Stradivarius for only two weeks and nearly died because of that. Speaking of whom, Ivan made a mental note to call Art again. *Catch up with him and all that.*

Ivan slid into his side of the booth. A server came by, dropping off a menu and asking him what he wanted to drink.

"Unsweet tea." If Grandma Yun were still alive, she'd say it was grammatically incorrect. She would have insisted, colloquialism notwithstanding, that it should be *unsweetened* tea. Ivan smiled. Grandma had been quite a character.

"Unsweet, huh. I always put sugar in mine," Ned said.

"If they make it too bitter," Ivan said. "But not at Barbara Jean's. They make tea just the way I like it here. I always get a to-go cup."

Ned placed his iPhone on the table, where the time was clearly visible even from where Ivan was sitting. "Looks like we have maybe an hour to eat and go. We'll drop you off at the store so you're not late back to work. Don't want you to get fired."

"Thank you, but I think we'll be okay. I swapped shifts with a coworker so I have until two o'clock."

"Matt fine with that?"

"Totally. He thinks that I should invite you to his antique store in case you see something you like."

Ned seemed amused. "He's business first and friendship later, huh?"

"That's Matt." Ivan put his hands down as the server came back with fresh rolls. He took their orders.

"Shall we say a blessing?"

"You do it."

Nervously, Ivan said a quick prayer. God knew he was eternally grateful for food. He figured that the fewer words he said, the less he had to retract later on. Not that it was a big deal; Ned went to the same church he did, and he probably had heard both long and short prayers.

"Speaking of business," Ned began. "What are your plans?"

"Plans?"

"For your career."

"My career?"

"Stop stalling. The clock is ticking."

Oh boy. That makes it worse. "Uh... Truth be told, I'm at an impasse."

"And?"

"And? I'm stuck, sir."

"So you're working in a thrift shop to regroup and gather your thoughts."

"It's not that heroic, Ned."

"I'm not letting my daughter marry a loser."

Loser? Maybe that's what I am. "I'm trying not to be one, sir."

"Try harder. How do you think I'm where I am today? Hard work. Back-breaking hard work."

"I thought you were born with it."

Ned laughed. "Then you don't know my dad. He made me work my way up before he gave me a dime."

"I think I would've liked your dad." Ivan's fried cod came and the big platter provided a barrier between him and Ned across the table. He watched the server place two giant crab cakes in front of Ned. They looked better than his cod. They made his mouth water.

Coveting is a sin. He could hear Grandma Yun clearly in his head.

"Let me rephrase my question." Ned cut up his crab cake. "You spent four years at Juilliard on a full violin scholarship. You spent two years touring with a crossover string ensemble."

"Jade Strings." *Then Grandpa Otto dropped dead. Grandma Yun broke a hip.* His concert violinist career ended.

"You spent six years teaching strings." Ned chewed slowly, as if to give Ivan time to think. "Do you see a pattern there?"

"A pattern, sir?" Ivan wasn't sure if he could enjoy the cod and think of patterns. Sure, there were patterns in music, but he couldn't eat and do that either.

"Brin said you've been playing violin since you were four years old."

"That's correct." Ivan wasn't sure what Ned was getting at, but considering the seconds and minutes on the iPhone on the table, all things would be clear soon. He decided to keep eating and be done so he didn't lose his appetite in case the news was bad.

Lord, don't let me lose Brinley.

"Look, son. I'm trying to help you think through this."

"I'm drawing a blank."

"Hence your impasse. We need to remove the blockage so you can move on."

Move on? As in—move on from what? From whom?

"What are you going to do when your wrist heals?" Ned asked.

"It may not completely heal."

"Have faith, you idiot." Ned chuckled.

Did he call me an idiot?

Ivan wondered if he should walk out. Then he realized that Ned was right. He had been an idiot. Many musicians were in worse situations than he had been and they had all survived.

Uh, name one.

"It's just a broken wrist." Ned wasn't finished. "It'll heal."

"Could take a long time."

"You're defeated even before you begin."

Ivan thought he had a good point there.

"Trust God. Don't lean on your own abilities, understanding, and point of view. Trust God. Trust His wisdom, His sovereignty. Do you know Proverbs 3:5-6?"

Ivan's fork stopped in midair. It was the verse

that Brinley had given him at Christmas and that the Seaside Chapel men's Bible study group had discussed back in December before his accident.

"Pastor Gonzalez said that it would be good if I can memorize some verses," Ned continued. "I carry this verse around with me. He might check up on me, you see, and I don't want to fail the test."

Pastor Gonzalez told Ned to memorize the verse. Ned told Brinley to memorize the verse. Brinley wrote it on a bookmark for Ivan.

What is God saying to me?

Ivan brushed off the thought. "I never thought you're the kind of person to go around quoting scripture, Ned."

"It's pointless to know scripture if you don't apply it. But there's more. The seventh verse in the same chapter says something remarkable."

"What?" Ivan finished his cod, all the sides that came with it, and every breadcrumb. He had thought he'd lose his appetite, but the opposite happened.

"Here is the seventh verse. 'Be not wise in thine own eyes: fear the Lord, and depart from evil.' Got that?" Ned read aloud. "Pastor Gonzalez says we have to learn to differentiate man's wisdom from God's."

"Obviously, I need to trust God and seek His wisdom." A lesson Ivan had been trying to learn the last four months.

Poorly.

~

"What are you going to do when your wrist heals?" Ned asked. "We're discussing your future with my daughter, Ivan. I want to know where you're going with her."

I knew it. He has doubts about me. Frankly, I have doubts about myself too.

"Give me a minute to get the words."

Ned nodded.

Well, he's going to be my future father-in-law. Eventually I'm going to have to face him.

Here goes nothing.

"I used to think, fresh out of college, that I'd tour the world doing classical and crossover concerts. I did that for two years straight. In my early twenties I had plenty of energy and zero care. Now that I'm thirty, I'm thinking more of staying in one place and raising a family. I don't think Brin would want to live in a touring bus all year long or in hotel rooms."

And with kids, that could be hard—

Ivan cleared his throat.

Wow. Kids with Brinley.

Ivan couldn't wrap his mind around that. He'd have to pinch himself later to make sure it wasn't a dream.

"You know Brin is not into traveling all that much."

"Yeah. She said that."

"You'd do best to remember that before you drag her all over the world."

"Don't worry about that." Ivan let the server take

his plate. He held off on desserts. "I'm praying about where to go from here. Clearly, I can't be working in a thrift shop the rest of my life—no offense to those who do, you know, like Matt—and obviously this is only a temporary situation for me. I think I would like to reopen my music studio."

"Sounds like a plan."

"You're a businessman," Ivan said. "Any advice for me? I mean, free advice. I can't pay you."

Ned laughed. "A steak dinner suffices."

"That, I can do." *But I can't afford Kobe steak. He'd have to settle for rib eye or something.*

"You can easily reboot your music studio. For example, you can rent a cheap house, live upstairs and teach music downstairs."

Ivan wondered how much Ned knew about his renting Grandma Yun's old house from Brinley.

"Or you could try to find a job managing someone else's music studio until your wrist heals."

"Good idea. I hadn't thought of that."

"Can you teach anything else other than violin?" Ned asked.

"Piano."

"There you go. It'll hold you over until you can teach violin again, right?"

Ivan tried to remain stoic. "If I can get enough students."

"How many did you have?"

"Forty."

"That many."

"It took six years to build that up." *All gone now.*

"Their parents all wanted their kids to take violin lessons from someone who'd gone to Juilliard and toured the world for two years. But now..."

"Now you find new students. Have you prayed and asked God to show you who your new students are?"

Ivan wondered how much to say. *Well, why not?* "Been thinking of targeting adult students."

"Not a bad idea. My wife, for example, has been wanting to play the piano all her life. You could teach her."

"Teach Brin's mom?"

Ned chuckled. "Don't look so startled. A student is a student."

"Right."

"She has friends who might want to take lessons too. Group lessons. Individual lessons. Whatever is suitable, right?" Ned drew back from the table. "Leverage your portfolio. Twelve years of strings, son. Put all that resume to good use."

"Yes, sir."

"A lot to think about. As your financial advisor, I'm recommending you talk to my accountant."

"Oh, I can't afford that."

"Don't worry about it. I'm being selfish here, Ivan. I want to make sure you don't drag my daughter into debt."

"I won't. Don't worry."

"We have fewer than two months left before the wedding. I want to know that you have a sensible financial plan going forward."

Ivan drank his tea slowly to avoid having to answer Ned's question. Too bad for him, Ned was patient. He waited until Ivan looked up.

"Uh, yes. I need to figure out how to pay off my debts and increase my income."

"Talk to my accountant about the first part," Ned said. "But increasing income. That's my department. Let's brainstorm. You have a good idea there about looking for new students."

"I don't have a choice." It would be bad form to steal students back from their new music teachers. Ivan knew he had to find new students. So far all his students had been kids who might or might not want to continue music past middle or high school. Most music teachers would target younger students. He could serve older ones. "Besides, some people at church told me they wished they had taken violin or piano lessons when they were younger."

"Or at least paid more attention when they had taken those lessons." Ned snorted.

"I hear you." Things were churning in Ivan's mind. "Someday I could expand my studio, add instruments, teachers, workshops, maybe even scholarships for students to go to college, that sort of thing."

"Scholarships?" Ned asked for a refill of his drink. "Maybe I could help with that."

"Oh no, I couldn't possibly accept—"

Ned raised a palm at him. "Ivan."

"Yes, sir?"

"Don't question God's provision. Just say *thank you*."

Sigh. "Thank you."

"In case you didn't know, I give out scholarships all the time through my various foundations."

"That's generous of you, Ned."

"What can I say? I'm a nice guy. I like my steak medium rare, please."

"Taking orders." Ivan finished his tea. As per usual, Ivan asked for a to-go cup filled with more tea for the walk back to the thrift shop and glanced at Ned's iPhone. It was 1:35 p.m.

"Almost time for me to get back to work. Appreciate the lunch, sir. Thank you for getting my mind thinking through the fog."

"One more thing." Ned tented his fingers. "I have a special wedding gift for Brin. Maybe you can help me deliver it."

"Anything for Brin."

"Not sure if you can handle it."

"Try me."

"You need to do some things to make this happen."

"Name them. I'm game." Ivan wondered at his own words.

"How's your therapy coming along?"

Ivan cringed. "Tough."

"My entire wedding gift depends on your wrist. You must get that wrist working again. Brin tells me you're not able to do the vibrato yet."

"No, sir." Ivan turned his left wrist, palm up

facing him. The pain was still there though not as much as two months before. The splint only masked it from the world. "My recovery is long and painful."

"You have seven weeks to get well, son."

That would lead us to early June when—

"I'm afraid you'll have to ask someone else, sir. I may never be able to play violin again. A left-hand violin, maybe."

"No can do. This one requires a right-hand violinist. That's the way it goes."

"Tough, then."

However, it gave Ivan an idea for a future angle in his music studio offerings. Hmm. Music therapy had never sounded this good. He checked off a few ideas in his head. *Wow, Lord. Maybe there's a new career for me yet.*

"My daughter seems to think you're improving every day. Maybe you need some more motivation to get that wrist well."

Ivan thought of Bach's "Air." That hadn't been enough. What could possibly top that?

"Has Brinley taken you to the warehouse?" Ned asked.

"What warehouse?"

"Ah, she hasn't told you."

"Told me what?"

CHAPTER SEVENTY

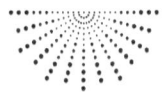

"*I* was thinking aloud, Brin." Ivan could not believe what he was seeing. The whole warehouse had been gutted, windows cleaned to let the sunlight in, and scaffoldings were everywhere up against the taller windows. Clearly, Brinley's crews had been here. "Tell me you didn't buy this warehouse."

"You wanted a music studio." Brinley's lips quavered.

"I wanted to rent a *section* of the first floor. You bought the entire building."

"Maybe we could expand the music studio."

"Sure we could."

"But?"

Ivan's shoulders sagged. "If you keep buying things, you're going to run out of money. Ask me how I know."

"It was at half price."

"Millions of dollars." Ivan remembered his old statistics on the warehouse. The property might have appreciated, but he doubted by much.

"I didn't want to lose the warehouse," Brinley added. Ivan saw the relief in her eyes.

"Is it the warehouse per se or the memory of our conversation of it?" He put his good arm around her shoulders. "Know what I think, Brin? I think you don't want to lose the memory of our moment together at the lighthouse when we looked over the pier and saw this place."

Now Brinley was visibly in tears.

Ivan cupped Brinley's face in his hands. His left wrist still hurt a bit if turned the wrong way, but what bothered him more right now was what he could see written on her face.

She doesn't want to lose me.

Ivan lowered his lips.

She didn't protest.

And he kissed her gently, sweetly, then ravenously. The way he had wanted to on their first evening together, after the party, in the moonlight, on the terrace, all that, before life got complicated.

Forehead to forehead, he paused to take a breather. "How's that for a new memory?"

Brinley smiled.

Ivan tried to think of how he could tell her what he wanted to say in such a way that she wouldn't be offended.

"I like your idea of putting me on a budget," he began. "Matt is doing wonders with my finances. I'm on a path to becoming debt-free. I'm happy to see that I'm starting to keep more than I spend."

"Good for you, Ivan."

"So." Ivan drew her closer. "We need to put you on a budget too, Brin."

Brinley gasped.

Then she seemed to calm down. "Touché. Should've seen that coming."

"I want to be sure we can afford our kids—future kids, plural hopefully—in college."

Brinley chuckled. Then turned somber: "I'm proud of you, Ivan."

"Not me. Be proud of God. He never left me nor forsook me even when I pumped my fists at Him and spat at His face, so to speak. Now I am experiencing a new journey of trusting God, not only at the point of salvation, but for the rest of my life."

"The prodigal son comes home."

"With a wife."

"Hey, we're not married yet."

"In less than two months we will be. Let's practice our PDA." Ivan waited for her to react at his suggestion. She didn't seem fazed by the idea of a public display of affection.

"But it has to be in public," she said.

"Huh?"

"We're alone in this warehouse."

"You mean we have to kiss outdoors?"

"Yeah? Public?"

So they went outside, and Ivan kissed her until it was time to go home.

~

The horsehair on the bow looked pretty decent. The strings, on the other hand, were bad. Ivan would have to replace them. No biggie. The lower bout was scratched, but Ivan didn't care. Soon, when he had saved up enough money, he'd send it to a luthier to be revarnished.

What mattered most to Ivan was that as he trusted God anew, God began to provide surprises in unexpected ways to cheer him up and encourage him to keep working through his wrist therapy to get well.

Like this violin, for example. A blessing.

And earlier today, the warehouse. Another blessing. A big one.

"What do you think?" Matt Garnett sat down on the floor in Ivan's family room and popped the top of the soda can.

"There's a chair over there." Ivan pointed to the other folding chair. Outside the windows it was dark and approaching ten o'clock. He had just come home from working at the thrift shop when Matt called, saying he was driving into St. Simon's and wanted to drop something off at his house.

"Nope." Matt propped himself up against the wall. "The last time I sat on one of those, I fell through."

"Some man you are." Ivan laughed. He continued to examine the old violin on his lap. "I still can't believe you got this for two hundred dollars.

You sure you don't want to get it appraised, auction it off?"

"Either way, what does it matter?" Matt said. "I'm giving it to you. Now someday you can sell it back to me for list price. Then I'll do something about it. So you think the label is authentic?"

"As far as I can tell. Made by Ira J. White. 1863. If this is real, you've made a terrific find. I'd say it's worth over two or three thousand dollars."

Ivan had heard of Ira Johnson White and his brother Asa, American luthiers who had produced respectable violins in the nineteenth century. It would be an honor to play an American-made violin.

"A big if. Can it still play?"

"Yeah, as soon as I get new strings for it. Looks like the horsehair still works, but I think I'll replace that too." Ivan placed the bow and violin back into the case. The case was probably why the bow hadn't been lost. He clicked the lid shut. "I don't want you to just give it to me, Matt. I'll pay you the two hundred in installments. Okay with that?"

"Whatever, dude."

"I insist. Thank you for this. Appreciate your thinking of me on your trip."

"I wasn't thinking of you most of the time, dude. I went to that house because the owner said the grand-father had died and left a collection of 'junk' he wanted to get rid of. In truth, I stumbled onto that violin, and only then did I think of you."

"Stumbled onto it? I think it was more like providence."

Matt lifted up his soda can. "Yep. God provides. It was my last stop. I almost decided to skip that route because it was raining and I'd been living in that old van for two weeks and getting van fever."

"But God."

"Right. Always God. And here we are."

"If I pay you fifty dollars four times, it'll be taken care of."

"Deal." Matt stretched out on the floor. "I'm dead tired."

"You could've waited until tomorrow to give me this. I'll be at work at eight o'clock."

"A thank you would suffice."

"Thank you, Matt. You're a good friend."

"I thought I was your best friend."

Ivan smiled. "And best man."

"How's the therapy coming?"

"If I say painful, it's an understatement. I'm quite confident my wrist will eventually heal, but the therapy could kill me before then."

Matt didn't say anything.

When Ivan turned to see what was happening, he saw that Matt's eyes were closed. Slowly he began to snore.

~

*E*very physical therapy morning, Ivan prayed doubly hard—sometimes harder—as he parked outside Vittorio's boot camp. He still didn't have his own car, but Matt was gracious enough to let him borrow his on therapy days, and to and from work.

He would come fifteen minutes early to prepare himself. The spurious name tacked onto the wall next to the front entrance of the center got him every time. East Beach Therapy Center. The center was neither east—it was at the south end of the island— nor was it beachy at all. *Beach* implied a life of vacationing comfort. This was no beach. This was all pain. Pure pain.

Three times a week Ivan prayed for mercy and for God to spare his soul as he dragged himself to EBTC to have his wrist tugged and pulled and bent into compliance with human physiology. Sometimes Ivan wondered if he should—

"Art! What are you doing here?" Ivan stepped into the lobby and let the door shut behind him on its own. He went straight to Art and shook his hand. "You look good for a man near death."

"That was four months ago. I'm back at work now."

"That's terrific. You seemed to have lost a bit of weight there." Ivan had spoken to Art a few times since the Savannah attack, notably over New Year's, but they hadn't visited each other for reasons best left buried.

"Are you saying I was fat?" Art asked.

"I'm saying you're ripped now. I'll never be that buff."

"I would have to agree with you."

"Hey..." Ivan decided to let it slide. "So. To what do I owe this visit?"

"To whom. Mr. Brooks wants me to look in on you. See if you're making any progress."

Brinley's dad. "Why?"

"Apparently he has a vested interest in you. I'm going to stay with you through your session today, and then we're going for a ride."

"A ride?"

"Yes. Mr. Brooks wants you to see something. Then I'll drop you off back here."

"You want me to follow you so you'll save a trip?"

"No."

"What? Ned's afraid I'll run off? In Matt's car on its last leg?"

"Something like that."

"How long are you staying with me? All afternoon?"

"And the next month or so."

"What?" Ivan was curious now. "What's going on, man?"

"You'll have to ask Mr. Brooks that," Art said as Ivan spotted Vittorio waving to them through an inside door.

"Let the torture begin," Ivan muttered under his breath.

CHAPTER SEVENTY-ONE

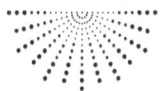

$\mathcal{A}$lmost two months later, Brinley Brooks stepped out of Seaside Chapel into the lovely flower garden, into the breezy June outdoors to the sound of gulls and seabirds in staccato beats against a backdrop of ocean waves crashing on the shore and then ebbing away. Above her, pelicans flew, silently gliding through the air and heading south through a blue sky with whispers of clouds like brushstrokes.

God's brushstrokes.

The early morning air smelled fresh and clean. Brinley closed her eyes, basking her face in the warming sun. She could stay on St. Simon's Island the rest of her life if life were like the last two months after Ivan's proposal. Throughout the months of April and May, the duo had spent a lot of time together, getting along, and getting busy with the warehouse renovations and the rebuilding of Ivan's student list. For now, his new students met him at Yun's old house but eventually they'd all move to the warehouse studio on Pelican Road.

Now, in early June, before St. Simon's Island baked in the summer sun, before throngs of vacationers descended on the island, it was time to tie a wedding bow to their relationship.

Brinley paused to give thanks to God.

Her breath caught when a distant violin solo rose above the sounds of the summer morning, above the rolling waves and squawking gulls, above the rapid beatings of her heart.

Our song.

It was coming from the pavilion, a siren song calling to her, filling her mind and heart with memories of that dinner party before Christmas when she'd felt a connection with Ivan, of New Year's Eve kisses and winter heartbreaks and spring restorations.

She wondered which SISO violinist was doing the honors. That was an unexpected surprise that the wedding planner must've thrown in. Brinley hadn't wanted any violin at the wedding because she was afraid it would make Ivan sad that it could be a very long time before his tendons and wrist were healed enough for him to play the violin the same way he used to.

Now this piece coming over the warming breeze sounded almost as good as Ivan playing it that evening in December.

Surely Ivan must've approved it. Or someone was

playing a trick on their emotions. Whatever. It was too late now. Brinley told herself to go with the flow.

Give me strength, God, to last through the ceremony so I can relax.

"Ready to go, Brinley Brin?" Dad tapped his walking stick. He was determined to walk her down the aisle and so here he was. In typical Dad fashion, the walking stick itself was more expensive than her wedding gown. Brinley had practiced walking in her laced tulle trumpet gown of pure white silk, but she still prayed she wouldn't trip and fall on the boardwalk before she reached the pavilion and beach.

Brinley linked her arm with Dad's, and they made the slow procession down the sidewalk, onto the boardwalk. All the time Bach's "Air on the G String" grew ever louder, pushing away all other sounds of the seaside.

Too bad Ivan hadn't played any violins lately. Or at least she hadn't heard him play. Every time she had asked, he said he was getting his wrist strength back. Brinley had been praying for his wrist to heal completely, but it was all in God's hands now.

She was grateful, however, that Ivan hadn't abandoned music altogether. In the two months since he had reopened his music studio, it was all coming along nicely. Business had picked up after he renamed it Yun McMillan Studios and started advertising to unexpected places.

And surprise, surprise, Mom was taking piano lessons from Ivan. She'd been so enamored by Ivan's charm and teaching ability that she had been telling all her friends up and down coastal Georgia about her new music teacher. Pretty soon those friends were practicing hard so they could play a severely simplified version of Franz Liszt's "Liebestraum No. 3" on their Christie's or Sotheby's concert grand finds.

Brinley inched forward at Dad's pace. Between the sea oats and dunes, the boardwalk seemed to stretch forever. She was determined to get to the pavilion and beyond, where everyone was waiting for them on the beach this beautiful, clear, sunny, bright morning.

"Remember, Brinley Brin." Dad choked up. "Your husband should love you as Christ loves the church and sacrificed Himself for her. If Ivan falls short, call me, and I'll whack him with my new diamond-encrusted titanium walking stick."

"Dad!" Brinley wiped a tear from her eye. "You're messing up my eyeliner."

"Nah. You look beautiful."

The closer they came to the pavilion, the louder the violin solo was. It was a deep, clear, distinct sound that only—

And then she saw him.

He was all she saw.

The sea and surf and sky behind him vanished into the clouds.

All Brinley saw was Ivan standing in the sand, his left hand out of a brace, fingers moving up and down the strings of what looked like a very old violin.

Brinley's knees buckled and she tightened her

grip on Dad's arm as they stepped off the pavilion and onto the packed sands of St. Simon's Island. She didn't even think about bits of sand getting into her toes and into the laced hems of her wedding gown. All she could think of was his wrist.

Thank You, God, for healing his left hand.

All those months of therapy and wrist rehabilitation had paid off, but Brinley hadn't expected him to play their song this soon. Coming out of the church building and hearing it, it hadn't crossed her mind at all that Ivan himself would be doing this. He must've been practicing for weeks. She knew the wrist had been giving him trouble still. He had been in pain every time he turned it.

Why is he doing this now?

Brinley inched toward Ivan, the measures and melody all running together, louder and louder in her ears as her heart beat faster and faster.

She quickened her pace down the aisle between two groups of white folding chairs.

Have to get to him!

Somehow Dad kept up with his walking stick, drawing lines on the sand.

There, at the end of the aisle, a simple arch framed Pastor Gonzalez. Ivan kept his eyes on her and his fingers on the violin. Behind him, Quincy was on the cello, providing accompaniment. Behind the arch was the sea and sky. The sun rose higher.

Brinley smiled at Ivan as he continued his serenade. His eyes sparkled in the sunshine. Those brownish, greenish, dark hazel eyes of his were on her. He grinned.

Thank God that's not a grimace.

Walking down the aisle, Brinley spotted a dark-haired woman in her fifties standing in the back. She was looking straight at Brinley. She had Ivan's nose. Or Ivan had her nose. And those soft curls in her hair reminded her of Willow's. There was Willow, two rows up near Skye Langston and Olivia Gonzalez. Across the aisle, Tobias Vega winked at her, and his dad waved. Somewhere, Brinley would like to think that Megan Zimmerman was here too, and not at the office this fine Saturday

Brinley smiled to Zoe and Diehl near the front, sitting beside Aunt Ella and her beau, Hiram, who had miraculously overcome his cancer. Aunt Ella's dementia had progressed to the point that she rarely left the Brunswick Senior Living Community, except when Hiram was with her. Next to them, Mom sobbed quietly into her embroidered French silk handkerchief.

Everyone was here.

Everyone except Yun McMillan...

But Brinley's thoughts went back to the woman in the back she had passed by. Could that be Jade McMillan? Brinley turned to her again. The woman smiled back, nodding. It was Ivan's smile. And Yun's.

Does Ivan know?

There he was, still playing in perfect time. He had timed it so well that he finished playing the last note as Brinley reached him. She figured he probably picked up the pace or slowed down as she made her way across the sand toward him. She suspected that Dad was an accomplice in the scheme. Ivan probably timed the tune according to his pace.

When Ivan put down his violin, Brinley squinted at it. The carvings on the side. She recognized those.

Could it be?

She watched Ivan hand over the violin and bow to Matt Garnett who looked spiffy as his best man. He put it into a carved dark brown leather case which Brinley had seen before in photographs.

She stared at the leather case. It had that distinct design. Hard to believe the 1698 Damaris Brooks Stradivarius was finally home. She turned to Dad as if to ask something, but when she saw that Dad could barely speak, she clammed up as he handed Brinley's hand to Ivan.

Ivan leaned down to her ear as if he'd sensed her thoughts and whispered, "Our song on the Damaris Strad as I've promised."

Brinley wished she hadn't nixed the veil. It would have veiled her tears. Her voice was a whisper. "All this time...?"

"Only the last several weeks," he whispered in her ear. "We'll talk all about it later."

Pastor Gonzalez cleared his throat. "No kissing yet."

Everyone laughed.

Realization struck Brinley. This was *the* wedding present from Grandpa Brooks. The one that he had promised her more than ten years prior if she kept her end of the bargain. And she had, with much heartache along the way. Had her vow of purity been worth it?

Yes!

But not for the heirloom violin.

She gazed at the man of her dreams. So peaceful and tranquil was his mien. So happy to be there.

She was too. And she knew then that they were God's gift to each other. Their journey continued, but oh, how far had they come as Ivan learned to trust God for his career and family, and as Brinley learned to trust God for Ivan and their future together.

Brinley locked her gloved hand in Ivan's warm and strong and steady fingers as they moved forward toward Pastor Gonzalez, toward new beginnings, new seasons, and a new life together as husband and wife in Christ, the glory and joy and music of their hearts.

~

DEAR READER:

Thank you for reading *His Longing Heart*. Did you enjoy the story of Ivan and Brinley? If so, you might also enjoy the next novel, *His Wake-Up Call*, the story of Ivan's friend, Sebastian Langston. In trying to win back his ex-fiancée, restaurateur Sebastian cooks up an idea to rent a girlfriend. Who in the world would agree to help him?

His Wake-Up Call (Seaside Chapel Book 2)
JanThompson.com/wakeup

JOIN JAN THOMPSON'S BOOK NEWS MAILING LIST

Sign up for my mailing list to keep up with my publication news. In addition to beach romances, I also write romantic suspense and near-future romantic thrillers.

Subscribe to Jan's book news:
JanThompson.com/newsletter

A FREE EBOOK FOR YOU!

A Christian beach romance novel, *Ask You Later* is the story of artist Leon Watts, who returns to Tybee Island and Savannah to jump-start his fledgling career. This novel is a part of the Savannah Sweethearts collection, and happens one year before the Seaside Chapel series begins.

Download this FREE novel now:
JanThompson.com/ask-seaside

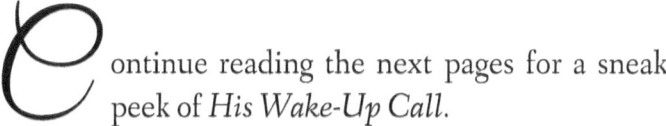ontinue reading the next pages for a sneak peek of *His Wake-Up Call.*

THE NEXT NOVEL IS HIS WAKE-UP CALL

SEASIDE CHAPEL BOOK 2

Single thirty-something Sebastian Langston hires his sister's best friend to be his fake girlfriend for the summer in order to win back his ex-fiancée whom he lost to a billionaire.

THE DESPERATE JILTED MAN...

Restaurateur Sebastian Langston cannot believe that his ex-fiancée, Talia, would leave him again. They've broken up so many times that he is sure she'll return to him...until he sees her with a billionaire. Now he has to fight to get her back. Sebastian cooks up an idea in which he hires a beautiful girl who can make Talia jealous. Poor starving harpist Emmeline O'Hanlon needs money and seems willing to help him reach his objectives.

THE DREAMY RENT-A-GIRLFRIEND...

When her best friend's older brother offers her an unusual proposition, Emmeline has no idea what she is getting into. However, her van is dead, her rent is due, and she is forced to take the job. The short-term business agreement would only last one summer, or so Emmeline thinks. More than money for graduate school, she needs Sebastian's funding to resume the search for her long-lost brother. Sebastian promises to enlist one of the top private investigators in the region to find Claude. In return, all she has to do is smile and make Talia jealous. How hard can it be?

THE DUET THAT CAN'T GO WRONG...

So begins this ill-advised scheme to drive Sebastian's ex-fiancée back to him. He thinks his plan-on-a-whim will succeed because it has to. He will turn thirty-four next September, and he wants to be a father by the following summer, preferably to the first of a passel of Talia's future children. As they keep up the ruse, Emmeline's ethereal harp starts to sound like a siren song that distracts Sebastian from his goals.

Soon, he rows away from his lane and begins to forget his original purpose for hiring her...

His Wake-Up Call is the second novel in *USA Today* bestselling author Jan Thompson's Seaside Chapel Christian small-town beach romance series. This book is the expanded second edition of the previously published *Step with Me*.

Continue reading for a sneak peek of Chapter 1...

HIS WAKE-UP CALL CHAPTER 1 SNEAK PEEK

SEASIDE CHAPEL BOOK 2

Six months after his fiancée left him for a billionaire, Sebastian Langston still wanted to get her back. His goal spun in his head as he mindlessly drove through the streets of St. Simon's Island, heading to the Fire Pit Service at his church.

Even though his bank account was way smaller than Jared Urquhart's billions, Sebastian felt that he had a chance because he had a long history with Talia, who had dumped him several times and yet still returned to him after she was exhausted with her new boyfriends.

Sebastian represented someone dependable who was always there for her, offering her a shoulder to cry on whenever life was hard. Was life really hard for Talia? What could be easier than withdrawing money from a trust fund every month to spend it all on entertainment?

Still, he always took her back. Surely she would return after she realized the errors of her ways.

Any day now, Talia. Come home!

After months of missing her, Sebastian got worried. Talia hadn't called. She hadn't shown up at the business meetings at the restaurant they both co-owned on Jekyll Island next door.

His sister, Skye, told him to let her go. If she was sleeping around, she was not the kind of woman he would want to marry and have kids with, was she?

Still, Sebastian held out hope that Talia would show up at his front door as she had done countless of times before.

Talia would beg for forgiveness. Of course, he'd forgive her.

She would ask for a fresh start. Sure, no problem.

She would whisper in his ear about her undying love for him. He would lap it all up.

All those boyfriends of hers hadn't lasted as long as her relationship with Sebastian. Someday, Talia would stop running off and they could marry and start a family. Sebastian could imagine how beautiful their kids would be...

This time, it seemed different for Sebastian. It felt like he was going to lose Talia forever, that her wandering days had led her far away from him, that Jared had so much more to offer her. Free plane rides around the world on his private jet, for example. Or vacations in the many Urquhart summer homes in Europe.

Sebastian had none of the above—except for his stable love and dependability, both of which money could not buy.

Take that, Jared.

Maybe it was time to spice it up a little. But how?

Sebastian found himself in the Seaside Chapel parking lot. *How did I get here? Did I run any red lights?*

He parked his SUV as close as possible to the pavilion behind the church buildings. There were two buildings in all: the main Seaside Chapel sanctuary and the one-hundred-year-old wedding chapel.

Sebastian had been eyeing that wedding chapel for a long time. He had catered wedding receptions both in its basement and outside on the grounds. Someday, he would like to be married there.

Soon, he hoped. He wasn't getting any younger. He wanted a passel of kids with Talia. He'd talk to her about that after he got her back.

Sebastian grabbed his Bible and iPad from the backseat and made it halfway down the boardwalk toward the pavilion before he started wondering if he had locked his vehicle. He clicked his key fob a couple of times, but it was too far away to send a signal to his vehicle. Maybe the key fob battery was dying down.

He drew a deep breath and debated whether to walk back to manually check his SUV doors or leave them alone. After all, St. Simon's Island was a safe place with very low violent crime rates.

While he was trying to decide, he found himself already walking back to his SUV. Apparently, his legs had a mind of their own.

Seconds later, he confirmed that his SUV was actually already locked.

He stepped aside to let a familiar truck by. It parked a couple of vehicles away. Benicio Ketteridge and Matt Garnett stepped out of the truck.

Sebastian walked toward them as Matt opened his extended cab door to retrieve a guitar.

"You missed dinner with us and Tristan," Matt said.

"What dinner?"

"This evening. Ivan couldn't make it, so it was just the four of us," Matt reminded him.

Benicio ambled toward Sebastian. "You were supposed to pick up the tab for dessert."

"That's today?" Sebastian checked his phone. "It doesn't say."

"We moved it from Monday, remember?" Matt closed his doors and locked them.

Sebastian scrolled up. "Oh. Forgot to change the date. Sorry, guys. I'll pay for dinner next time."

"You'll pick up the tab for the entire dinner?" Benicio slapped Sebastian's shoulder. "You're the man."

Sebastian followed Matt and Benicio as more

vehicles filed in. The church parking lot was almost full. It was the beginning of summer, the weather was warm, and the Wednesday night outdoor service was a hit this time of year, not only for regular church members but also for visitors to the Georgia coast.

Sebastian turned his head when he heard a noisy engine that sounded like it was about to fall out. It seemed to come from an old, decrepit van. When it passed by him, he noticed that his sister's close friend was at the wheel. Her hair was tied up in a knot on top of her head, but little curls dangled all around her face.

A harpist, Emmeline O'Hanlon was one of the three musicians in Treble Trio. The other two being Sebastian's sister, Skye—who organized the group and was the lead singer—and Avery Chung, who played the trumpet and didn't sing. Lately, Ivan's wife, Brinley, would play accompaniment for them at the piano, although she was not considered a permanent member of the group yet.

That was pretty much all he knew or cared about the trio. However, Skye had told him a lot about Emmeline and Avery, who were both still single—not that it mattered to Sebastian. In fact, he hadn't seen those two ladies much except when they sang at church or at a wedding his restaurant catered.

Emmeline climbed out of her van, wearing a loose-fitting empire-waist dress with a modest neckline and delicate flower prints on it.

She had indeed changed.

Sebastian recalled that a year before, all Emmeline had ever worn were form-fitting clothes that made her look like she was at the gym all day long—and left nothing to the imagination. She had hung all over Ivan McMillan, who had no long-term interest in her. After Ivan's wedding to Brinley, Skye told Sebastian that Emmeline had spent some time with her parents in Atlanta. Perhaps she reformed then.

A ping from his phone made Sebastian check his notifications. Skye asked him to save her a seat because she was going to be late.

A personal chef, Skye would always be late to the Wednesday night service until she could find another chef to handle preparing dinner for her clients that evening.

Sebastian walked briskly toward the pavilion, and found almost all the back seats occupied. He ended up sitting in front of the podium, where Benicio was welcoming guests.

The former US Army chaplain was now an associate pastor at Seaside Chapel, working primarily with the teens in youth camps and mission projects. Sebastian wondered how a bachelor with no kids of his own would be able to handle other people's kids.

Kids.

Someday, Sebastian wanted to have kids with Talia.

Yeah. Talia.

Unfortunately, she was gone. How on earth could Sebastian get her back? What would make her leave that billionaire playboy and return to Sebastian?

Perhaps all was not lost. Talia was still Sebastian's business partner at their thriving Saffron on Jekyll. He could still see her on a professional basis.

Granted, Sebastian worked hard to make the restaurant popular with both the locals and island visitors. For the most part, Talia was a hands-off partner who pretty much let Sebastian do whatever he wanted.

Hmm...

Sebastian wondered how he could make Talia jealous. That was one of her weaknesses. Could he use that to his advantage?

He looked to find Benicio staring right through his mischief. Did pastors have x-ray vision?

Worse yet—God would see it all. What if God looked inside Sebastian's heart and read his mind?

Still, he wanted Talia back. If he could get her back in his arms, he could worry about the rest of it later.

The rest of what?

Ramifications of dating an unbeliever, for example. Well, he had prayed for her salvation. Wasn't that enough?

When Sebastian looked up again, his sister was walking toward him. Skye plopped herself down on the seat next to him just as her phone rang. She sent it to voicemail and muted the phone.

"You made it out of the kitchen alive," Sebastian whispered in Skye's ear.

She shook her head and rested it on his shoulder for a split second before sitting up straight again.

"How about I send you a chef for a few weeks until you find a permanent one?" Sebastian asked.

"You would?" Skye looked surprised.

"I'm selling the catering business anyway, and I've already told my employees."

"Did they quit on the spot?"

"Some have started looking for a new job, but Chef Joseph is transitioning to Sage Café, though I don't know if he'll like it there. He might be a good fit for you—although I don't want to push him your way."

"I've worked with him before," Skye said. "Will you ask him? I just need an extra hand for the summer."

"I'll talk to him." Sebastian squeezed his sister's shoulder.

"Any prayer requests?" Benicio asked through the microphone.

Sebastian sat through at least half a dozen serious prayer requests from those in attendance, ranging from life-threatening illnesses to deaths. Argo Perry's cancer had returned. Hayden Hartley's grandmother had fallen and broken her hips. Matt's brother needed a better-paying job.

Sebastian wondered if he should say, "My fiancée left me—again."

More hands went up. Benicio pointed to someone sitting somewhere in the back. "Emmeline."

Sebastian could not see her from where he was sitting, but he could hear the concern in her voice.

"Please continue to pray for my missing brother,

Claude. My parents' wedding anniversary is coming up, and it would be a miracle if Claude comes home." Emmeline's voice cracked. "It has been five long years."

"We'll keep praying. God works miracles," Benicio said. "Let's go to the Lord now."

Sebastian could hear Emmeline sniffle—or someone did.

It tugged at his heart.

And he didn't know why.

~

His Wake-Up Call (Seaside Chapel Book 2):
JanThompson.com/wakeup

Seaside Chapel:
JanThompson.com/seaside

Subscribe to Jan's mailing list for book news:
JanThompson.com/newsletter

ACKNOWLEDGMENTS

Many thanks to my Georgia Press publishing team for keeping up with my writing schedule.

I appreciate my copyeditors and proofreaders: Pauline Nolet and Lenda Selph for the first edition, and Lesley Ann McDaniel and Judy DeVries for the second edition. Thank you very much, ladies!

A special thank you to my loyal readers who have been with me from the beginning. Your enthusiasm for every book I write is encouraging and inspiring.

I am grateful to God for my husband and son for their support and encouragement. I also thank God for my parents and my three brothers for my happy and memorable childhood. I'll always remember my beloved mother and my late father for having instilled in me the love of reading and writing from a very early age. I miss my father here on earth, but I will see him again in heaven someday.

Most of all, I am eternally thankful to my Lord and Savior, Jesus Christ, who died on the cross to save me from my sins and rose again from the grave to give me eternal life. Without Him, I can write nothing (John 15:5).

Joyfully in Jesus,
Jan Thompson
John 3:16

READ A FREE EBOOK IN THE SAME STORY WORLD

Set in Georgia, South Carolina, and Tennessee, this clean and wholesome Christian romance tells the story of art gallery archivist Sheryl Breckenridge and world-famous sculptor Winton Pace. Read this ebook for free!

Time for Me (A Vacation Sweethearts Prequel)
JanThompson.com/time-free

BOOKS BY JAN THOMPSON

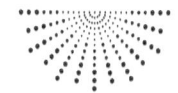

CONTEMPORARY CHRISTIAN COASTAL AND
BEACH ROMANCE

Seaside Chapel (7 Books)
JanThompson.com/seaside
Savannah Sweethearts (12 Books)
JanThompson.com/savannah
Vacation Sweethearts (8 Books)
JanThompson.com/vacation

CONTEMPORARY CHRISTIAN CITY
ROMANCE

Midtown Christmas (4 Books)
JanThompson.com/christmas

CHRISTIAN ROMANTIC SUSPENSE

Protector Sweethearts (6 Books)
JanThompson.com/protector
Defender Sweethearts (6 Books)
JanThompson.com/defender

NEAR-FUTURE TEHNOTHRILLERS WITH
CHRISTIAN ROMANCE

Binary Hackers (4 Books)
JanThompson.com/binary

Subscribe to Jan Thompson's mailing list:
JanThompson.com/newsletter

SEASIDE CHAPEL

Welcome to *USA Today* bestselling author Jan Thompson's Seaside Chapel Christian beach romance series. These novels are set on real-life St. Simon's Island, Georgia—a beach town where history is all around and the future is a moment away—and the neighboring fictitious Seaside Island, where the rich and famous live.

Savor the small-town atmosphere and the warm southern beaches of St. Simon's Island and the idyllic Golden Isles along the Atlantic Ocean. Enjoy the music of the orchestra and hymns of the church, and hang out with our Christian friends who attend Seaside Chapel, a little church by the sea known for its beach weddings and fair share of love and life.

As these Christians grow in their knowledge and understanding of God, they are tested in their spiritual maturity, their love lives, and their relationships with others. Share their heartaches and healing, and cheer them on as they celebrate faith, family, and friends.

~

JanThompson.com/seaside

- Book 0 (Prequel): *His Surprise Proposal*
- Book 1: *His Longing Heart*
- Book 2: *His Wake-Up Call*
- Book 3: *His Morning Kiss*
- Book 4: *His Quiet Serenade*
- Book 5: *His Waiting Love*
- Book 6: *His Beach Retreat*

SAVANNAH SWEETHEARTS

Welcome to the new south! From *USA Today* bestselling author Jan Thompson come these clean and wholesome, sweet and inspirational Christian romances set on the romantic beaches of Tybee Island and in the coastal town of Savannah, Georgia. Meet a group of multiracial and multiethnic church-going Christians who love the Lord, work hard in their careers, and seek God's will for their love lives. Against a backdrop of ocean, sand, and sun, these inspirational romances showcase aspects of the human need for God and for one another. Have some tea, settle in a comfortable reading chair, and enjoy these sweet celebrations of faith, hope, and love in Jesus Christ.

JanThompson.com/savannah

- Book 1: *Ask You Later* (Artist Romance)

- Book 2: *Know You More* (Multiracial Romance)
- Book 3: *Tell You Soon* (Asian-American Romance with Suspense)
- Book 4: *Draw You Near* (International Romance)
- Book 5: *Cherish You So* (Wheelchair Billionaire Romance)
- Book 6: *Walk You There* (Old-Meets-New Tour Guide Romance)
- Book 7: *Love You Always* (Romance with Suspense)
- Book 8: *Kiss You Now* (Multiracial Romance)
- Book 9: *Find You Again* (Multiracial Romance)
- Book 10: *Wish You Joy* (Christmas-Themed Romance)
- Book 11: *Call You Home* (Deaf Chef Romance)
- Book 12: *Let You Go* (Asian-American Romance with Suspense)

Read *Ask You Later* (Book 1) for free:
JanThompson.com/ask-free

VACATION SWEETHEARTS

Travel with our friends from Savannah, Georgia, to the coast and to the mountains. Cheer them on as they celebrate the immeasurable grace and undeserved mercy of God through Jesus Christ.

The Vacation Sweethearts novels are a spin-off of Jan's Savannah Sweethearts series, and fans will recognize familiar faces from Riverside Chapel, a church in the coastal city of Savannah, Georgia. In fact, we might even visit the beach town of Tybee Island from time to time to visit old friends and beloved families...

∽

JanThompson.com/vacation

- Book 0 (Prequel): *Time for Me*

- Book 1: *Smile for Me* (Beach Romance in the Bahamas)
- Book 2: *Reach for Me* (Romance with Suspense in the Smoky Mountains)
- Book 3: *Wait for Me* (Romance with Suspense on a Cruise Ship)
- Book 4: *Look for Me* (Romance with Suspense in a Florida Beach Town)
- Book 5: *Pray for Me* (International Romance in the City of Atlanta)
- Book 6: *Care for Me* (Small Mountain Town Romance)
- Book 7: *Cheer for Me* (International Romance)

✦

Read *Time for Me* (Prequel) for free:
JanThompson.com/time-free

CHRISTMAS SWEETHEARTS

Welcome to Christmastown, that holiday decorating company that is now run by Cyrus Theroux and his lovely wife, Amy Untermeyer-Theroux. Their story is first told in *Wish You Joy* (Savannah Sweethearts Book 10), the prequel to this Christmas Sweethearts series.

When this holiday romance series begins, Amy's Christmas Tree Farm and Christmastown have merged their daily operations at their Savannah headquarters.

JanThompson.com/christmastown

- Book 1: *Wish You Faith*
- Book 2: *Wish You Hope*
- Book 3: *Wish You Peace*

MIDTOWN CHRISTMAS

Big city romance, small town feel. Four Christian couples minister at Midtown Chapel in metro Atlanta, and Midtown Village, the community of tiny homes for needy families. From November to January every year, this place turns into a Christmas Village for a small-town feel right there in the metropolis of Atlanta, Georgia.

- Book 1: *Let Me Hold You* (Levi Theroux and Maggie Jacobs from *Pray for Me*)
- Book 2: *Let Me Adore You* (Erika Song from *Look for Me* and Hiroki Yamada from *Walk You There*)
- Book 3: *Let Me Honor You* (Forsythia McDevitt from *Call You Home* and Owen Grayson from *Find You Again*)
- Book 4: *Let Me Love You* (Leila Patel from *Find You Again*)

PROTECTOR SWEETHEARTS

Private investigator Helen Hu and her associates specialize in searching for missing persons and hunting for lost treasures. Join them in their adventure suspense around the world in *USA Today* best-selling author Jan Thompson's Protector Sweethearts, a series of Christian Romantic Suspense with a side of mystery.

Protector Sweethearts is a spin-off of Savannah Sweethearts and Vacation Sweethearts.

JanThompson.com/protector

- Book 1: *Once a Thief*
- Book 2: *Once a Hero*
- Book 3: *Once a Spy*

- Book 4: *Twice a Fighter*
- Book 5: *Twice a Convict*
- Book 6: *Twice a Soldier*

DEFENDER SWEETHEARTS

Defender Sweethearts is a sister series to the Protector Sweethearts Christian romantic suspense collection. While the heroes in Protector Sweethearts search for lost treasures and lost people, the Defender Sweethearts novels focus on protecting the helpless and hopeless. The main characters in Defender Sweethearts come from the supporting cast in Protector Sweethearts.

JanThompson.com/defender

- Book 1: *Never a Traitor*
- Book 2: *Never a Hostage*
- Book 3: *Never a Fugitive*
- Book 4: *Always a Maverick*

- Book 5: *Always a Champion*
- Book 6: *Always a Guardian*

GUARDIAN SWEETHEARTS

Guardian Sweethearts is a collection of Christian suspense novels in between other books in Jan Thompson's story world. These sandwiched stories feature married couples who met in the books before the present ones. Therefore, the books in this series are both prequels and sequels or preludes and postludes.

JanThompson.com/guardian

- Book 1: Once Bitten, Twice Shy: A Christian suspense novel in between Tell You Soon (Savannah Sweethearts Book 3) and Once a Thief (Protector Sweethearts Book 1)

- Book 2: Check Once, Check Twice: A
  Christian suspense novel in between
  Love You Always (Savannah Sweethearts
  Book 7) and Never a Traitor (Defender
  Sweethearts Book 1)
- Book 3: Going Once, Going Twice: A
  Christian suspense novel that comes after
  Reach for Me (Vacation Sweethearts
  Book 2)
- Book 4: Fool Me Once, Fool Me Twice:
  A Christian suspense novel that comes
  after Wait for Me

BINARY HACKERS

Like more suspense with your Christian romance?
Like to read suspense thrillers? If you're looking for
clean near-future romantic suspense without
compromising the Christian faith, these books are
for you.

From *USA Today* bestselling author Jan
Thompson come these inspirational near-future
cyberthrillers combining technothriller and romance,
starting with Binary Hackers that feature computer
specialists living at the edge of cyberspace, where
they have to juggle being law-abiding truth-telling
Christians while carrying out their assignments by
any and all means possible.

The Binary Hackers series is set in the same story
world as Jan's other books, and characters from the
other series may make cameo appearances in this
series and vice versa.

JanThompson.com/binary

- Book 1: *Zero Sum*
- Book 2: *Zero Day*
- Book 3: *Zero Base*
- Book 4: *Zero Trust*

ABOUT JAN THOMPSON

USA Today bestselling author Jan Thompson writes clean and wholesome contemporary Christian romance with elements of women's fiction, Christian romantic suspense with an air of mystery, and inspirational international thrillers with threads of sweet Christian romance. Jan's books are for readers who love inspiring stories of faith, hope, and love in Jesus Christ.

Raised on a tropical island in the eastern hemisphere, Jan now lives and writes in the western hemisphere. Her international background gives her a unique multicultural and multiracial perspective to her novels and books. The island has never left her, and she reminisces about beach life in her beach romance novels.

When Jan is not busy writing small-town stories, she writes big-city romantic suspense and international technothrillers, a nod to her previous career in computer science. She weaves technology with human interests, reflecting the current and future digital world. And romance. There's always romance.

Beyond the printed page, Jan is a wife, mother,

avid reader, former quilter, erstwhile pianist, occasional artist, and chief of staff to the family cat.

Find out more about Jan Thompson:
JanThompson.com

Subscribe to Jan's book news mailing list:
JanThompson.com/newsletter

*For God so loved the world
that He gave His only begotten Son,
that whoever believes in Him
should not perish
but have everlasting life.*
—John 3:16

www.ingramcontent.com/pod-product-compliance
Lightning Source LLC
Chambersburg PA
CBHW030738030726
47497CB00001B/29